BRIGHT CITY
LOST SOULS

A Luke Kelly Crime Story

Graham Storrs

Dedication

This book is for my wife, Christine,
who is simply the love of my life.

Chapter One

The clock on the wall showed 10 a.m.. It was a cheap clock I'd bought from K-Mart and it ran fast. I glanced at my phone and saw the time was really nine fifty-four. I thought about going over and setting the clock right but what would be the point? It would be wrong again the next time I needed it. If I wasn't spending so much on this stupid office, I could afford a better clock. And, of course, Ronnie had talked me out of hiring a receptionist. But, if I'd done that when I wanted to, I'd be throwing money into this venture at an even faster rate and Ronnie's scorn would have been even more unbearable. On the other hand, if I hadn't let myself be browbeaten by his constant ridicule, I'd probably have bought a decent clock in the first place.

Outside my window, I could see the busy streets of Toowong, three storeys below me. It was late spring and every shop had Christmas bunting out. I should probably get some for the office. It would be my first Christmas without Chelsea, almost a year since she was murdered. I'd got through Valentine's Day, her birthday, my birthday and our anniversary since it happened. How hard could Christmas be?

The tap at the door made me jump. I dropped my phone onto the desk. I'd been re-reading Bertrand Russell's *History of*

Western Philosophy on it, the book that had started my lifelong interest in the subject. More accurately, I'd been staring at the same page on the Stoics for half an hour, my thoughts skipping away in all directions each time I tried to focus.

"Sorry," said the woman in the doorway. She was holding the door handle with one hand and had the other poised to knock again. "I didn't mean to startle you."

For a moment, I stared at her, open mouthed. Probably every male private investigator has a fantasy that, one day, he'd be sitting in his office and in will walk The Beautiful Blonde. She'd be sultry and mysterious. She'd sit across the desk from him, cross her perfect legs and take a long cigarette out of a silver case, waiting meaningfully for him to light it. Of course, this was not it, but it was probably as close to it as I would ever get. The woman in my doorway was tall, blonde and very, very beautiful. She glided in on long legs and sat in the chair I proffered with the languorous grace of a supermodel. She was dressed in something that hugged and flattered her and probably cost more than my car. She seemed only slightly discommoded by my impression of a starving man confronted by a banquet. My guess was she met this kind of reaction all the time.

"Luke Kelly?" she asked.

"I – Yes! I am. I mean, hello. I... er..."

"You investigate murders, I'm told."

"I, er, well, yes." That is, I would if anyone had ever asked me to. So far my business had been a handful of missing persons, an arson, a crazy guy poisoning people's pets and that was it. "Can I just ask, who told you that?" If this job was coming to me by word of mouth, it was the very first time and quite a milestone.

"I'd rather not say," she said and smiled. "I'm guessing

that you're the philosopher and your partner's the tough guy."

It was all deliciously perplexing. She wasn't just a blonde, she was a mysterious blonde. It crossed my mind that it was an elaborate practical joke and sometime down the line I was going to end up in the middle of Elizabeth Street in my underwear. The thought that this was Ronnie having a laugh at my expense sobered me up.

"Perhaps we could start with you telling me who you are and then we'll see how I can help you?"

"OK. I'm, er, Margaret Preston and I—"

The hesitation was so obvious my suspicions ratcheted up several notches.

"You're Margaret Preston? Like the famous Australian artist?" She blinked and her lovely mouth fell open. Clearly unhappy that I'd seen through her brilliant ruse, she didn't seem to know what to say next. I said, "Look, I don't know what this is about but if it's some kind of joke, you might as well come clean now. You seem like a nice person and you're obviously not used to telling lies, so it's probably best you just tell me what's really going on here."

"Bugger," she said, frowning deeply. Then in an instant, she was smiling again. "You're a pretty good detective, aren't you? I want to hire you."

I tried not to look completely incredulous. "Really? We're just pressing on as if nothing happened?"

She waved a hand, dismissing anything so trivial as social awkwardness. "Look, I'm not going to tell you my real name, so let's just go with Margaret, shall we? The thing is, Luke, someone has murdered a friend of mine and the police are useless, so I'd like you to solve the case and bring the killer to justice."

I sat back and regarded her for a moment. It was hard to get past how beautiful she was. I know it sounds incredibly shallow but it's the truth. I suppose men just want to think good things about beautiful women and I'm sure there are a million excellent evolutionary reasons for that. Even while my neocortex was telling me this was a spoilt, privileged woman, so used to getting what she wanted that men like me were simply tools to be used, some part of my hind brain, my lizard brain, was saying "Don't throw her out, you fool. Show her your bright plumage. Spray her with pheromones!"

Being the man I am, my neocortex won. But, to be honest, there was a struggle.

"Margaret," I said, pointedly. "The sad reality of my business is that private investigators get to work on the cases the police aren't interested in; missing persons over a certain age, probate matters, divorce cases, domestic cases, Centrelink fraud, old and hopeless cases... You get the picture. If a child goes missing, they're all over it like a rash. If someone is murdered, they pile into it like a rugby scrum. The fact that the police aren't interested in your case tells me they don't think it was a murder."

She goggled at me, open mouthed. Not the reaction I was expecting to my brush-off.

"Gosh, you're amazing!" she said "That's exactly right. They think it was a suicide. I told them it wasn't. I knew Sonny. He'd never do a thing like that. He'd consider it terribly bad taste."

"Sonny?" I asked, biting despite myself.

"It's short for Everson. Everson McKinley."

I tried to pull back. "I'm sorry your friend—"

"Oh, he wasn't my friend. Not as such. He was my tutor at uni. I did a Fine Arts degree." *Of course you did.* "That is, I started one. The thing is, he was so lovely to me and I got to know him really well and I just know he would not kill himself."

She seemed genuinely upset about it and I wanted to let her down gently. "I'm guessing all the evidence points to suicide and that's why the police are reluctant to investigate."

"Evidence!" She waved it away as if it was nothing. "All they can talk about is evidence." She leaned towards me, fixing me with her heart-stopping blue eyes. "I *know*."

She seemed so absolutely certain I didn't dare argue with her. Instead, I moved the conversation sideways. "Which cops have you spoken to?"

She sat back, draping her arms over the chair as if she were posing for a photograph. "All of them. They're all as stupid as each other. Tim Pearce wants to help me. He's such a darling. But he's not even in homicide these days. So he can't actually do anything."

"So, who in homicide did you talk to?"

She scowled at me. "Everyone! From the tea boy to bloody Gomez."

"Gomez?" I thought I knew the names of most of the senior cops in homicide but this was a new one.

"Adams. Chief Inspector Adams. Trevor calls him that. It's some kind of boomer joke."

"Trevor? Is that Detective Inspector Trevor Reid?"

"Oh, you know Trevor? He's a sweetie, isn't he?"

No, he's two metres of bone and gristle who tried very hard to put me away for Chelsea's murder. He's single-minded, stubborn, aggressive and dumb as a bag of hammers.

Smiling, I said, "What about Detective Sergeant Bertolissio? Have you spoken to her?" If anyone would give this woman's allegations a fair hearing, it would be her.

5

"Her? She's the worst of the lot! 'Bring me some evidence, M – er, Margaret, then we can do something.' 'Well, how am I supposed to get any evidence if the cops won't look into it?' I asked her. She laughed but I insisted she tell me. And do you know what she said?"

I shrugged and shook my head. I was still struggling with my amazement that my mystery blonde seemed to be on such intimate terms with Queensland's finest that she could harass and browbeat them, and share inside jokes about a DCI with grim-faced DI Reid.

"She said I should hire you. That's what she said. So here I am and, I have to say, it looks like I'm wasting my time."

I scrunched up my face, trying to get my head around what was going on. "You're saying that DS Bertolissio actually told you to hire me to look into an alleged crime she doesn't actually believe happened."

"Yes."

It wasn't a very helpful answer. It didn't explain anything. "Why? Why would she do that?" At the very least it must be a breach of some kind of ethical code for a cop to recommend a particular PI.

The mystery woman shrugged. "I suppose she must think you're good at this."

I couldn't help giving a snort of laughter. Alexandra Bertolissio knew exactly how badly I'd screwed up the investigation of Chelsea's murder and how close I'd come to getting myself and Ronnie killed as I blundered around back then. Was this some kind of payback, dumping this gorgeous but irritating pest on me? She hadn't seemed like a woman who bore grudges. And I thought we'd parted on pretty good terms despite everything. We'd bumped into one another from time to time during Kurt Opperman's endless trial and she had always seemed friendly.

Could it be she had some reason to believe Blondie that I didn't know about? Something the woman had told her? Some fact or clue that didn't itself amount to evidence but maybe pointed to something that gave credibility to the woman's belief that a murder had been committed?

I looked at my Mystery Blonde with a new interest. She had crossed her long legs and was tapping the air with one foot, impatiently.

A real murder to work on. Ronnie had said it would never happen. But here was a living, breathing, foot-tapping client, ready – no, eager – to pay us to investigate it. I told her our daily rate. She didn't bat an eye.

"So you'll take the job?"

I opened my desk drawer and picked off the top two documents from the pile in there. "This is our standard contract. If you'll just sign both copies where it says 'Sign Here', we can get started right away." She gave me a smile brighter than the Brisbane sunshine. Dazzled, I smiled back.

* * * *

"I tell you it was like the opening scene of *The Maltese Falcon* or something."

"What, so now you're Sam fucking Spade? Did you even see that film? Nothing good came of that meeting."

Ronnie was being his usual irritating self. We were having lunch in the mall where our office was sited. I'd called Ronnie at home and told him the news as soon as Blondie had left. Reluctantly, he'd agreed to let me buy him lunch.

"Well, Lauren Bacall in that other movie then, the one where Bogart's a ship guy and there's a revolution going on, or… You know the one."

"I'll just type that into Google, shall I?"

"Yeah, well, maybe we're getting off the point. The thing is, it's a job – and not just any old job. This could be the one we've been waiting for all year."

"A Christmas miracle," he said.

"Well, a gift horse, anyway. And what don't we do with gift horses?"

"Shut the fuck up. What do you know so far?"

I had been expecting that. I opened my laptop and turned it to show him. "This is the victim, Professor Everson McKinley, aged fifty-six, taught Art Appreciation at university, three books on the subject to his credit, as well as a lot of academic papers on the Pre-Raphaelite painters, affectionately known to his students as "Sonny", died at home on the night of November 4, suspected suicide, shot himself in the head with a twelve bore shotgun."

"Fuck," Ronnie said, his face a mask of disgust. "I wouldn't want to have to clean that up."

"He was well off. Lived in a big house on the river at Chelmer. Not far from here if you fancy a look. Don't know about family yet, or who gets all the loot."

"Why'd he do it?"

"If he did it."

Ronnie gave me a tight smile. "Why is he supposed to have done it?"

"November 4 was the anniversary of his wife's death. She died of cancer a year ago."

He gave me a level stare. "It's the anniversary of Chelsea's death soon. You going to top yourself?"

"What? No! Why would you even ask that?"

"Just curious." He gave a heavy sigh. "Right-o, then. Let's

go take a look at how the other half lives."

He stood up and so did I. "Does that mean you agree we should take the case?"

"Mate, you already took it. You signed a contract."

"Which is full of escape clauses."

He frowned at me. "It's your business, Luke. I'm just the consultant, remember?"

"Yeah, well, consult then. Tell me if you think we should do it."

"I think it's a complete waste of time but if some dumb blonde is willing to pay you to waste your time, and you're willing to pay me to waste mine, why the hell not?"

"She's not a dumb blonde. She seemed quite bright."

He grinned. "I see. She flattered you."

"No! Not at all. Well, I suppose she mentioned how astute I seemed. A couple of times."

"Right. And did she flutter her eyelashes at any point?"

I made for the till to pay. "I don't know what happened to you to make you so cynical but I reckon you've had that leathery, wrinkled old heart broken at least once." I stopped. I'd forgotten that Ronnie had once told me he'd been married. I'd never found out what had happened. Never asked. "Shit! I'm sorry, mate. I didn't mean to be such a dickhead." We were at the till by then and the young woman standing behind it was staring at us.

Ronnie shook his head in despair and walked away, saying, "Just pay the bloody bill, you wanker."

* * * *

Anyone listening to us talk would think that Ronnie and I hated each other. And, I suppose, in some ways, we did.

Neither of us would ever have chosen the other for a friend. We were just so completely different – in our attitudes, our personalities, our experience, our ages, even our physical build. And yet circumstances had thrown us together hard enough that we'd just sort of stuck. I suppose you could say it was a complicated relationship. One day, I promised myself, I'd sit down and puzzle it all out. Until then, we each gave the other something we needed, I supposed, and we just rubbed along in order to get it.

I was reflecting on this as we rolled into the drive of the late Everson McKinley's home. It was, indeed, a large house. Massive, actually. The kind of property that sells for millions. The river wasn't visible from the front but the air had a freshness to it that lifted the spirits. The double door under its pillared arch was enormous, glossy with black lacquer and heavy with ostentations brass door furniture that drew the gaze away from the discrete electronics. The drive was a gravelled road you could drive a B-double down. It swept past the front of the house in a grand loop and a side road went off to what might have been a garage block attached to one wing of the elegant mansion. There was a red BMW convertible parked near the door, looking mean and expensive. All around us were neatly-trimmed shrubs and a sprinkling of statues in a well-tended lawn. *Grounds*, I thought. This house had grounds, not a garden.

I rang the doorbell. I don't think I could have lifted the brass knocker, it was so large.

"Please wait," said a disembodied voice. "Someone will be with you shortly."

"Cute," Ronnie grumbled.

We waited perhaps a full minute before a man in his late twenties opened the door. He was good looking and well built with wet, tousled hair and a bathrobe.

"G'day," Ronnie said with a smile. "Are you the new owner?"

The man looked us both up and down. "Who are you?"

"I'm Ronnie Walker, this is Luke Kelly. We're investigating the death of Everson McKinley."

He thought about that for a while then said, "Hang on," and closed the door on us.

Ronnie put his ear to the door. Shocked by his impropriety, I nevertheless followed suit. From inside, I heard the man call, "Hey Offie, it's the cops again." A woman's voice joined his and they spoke inaudibly for a moment. Ronnie pulled back and so did I. Seconds later, the door opened again and a young woman glared out at us.

"What?" she demanded.

She was much younger than the man – nineteen or twenty, I'd have guessed – with short dyed-black hair, freckled skin, and a trim, narrow-hipped figure. I can say that with confidence because all she was wearing was a wet swimsuit.

Ronnie's smile clicked into place. "Good afternoon. Are you Ophelia McKinley?" It was a brilliant guess, I thought. If this was, indeed McKinley's daughter, he might well have named her after Hamlet's tragic girlfriend, the subject of so much interest to the Pre-Raphaelites he studied.

"I'm busy, What is it now?"

"I'm sorry to interrupt," said Ronnie, without a trace of sarcasm. "We'd just like to ask you a few questions about your father's death."

"You've got a nerve. I told the last lot I didn't want to see any of you again. Do I need to call my lawyer, or will you just piss off right now?"

"I think there's been a misunderstanding, Ms McKinley.

We're not cops. We're private investigators from…" He hesitated. His lips tightened and his throat constricted. He seemed to be physically forcing himself to say the name. "…the Systematic Doubt Agency." It took him a moment to recover. "We have been hired to look into Professor McKinley's death."

Ophelia looked shocked. "You've been hired to… By who?"

Whom, I thought, reflexively but managed to keep my mouth shut.

"I'm sorry but we cannot divulge the names of our clients. However, I can tell you that our client was a friend of your father and is very unhappy with the police decision to treat his death as a suicide."

Ophelia was frowning deeply. She studied us both as if she had just noticed we were standing on her porch. Slowly, seeming a little dazed, she stepped back and held the door open for us. First Ronnie, then I walked past her into the enormous hallway.

Ronnie introduced us again and offered our condolences for her loss while I gaped at the grandeur around us. The hallway reached up to the roof and was probably large enough to fit a two storey town-house inside. A staircase wide as a country road was the centrepiece. It swept up to a landing then split and curved away over my head. Following its aerial journey, I discovered a chandelier or, rather, a cloud of crystal prisms the size of a delivery van, floating in the void above us.

"Let's go into the library," Ophelia said and I forced my gaze back down to earth. I heard a strange sound and it took me a second to realise it was someone diving into a pool. Which explained where the handsome fella had gone. I

followed Ronnie who followed Ophelia across the tiled floor
to a large, wooden door and through it to the high-ceilinged
library. It was ridiculously large, bigger than my whole unit.
Along one wall were tall, arched windows that filled the room
with light. There were tables and armchairs in islands under
every other window. On the other wall were bookshelves,
deep alcoves from floor to ceiling that must have contained
thousands of books – perhaps tens of thousands. As we took
seats at one of the tables, I saw that outside were more
statues in a lawn that sloped down to the river.

"Nice place," Ronnie said.

"Nice enough to kill your own father for," she said. "At
least that's what the cops have been insinuating, the
bastards."

"DI Trevor Reid?" Ronnie said, looking sympathetic.

Ophelia's face set. "No, some ugly fat bitch called Marr."

"But they still believe Professor McKinley killed himself?"

"Yeah." She seemed resentful of the fact.

"But you don't," I said.

She looked at me sharply. Then she stood up. "He wasn't
the kind. And there was no note. And Come on, I want to
show you something."

We followed her out of the library through a door at the
far end. It led directly into a spacious office. It too had the
high arched windows and the views across the lawn to the
river. The glass desk was set in front of the wall opposite the
windows so that the professor could sit in his high-backed
leather chair and look out. There were bookshelves in this
room too but it had a more relaxed and informal feel than the
library. On the desk were a couple of trays with papers in
them, a lamp, and a glass desk tidy with a couple of nice pens
and other odds and ends in its various compartments. A

single photo in a glass frame showed McKinley, a much younger version of Ophelia and a woman who might have been her mother. They were at the beach and looked very happy. There was no computer. The police had probably taken that. The walls, like all the walls in the house, were hung with paintings. Some were reproductions of famous works, others looked original. The only bare space was behind the desk. A rectangle of less-faded wall about two metres by three clearly marked where a very large painting had once hung. There was damage to the plaster, as if someone had been chipping randomly at it with a small pickaxe and had then scrubbed the whole area furiously. I glanced at Ronnie and he was staring at it, too.

"It was an Archer," Ophelia said.

"Like… a picture of a bowman?" I asked.

"No, a James Archer. He was a painter. A Pre-Raphaelite, of course. This particular canvas was called *The Lady of the Lake*. He did a lot of Arthurian stuff. I hated it – gaudy and sentimental – but Daddy thought it was the most beautiful thing he had ever seen. You should have heard him rhapsodise over it. It was his most prized possession – apart from some stuff he kept in the bank.

Ronnie nudged me and showed me a picture on his phone. It was all rich colours and ladies in cloaks. A king – Arthur, I supposed – lay dying beside a lake reaching up to a woman who stood over him. The figures were slightly stylised and the mood was maudlin and melodramatic.

"It says here the provenance is disputed," Ronnie said.

"Didn't matter," Ophelia said. "He believed it was genuine and that was enough for him. The thing is…" Her nostrils flared as she drew a deep breath. "When he shot himself… his brains…" She stopped, her jaw working.

"The gun was pointing towards the painting," Ronnie said, as gently as I'd ever heard him say anything.

Ophelia nodded. She turned and walked a few paces across the room. It seemed wrong that she should be standing there wet and almost naked. It made her too vulnerable. I wanted to fetch her a robe or a sheet. I even glanced about for one.

"The point is," she said, turning to face us, her chin up. "He would never have harmed that painting. He couldn't have. Paintings were his life. More than that. He believed they were the embodiment of all that was good and beautiful in the human soul. He could no more destroy a painting than... than strangle a baby. Especially that painting."

"Were any of your father's fingers broken?" Ronnie asked. Ophelia and I both stared at him. "Did the police mention any damage to his hands?"

"No! Do you think someone tortured him?"

"No, not at all. Perhaps we should go back to the library?" Ronnie suggested.

It was a good idea. The room was beginning to upset me, let alone Ophelia.

When we were all seated again, Ronnie said. "Is it all right if we ask a few more questions?" The young woman nodded and he went straight into it. "I noticed the back of the chair wasn't damaged."

Again, she nodded. "The police said he must have been standing up when he... pulled the trigger."

"What time did it happen?"

"About ten p.m.. He was alone in the house. The housekeeper found him the next morning."

"Any sign of a break-in?"

"None at all. The front door was locked and the alarm was set."

"You don't live here?"

"I have my own place. I moved out when I started uni."

"Did you not get on with your father?"

"We – We started having rows after Mum died. We both agreed it might be better for our relationship if we had separate places. It did actually seem to help."

"Your mother died about a year ago?" Again a small nod. "Was he having difficulty with the anniversary?"

She shook her head, squirming with agitation. "He wasn't like that. Oh, he was sentimental and all that – I mean, just look at how he spent his life – but he wasn't, you know, superstitious about dates and things. I called him that morning, to check that he was all right. He actually laughed. He said, 'Offie, darling, if I could get through the very first day after she died, I can get through the three hundred and sixty-fifth.'" I caught myself nodding.

"Did he say anything else that day? Did he seem at all stressed or anxious? Unhappy? Frightened? Worried?"

She shook her head. "I just wish I'd said… more." A tear ran down her cheek and she dropped her head. Ronnie and I exchanged glances and he signalled with a tilt of his head that we should go. I nodded my agreement and we stood up.

"Thank you," Ronnie said. She looked up, startled, and stood too. The chair was damp where she'd been sitting in her wet cozzie. "We should get going." We all started moving towards the hallway. "Would it be OK to come back, or call you if we have more questions?"

She quickly went to a table near the door and wrote her phone number on a pad there. "This is my mobile. I'm only here to, you know, sort things out."

"Is this place yours now?" I asked as we entered the hallway.

She looked at me as if she'd forgotten I was there. She blinked. "Yes. I'm an only child. They read the will a couple of days ago."

"Did anyone else benefit?"

"Not really. There was a friend of his who got some porcelain figurines, a cousin who got a few thousand. Gifts for the staff. Stuff like that." She thought for a moment. "Oh and something about a shared investment that became the property of the surviving shareholders. I don't know. I wasn't really paying much attention. The house and everything else came to me."

"Would it be OK if we spoke to the lawyer about the will?" Ronnie asked. In response, she went back and wrote the name of the lawyer and the company on a new piece of paper.

In silence, we moved on to the door and she opened it. Ronnie and I stepped outside, but I still had one more question.

"The gun," I said. "Why did your dad have a shotgun?"

She shrugged dismissively. "It was just a family heirloom thing. A Purdy or something. Granddad used to shoot stuff when he had the Gold Coast property but that was yonks ago. It's all units and canal developments now. Dad kept the gun in a display case in his office. The key lived in his desk drawer. When the police found it, the case was opened and the key was in the lock. The gun was on the floor over there. No prints. Spent cartridges still in the barrels."

We said our goodbyes as we walked out onto the drive and I gave her one of our cards but, before we left, Ronnie asked, "Do you have someone you can talk to about all this?" He pointed vaguely at the red sports car in the drive. "Apart from that guy?"

She pulled back. "That's Fraser's. He's my boyfriend."

"Darl, he handed you on to two complete strangers, left you alone with us, without even checking our IDs, or checking you were OK. I don't think he's focussed on your best interests. Don't you have a girlfriend, or someone at the uni?"

As the surprise passed, her face set. "You know what? My personal life is none of your damned business. And don't bother calling again. We're done." She turned and walked away.

I glared at Ronnie and spread my hands in a "What the fuck, dude?" gesture but he was staring after the girl.

"Ophelia," he called so she could hear him. "Your father was murdered. The murderer is still out there. For all we know, you could be a target too. You need to be careful – and make sure the people around you care enough to make sure you're safe."

Chapter Two

We drove into the city and parked in the Post Office Square car park. We crossed Anzac Square and grabbed a coffee and cake in the food hall. Ronnie had been quiet and moody all the way there and stared at the giant doughnut with sprinkles on the plate in front of him as if it might contain the answer to all life's mysteries. I mention this because it was very unusual for him not to wolf down any scrap of food in front of him. Finally, he lifted his grizzled head and looked at me, his pale grey eyes strangely dark.

"OK, it's a murder," he said.

I grinned back at him.

His brows furrowed. "Yeah, don't get all fucking cheerful about it. It was a nasty, vicious crime. Some bastard literally blew a bloke's head off in cold blood. If we go after him we put ourselves in the firing line. This could be dangerous."

It was my turn to frown. "What's up with you? I thought you loved chasing down killers. I thought it was the wind in your sails, so to speak. Now you're suddenly worried about how dangerous it is? That's not the ex-special forces, stealth and strength, full speed and take 'em, gung ho, mutant ninja—"

"Will you just shut the fuck up?"

We stared at each other in silence for a moment.

"So what's wrong?" I asked.

He looked away, sucked on his teeth, studied the ceiling and looked back.

"There's something I haven't told you," he said. I'd never seen him look so shifty.

"Well, I know you're not my real father, so—"

"Jesus! Will you shut up? I'm going for an operation."

"What?" It didn't make sense. I know Ronnie looked as old as Methuselah but he was as fit as a Mallee bull. I'd seen him take down two young thugs – one armed with a knife – in about ten seconds flat. What was he now? About sixty-five? Yeah, well that was pretty old, more than twice my age, but he had a gym in his house and I knew he worked out every day. And he was built like a brick dunny.

"I'm going in real soon now," he said, interrupting my skittering thoughts. "It's only day surgery but I'll be laid up for a while. I might – I might never be what I was."

"Jeez, mate, what the hell is it?"

"That doesn't matter. The thing is, it's a really bad time to be getting into all this. I've done a lot of murder investigations in my time and I can tell you, the people who commit murders are not the kind you want to be hunting from a wheelchair."

"A wheelchair?"

"I'm exaggerating. It's not that bad. But, look, you're a useless knob end. What are you going to do if you get into trouble and I'm not there to save your arse?"

Now he was just being rude. "Look, mate, your role in this company isn't to be my bodyguard. You're involved because I value your investigative skills and experience."

He dismissed that with a shake of his head and a small sneer. "You wouldn't be able to brush your teeth without someone to hold your hand. Me working as a consultant for you isn't because you appreciate my valuable input, it's because you wouldn't have a bloody clue what you were doing without me to tell you."

"Yeah, well, maybe that was true at first, but I've come along way since we started. I'm a lot better at this PI thing than you give me credit for. So, just you go and have your operation and don't worry about me. I'll solve the case. She'll be right. When is it, anyway?"

"Tomorrow."

"Tomorrow? And when were you going to tell me about it?" My guts churned. Tomorrow? For all my bravado, the idea of Ronnie suddenly being unavailable right at the beginning of such an important case, filled me with panic.

"Yeah, well, I've been meaning to."

"Fuck."

We were silent for a while. I studied the cake I wished I hadn't bought and he studied his gaudy doughnut.

"It'll be all right," he said. "We'll go see the lawyer after this and that should give you a list of suspects to start working through." It dawned on me why we'd driven into the city and I realised how much I was willing to just go along with what Ronnie said to do on an investigation, without questioning it. The fact is, I completely trusted him to know how to do this PI thing and had quickly learnt not to make my own stupid suggestions.

"By the time I'm up and about," he said, "you'll have seen everybody and we can look at the next step."

"How long will that be – until you're up and about?"

"The surgeon said I should rest completely for three days

and then I can get back to normal stuff but without any strenuous activity for a few weeks."

"So that includes not doing any Kung Fu on murderous thugs, I suppose."

"It's mostly Krav Maga but, yeah, I reckon that would be out. We didn't discuss it specifically."

"But I can still, like, call you?"

"It's only a few days, really."

"Right. And I can come round. Bring grapes."

"If I have to put up with you visiting, bring rum."

"So, do you, like, need a lift to the hospital, or something?"

"Nah, mate, it's all sorted. One of my mates from the club is driving me there and picking me up."

I didn't know any of the people he socialised with at the Dogsbodies Club. They were all crumblies like Ronnie and got together to organise dog shows and talk about their fancy breeds. It was a world of surreal strangeness that I didn't want anything to do with. My own hobbies included arguing arcane matters of epistemology on Internet forums and taking an online forensic science course. It had been a bit of a disappointment to discover that the friends Chelsea and I had had before she died, were all Chelsea's friends really, and the people I knew from uni were all troglodytic introverts – much like me – and never called, never organised parties, and had to be bullied and cajoled into even going to the pub. I wasn't exactly friendless but I didn't really have a social life, either.

"So, what do we know?" Ronnie asked, breaking my reverie.

I tried to marshal my thoughts. "I dunno. Not much. It actually does look like suicide. No note but…"

Ronnie sighed. "OK, let me have a go then, hey? First off,

McKinley was loaded and, while the upside of being wealthy is that beautiful women with low self-esteem want to marry you, the downside is that everyone in your immediate family and many business acquaintances are likely to profit from your death. On top of that, there are probably people who will hate you for what you did to them to acquire your wealth and there are lots of people who will just hate you for having lots of stuff while they've got nothing. So, even without us knowing a thing about McKinley except that he had a spectacular house, we know there's a large mob out there with motive to kill him. So?"

He paused, expectantly. I bridled at being treated like a student in class but I played the game anyway. "So we need to check the will, find out who benefits. Look at his business dealings, see who owes him money, see who he's screwed over the years who might have a grudge." I quailed inside at how much work that would be.

"Good lad. Next, we know that whoever killed him was let into the house and knew enough to set the alarm when they left. That suggests close family and close friends, as well as cleaners, contractors, the security company, and so on."

"Or it just means whoever shot him made him explain how to set the alarm first. Or that there was another, unsecured way in and out of the house."

"Or that someone hid in the house, killed him, then hid again until it was safe to leave." I frowned hard, trying to work out whether he was seriously suggesting such a scenario. "The point is, we can sit around and dream up all kinds of improbable ways to kill McKinley but the only one that helps us expand our pool of suspects, is the one where he knows the killer."

"Yeah, that's all right for you to say. You'll be lying in bed eating grapes."

"Drinking rum."

"Whatever. Thing is, I'd rather be cutting down the number of suspects so I don't have to interview half the city."

He shook his head. "Too soon. It'll do you good to get out and about. You spend too much time sitting in the office. You'll end up with an arse as fat as a pollie's pension plan."

"Just leave my arse out of it. Why don't you try explaining why we're so convinced it was murder?"

"Right-o. Number one, a shotgun's a bloody awkward thing to top yourself with. Do you know how long those things are? And how heavy? And what the recoil's like? I know McKinley was a tall bloke but—"

"How do you know?" I didn't remember that coming up at all when we visited his daughter.

"I've seen him in group photos online. He looks like he was at least six feet, probably a bit more. So he probably could have done it with a bit of a struggle but…" He shook his head. "Number two, the angle of the shot."

"But we already figured that one out. If he'd been in his chair, it would have—" Suddenly I saw it. To hit the painting while he sat at his desk, he would have had to hold the shotgun at a steep angle, pointing upwards, with the barrel under his chin. It would have been a very natural angle for the long, heavy weapon. He might even have taken some of the weight by grasping it with his knees. We knew he hadn't done that because the headrest on the chair wasn't damaged. So he would have to have shot himself standing up. In my imagination, the angle of the gun wouldn't have changed. Why would it? It would seem natural to put the barrel under your chin. But, if he'd done that, the shot would have hit the ceiling, not the painting and the wall. There had been no damage on the ceiling. So he must have held up the gun to a more horizontal angle. If Ronnie was right about the weight and the length – and he probably was – that had McKinley shooting himself in the face, holding the shotgun very awkwardly. It wasn't impossible that that was what he'd done but it did seem very odd.

"That's why you asked about broken fingers," I said. "But his hands were OK. On the other hand, someone pointing a shotgun at McKinley's head with the stock against their shoulder would be holding it at exactly the right angle."

Watching my face, Ronnie shook his head. "It's painful to watch sometimes but all the parenting books say it's better to let them work it out for themselves."

If I didn't know he could kick my arse with no trouble despite my almost forty year age advantage, I'm pretty sure I'd have taken a swing at him long ago. As it was, I attacked his argument instead. "If what you're suggesting is true, the cops would have worked it out by now. They can work out lengths and angles just as well as we can."

His grin broadened. "What you always fail to understand about the coppers is that, with one or two rare exceptions, they are as lazy and shiftless as any other group of workers in the world. Yes, it would be harder and less likely for him to shoot himself holding the gun up like that." He mimed the position. "But it's not impossible and, if that's the only piece of evidence that contradicts their nice, easy, low-effort theory that he killed himself, they've got a great incentive to discount it. I mean, look at you. You're all gung-ho for a murder investigation but, when it comes to all the hard yakka of eliminating dozens of suspects, your enthusiasm deflates like a pricked balloon. Don't try and deny it. I saw your face."

I closed my mouth. "Yeah, all right, that's sort of plausible but it's not the only contradictory evidence, is it. There was no note."

"True. That was my point three. But there's plenty of suicides without notes."

"Then there's the picture – the disputed James Archer *Lady of the Lake* which he would never have damaged."

"And that was point four. Thing is, anyone in a mental state where they'd kill themselves might not be too bothered about what collateral damage they did."

"But Ophelia said—"

"Which takes me to point five. His daughter said he was fine. He had no reason any of us is aware of to want to kill himself. His motive for the self-murder is completely lacking, the evidence that he did it is thin and contradicts Ophelia's statement, and the means he used raises its own doubts."

"All right, all right, you've made your case – almost. There's plenty of reason to doubt that he killed himself but the only real reason we have for thinking someone else did it was the angle of the gun."

"And all the money to be gained."

"Yeah, I don't know if that—"

"Well, you'll find out soon enough when you start talking to people, won't you?"

The conversation, having moved away from his hospital visit to the murder, seemed to cheer him up and he rapidly polished off his doughnut.

We left the food hall the way we'd entered, through Anzac Square, and turned down Anne Street towards the river and the offices of McKinley's lawyers. It was a cramped little dump, like so many CBD offices that weren't in new buildings, but I reckoned the size of the rent must be impressive enough to make up for it. We went up to the second floor in a lift with brass doors that rattled and lurched all the long, slow way. It gave us a quiet opportunity to talk.

"So, are you nervous?" I asked Ronnie.

"What, about talking to a shyster?"

"No, about your operation. You still haven't said what it is."

"You still haven't asked."

Yes, I have. It was my first question. You changed the subject."

"Yeah? What does that tell you, hey?"

"You know what?" The doors slowly opened into a corridor that might have been from a BBC period drama. "You don't deserve sympathy. You're a cantankerous old—"

"This way," he said and walked away up the corridor.

He pushed through a half-glass door, with the lawyer's name on it and I trailed in behind. We were confronted by a middle-aged lady and a small reception with chairs and magazines.

"Mr. Drew?" the receptionist asked, smiling.

Ronnie smiled back. "Am I late?"

"Nothing to worry about. Mr. Morley will see you now." She indicated a wooden door with a small name plaque on it. Ronnie thanked her and went in. Astonished at the man's effrontery, I again followed him in, closing the door behind us.

The lawyer greeted Ronnie as Mr. Drew and they shook hands.

"I'm afraid there has been some kind of mix-up," Ronnie said, pretending to be baffled. "My name is Walker, this is Luke Kelly."

"Oh dear," said Morley, flustered. He was one of those

rare people who actually looked older than Ronnie, with thin white hair in unruly streaks and a habit of squinting when he looked at you. "I really am terribly sorry." He made a move towards the door but Ronnie held up a hand.

"Actually, our business should be very brief. Perhaps, while we're waiting for the real Mr. Drew to turn up, you wouldn't mind just answering a couple of questions?"

"Questions?"

"Yes, about the late Everson McKinley's will. We have been authorised by his daughter, Ophelia, to clarify a couple of things."

"Ophelia? Why would she—?"

"Mr. Morley, Ophelia McKinley believes that her father was murdered. The police stubbornly insist it was a suicide. Our client has engaged us to investigate the circumstances of his death." The implication that our client was Ophelia was strong but Ronnie hadn't actually said it. "I assume you will wish to continue to fill the role of family solicitor." And was that a veiled threat? Morley certainly seemed to feel it.

"Continue? Why, that is for Miss McKinley to—"

"So, it would be very helpful if you could provide us with a copy of the will, then we can get out of your hair."

The solicitor was slowly gathering his wits. "Oh no, I don't think that would be appropriate. Perhaps if Miss McKinley were to apply to me directly."

I expected Ronnie to retreat at that point but, instead, he smiled and pulled out his phone. "I absolutely understand. Would it be acceptable for her to instruct you by phone?"

"Certainly."

Ronnie nodded and began dialling. As he did he grimaced, then paused. He looked at me and asked, "She'll be all right, won't she?" I tried to play along, pulling a face I hoped would express doubt, hoping that's what Ronnie wanted. "The thing is," Ronnie said to Morley, lowering his voice and leaning towards him confidentially, "you're not Offie's favourite person right now. I don't know what it's all about but she was very upset this morning – something about retainers and value for money and new blood. You know the kind of thing. Probably just the grief talking. She's been in a terrible state. Only I just want to check that you really want to ask her to repeat her instructions right at this moment. I understand you're only doing your job but..." He rolled his eyes. "...you know how unpredictable young girls can be at times like this."

I have no idea what the McKinley family business was worth to Mr. Morley, but it was clearly enough that he wasn't going to risk upsetting his client. He put up both hands. "You're quite right. No need to bother her." He pushed a button on an intercom on his desk and asked the receptionist to make a copy of "the McKinley will" for us. Ronnie thanked him profusely.

"Have the police asked for a copy?" Ronnie asked as we prepared to go.

"Yes, they have. I thought it odd since, as you say, it is all cut-and-dried."

"Glad to see they're being thorough. Was there anything in the will, or at the reading, that struck you as odd?"

"No, nothing at all. There were a few gifts and the settling of business matters but, basically, it all goes to Ophelia."

"When did he make the will?"

"About five years ago."

"Any changes since then?"

"Nothing significant. When his wife was alive, everything would have gone to her and then to Offie on his wife's death.

When she died, he changed that so it all went to Offie. A technicality, really, considering it would have gone to Offie anyway, his wife having predeceased him. It was a very simple will for a man with so much wealth,"

"Did he leave anyone out you thought should have been in there?"

"That really isn't my place—"

"So there was somebody?"

Morley bristled at being interrupted. "No. There was nobody."

By the time we got out of the office, the receptionist was stapling together the photocopied pages.

I waited until we were in the creaky old lift before I dared breathe.

"You know you lied to him?" I said.

"Yeah, but not much. Only about Ophelia being mad at him. If it ever came to court, he'd have to explain why that made him change his mind about giving us the will instead of doing his duty to his client."

"You just think the ends always justify the means, don't you?"

"What, you mean like catching a cold-blooded murderer justifies putting the wind up a money-grubbing little shyster? Too bloody right mate."

We took the will back to the office in Toowong. Ronnie unstapled the sheets and made a copy, stapled the copy together and put it in the new case folder I'd set up. We then sat at the table I had optimistically bought from Ikea for client meetings and went through each page, marking every name we found in highlighter and transferring the names to a separate list. Using my laptop, Ronnie started searching for information about each of them. I offered to do that part but he said, "Screw that. We'll be here all day." So I was in charge of writing down the stuff he called out and adding it to our list.

In a very short while, we had six names with addresses, ages and occupations, and the size of each bequest, plus two names with mostly question marks against them, and no more information to go on.

"Add your mystery woman to the list," Ronnie said.

"She's not in the will."

"As far as we can tell. But she's a suspect anyway until we can clear her."

So I wrote down, "Mystery Woman," and guessed her age at twenty-five.

"I don't see how trying to get a murder investigated makes you a suspect." I grumbled.

Ronnie ignored me. "Write down the shyster, Morley. Just do it. And the daughter's boyfriend – what was his name?"

"Fraser," I said, sulking. I wrote it down.

He took the list from me and studied it. He didn't look very happy. The list included the housekeeper and the gardener, a couple of relatives and a couple of old friends. We knew who these were because the will contained phrases like, "To my old friend, Charlie," and "For her long years of devoted service, to my housekeeper, Maureen," and so on. It did not look like a promising list of suspects. As far as I could see, Ophelia was the most likely culprit and, as far as I was concerned, she had pretty effectively ruled herself out by telling us she thought her father had been murdered. I suppose Ronnie felt the same way.

"All right, then, let's take a squiz at his business dealings."

If the first list had been easy, the second was very hard. We started at the university where he lectured, looking for businesses that contributed to the department or sponsored events he was part of. Then we tried to find other connections between McKinley and those businesses – whether he was on the board, or they used him as a consultant, or whatever. It was slow and tedious and we got pretty much nowhere. There was one company, an art gallery in Fortitude Valley, that he seemed closely connected to, but little else. I wrote down its name, Carnarvon Fine Art, and its address in Arthur Street.

Googling McKinley brought up the usual tsunami of information which, when we'd filtered it and chased up loads of dead ends, led to us adding a couple of charities he was associated with. And that was it.

"OK, I'm going to shoot through," said Ronnie, standing up. "There's stuff I need to get sorted for tomorrow." He waved a hand at the papers strewn across the table. "You've got enough there to keep you busy, I reckon." His eyes lingered on the notes and lists.

"I'll come round and see you. Day after tomorrow, hey? Give you an update." For some reason, I felt really bad that he hadn't told me about it, like I'd let him down, somehow. "You don't want to tell me what it is?"

"Nah. It's just me getting old, that's all. I'm sorry about this. Bad timing. Try not to get yourself killed while I'm away. And if… Yeah, well, you've got my number."

I watched him leave feeling an odd kind of melancholy. Ronnie Walker was a tough guy. Even at sixty-five, he was hard and mean. I'd seen him beat up blokes half his age and less. Two at a time! He'd been in the British Special Boat Service – the Royal Navy's elite special forces regiment – and he'd served as a cop in Brisbane. Manliness wasn't really a concept I understood. My own background was solidly academic. But maybe I could understand how a man like Ronnie might feel about his body ageing and failing by imagining what it might be like to feel dementia creeping up on me, not being able to remember all the masses of useless detail I always could, not being able to make the fine conceptual distinctions I prided myself on, not being able to make the creative leaps of reasoning that so thrilled and excited me. It would be frustrating, then frightening and, ultimately, depressing. Was that what Ronnie was going through?

I cleared up the papers, went back to the main list of suspects and added phone numbers where I could. It wasn't close of business yet, so I busied myself making calls to set up appointments for the next couple of days.

Ronnie hadn't told me what was wrong with him because he was ashamed. He felt that illness – any kind of weakness – diminished him. I thought it was telling that he'd let one of his dog club mates drive him to the hospital and back but wouldn't let me. Maybe it was because his peers would understand. They'd know from their own experience that there was nothing you could do about ageing but endure it. Maybe it was because he thought I might gloat. I'd always teased him pretty cruelly about his age. Practically every insult I ever gave him had the prefix "old" in it. Jeez, was I an ageist? If he'd been black or disabled, would I have kept harping on that, too? I wanted to go round to his house and tell him I was sorry. Could I explain it was just casual ageism, not deliberate or malicious ageism? I'd heard people justifying their racism like that. But, thinking about it, maybe that was even worse. Maybe thoughtlessly embodying the cruel attitudes of a heartless society just made me a mouthpiece for a crass culture, another mindless drone, programmed by the haters to internalise their poison?

I burst out laughing, suddenly hearing Ronnie's voice in my head saying, "Shut the fuck up, will ya? Is that the kind of drivel that passes for philosophy these days?"

* * * *

By noon the next day, I'd spoken to three of McKinley's beneficiaries – the gardener, the housekeeper and the friend who got the porcelain figurines. It meant going back to McKinley's house but that had to be done. I was pretty sure I could persuade Ophelia to be friendly again but I didn't get the chance. She and Fraser had left early, Mrs. Roberts, the housekeeper told me, and she had no idea when they'd be back.

I hit it off pretty well with Mrs. Roberts, which is kind of unusual for me, but she was such a friendly, chatty type, she probably hit it off with everybody. She was a strong, wiry woman in her fifties, with more than a trace of a Scottish accent. She had been with McKinley for twenty years and didn't have a bad word to say for him. The "wee gift" he left her seemed pretty paltry after so much devoted service, but who was I to judge? Certainly, Roberts seemed very pleased with it. And Ophelia had asked her to stay on and look after the house, "So all's well that ends well, eh?"

She didn't like the idea that her former employer would kill himself.

"I used to call him the Laird," she said, fondly. "It was a kind of a joke, but I think he liked it." She winked at me and laughed. "But he was a fine gentleman, you know. The kind you don't see any more." Considering Roberts would have been young in the seventies and eighties, I wondered just what golden age of great gentlemen she was harking back to. "There is no way on God's green earth that man would have killed himself," she concluded.

"But if he didn't kill himself, you're saying someone murdered him, Mrs. Roberts. Who could have done that?"

She bristled, as if I'd caught her out in a logical fallacy. "Burglars and thieves," she said. "Some young druggies, running around like crazed animals."

As carefully as I could, I said, "But you've seen the house. There was no sign of a break in, no damage, nothing stolen. It really doesn't look like a burglary. Or have you seen something the police missed?"

"The police!" She snorted in disgust. "Barely out of kindergarten most of them. Ordering me around as if they had the right to. I wouldn't trust anything they say."

"I don't," I said, establishing common ground. Ronnie had given me lessons in interviewing because he reckoned I was a "useless prick with all the social skills of a brain-dead wombat." Establishing a rapport was one of the first things he emphasised and, I had to admit, it had being going quite well with Mrs. R. "The police think Mr. McKinley shot himself but I think they're just being lazy, not looking deeply enough."

She looked at me suspiciously. "So you think he was murdered, do you?"

"Yes, and I was hoping you could tell me who did it. Did he have any enemies?"

"Enemies? Why would a man like that have any enemies?"

"What about his daughter, Ophelia? They argued, didn't they? She left home to get away from him."

And then we weren't getting on at all any more. "Offie? Are you out of your mind, man? Ach, she's a wild one and no mistake, always was, even as a nipper, but there's not an ounce of malice in that poor child's body. Not an ounce. If that's what passes for detective work these days, young man, we've all come to a sorry pass. A sorry pass indeed." She stood up, agitated. "Now, if you'll excuse me, I have work to do. You'll find Dedwin in the garden somewhere – probably in his shed, hiding."

Dedwin was the gardener and I did find him in a small wooden hut at the side of the house. He was a short, stocky man, probably in his seventies, stooped and shuffling. His skin was nut brown and wrinkled and he smelled of dust and oil. He complained about the heat and the amount of work he had to do at great length in a mumbling country accent so thick I could barely understand half of what he said. It was clear from the first minute that I was wasting my time. All he seemed to know about McKinley was that he'd been a "top bloke" and he was "worth a few bob." Yet he seemed happy to believe his former boss had killed himself, mainly on the grounds that "money ain't never made any fucker happy."

The bloke with the porcelain figurines, Darren Constance, worked in the CBD. He was another fifty-something. *Silver fox*, came to mind when I met him in a café beneath the bank he worked for. He was medium height, slim and dapper. He wore a tailored suit and a bold, yellow tie. He told me he was in risk management at the bank and I made a mental note to google that as soon as he left.

"You collect porcelain figurines?" I asked, for want of anything better to say.

"I collect all kinds of things," he said with a wolfish smile.

"How did you meet Everson McKinley?"

"At a gallery. We got chatting and he mentioned he had a few pieces. I went to his house to see them and fell in love.

Nothing valuable. We're not talking Lladro or even Royal Doulton you understand, but fabulous pieces all the same. Sonny wasn't a collector, of course, he only had them because they came to him from his father. His real passion was paintings. He got me quite fired up about his pre-Raphaelites for a while but you have to know what you're doing and I never had the patience to learn it all. Even with Sonny's help I made some very rash purchases."

"So you became friends?"

He looked at me curiously, a little frown creasing his broad forehead. "We shared far more than just a passion for fine art," he said, meaningfully. I nodded as if I understood but it wasn't until half an hour after he'd gone that it struck me he'd just told me they had been lovers.

"Do you have any idea why Professor McKinley might have killed himself?"

"I can't believe he did. He wasn't that kind of man. I know it's a cliché but he loved life."

"When was the last time you saw him?"

"Oh, probably a year ago now. So, yes, I suppose things could have happened to make him…" Again, I was slow on the uptake. McKinley's wife had died a year ago. But I bumbled on.

"Is it possible that someone would want him dead? Can you think of anyone who hated him? Anyone who held a grudge? Anyone he'd crossed swords with?"

He gave a quick shake of his head, almost a shudder of distaste. "Sonny wasn't like that. He treated everybody fairly. It's hard to explain to someone who didn't know him but he was an aesthete. To behave shabbily towards anyone would have seemed sordid to him. Ugly." He fell silent. "I miss him so much."

Chapter Three

Lunch was a sandwich from a shop in the mall, eaten in my office while I wrote up the notes of my three interviews. I was feeling low. It felt like I'd wasted the morning, got nothing of any value, and was getting nowhere with the case. It didn't help that I'd missed a key opportunity to explore Darren Constance's relationship with McKinley. Being the bloke's lover and then the affair ending just when McKinley's wife died, just screamed potential motive but I'd let the whole thing pass right over my head. The other two weren't so dramatically stupid but I'd managed to piss off Mrs. Roberts, despite a friendly start and a chatty witness, and I'd given up on Dedwin, the gardener, mostly because I'd written him off as a bloody galah.

I closed my eyes and fell back in my chair. I was really bad at this stuff. Really, really bad. The handful of small cases we'd had in the past year, hadn't prepared me at all for running a murder investigation. Mind you, the training sessions I'd had with Ronnie on procedure and technique were a joke. Most of them had ended up in shouting matches anyway. Ronnie was a bloody useless teacher and I was far too willing to get into a blue with him when he turned snarky and insulting. And maybe you couldn't learn that kind of thing anyway. Maybe it was something you had or you hadn't, like being a good joke teller, or having good hand-eye coordination. Ronnie wouldn't have screwed up the way I did that morning. And I could not imagine Ronnie acquired his skills by being a good and diligent student.

"Are you… asleep?"

I almost fell off my chair with the shock of hearing a voice right there in the room with me.

"I – I was thinking," I said, sounding ridiculously defensive, as if I really had been sleeping.

As I grabbed up the remains of my sandwich and dumped it in the bin, my Mystery Woman watched me fumbling from across the desk. With an effort, I made myself stop doing stupid things and focus on her. She was twice as beautiful as I remembered her. She wore a bright, summer dress that hugged her torso, caressed her breasts and swooned over her hips.

"Hello," I said. "How are you doing?"

She seemed amused. "May I sit?"

"Of course! Of course! Please do!"

I understood McKinley perfectly now. He had turned into a slobbering moron on meeting this woman and, in the aftermath, had seen only one way out of his acute embarrassment and shame.

"How's the case coming along?" she asked.

I sat and blinked while my brain finished turning somersaults and settled down again. This was the client. This was our most important case ever. I needed to chill.

"It's good. Very good. We've… er…" What the hell had we been doing? Oh yes. "We've established a preliminary list of suspects and I've been out this morning interviewing some of them."

39

"Good," she said, nodding. "Do you mind telling me who you're looking at?"

I reached for the suspects list but remembered just in time that she was on it. "It's just a preliminary list," I said. "Everybody with any connection to the deceased is on it. It will be clearer in a couple of days when we've managed to eliminate a few of them."

"So, no prime suspect yet?"

"These things take time."

"Of course. Have you spoken to the police, yet?"

It was an interesting question. "Not yet. I'd like to be more familiar with the people involved before I give the cops the opportunity to tell me to piss off."

She smiled. "Only I've heard they're going to close the case very soon."

"Really? Who did you get that from?"

"Tim. Tim Pearce."

"Yes, you mentioned him. He wants to help but he's not even in homicide."

"Wow, you have a really good memory."

"It's quirky. However, I do remember you gave me a false name when you were here yesterday."

She smiled. "O gosh, I've forgotten what I said now."

"Margaret Preston."

"Right. What's wrong with that?"

"You also said that Sonny McKinley was your tutor at the university. Was that false, too?"

"Oh no. He really was. More like a mentor, actually. He was so lovely."

Well, at least that squared with what everybody was telling me. "Do you know McKinley's daughter, Ophelia?"

She wrinkled her nose, giving me severe cuteness

overload. "Not really. Sonny introduced us once at his place but she was just a teenager. Not a friend or anything."

"Did you know she inherits everything?"

She pulled back in surprise. "You're not saying little Offie is a suspect?"

"Not so little any more. And she and her father appear to have fallen out after her mother's death. Do you know what that was about?"

"Not a clue but that sort of thing puts a terrible strain on families."

Her sky-blue eyes wandered away from me as something obviously filled her thoughts. Perhaps she was talking from personal experience.

"Won't you please tell me what your name is?"

She came back and smiled. "I suppose you're worried about getting paid."

"It never crossed my mind," I lied.

She reached into her handbag and brought out an envelope stuffed with cash. She placed it on the desk. I looked at it, then at her.

"It should keep you going for a few days," she said. "Happy now?"

"Thank you, but that wasn't my concern at all. Mostly, I'd just like to be able to confirm your story. Just to be thorough, hey? Tick all the boxes?"

She stood up and gave me another thousand megawatt smile. "If you're any good, I'm sure you'll work it out soon enough."

She left before I could leap around the desk to shake hands. I stood in a cloud of her perfume, watching the empty doorway.

What the fuck? I asked myself. Okay, she was stunning. She wasn't just beautiful, she was supernormal. Everything about her said sex, in fact, shouted it so loud you couldn't hear yourself think. But what was more worrying than her astonishing animal magnetism, was my own reaction to it. I wasn't the kind of bloke who turned to stare at women in the street, who made obscene suggestions to girls at parties, or who made a bee-line for the hottest chick in the bar. I was... well... normal, not a perv, or a misogynist, or a creep. Yet somehow this woman brought it out in me.

I sat back down in my chair and let my head fall onto my arms on the desk. What was wrong with me? Yes, I wasn't the most socially skilled twenty-something on the planet but I'd always been a civilised human being around women. In fact, I'd had a beautiful, intelligent, strong girlfriend in Chelsea and, while she'd probably thought of me more as a cute pet than a Real Man, we'd had a more-or-less grown-up relationship. Kind of. Anyway, I hadn't been a leering douchebag. And yet, there I was, reduced to drivelling imbecility by the mere presence of a goddess in human form.

I supposed I should congratulate myself that I'd still been able to ask a few sensible questions.

"Are you... asleep?"

I sprang into an upright position, sending my chair rolling backwards. I flailed awkwardly, trying to bring it under control. Karen Cha stood where the Mystery Woman had been just minutes ago, watching me with her head cocked and a twinkle of amusement in her large, dark eyes.

"I – I was thinking," I said. She chose not to comment.

Karen was employed by Chelsea's company, that is, by the one I had inherited when Chelsea died and which I had very little to do with – mainly because I found it hard to understand what they did and didn't want to mess it up. I'd placed it in the safe hands of Kazima Abbas, Chelsea's friend and Finance Officer and had never regretted the decision for a moment. Kazima had flourished in the CEO role, the company had expanded, business was growing fast, and the profits I had taken at the end of the financial year had been ridiculously large. I told Kazima to keep most of it and re-invest it. She explained that they'd already put enough aside for planned growth and that, if I didn't take the money, I'd effectively be buying more of the business and my profits would be even larger next year. I decided to put the money into my private investigation business, Systematic Doubt, instead because god knows, it wasn't making enough to pay the rent, let alone Ronnie's consultancy fees.

Karen Cha was the tech support guru at the other place. Brilliant, unflappable, elegant and, as I discovered while chasing Chelsea's killer, a very accomplished hacker. I'd asked Karen to set up the IT for Systematic Doubt and she'd become the go-to IT guy for Ronnie and me. Not that there was much IT involved – a server, couple of laptops, a couple of phones, an Internet connection and router, a website and some email addresses, and that was it – yet even that was enough complexity that I struggled to understand it all. I suspected there was more but Karen wisely kept the detail from me. She had it all documented in a file that she printed off for me and which I stuffed into the back of the filing cabinet without reading.

"IT trouble?" I asked, recovering what was left of my dignity. She took the seat opposite me, sitting primly with a straight back and her hands in her lap. She was about my age but looked like a teenager.

"Not this time." She seemed reluctant to speak.

"So how can I help?"

"Are you busy?"

Considering she thought she'd just caught me sleeping in the office, it was a very politic question. "We've got our first murder case," I told her, grinning. She knew full well what that would mean to me. She and I had spoken often over the past year, not just in the office but at staff dos that the other place seemed to run every month or so – birthday parties, contract celebrations, barbies, even a wedding.

"Wow. Is Ronnie out working on it?"

And that was another odd thing. She got on really well with Ronnie. It didn't make any sense. He was a miserable, curmudgeonly, scruffy, foul-mouthed, culture-free zone, while she was refined and delicate, always immaculately presented and polite to a fault. Yet, there it was: Beauty and the Beast.

I explained Ronnie's hospital visit and she immediately said, "I should go to see him. What do you give to sick people in Australia?"

"I'm sure he'd love a good book for his convalescence," I said. "Something mushy and romantic." She frowned, clearly not believing me, but did not contradict me. "I'm going over to his place this evening after work. Maybe I could pick you up?"

She didn't respond and the silence dragged out into an abyss of awkwardness. It was too much like asking her out on a date. Far too much. We didn't have that kind of relationship. Nothing like. Why on earth had I said that? Was I asking her out on a date? Why would I even think that? What was wrong with me? Far too late, I said, "Or not. Maybe I'll see you there. Or something…" She nodded, looking uncomfortable. *Change the subject, you moron!*

"So, why did you come round if it isn't an IT thing?"

Like a drowning woman, she clutched the life belt I'd thrown. "I need to ask you a favour."

"Anything. Anything at all. You know that." She had saved my life that time Chelsea's killer had me captive and I owed her everything. Yet she had not asked for a single thing in a whole year. "I'd be happy to help."

"But you have your big case at last. My timing sucks."

"Don't worry about that. Whatever it is, I want to help."

She nodded to herself and looked down at the desk. "You remember when I did some hacking for you last year."

"Of course. You were brilliant."

She ducked her head even farther. "You remember me saying I'd been forced to do that kind of thing before, back in Hong Kong?" She glanced up to catch my nod. "Well the man who made me do that was my Uncle Lau. He is a very bad man. He knows lots of bad people and has a great deal of influence."

"He's asked you to work for him again," I said, seeing where she was going.

She nodded slowly. "But I don't want to. It is part of why I left home in the first place. I don't want to be a criminal like him and his friends. I just want to be free of all that."

"Can he make you?" I asked, imagining some of the ways he could. Her whole family was still living in Hong Kong.

"He has threatened many things but I don't really think he would hurt his own family."

"So you've called his bluff. What changed to make you scared?"

"He's coming here. In a few days. He says he'll drag me home by my hair if necessary. He is a horrible, violent man."

"Have you spoken to the police?"

"No! You know what immigration is like in this country.

45

Well, perhaps you don't. He has threatened to reveal some of what I did in Hong Kong to the Australian Federal Police. I am here on a work visa. I hope to get permanent residence in a year or so. If there is even a suspicion that I was involved in criminal activity, my chances would be zero. They would deport me."

The only time I had ever seen her look the least bit upset was when her past in Hong Kong became an issue because I had asked her to hack a government website for me. Her fear of being dragged back into that life was written all over her face.

"What can I do?" I asked. "If you need money, or references or an intermediary or... anything, just tell me." I honestly didn't see how I could help her, but I wanted very much to try. "We should talk to Ronnie. He has all kinds of contacts I don't. I bet he could even get you a complete new identity if that's what you need." I'd heard him say as much in the past. It was a mark of how desperate she felt that she actually seemed to consider this. "Look, come with me to see him tonight. Seriously. I'll pick you up at the office. I'll text you from the car park when I get there."

She nodded again. "Thank you. I am very sorry to bring you this trouble at such a time."

"Helping you is my top priority." I tried to lighten the mood. "Half of Brisbane could be murdered and it wouldn't change that."

"I should go back now. I'm here on my lunch break."

"Don't worry about it. I have a lot of influence with the boss." She gave me a weak smile and stood up. I stood too. "We'll sort this out, Karen. Uncle Lau will not make you go back, I promise."

* * * *

My afternoon interviews were with McKinley's charities and the art gallery in Arthur Street. I phoned the charities and thanked the heavens I hadn't wasted my time visiting them in person because all I got from them was that McKinley had been a valued patron and that nobody there really knew him personally. Well, they had been long shots at best. The art gallery, I visited in person, leaving the car in the CBD and walking out to Arthur Street for the exercise.

Carnarvon Fine Art was a small, boutique gallery, with polished wooden floors and white-painted walls on which a couple of dozen paintings hung under bright lights. I wandered around briefly, not particularly liking anything I saw, until a cadaverous creature in a floral dress materialised at my elbow.

"I see you're admiring the di Rossi," she said in a husky, English accent. Her eyes were like something from an Oxfam poster. Her lips a bloody slash beneath them. The tight skin on her face made it look as though her skull had been vacuum sealed for freshness. The gold bangles on her skeletal wrists threatened to fall off at any moment.

"No, actually, I'm just—"

"Magnificent, isn't it?"

I looked again, in case I'd missed something but, no, it was the same set of colourful blotches I thought it was.

"Cheerful," I said, trying to enter into the spirit.

"Yes! You've captured its essence in a single word. How perceptive. What a marvellous talent this young man has."

I assumed she was talking about the artist, not me. "I'm actually here to see someone," I said, reluctant to interrupt her aesthetic rapture. "Tony Rushton? He owns the gallery?"

She stepped away, regarding me in a new light. "I'm Antonia Rushton. How may I help you?"

"Oh, I'm sorry. It was written with a 'y' and I just assumed…" She watched my fumbling apology with a pained expression. I took a breath and held out my hand. "I'm Luke Kelly. I'm a private investigator. I'm looking into the circumstances surrounding the death of Everson McKinley."

Frowning, she held out a long, fragile hand and I shook it, carefully. "I still don't quite understand."

I had a sudden feeling of wasting my time. If this woman could even lift a shotgun to shoulder height, the recoil from firing it would have shattered every bone in her body. I fought the urge to go.

"Mr. McKinley was a partner in this gallery, I believe."

"Sonny shot himself. That's what the police said. Why are you here?"

"My client believes the case is not so cut and dried. I've been engaged to find out."

"And who is your client? Offie?"

"I'm afraid I can't say. Was Mr. McKinley your partner?"

"Sonny was one of several investors. He wasn't much interested in emerging artists himself but he believed he should support those of us who are. He had very little involvement with the business. He attended some of our more important exhibitions, provided his professional expertise in evaluating new work, when asked, which was not often, and we knew each other socially." She closed her eyes, her lids moving with a strange slowness. When she opened them, she said, "If you must know, our friendship had been a little strained lately because of the FABClub affair but he was far too much of a gentleman to blame me, even though I'd made the introductions."

"What's the FABClub?"

She sighed as if it was all too awful. "The Fine Art Buyers Club. It's a bit of a craze at the moment. People with money get together and buy art pieces as an investment. A half-dozen people with fifty-thousand each can buy something really worth having. They don't exhibit their pieces, or even hang them at home, just put them in vaults and let them appreciate. Rather tacky, really. These little investor groups like to have at least one member who knows the art world and can help make sure they don't get fleeced. Sonny was quite tickled by the whole thing, at first. The FABClub bought quite a few pieces, I gather. But the other people in the club were not really Sonny's type, you understand. Investment bankers, property developers, mining magnates, that sort. They had a falling-out over something." She waved a hand. "Don't ask me what but it was rather acrimonious, I believe. Sonny was in quite a sulk about it for a while. But he wasn't the sort to hold grudges."

I asked for a FABClub contact and she gave me the name and address of Nick Kryou, a property developer with offices in the CBD.

"Do you know if Mr McKinley had any enemies?"

"No! Of course he didn't! If you'd known him, you'd know what a silly question that is."

Yet someone had put a gun in his face and deliberately blown his head off. I pondered that as I walked back to the city centre. Everson McKinley was a nice man. He was well liked. He did charity work and supported young artists. No-one who knew him had a bad word to say about him, even his rather prickly daughter. An ex-student was paying me to find his killer. So how does a man with no enemies end up being murdered in cold blood?

I fell into a café to recharge and think about the investigation. I still had lots of people to see – not least whomever I might find at the university – and my day's talking had added another name to the list: Nick Kryou. But, first, I wanted to talk to the police. That is, I didn't want to but I knew I had to. The nearest thing to a friendly copper I knew was Alexandra Bertolissio, but this wasn't her case. I needed to find this DI Marr my mysterious client had mentioned, the woman who was actually making such a pig's ear of the investigation, and talk to her about it.

It was a hot day and the central police station was at the opposite end of town, so I walked slowly and it was mid-afternoon before I was at the reception desk asking if I might speak to the officer in charge of the Everson McKinley suspicious death case.

They made me wait in the lobby, among the universally miserable-looking denizens of that place. I suppose that, after fifteen minutes waiting, I looked just as miserable as everyone else. When a balding, middle-aged man appeared from a side door and, holding it open, called out my name, I felt quite guilty that I was being seen before many who had been there before I arrived.

"So, you've got information in the McKinley case?" he asked without introducing himself. He was still holding the door open and I supposed this was a test I had to pass before he'd take me inside.

"Yes, I do," I said, confidently.

He looked me up and down. "I'm Detective Sergeant Bronski," he said. "We've met." He signalled me to go in with a tilt of his head and I followed him to a small interview room, all the while wracking my brains to remember when I might have had the pleasure. It hit me as I sat down opposite him, the memory triggered, no doubt, by the similarity to the previous occasion.

"I remember now. You were on Reid's team investigating my girlfriend's murder." He'd been present for just one interview but, since I had been their chief suspect at the time, it was hardly surprising I had been more memorable for him than the other way round. I vaguely recalled he had a different job description back then. "You've been promoted," I guessed.

He frowned at me but said nothing. It got my back up. Would it hurt these bozos to show just a little basic civility beyond what was absolutely mandated by their procedure manual?

"So, what can you tell me, Mr. Kelly."

"Doctor."

"What?"

"It's Doctor Kelly. Remember? Your boss thought I was an evil mastermind, arrogantly sneering at you all as I pulled off the perfect crime."

"What do you want, *Doctor* Kelly?"

I thought about stringing it out a bit longer, just to wind him up. Why was it that the cops brought out the worst in me? But I decided not to indulge myself and just get on with it. "I've been investigating the Everson McKinley murder and I thought I'd come and share what I'd learned."

"You've been what?"

I pulled out a business card and put it on the table in front of him. "I'm a private investigator now."

He picked up the card and studied it. "Systematic Doubt? That's what you're calling yourself?"

"Don't you like it?"

"Nah, it's bloody stupid." He grinned at me. "Just offering

my professional opinion."

It was irritating. No-one liked the name except me. "Anyway, my client instructed—"

"What? You got a client? With a name like that?"

"My client asked me to look into McKinley's death. I've come to the conclusion it was murder, not suicide."

He sat back in his chair and studied me. "Bit of a figjam, ain't ya? You think you can do our job better than we can, just 'cos you got lucky one time?"

It was actually a very good point and essentially true. "Do you want to hear what I have to say?"

He shook his head, sadly. "Let's see. Do you have solid evidence that there was anybody else in McKinley's home at the time of the murder?"

"No but—"

"Do you have anybody else's prints on the gun except McKinley's?" I didn't answer. Only the police would know that and I assumed the question meant they hadn't found any. "Have you found any evidence of a break-in? And evidence of theft? Anybody with a motive who doesn't have a rock-solid alibi? No? I didn't think so. In which case, no, I don't want to hear what you have to say." He stood up. The interview was over. "Thank you for your time, *Doctor* Kelly. We're always happy to hear from concerned citizens."

I stood up too. "All right, I don't have any evidence, but there was no note, the angle of the gun was all wrong, he damaged his favourite painting, not one person I've spoken to said he was in a mood to do such a thing. Doesn't that just feel wrong to you?"

He opened the door and waited for me to leave. "You can go back and reassure your client that her father was not murdered. We've run a very thorough investigation – a professional one – and come to the conclusion that it was suicide. If she'd like to talk to DI Marr about any lingering concerns she has, I'm sure her door is always open."

"DI Marr is the senior investigating officer?"

"She was. We closed the case this morning."

"Ophelia McKinley isn't my client."

It was the first thing I'd said that had given him pause. He frowned. "So who is it?"

"I'm afraid I can't say. But Ophelia isn't the only one with doubts. I hear there was a woman trying to get you to see sense, making a nuisance of herself. A former student of McKinley's."

He grinned. "You mean Mel?"

I shrugged. "I don't know who she is, just a description: tall, blonde, late twenties."

"If you'd ever met her, you'd know that does not do her justice. Mel can come and make a nuisance of herself any time she likes. As for you, Miss Marple, it's time you shot through. Some of us have real police work to do."

"What's her full name? This Mel woman. I'd like to talk to her."

"Yeah, you and me both. Why don't you ask your buddy, Al?"

"Al?" I didn't have any friends called Al.

"Detective Sergeant Alexandra Bertolissio."

"Ah, right-o. I'll ask her then. Or you could just, you know, tell me."

"It'll be better coming from Al."

"No probs. Could you let her know I'm here, please?"

"Do I look like your bloody slave? Go see the desk."

He practically booted me out of the door and back into the reception area. I sat down in the waiting area again, not because I was going back to the desk – I'd already decided I'd give Bertolissio a call – but because I wanted to update my notes before I left. I tapped at my phone, pulled out a folder called "QPS" and opened an org chart that I'd been compiling. It had various tree diagrams – like a large, fragmented family tree – representing the various departments of the Queensland Police. I added DI Marr and DS Bronski, linking Marr to DCI Adams who ran the homicide team. I linked Marr and Bronski to the McKinley case. Then I opened the case file and updated the client name from "Mystery Woman" to "Mel X". With just the first name, I could probably find her now, knowing she had been a student of McKinley's at UQ. But it would be much simpler just to call Bertolissio.

I put all my apps away and headed for the door. My phone rang as soon as I put it in my pocket. It was Bertolissio.

"Hi, Luke. How are you dong?"

"Good. Yourself?"

"Bronski just passed my desk and told me you were here. I'm taking a break. Fancy a coffee?"

"Sure."

"I'll be down in two."

She was down in one and we walked out to a café on the far side of Turbot Street, taking almost five more minutes to cross the busy road and walk fifty metres. I ordered the drinks and she waited at a table for me to join her. The café looked like it was closing soon and we were the only people in the place.

"So…" She seemed a little hesitant. "Your new client is my sister, Mel."

"What?" That was impossible. Bertolissio was small and dark – my exact stereotype of a second-generation Italian-

Australian. My client, Mel, was tall, blonde and blue-eyed. The detective was pretty enough but Mel was…

"Yes, a lot of people react that way. Not much family likeness. And, before you ask, same mother, same father."

She sat quietly, watching me, as I struggled to get my thoughts in order.

"Your sister is paying me to look into McKinley's murder? Why would she do that?"

"I'd be more concerned about how she's affording it. Don't let the clothes and designer accessories fool you. Men like to give her presents. I'm sure you understand. But she's not usually reliably employed."

I put that aside for later analysis. "Did you know?"

She shook her head. "I knew she was thinking about getting help elsewhere. I did discuss you and Ronnie with her, in fact. She doesn't usually listen to me though. Even so, there are much worse people she could have turned to. Some of them are the same ones who give her such nice presents."

Again, to be dealt with later. "And… what do you think about her concerns about McKinley?"

She pursed her lips. "You've met Bronski. You haven't met Barr yet. She's ambitious. She's in a hurry. She's determined to have the best clear-up rate in the department."

"So, she's sloppy?"

Bertolissio shook her head. "Not exactly. Just not willing to complicate what she sees as a straightforward case. To be fair, most coppers would think she came to the right conclusion about McKinley."

"What about you?"

"I have learned not to underestimate Mel's instincts about people – except when it comes to boyfriends."

"Was McKinley one of her boyfriends?"

"She says not – although he has the right financial profile."

"Have you seen the file?"

"I'm not on that case but I might have taken a peek from time to time."

"Do you think he was murdered?"

"I think there is a possibility. Personally, I wouldn't have closed the case until I'd answered a few questions."

"Like what?"

"Like why was there no security footage for the night McKinley died? Have you been to his house yet? The entrances and grounds are full of cameras. Yet they were all turned off just after McKinley died. Turned off using an app on McKinley's phone. The phone that was found in his pocket. And the recordings were deleted for the preceding two hours."

"Did he do that often?"

"I don't know."

"Could anyone else have accessed the system?"

"I don't know."

"Why do you suppose Ophelia didn't mention it?"

"She might not know anything about it. The system was not turned back on again. Investigators don't always share every detail of an investigation with potential suspects."

"And the fact that Ophelia didn't start it up again might mean she doesn't know it's off, or she doesn't know the codes to get it working again." I felt very stupid not knowing all this already. "What else?"

"I'd have looked into McKinley's business dealings. The art world can be a very shady place. Lots of money sloshing about. Lots of opportunities for fraud and other kinds of theft."

"Didn't Marr look into that?"

"No. No need if it was a suicide."

"I've made a start there but I haven't learned much. He seems like a nice bloke who didn't really do bad stuff. His money seems to have been inherited from his father."

"I'd also be talking to his colleagues at the university. If there was the kind of interpersonal friction that gets people killed, a university is as good an incubator as any."

"That's on tomorrow's to-do list."

She fell silent. "Thank you," I said, "for talking to me. Ronnie's... got medical problems and he's out of commission. He got me started but I've been on my own and floundering a bit."

"She'll be right," she said with an encouraging smile. "You seem to be doing all the right things."

Except I missed that the cameras were turned off. "We'll see."

"Give Ronnie my best. You'll be seeing him tonight, I suppose."

"That reminds me. I need to get some grapes or something."

She laughed. "Get him a book. No-one really wants grapes."

"Yeah, I'm not sure a book's the go, either. Not for Ronnie. Maybe an *Arms and Ammo* magazine or something."

She laughed again and it struck me that maybe Mel wasn't the only beauty in the Bertolissio family. You just had to spend more time with Alexandra to discover it. She pushed back her chair.

"I have to go now. Good luck with the case."

I watched her go and sat for a while brooding over the dregs of my coffee. When the staff started putting chairs on tables ready for closing, I got up and left.

Chapter Four

Karen and I turned up at Ronnie's place at about six. There was a little blue car already parked in the drive so I found a spot in the street. An old woman with lots of beads, long grey hair and a floor-length loose dress answered the door. She greeted us like old friends and talked non-stop as she led us through the house to the patio at the back. By the time we reached him, we were fully briefed on his condition. It seemed Ronnie was doing very well, considering ("The poor darling") and everything had been a complete success ("They can work miracles these days"). "But don't expect his usual cheery self 'cause he's still a bit crook. Have you eaten yet? We were going to get a carry out. I said I'd cook but Ronnie won't hear a word of it, bless him. 'I'm not having you run around after me like a mother hen, Maggie,' he said. Hey, darl, we've got company."

Ronnie was on one of the sun loungers, an esky full of stubbies at his elbow. He looked old and tired and I felt a wave of sadness at the sight. Until he spoke.

"I see you two have hooked up at last. Always thought you would. Of course, you're too good for him, love. You could do a lot better, trust me."

Karen and I burst into denials simultaneously. She seemed quite distressed and even took a sideways step away from me, to emphasise her position. Ronnie just grinned, enjoying the performance he'd triggered.

"He's only kidding," I said to Karen. To Ronnie, I said, "I see the surgeons didn't remove your defective sense of humour."

Ronnie indicated the esky. "Help yourselves. You've met Maggie."

I turned to Maggie, who was smiling indulgently. "I'm Luke. This is Karen. We just came to pay our respects but it looks like the old bastard survived, so we'll have to cancel the celebration now." She laughed raucously. I took two beers out of the esky and passed one to Karen. We pulled up a couple more sun loungers and everyone sat down. "So, I'm guessing you're one of the Dogsbodies, Maggie?"

"Proud mum to four fur babies," she said.

I smiled at Ronnie. "How come you don't have any fur babies, mate, since you're such a big fan?"

"A dog's a big commitment," he said. "And I've got enough on my plate looking after you. Now, give Maggie your credit card so she can order us some nosh. Maggie, be a love and bugger off for a bit until the food comes. I need to talk to these two about confidential business stuff."

Maggie took my card and disappeared into the house.

"She's nice," I said, pointedly.

"Yes, she is. Now, let's hear how badly you've been stuffing things up while I've been gone."

"First you need to hear what Karen has to say. She's been having a bit of trouble and needs our help." Ronnie was as sensitive as I was to the debt we both owed her. His full attention switched to her immediately. Suddenly reluctant again, she hesitantly retold the story of her Uncle Lau. Ronnie listened in silence, sipping his coldie. When she finished, he was quiet for a while.

"Any chance he's bluffing?"

Karen shook her head.

"There are only three things to do then. One: you could have him bumped off. I could probably arrange that."

Her eyes flew open. "No! He is my mother's brother. It would not be right."

I was shocked that her main reason for rejecting the suggestion seemed to be that the victim was a close relative.

"Good," said Ronnie. "Because I've had a gutful of murdering people. Two: you could disappear. I could help with that, too."

She shook her head, eyes down. "I've already run seven thousand kilometres to get away from this. I think that's far enough."

Ronnie nodded. Her response seemed to satisfy him. "So you've decided to fight, hey?"

"If I can. I just don't see—"

'The basic principle is you make it so that if he tries to expose you, it will hurt. We need to be able to threaten Uncle Lau with something so terrible, he won't dare touch you. So, what have we got?"

Karen opened her mouth and drew a long breath but didn't say anything.

"The bloke's a crim, hey?" I said. "There must be some evidence of that. I hate to say this but, couldn't you hack his computers?"

She sagged a little. "I would have done that if it was possible but I helped him set up his network security. Everything important is air-gapped. There's no way in."

"Air-gapped?" I asked.

"No connection to the Internet. You'd have to be right there in the same room with one of his computers to be able to access it."

Ronnie didn't seem to think this was a major obstacle. "But, if you could get in, you'd know what to look for, where to find the good stuff, right?"

"Yes, of course. I set up his file system, his security, everything. I even have back doors into key parts of the network. I doubt that the setup has changed much since I left."

"Back doors?" I asked.

"Jeez, mate, go read a book that wasn't written by some dead Greek. Everybody in the world knows this stuff, except you." I scowled at the miserable old bastard but didn't argue. I had to admit, there were gaps in my general knowledge and all things computer-related was one of them. Maybe he was right and I should go learn something about cybercrime.

I heard Maggie answering the door to the delivery guy. Ronnie waved Karen closer and I wondered again what he'd had done that meant he couldn't lean towards her. "Let me work on this," he said in a low voice. "I've got your number. I'll call you when I've got something."

Karen answered, also in a low voice, "Whatever it is, I'm not going back there."

He was about to reply when Maggie came out onto the patio. "Grub's up, guys."

"Maggie, you're an angel," Ronnie announced, loudly. "Luke, get me up."

"I'll bring it out to you," Maggie said. "The surgeon said to keep you off your feet."

He gave her a broad wink. "What he said was to sweep me

off my feet, and you did that years ago, darl. Luke. Get here."

Maggie pulled a mock-cross face and went back into the house. I got the impression she was well used to his ways. Karen hurried after her. I helped Ronnie stand up. When I tried to support him as he walked, he batted me away. To be honest, he looked OK and, although he moved slower than usual, he didn't seem to need me.

We arrived in the kitchen in time to hear Maggie telling Karen she'd ordered Chinese. "I didn't mean to be culturally insensitive or anything, it's just that it's Ronnie's idea of comfort food."

Karen reassured her that no offence was taken and we all sat down to eat. Maggie kept up a stream of chatter – mostly anecdotes about what her friends and relatives had been doing recently. I kept trying to steer the conversation round to Ronnie and The Dogsbodies, my fascination with this weird other side of my partner's life getting the better of my resolve to avoid it. But each time she started to tell us anything interesting, Ronnie deftly moved her onto some other topic. He and I duelled like this until the meal was over and tidied away.

"Well, I'm going to shoot through," Maggie declared once she had made sure everything that could possibly be done for Ronnie's comfort had been done. She offered Karen a lift and for some reason I felt put out when Karen readily accepted. I'd assumed I'd be taking her home but, now that I thought about it, there was no particular reason for her to stay. So I saw them off and helped Ronnie back to his recliner on the patio.

"So, what's the deal with you and Maggie, then?" I asked, handing him another coldie.

"Wouldn't you like to know?" He winked at me.

"Oh god, now I'm thinking about disgusting old people sex."

"Yeah, right. So much worse than embarrassing young people fumblings. Why don't you get your head out of your daks for a minute and tell me what you've been doing about the case."

So I sat back, stared into the sky and told him from beginning to end. He didn't say a thing, just listened, until I told him about my Mystery Woman being Bertolissio's sister. That made him snort.

"How did I do?" I asked. The recitation had felt like a listing of my shortcomings as an investigator. Each new failure to elicit anything useful from anyone at all was like an extra weight on my chest and, in the end, I felt I might sink through my chair and into the soil below. "The thing is, I really needed you out there. I was just completely out of my depth. That copper, Bronski, was right; it was amateur hour. The only thing I got right was finding out who the client was – and that was just an embarrassment. If I'd spent less time drooling over her and more forcing her to come clean, it would never have got to that point in the first place. I don't know what's wrong with me. Maybe I'm not cut out for this."

Ronnie sighed. I looked across at him, ready for the insults and jokes to begin. He looked back at me, his expression unreadable.

"Mate, you did just fine. You did the footwork. You crossed off names. Ninety per cent of this stuff is just boring crap. You're right, I should have been there. Our first big case and here am I with my feet up having a beer. And don't forget I was there when we forgot to ask about the security footage. That one's on me."

"Nah, you were distracted. That's fair enough. I didn't

have any excuse at all."

He stared past his feet to the dark lawn beyond. "I hate being fucking old." He sighed again and his chin came up. "Never mind. We'll do better tomorrow. You've written it all up, hey?"

"Yeah, everything except the meeting with Bronski and the phone call from Bertolissio."

"Good. Get those on the case file and I'll go over them more carefully. Right now I'm fucking knackered. You should piss off and I'll see you tomorrow."

"Er… Do you want me to help you into bed or anything?"

"Fuck off." He sounded genuinely affronted.

"Right-o. I'll just, you know, bugger off then." I stood up to go. "When shall I come round tomorrow?"

"Don't. I'll meet you at the office. You're off to the uni first thing, I suppose. So I'll see you about lunchtime, yeah? Bring something edible back with you."

I left him brooding on the patio and made my way home.

* * * *

The main campus of Queensland University is a big, sprawling site with the suburb of St Lucia on one side and the river on the other. I'd have liked the place better if there was ever anywhere to park that didn't cost an arm and a leg. Still, I had an enduring fondness for the old place. It was my *alma mater*. I had done my undergrad degree and my doctorate there and, if I didn't exactly love it, I would always feel an intimacy with it as the site of so many of the major emotional moments of my life.

Most of all, it was where I met and courted Chelsea. As I stood in front of the big map of the campus just outside the multi-storey car park, looking for where a fine arts lecturer might be found, the lines and labels spoke to me of blossoming love and the agonising, delicious yearning of finding someone so wonderful and feeling she might, just might, like me too. So much of that map was overlaid with memories it was almost impossible to focus on the job I'd come to do.

It was nearly a year, a full year, since Chelsea had died and the pain was still lurking inside, ready to ambush me at any moment. I didn't cry much any more but the tears were always there, just behind my eyes.

"Can I help you?"

It was a young woman. Probably too old to be a student. More likely a research assistant or a very young member of staff.

"I'm fine," I said, quickly wiping my eyes. "I studied here. I know the place pretty well."

"And yet, here you are, staring at the map."

"It… brings back memories. I suppose I was, just you know…"

"Right-o," she said, a little dubiously. "I won't interrupt you then."

She walked on a couple of paces before I called after her, "Actually, I could do with some help." She stopped and turned, her eyebrows raised. "I'm looking for the arts department – or something like that. Fine Arts? Art History? I dunno. Somewhere that would have a lecturer in fine arts."

She gave it some thought. "There's the Art Gallery but I can't think of any courses. QUT has a Fine Arts degree."

God damn it! I had the wrong university. When Mel Bertolissio had said she'd studied under McKinley "at uni', I'd just assumed she meant The University of Queensland. It was where I'd studied. It was what I thought of when someone said "uni". But there was another – The Queensland University of Technology – which had its campus miles away in Kelvin Grove. Mel must have meant that. I gave myself a moment to fully acknowledge what a total bloody drongo I was before thanking my kind stranger and saying I'd try "the other place." As I stomped back to my car, I made a vow never to set off anywhere on spec again without first looking it up online.

I was still beating myself up when I got to the Kelvin Grove campus and I realised I'd done it again. I hadn't checked which of the QUT campuses the art department was on. I knew of at least two. For a moment, it completely floored me. I felt like I might just give up and go home. I sat in the car park and asked myself if I was really cut out for this life. Frankly, if I couldn't do anything as simple as check a bloody address before I went haring all over town, I should seriously consider not taking anybody's money for what I did. Yesterday, I couldn't interview a suspect without forgetting to ask the important questions. Today I couldn't even find a suspect to interview because I was randomly driving all over the place. When Mel Bertolissio first walked into my office, I'd felt like Sam Spade. Now I felt more like Dirk Gently.

Having a card that said "Private Investigator" didn't make me one. Even having the license wasn't good enough. To be a PI, I needed to actually act like one, sniff out clues, find crims. I pulled one of my cards out and looked at it. Ronnie was right. The name was shit. "Systematic Doubt"? I might as well have called it "Bunch of Clowns", or, better still, "This Guy is a Useless Dickhead".

I needed Ronnie. That was the long and short of it. He was the one who knew how to do this stuff. He was the one who always had his head in the game and didn't make stupid mistakes.

Except when he did.

He'd forgotten to ask Ophelia about the security camera footage. Yes, he'd had an operation looming. For all I knew, he'd been feeling ill. He had excuses – unlike me – but that wasn't much consolation. Ronnie was getting older all the time. This kind of thing was only going to happen more and more often. I'd based this whole venture, my whole life plan, on being able to rely on Ronnie. Now I saw that might have been a foolish thing to have done. Was that why I was so rattled? Was it because I was scared that my training wheels had come off and now I was wobbling along on my own?

It was an annoying thought. I'd been doing this for the best part of a year and I thought I'd been doing all right. But maybe I hadn't. Maybe Ronnie had been carrying me the whole time. Maybe I really was a useless prat and couldn't even find a public building without someone to hold my hand.

Angrily, I pulled out my phone and started typing. It took, literally, ten seconds to get the address of the building housing QUT's "Creative Industries Precinct". I drove there and, by a miracle, found a space in the pay and display car park. I bounded out of the car and stomped over to the building. Being in a bad mood already, I was not impressed by the quirky, modern concrete block design, nor the somewhat oppressive, predominantly brown, interior colour scheme. I wandered around the mostly empty building, asking everyone I bumped into for directions to someone who could answer my questions. I ended up in the office of a senior lecturer, Dr. Scott Armitage, who seemed flustered and busy. He was clearly about to dismiss me until I handed him my business card.

He stopped and read it, his brow furrowing. When he looked up at me, he said, "A private investigator. How exotic. And you're a doctor. A doctor of what, I wonder. Criminology? Forensic Science?"

"Philosophy."

"Goodness me. Is that what people do with their philosophy degrees these days? Who'd have guessed? And you're here to grill me about poor old Sonny? I thought he'd shot himself or something. Are you telling me it was foul play?"

He showed me to a seat and sat himself down opposite me across the desk.

"I'm looking into that possibility," I said. "I gather that you are now the acting professor."

He pulled back in mock horror. "It's a fair cop, guv'nor. I did it to get control of his vast academic empire."

He was the first person I'd encountered who saw any humour at all in the situation and it gave me a prudish feeling of distaste. I said, "If anyone from this department did kill McKinley, I'd hope they had a better motive than that. There are, what, about ten lecturers in the Visual Arts program?"

"You've read our prospectus, I see. Ah well, perhaps I won't achieve notoriety today after all. Was that an example of..." He looked at my card again. "...Systematic Doubt? You do it very well."

Cheeky bastard. Ronnie was so right. I needed a new business name.

"Do you mind if I ask you a couple of questions?"

"Not at all. It's quite exciting. We had the police in, of course, but they weren't half so interesting. Fire away."

"How well did you know Professor McKinley?"

"We worked together, attended social gatherings, bumped into one another at exhibitions, went to a couple of conferences together. That sort of thing. He was my boss. We weren't mates but we were colleagues."

"Was he mates with anyone on the staff? Anyone in particular?"

"Not really. Very pleasant bloke and all that. Friends with everyone. But not anyone in particular."

"What about anyone else, maybe in a different department?"

"Nope. No-one I'm aware of. Sonny was an aesthete. The very idea of having to talk to an engineer or a scientist would make him shudder." He laughed at the image he'd conjured for himself.

"You didn't like him much."

"What on earth makes you say that? We got along just fine."

O-kay. "What about the students?"

He rolled his eyes. "They all loved him. He spooned them a heady mixture of romanticism and traditional aesthetics, *l'art pour l'art* with a heavy dollop of *le mal romantique.* Everybody left his lectures feeling like Baudelaire with a paintbrush."

I had little idea what he was on about but I took the mildly snide tone on board and let the rest pass. "Were there any students in particular under his spell? Girls? Or boys?"

He laughed again. "If you're looking for torrid affairs and sexual passions, you're definitely looking under the wrong rock here, Dr. Kelly. Sonny was straight as a die. Definitely not the type to prey on pretty young things of either sex." He looked away and seemed, for a moment, to weary of his brittle, jousting facade. "Honestly, he was a good bloke. He did his job well. Played a straight bat. If anyone did kill him, it wasn't a pregnant teenager, or a jealous husband. That wasn't Sonny."

For form's sake, I asked him where he was on the night McKinley died.

"At home with the wife and bubs," he said and I wrote it down, not expecting I would ever attempt to check it. "Goodness, does that mean I'm a suspect after all?" The façade was back up again.

"At this point, I can't rule you out," I said, throwing him a bone. I got up to leave. "By the way. Do you remember a student here called Mel Bertolissio?"

"Have you ever met *La Belle* Mel?" he asked in reply.

"Yes, I have."

"Then you will know that no male over the age of twelve would ever forget her."

"Was she a particular friend of McKinley's?"

"Not the way you mean but yes, the lucky bastard had her in his tutorial group and they forged quite a bond. I can see why. He was the only man on campus who wasn't drooling over her. She probably felt safe with him in a way a woman like that doesn't often encounter. What has she got to do with it? Is she a suspect, too? She would make a fabulous *femme fatale*. Please tell me it was her."

I thanked him for his time and got out fast.

Poking around in dead people's lives was both fascinating and sordid. I imagined that Scott Armitage would enjoy the work – probably far too much. I tried to shake the slightly soiled feeling that talking to him had given me. I sat in my car and ran over our conversation, sifting it for any useful information. There wasn't any. Just more confirmation that Everson McKinley was a good bloke and no-one had any reason to kill him.

I drove back to Toowong and parked. On the way up to my office, I stopped off in the food hall and bought some pies and chips. It wasn't quite lunchtime but, if Ronnie was waiting, he'd be ready to eat. I'd never known him turn down a free feed.

The office, when I finally arrived with my cloud of fast food smells, was transformed. The whiteboards were up and full of pictures, writing and arrows. The tables and desks were strewn with documents. Even the floor and chairs had documents on them, as if they'd been dropped onto the tables from the ceiling and had rained down everywhere. In the midst of it all, Ronnie was slumped in my office chair like a god of chaos on his throne. He was staring at the whiteboards in a kind of trance but slowly rose to consciousness as the smell of meet pies reached his nostrils.

"About bloody time, mate," he said, focussing on the carrier bag, not me. "Let's have it, then." He swiped a hand across the desk, clearing a space. Photos and printed web pages tumbled to the floor.

"Feeling better?"

"Mate, I feel like they scooped out my insides with a ladle and sewed me back together with barbed wire. But she'll be right. As my old lady used to say, it's only pain."

"She sounds lovely. I see you've been busy."

"Flat out like a lizard drinking since the minute I got here. Did you bring any beer?"

"I brought coffee – and I'm not sure you should even have that. Of course, if I knew what they'd done to you, I'd know how to look after you."

"You? Look after me? That's a good one." His face disappeared into a steak and kidney pie.

I gave up on the conversation for the time being and went

to the whiteboards. McKinley's photo was at the top of one, with his name and the with label, "Victim", under it. There were lines leading down to Ophelia ("Grumpy Daughter"), a rectangle with no photo for Ms Roberts, the housekeeper ("Loyal Retainer"), another empty rectangle for Dedwin, the gardener ("Simple Son of the Sod"), an incredibly flattering shot of Antonia Rushton ("Undead Business Partner"), Darren Constance ("Porcelain Fancier With Benefits") and what looked like a publicity shot of Nick Kryou ("Property Developer Business Partner"). Kryou had a link to the second board where a circle was labelled "FABClub". Ophelia had a link to a picture of her boyfriend, labelled "Fraser X, Dickhead".

"Very mature," I said, turning to Ronnie. He grinned back at me, his mouth full of chips.

Also on the second whiteboard was a list of the police personnel involved. There was a picture of Mel Bertolissio that did not do her justice with a thick black link to her sister Alexandra. The label on the link said, "WTF?" There were also a few unanswered questions, such as, "Who turned off the CCTV?" and "How good is Ophelia's alibi?" There was also a list labelled "To Do" which had "Interview Kryou," "Interview the FABClub," and "Redo all of Luke's interviews."

"Put your university interviews up," Ronnie said.

I sighed and drew a new link from McKinley to a new rectangle. I wrote "colleague" on the link and labelled the rectangle, "Dr. Scott Armitage, Harmless Creep". I noticed that Ronnie had already added the link between McKinley and Mel.

"Is that it?"

"Armitage was a gossip and snide bastard and the worst

thing he had to say about McKinley was that he was a good bloke. I didn't bother asking anyone else." Ronnie shook his head, sadly. It made me defensive. "I told you. I'm really crap at this."

"That's a great argument for not doing your job properly. I wish I'd thought of that fifty years ago. It would have saved me so much hassle."

"You know what I mean."

"Sadly, I do. All right, so you're not a people person…"

"Pots and kettles, mate!"

"Why don't you turn your mighty analytical brain to solving the case?" He waved half a pie towards the boards. "That's everything we know. Use it to tell me who did it?"

I lifted some paper from a chair and put it on a table. Sitting down heavily, I said, "I have no idea. The guy was loved by all. I'm beginning to think he really did kill himself."

His face fell and his brows met. "And I'm beginning to think you bought your philosophy degree from an American online university for fifty bucks. Everyone on that board had the opportunity to shoot him – as far as we know – and most of them had a motive."

"What? Who? Name one – apart from Ophelia."

He lifted a hand and began ticking them off on his fingers. "One: Darren Constance, the jilted lover."

"We don't know he was jilted."

Pointedly, he said, "No, we don't, do we? Two: Scott Armitage, the man whose promotion went to McKinley."

"I never said that."

"And you didn't ask, did you? Three: The beautiful Ms Rushton, whose business is dying for want of more investment."

"We don't know that." He didn't need to point out why

we didn't know it. Deflated, I said, "And she's not that hot, unless you're into necrophilia."

"And then there's our Mystery Woman who threw herself at McKinley, then plotted revenge after he cruelly rejected her."

"You're just making stuff up."

"In the absence of actual evidence, what the hell am I supposed to do? Go out and get me some facts and I'll start winnowing the pack. But don't you dare tell me you think he might have killed himself. That might do for DI bloody Marr and her flying monkeys but you know better. The angle of the gun. The damaged painting. The absence of a note. The interrupted security footage. The testimony of everyone who knew him that he wasn't the type. Marr might prefer to close a case rather than chase her tail for no likely result, but we will only be satisfied when we've reeled in our fish and he's belly up on our chopping board with his guts in the bin. Isn't that right?"

He waited, glaring at me, clearly expecting an answer. "I was only joking," I said, feebly.

He sat back in his chair and shifted uncomfortably. "I hate being old and fucking useless," he said.

I didn't know what to say. I felt miserably guilty for having been such a useless prick. I could see he was champing at the bit to get out there and do all the things I wasn't doing properly. Yet it was also obvious that even coming into the office and shuffling some papers had left him feeling tired and in pain.

"You'll get over this," I said, not sure which of us I was trying to console. "Look, just talk me through it a bit, help me get things straight, then I'll be right to be a bit more effective tomorrow, hey?" He nodded, a sour look on his face. "I'm going to step up, mate, I promise." His expression didn't change, so I changed tack. "You shouldn't even be here. You should be at home with poor, long-suffering Maggie bringing you cups of Milo and changing your colostomy bag, or whatever."

He immediately rose to the bait. "Cheeky little sod! Even if I had a bloody colostomy bag, I'd be ten times the man you are. And as for Maggie..." He saw me grinning, stopped suddenly and laughed. "You little fucker." He took a moment and, in a much better mood, said, "All right, let's see if we can turn this into something resembling a proper investigation – despite all your efforts."

* * * *

I drove Ronnie home and went back to the university. I interviewed two other staff members and a couple of students before Dr. Armitage ran into me as I sat in an open area, making notes.

"Still here?"

I stood up. "A gumshoe's work is never done."

He grinned. "I like the Aboriginal word for it: 'featherfoot'."

I hadn't come across the term before. "Because we tread lightly?"

"Because the tribal investigators wore emu feathers on their feet to disguise their footprints?"

"I must pick up a few emu feathers next time I'm in Woollies."

He laughed but his eyes watched me carefully. "So, confirming my story, hey? How did I do?"

"It seems everyone here liked Professor McKinley. I was

going to come by and ask you a couple more questions. Do you have time now?"

"Sure. Can you walk with me while you ask them? I'm on my way to a meeting and I don't want to be too late."

We left the building and wandered up the road at a leisurely pace.

"Have you been on the staff long?" I asked.

"About five years."

"Really?"

"You sound surprised."

"No, no. It's just… You seem like an ambitious man. How come you're just a senior lecturer and not a head of department somewhere?"

"Like here, you mean?"

My heart sank. I was so transparent. Nevertheless, I pushed on. "Yeah, for example."

"Are you really that hard up for a motive? Or do you particularly want to pin it on me for some reason?"

"That's a little paranoid. I'm just looking at all possibilities."

He stopped and I stopped with him. "Right. And here's a little interview tip: don't call the people you're interviewing 'paranoid'."

Shit! "I'm sorry. I didn't mean it like that. Look, I really do want to just tick all the boxes. It's nothing personal. I'm just… I'm basically a philosophy wonk who ended up doing some very strange shit that, probably, I'm not really very good at and just doing the best I can and screwing up every time I open my mouth So, please don't take offence if I say dumb stuff. I just want to find who killed McKinley and I'd really like your help."

He watched me throughout my pathetic confession with a

look of astonished puzzlement on his face. I expected him to laugh, or jeer, but he didn't. He just said, "I've got family here. Family's important. I'm not going elsewhere just to chase fame and fortune. Besides, Sonny was the right man for the job. He did it well. I respected him."

I stared at him for a moment, as amazed by his response as he'd been by mine. "Thank you. That's... Thank you."

"Right-o." He pointed at the building we had stopped near. "That's me. Good luck with the case."

"Thank you," I said, again. He turned and began to leave. "Just one more thing."

He turned to me, smiling. "Is that technique, or did you really just think of something?"

Flustered, I said, "I – I don't really have any technique."

He nodded. "Quickly then."

"Have you ever heard of the FABClub? It was some kind of investment group that McKinley was involved in."

He pursed his lips and shook his head. "Never heard of it. That all?"

"Yeah. Thanks."

Chapter Five

I was driving back to the CBD when the phone rang. It was an unknown number.

"Luke Kelly," I said, trying to sound professional. The call was on my work phone and that meant it might be a client.

"Hi, it's me." I didn't recognise the voice.

"You?"

"Mel."

"Oh, Ms Bertolissio. How are you?"

"Not so good, Luke. I've had my sister giving me grief all day about going to you about Sonny."

"I thought you said she—"

"Have you got a big sister, Luke? Or a big brother?"

"No. Only child." It wasn't quite true. I had a step-sister. But I didn't want to get into all that.

"Right. Then you cannot imagine the lifelong torment of having someone who thinks they can run your life better than you can."

"But I thought…"

There was a pause. "I might have misled you a teensy bit. Sorry. What she actually said was… Well, it's best I don't say."

I turned off the road and started winding my way up a

multi-storey car park.

"How can I help you?" I asked, trying to keep the bitterness out of my voice. I had been hugely flattered that the detective had referred her sister to us. Now it seemed more like she'd warned her off.

"Oh God, you're not going to get all sooky now, are you? I hate it when men sulk."

I took a deep breath. "I'm good. Was that all you called about?"

"Yes. No! I wanted to know how the case was going. Have you caught him yet?"

"Him?"

"The killer."

"What makes you think it's a man?"

"It's always a man." She sounded quite scornful that I didn't know such an obvious fact.

"Right. OK. Well, we've interviewed the people he worked with, his domestic staff and family, a business associate, and a former lover."

"What?"

"Did you know Professor McKinley was gay? Or, at least, bi?"

"No! Wow, you're really turning over the stones, aren't you? It's – it's quite horrible."

Yes, it is. "But we don't have any leads at all yet." I listened to the silence for long enough to feel thoroughly rebuked. "By the way, while I have you here, can I just ask you where you were the night McKinley died?"

"I was at home. Well, not my home exactly. I've been staying with a friend."

"What time did you get home that evening and when did you next leave the house?"

"You're talking as if I'm a suspect." She sounded more surprised than outraged.

"I just want to get a picture of where everybody he knew was that night."

"I suppose. Well, I got in about tea time and stayed in all evening and didn't go out again until the next morning."

I found a parking spot at last and, wheels squealing on the concrete, turned into the space.

"And your friend will confirm this?"

"Of course!"

"Perhaps you could give me his name?"

"*She* is a woman. And perhaps you should remember who's paying for your time."

Bugger! There I go again. "I'm sorry. I just… You're quite right. That was…"

"So what's next?" She sounded rather frosty.

"Right now, I'm off to interview another of McKinley's business associates. Did he ever mention something called the FABClub to you?"

"No. It sounds kind of retro though, doesn't it? Like a Sixties swingers club."

"I suppose it does but this seems like it's some kind of investment group for buying up paintings."

"Oh. Boring."

"Yeah, probably. Anyway, I'm off to see one of the members. The thing is, I'm pretty sure he's going to tell me what everyone else has already told me: Sonny McKinley was a good man and nobody had any reason to kill him."

"I know," she said. "It's so weird. Everybody loved Sonny but—"

"But he'd never kill himself." I'd been firmly impaled on the horns of that dilemma for a couple of days now and it was driving me mad.

"Right. So, then what?"

Very good question. "Then my partner and I need to consolidate the information we have collected and determine our next move."

There was a silence at the other end that I could only imagine was disappointment. I wondered what might happen if we really did hit a brick wall, no more leads to follow, no more inspiration, no more vaguely-related people to interview. What would we do? Call Mel and say, "Sorry, we don't know who killed your friend and we're too useless to work it out. Have a nice day. The bill is in your email."? Would I have the effrontery to do such a thing, or would I go on in a hell of embarrassment, pretending to be making progress until I could stand it no longer?

"So, I'll call you again tomorrow, then," Mel said, breezily. "And you can tell me how it went."

"Er, yes. Yes, of course." Oh God, had I taken my first step on the road to perdition? The case was going badly. Really badly. I was getting nowhere. I should have told her the truth. At what point should I call it a day? How would I know when I'd reached the point where I was just treading water, just going through the motions with no benefit?

I felt a rising panic. I needed to talk to Ronnie about this. But what would Ronnie say, "Work harder you useless bell end," or something like that. Ronnie was not a quitter. He was the kind of bloke who would push on past the point of no return, and keep on pushing until something snapped and the case finally unravelled. Or until he ended up in a psych ward.

No, I couldn't talk to Ronnie. I needed somebody more… sane.

I told the car to phone DS Bertolissio.

"Luke. Is everything OK?"

"Yes, yes. Fine. Well, not quite fine exactly. Look, can we meet up? Can I buy you a drink after work or something. When do you get off?"

"A drink?"

"Oh, no, not like that or anything. Not that I wouldn't… I mean… I just want to talk. To ask your advice about something?"

"About the case?"

"Yes. I mean, no, not really, more about cases in general."

"About cases in general?"

"That's it. Yeah? Is that all right?"

She didn't speak for several seconds. "Luke, are you on something?"

"What? No! Never. I mean, I don't."

"Only you seem a little… disjointed."

"No. Honest. I'm just sort of freaked out about something. That's why I need to talk. To get a different perspective."

There was another long pause. "OK." She gave me the name of a smart bar in a CBD hotel that I vaguely knew and I thanked her profusely. "Six thirty," she added. "I won't wait long, so don't be late."

* * * *

Nick Kryou had his offices in a megatower in the CBD. The sign on the door said "NKPD plc" which sounded a bit like a US police department but I reckoned it stood for Nick Kryou Property Development. There was a large reception area full of models of hideous buildings – most of which seemed to be hotels beside tropical beaches – with a curved and illuminated reception desk on the far wall. A young man in what might have been a security guard's uniform, sat behind the desk, watching me with suppressed hostility. Perhaps I didn't look like the usual kind of visitor – the Council planners, the investors, the politicians – he was used to. In my shorts and Tee, I probably looked more like one of the leftist greenie types that chained themselves to heritage buildings, or two-hundred year old gums whenever Kryou and his mates passed by. Worse still, I might be a reporter from the Guardian or the ABC.

I gave the suspicious guard a disarming smile. In return, he grudgingly asked if he could help me.

"I'm here to see Mr. Kryou," I said. "I called earlier. Doctor Luke Kelly."

He frowned at me as if I'd added, "I'm a Martian by the way." He looked down at a printed list then back up at me. Without losing the frown, he said, "One moment, please," and called Kryou on the internal phone to announce me. Kryou obviously gave him sufficient reassurances because he finally hung up and pointed to a frosted glass door in a frosted glass wall. "Through there. First door on the right."

I walked to the door and it buzzed and clicked open. Nick Kryou's office door was open and he jumped up to greet me with none of the caution his minion had shown.

"Come on in," he said, shaking my hand and leading me to a comfortable chair at a small glass table. He was a tall man, almost bald, with a wide, cheerful smile beneath intense, watchful eyes. His skin was a smooth, rich tan and his voice was deep and warm. "It was such a shock to hear Sonny had died."

I nodded. "When did you hear about it?"

He settled himself in a chair opposite me. "Not until his lawyer called me."

"You were part of the same investment group."

He laughed. "Yes, the FABClub. Not my idea, the name, but you've got to call it something."

"It was the FABClub I particularly wanted to talk to you about. Has it been going long?"

"Not really. A couple of years. It didn't really get going until Sonny signed up. Then we were quite active for a while until... Well, I suppose you know, Sonny fell out with the rest of us. I think all the crass commercialism got on his nerves." He smiled, quite charmingly. "All the rest of us wanted to talk about was money and valuations and return on investment. All he was interested in was the artistic value of our acquisitions. It's like he didn't get the point, you know?" He laughed again. "Anyway, that was the end of it really. Without Sonny, the rest of us are just a bunch of philistines. We wouldn't know which way up to hang most of what we see at auctions. So it all sort of died out. Pity, really. I liked Sonny. We all did. If he could just have seen what we were doing as building an investment portfolio and not starting an 'important collection', or whatever he thought he was doing, it would have been a helluva lot easier all round."

"So the club isn't active any more?"

"Not really. We've still got a load of pictures in a storage unit somewhere, and we're all still hoping for a payout, one day."

"A payout?"

He looked at me as if appraising my soundness. "What do you know about investing in art?"

"Almost nothing."

"Well, here's the important fact. Buying art is like buying

gold or diamonds. You don't make any money from it unless it appreciates in value and you can sell it. On average, art brings in about seven-point-five per cent. That means you'd most likely do better on the stock market. However, if you know your art, you can increase those odds a lot. The FABClub was founded by a bunch of us who just wanted a hedge in uncertain market conditions. However, when Tony – you've met Antonia Rushton, haven't you? When she introduced us to Sonny McKinley, we were in a whole new ballpark. He knew the art world inside out. He was the kind of bloke who could pick us a winner – you know, like some blokes know their horses, or have a nose for the stock market? It was practically certain we'd beat the odds with Sonny on board. But…" He made an expansive shrug and fell back in his seat. "It wasn't to be. Still, as I say, we've got a few pictures in the bag and, according to the terms of the club agreement, we'll drag an expert in after ten years to give us a valuation. I'm hoping for good news."

"That agreement… When Professor McKinley died, his share of the paintings was divided among the rest of the members. Is that right?"

He laughed. "Has to be that way. You can't have us sell up the whole investment every time someone carks it. Some of our members are not exactly ankle biters."

"Do you have a list of the names of all the members I could have?"

He thought for a moment. "Tell you what, why don't I just give you a copy of the agreement. Everybody's names and addresses are on there." He picked up a phone on the desk and poked a couple of numbers. "Shiels, there's a folder in my personal files called FABClub – all one word. – with a file inside called Agreement, or something like that. Can you print off a copy and bring it in? Thank you." He gave me a smile. "Shouldn't be long. Speaking of which, do you have many more questions? I was hoping to get off home at some point."

"Just one, really. Would it be possible to tell me what the value of the club's investments is at the moment?"

He thought about that, too. I had the impression he thought carefully about everything he said.

"I see. You want to know if Sonny's share was worth bumping him off for. Am I right?"

It seemed unlikely that it had taken him this long to understand the reason for my visit, but I humoured him. "That's right. My client believes McKinley was murdered but so far we have been unable to find a motive."

He laughed again. "Well, I'm afraid you've drawn a blank here, mate. Our total investment through the club is about three hundred thousand dollars."

"That seems like a lot to me."

"But Sonny's share was only a seventh of that. Forty-two thousand and change. Split that among the remaining members and it's about seven grand apiece. I don't like to boast but that kind of money is peanuts. You won't find anybody in the club who thinks seven grand is worth crossing the street for, let alone murdering someone."

I didn't understand. "So, you each put up forty-two thousand, with the expectation of making seven-and-a-half per cent – that's three thousand and something – but seven thousand isn't worth having?"

He looked a bit put out but that was possibly just because I needed him to explain something he felt was obvious.

"When you invest money, you're always trying to maximise your returns and minimise your losses. It's a kind of gamble but, to be honest, a pretty safe kind. You diversify, you hedge, but you're always looking for the little windfalls. Also, if I'm honest, you try new things just to make it more interesting. That's what the FABClub was about. In a way, it was more like having a flutter at the casino than a serious investment. Forty K is the kind of sum each of us wouldn't miss much if we got our fingers burned but it was also enough to leverage a decent return if things went well. And worth it to have a bit of fun. Do you see? If I killed off all six of the others and got the full three hundred grand, it would be nice but three hundred is what my new Mercedes cost. Would you kill six people – some of them friends – to get a new car?"

"I guess not." I stood up. "Thank you for your time, Mr. Kryou." He stood up too and gave me a well-practiced handshake. A woman came in, dropped a document on the table and left. Kryou picked it up and handed it to me. I looked at it, not really seeing the words.

"You sound as if you liked McKinley," I said, suddenly reluctant to leave.

"He was a good bloke. Funny too, when he was in the mood. Good company for a professor." He laughed again.

"So which of the club members did he fall out with? I gather he was very upset about it all."

He pulled in his chin in surprise. "No. There was no falling out. Just a disagreement about the aims of the club. We're all business people. Well, except Sonny. It wasn't working out, so we agreed to part ways. Nothing to be upset about. These things happen."

I took my leave and, checking the time on my phone in the lobby, ran from Kryou's building to the hotel where I was supposed to meet the detective. I arrived fifteen minutes late, sweaty and dishevelled.

She was at a table with a glass of wine in front of her. She looked remarkably cool and demure for a woman who should be fuming. I hurried over and began my apologies but she waved them away.

"It's OK. I only just got here. I guessed you were one of those people who turns up late all the time, so I planned accordingly."

While I was wondering how I should take that, a man about my age appeared at my shoulder. He wore tight black slacks and a loose, dark blue satin shirt. His shoes were impressively shiny and his hair was full of what people who use it call "product".

"I'm terribly sorry, sir, but this establishment has a very strict dress code." He looked down at my bare feet and the thongs I was wearing as if that would explain everything.

"What?" I asked, genuinely confused. Were there really places so up themselves they thought they could tell people how to dress? I'd assumed that was just something in films from bygone times, or maybe British or American snobbery. I'd never encountered it in Australia before and could hardly believe it was happening.

"It's all right, Miguel," Bertolissio said. "He's with me. We won't be long, I promise."

The bloke looked at me with a pained expression, then turned to the detective. "Of course. Anything at all. I'll send someone to take the gentleman's order."

He marched smartly away. "What the hell was all that?" I asked, sitting down.

"I should have mentioned the dress code here. Miguel is very fussy about it."

"He seemed more punctilious about keeping you happy. I

didn't know the police had that much power in this town."

She laughed – even though I hadn't meant it as a joke. "It's nothing like that. I did Miguel's father a bit of a favour a couple of years ago. Since then, the whole family has been treating me like royalty. It's a bit awkward sometimes, but I like coming to this place. It's quiet and not many cops come here."

I looked around and began to take in the generally well-heeled clientele. "Plenty of crooks though, I bet."

A waitress appeared, dressed so well she could have been someone's date, and took my drinks order.

"You wanted to see me," Bertolissio said. "You sounded distressed."

"I was having a moment of self-doubt. I get them about every five minutes since I started this case."

"The Everson McKinley suicide?"

"The Everson McKinley murder." She gave a slight tilt of the head which could have meant anything "You told your sister not to use us." I don't know why I decided to start with that. I suppose it had been bugging me.

She sipped her wine, no doubt deciding how to reply. "Mel can be a bit impetuous. And headstrong. There's little I can do to stop her when she has a bee in her bonnet like she has about McKinley. She was determined to see a private investigator and she knew about you from last year. I just thought it might be better for her to use a more experienced firm. She has a way of dragging everyone around her into some quite bizarre escapades. Especially men. I thought you might be particularly vulnerable."

"What? Why?" So, she had told Mel not to use us? Because I'd be particularly vulnerable? What the hell?

She looked at me with a sad expression. The fact that I

didn't know why, her drooping brows said, was precisely what made me easy pickings for her sister. It's horrible to have someone you admire so much tell you you're a naive idiot. I couldn't meet her eyes and found escape in quaffing half my beer.

"You wanted to see me about something," she said again.

I put down my beer and tried to remember why this was a good idea. "It was nothing, really."

"OK. If you don't want to tell me."

I felt like an even bigger idiot. Beginning to feel angry with myself, I said, "I feel like I'm spinning my wheels on the McKinley case. I just wondered if you had any good advice on knowing when to call it a day."

She had an unsettling way of looking at me as if what I'd just said might not have been what I really meant. Carefully, she asked, "Have you exhausted all your leads?"

"What leads? The man was loved by all. No-one had any reason to kill him."

"Except whoever did it."

"Yeah," I said, watching the bubbles in my beer.

She sighed and put down her glass. "My guess is, you have barely scratched the surface of McKinley's life, yet. You don't have the resources. You haven't seen his bank statements, or his phone records, or his will…"

"Actually, I have seen that. It all goes to his daughter, plus a few small gifts and business settlements. Only Ophelia would have any motive if the will was a clue."

"My point is, with all the resources of the Queensland Police, we didn't manage to find any solid evidence that McKinley was murdered, so what chance do you have?"

She was right, of course. Maybe I was beating myself up for no good reason. "So, how do I know when to stop?"

She smiled. It was a subtle smile, a little sadness, a little conspiratorial wickedness, a little kindness. "Do you think McKinley was murdered? I mean, do you absolutely believe someone killed him?"

I thought about it. "I reckon. He may not have had any enemies but he didn't kill himself. That wasn't where he was. Someone, for some reason we haven't seen yet, went to his house, picked up that gun and deliberately blew him away."

She nodded to herself. "In that case, if I was working on this, the only reason I'd stop is if my bosses told me to and I couldn't find a way to work around them. In your case, I'd say you should keep going until Mel decides to stop paying you and then keep going as long as you can afford to. Or... until you catch them. That's the only way you're going to be able to live with yourself."

"You sound just like Ronnie."

She laughed. "Yeah, well, I hope I can keep my job longer than he did."

"There's always a place for you at Systematic Doubt if you need one."

She laughed again, ambiguously.

Chapter Six

I took a carry-out to the office and spent a couple of hours writing up my notes and tidying the place up. I'd had high hopes for the FABClub as a source of suspects but, as I looked up each member and added them to the whiteboard, I felt nothing but disappointment. They were all rich men, pillars of society, not the kind who would knock off an art teacher for an extra forty-thousand bucks. I had no illusions that rich old men couldn't also be murderers, it's just that it was hard to see any motive.

And that was becoming the theme of the whole investigation; no-one had any reason to kill Everson McKinley. He wasn't squeaky clean, of course. He'd had an affair with Darren Constance while his wife was still alive – but that had ended a year ago, when she died, and, apparently, without rancour. He and his daughter had fallen out badly enough for her to move out of the mansion but not enough that they didn't still stay in touch quite regularly, or for him to disinherit her. She had a rich boyfriend who might have seen her father's death as a way to get a bit richer. It was a long shot, but I should probably follow that up. And there was the FABClub – a bunch of bored rich men having what was, for them, a small flutter on the art market. Even for

McKinley, who was probably the least rich of them all, the stakes were small and, anyway, they'd all grown bored with that, too, after McKinley picked up his ball and went home.

With a heavy sigh, I snapped my laptop shut and headed out. It was late and the usual business service staff were all gone. In fact, I seemed to be the last to leave my floor. The white carpet and brown, wood-effect walls gave the corridor a creepy yet sumptuous feel as I plodded, almost silently to the lifts. My car stood alone in the basement car park. If I hadn't had that chat with Detective Bertolissio earlier in the evening, I would have wrapped it all up by now and written her sister a final invoice. And if I'd done that, perhaps I would not have this awful feeling of wading through treacle. If Don Quixote had suspected as strongly as I did, that he was, in fact, tilting at windmills, perhaps even his mighty heart would have quailed, the way mine did. It was all very well the detective telling me to keep at it because I knew it was the right thing to do but even the right thing could turn out to be impossible to ach—

"Kelly, you fucker!"

I jumped and spun to face the shout, realising, too late, that I'd been hearing quick footsteps behind me for the past few seconds. There were two men approaching me fast, almost upon me. One was broad and big-chested, not tall but powerfully built. The other was much taller, as tall as me, lean and hard, like a footy player. They both wore balaclavas. My heart burst into overdrive.

Scuffed boots, dirty jeans, work shirt, I said to myself. Ronnie had told me to do this if I was in trouble. It would help me remember what my attackers wore. I had no doubt I was about to be attacked. I stepped back and fetched up against my car in just two paces.

"You've been sticking your nose where it shouldn't be." It was the shorter one talking but it was the tall one who hit me in the stomach.

No jewellery, my inner voice said. *Blue eyes.*

"People want you to pull your fucking head in mate," Shorty said. The big one hit me in the face. Belatedly, I remembered Ronnie's other advice for this situation. I brought my hands up to cover my face just in time to block another blow. *Gloves*, I thought. *Work gloves.*

"So just mind your own fucking business, hey, cunt?"

The shorter one hit me in the stomach this time and I went down. Following Ronnie's instructions, I curled up into a ball, my back to the car so they couldn't kick my kidneys and spine, legs up to protect my ribs and belly. They both took kicks at my shins and forearms.

"Who sent you?" I asked and got another round of kicking in reply.

"Shut the fuck up."

The assault stopped. They took a step back. I peered up at them from between my arms. "This was just a warning. If we have to come back, we won't be fucking around. Do you understand?"

I nodded.

They considered this for a moment then the short one slapped the other on his arm and they turned and walked away. I didn't move until they were out of sight, then slowly, painfully unfolded my bruised limbs and got to my feet. I was trembling all over and my stomach felt like I'd heave at any minute. I leaned against my car for a while and checked for broken bones. I didn't find anything but I felt hollowed out and shaky. Blood was seeping through my jeans where my shins had been cut. I didn't look to see how bad it was. I didn't want to know. I heard a car engine start out of sight across the car park, a big, grumbling engine, like a large ute. I pulled out my phone and checked the time so I'd know when they left.

I sat on the car's bumper and waited for my nerves to settle. I thought about phoning Ronnie but couldn't see the point. I thought about phoning the police but, again, what was the point? I could go and find building security and get them to show me the car park surveillance footage. That way I might get a rego for the ute. I might even see their faces if they'd removed their masks before arriving or leaving. But what good would that do me? A couple of thugs had been hired to rough me up. I didn't want to catch them, I wanted to know who had sent them. If I could get that security footage, I might be able to track them down but I could spend days doing that and still get nowhere. Meanwhile I'd have been off the case as surely as if their threats had worked.

Had their threats worked? It was an interesting question. I was sitting in an empty car park, bruised and bleeding, feeling physically ill in the aftermath of the shock and fear I'd endured, slowly calming down and getting up the composure to drive home. Yet I had not once thought about giving up the case. I felt a little surge of pride in myself. Those two thugs had hurt me and scared me but they had not made me back down. I wouldn't say I was even more determined than ever but I was definitely not intimidated. I smiled and raised my head. That was a helluva thing. Who'd have guessed I had it in me? I almost couldn't wait to tell Ronnie.

Of course, Ronnie would have beaten up the pair of them and they'd be in police custody by now. I really needed him to show me some of his martial arts moves. This private investigation business was clearly more dangerous than I had expected. Ronnie understood the risks, though. He'd insisted I learn how to survive a beating. I'd glibly told him I'd be right, that I'd just stand back and watch while he took care of any trouble. But he'd insisted. And, by some miracle, I'd remembered what he taught me, even though I'd been cocky and dismissive at the time. Maybe it was his graphic descriptions of what a size twelve boot could do to a human kidney or spleen that had imprinted his lessons on my memory.

I pushed myself off the car. My legs were a little wobbly. It was irritating that I couldn't just shrug it off like people did in movies. I had a sudden flashback to my childhood. My mum was dabbing Dettol on a grazed knee and saying, "There's my big brave soldier." I climbed into the car feeling the urge to go visit her. She and Dad didn't live far away. It was a disgrace that I didn't go to see them more often. It's not like I was always so busy. But I couldn't go now, not with my jeans wet with blood and my face throbbing from whatever hideous bruise was forming there. They'd have a fit. God knows they were already worried enough about me and my inexplicable career choice.

I drove out of the car park on automatic, forgetting to check where the security cameras were placed. Whoever sent those blokes knew where I worked and, I realised, which was my car. They probably also knew where I lived. Addresses and occupations were easy to find. I'd gone to a lot of trouble to make my work address as accessible as possible so that customers could find me. But the car? Who would know to tell a couple of standover men to wait by a particular car?

I tried to remember all the people I'd seen since the case began and which of them had also seen my car. The answer was, almost all of them. And every one of them could have followed me or just watched me after I'd met them to see what car I got into. So that was a dead end.

So, did it mean that the killer was one of the people I'd already spoken to? It seemed like it must be but then I realised any one of them could have told others. Every potential suspect I had and plenty of other people could easily be aware of my investigation – and that was without other people, like the cops, or Mel Bertolissio, spreading it about. Again, that didn't narrow down the field. I thought about the diagram on the whiteboards at the office. That network of who knew who and why would be my best guide to who knew about the investigation but I had no way to guarantee it was anywhere near complete or accurate. Detective Bertolissio had been right; I was a one man band and this case needed loads more resources.

I got home and sat in the dark, trying to clear my head and think through the problem. Images of the attack kept intruding, along with all the things I should have done or said. I pushed harder to focus. The attack was new information. At the very least, it confirmed that McKinley had been murdered. But what did it tell me about the murderer? He or she was someone who knew how to find heavies when they needed them. Did that help? Not much. Probably anybody could hire a goon if they tried hard enough. But it must at least rank the suspects. The old housekeeper and the gardener were probably at the unlikely end of the scale while the property developer, Kryou, was at the likely end. But where was everybody else? Ophelia? Her boyfriend? The ex-lover? The art department staff? The lady at the art gallery?

I gave up. Even to me, the whole exercise was feeling ridiculous. I took a shower, cringed at the sight of the cuts on my shins and arms – which looked a lot better when they were washed clean – put on some shorts and a Tee, went down to retrieve the first aid kit from the car, and returned to dress my wounds. *There's my big brave soldier,* I told myself, as I stuck inadequately small band-aids on my legs.

* * * *

"And this all happened last night?"

It had taken Ronnie about two seconds, looking at the bruise on my face, to realise I'd been attacked. Two seconds later, he was dragging me off his porch and into my car so I could report it to the cops. It took him the whole trip from his house in Jindalee to the Indooroopilly Police Station in Moggill Road, to explain to me what a complete drongo I had been for not reporting it at once.

Then there was a young police sergeant called Tim Pearce sitting across the table from me, grappling with the puzzle of why I'd get beaten up in a car park and then just drive home and go to bed.

"I don't seem to deal with extreme situations very well," I told him. "I found a dead body once and I just sort of went into zombie mode for the next few hours."

The sergeant sat back in his chair and studied me. "I thought it must be you."

"What?"

He smiled. "We've actually spoken before. About a year ago. When your unit was burned down. I was the one who called you to break the bad news."

I looked at him again. He was a good looking bloke, about my age, with a wholesome, friendly manner. A vague memory of something my mysterious client had said on our first meeting surfaced.

"Are you a friend of Mel Bertolissio?" I asked.

Something like hope kindled in his eyes. "Why? Did she mention me?"

"Yeah, mate, but only to say 'even you' wouldn't help her with the McKinley case."

He looked deflated and sad for a moment. Then his brows furrowed and he said, "But you said yes. You're helping her. And that's something to do with why you got beat up last night."

I pulled out a business card and pushed it across the table for him. "All in a day's work." I saw the usual look of dislike when he saw the company name. "It's a work in progress, the name. Thing is, I'm a PI now and Mel hired me."

"But it's a suicide."

"Yeah, nah. The blokes who gave me a kicking last night were delivering a message. They wanted me to drop the investigation."

He thought about it for a while, still holding my card in front of him. "And is Al OK with this?"

"Al? Oh, Detective Bertolissio. Yeah, no worries."

"You know they're sisters, hey?"

"No, it's fine. I talked to, er, Al last night and she reckons as long as Mel's happy spending her money, she's happy too."

"But you haven't told the investigating officer about what happened?"

"You're the first to know."

He nodded to himself. "Right-o. Let's get your statement." And we were down to business. He took my statement, took some photos of the injuries, and told me he'd let "the team" know.

"I thought the case was closed."

"They might decide to re-open it," he said.

"What about my assault? Are you going to investigate it?"

He shook his head with a regretful smile. "See this uniform? I got that as a result of getting involved in another case involving our friend Mel. I don't regret it. What I did was the right thing to do. But I don't suppose I'll ever make detective again. So they'll assign a detective to your case and he or she will be in touch in due course."

"We should get a drink one day and you can tell me the sad story," I said on impulse. I liked this bloke.

He nodded, slowly. "Well, you know where to find me."

* * * *

Ronnie had still not calmed down when I rejoined him in reception.

"A bloody hour I've been waiting here. How long can it take to write, 'I got a walloping 'cause I'm a fucking muppet who can't be left alone for five minutes.'?"

"That's uncanny. How did you know what I was going to write?"

"Psychic. Right..." He took my arm and steered me firmly out onto the street. I winced and pulled my arm away. He regarded my show of pain with utter contempt. "Now you're going to tell me everyone you saw yesterday and every word everyone said." We crossed the road and went into the shopping centre where we were soon sitting in a café enjoying the kind of privacy that only seventy-decibel ambient noise can give you.

"It's all in my notes," I said. We used a shared notes app and he had access to everything I'd written after my interviews.

"I know. I read it. Now tell me it all in more detail, so I can see who you scared enough to set the dogs on you."

So I went through the day in detail, constantly bombarded by questions from Ronnie about what precise words someone used or what exactly I'd asked. We'd got through two coffees and a plateful of doughnuts by the time I finally finished recounting my final interview with Nick Kryou.

"Did you give him a card?"

"Yes, I give everyone a card."

"But do you remember actually giving him a card?"

"Yes, I do. He made some joke about the name."

Ronnie rolled his eyes.

"Well what would you call it?"

"AAA Investigations."

"You are so old school. No-one uses a phone book any more. They search online. You need a name that includes the right keywords."

"Like 'doubt' and 'systematic'?"

"All right. Maybe I need to rethink it. Tweak it a bit."

He snorted. "So who was it? Kryou? What was he like?"

"I dunno. Smooth. Slimy. Just what you'd expect, I reckon. He didn't seem like a man who would kill a business partner and then threaten me to keep it quiet. I wouldn't even know what someone who'd do that would be like."

"Same as everybody else, only a bit more self-centred, a bit less full of the milk of human kindness. Anyone could be a murderer in the right circumstances. Some people just find it a bit easier than others."

"Very helpful."

"You're welcome."

"Look, I've been through all this last night. I don't think me being attacked helps us in any way."

"Except—"

"Yeah, yeah. Now we know it really was a murder not suicide."

Ronnie scowled. He sat back in his chair. He stared at the remains of the doughnuts for so long I thought he was falling asleep.

"Are you OK?" I asked.

"Nice of you to ask. I'm healing nicely, thanks."

"I didn't – I mean, great. That's good. I could have done with you around last night." He looked at me under his brows. "No, I didn't mean. I was just saying…"

"Who else did you see last night?"

"What?"

"There was a gap. After you saw Kryou: before you went to the office. At least half an hour. So who else did you see? It wasn't Karen Cha because she was over at my place."

"Karen was at your place?" I suddenly remembered her problem with her uncle. It had gone right out of my mind. "Right. How's that going?"

"You first."

I hadn't wanted to tell Ronnie I'd been to someone else for work advice but now he was making such a big deal of it, telling him seemed the lesser of two evils.

"I met up with Detective Bertolissio. We had a drink at some bar in town."

He cocked his head and stared at me, puzzling it out. The downside of working with a Ronnie – one of them, anyway – was that he was a damned good detective. Almost nothing got past him.

"Well, you two are not screwing and you're not exactly mates, so it had to be something about the case. How am I doing?"

"All right," I said, surrendering. "I needed some advice. I knew what you'd say, so I went to Al. It's no big deal."

"What advice?"

I was hoping he'd get sidetracked by me calling her 'Al'. "I felt the case was at a dead end. I wanted to know how you decide when to give up and call it a day."

"When you've caught the bastard."

"You see? I knew you'd say that."

"And what did *Al*, say?"

"She said the same, pretty much."

"Great minds."

He went back to studying the doughnut crumbs. Just as I was about to speak again, he lifted his head and said, "So who's next?"

"What?"

"Ophelia and the dickhead boyfriend, I reckon. Do you think this FABClub thing has got any legs?"

"Not really. We should probably talk to all the members, just in case something pops out. Kryou is my favourite right now but only because he's a slimeball and he'd have the right contacts to have me beaten up."

"The uni?"

"Just teachers and students. No love triangles or moonstruck teenagers as far as I could tell."

"The undernourished beauty at the gallery?"

"A, Not a beauty. B, She doesn't benefit in any way. C... She just doesn't seem to fit. The gun. The alarm system. I don't know..."

"The gay lover?"

"Worth another look, I reckon. I only have his word that there were no hard feelings."

He thought for a moment. "Right-o. I'll take Kryou and

the FABClub. You have another go at the fair Ophelia and her bloke. If you've got time, put the gay lover through the mill. What was his name? We'll meet up at the office for lunch."

"Darren Constance."

"Right. Poncy name but what do you expect from a bloke who collects shepherdesses and crap like that?" He stood up. "Let's go then. You can drop me in town. It's on the way to the McKinley mansion."

It wasn't but I knew better than to argue.

Chapter Seven

Luckily, I had the sense to call ahead to get a meeting with Ophelia. It turned out she and her bloke were at a posh gym in George Street, not far from where I dropped Ronnie.

Before I went to see them, I made a call to my old mate, Dicko.

"Luke? Fuck me! How ya doing, mate? Still in the sneaking around for money racket?"

It was at least six months since I'd spoken to him and nearly a year since he'd driven me around during my pursuit of Chelsea's murderer. Dicko lived a chaotic, unstructured life of odd jobs and dodgy deals. He was a scrawny, unkempt young man of about eighteen, with a narrow jaw, wispy facial hair, and adolescent pimples that seemed like they'd never leave him. I had thought that, as a PI, I'd be able to give him occasional work and help him out but I'd only had a handful of jobs myself and, the one time I'd used him to help follow a suspect, his ludicrous, bright yellow car had been towed and impounded for illegal parking.

"I'm good, mate. How are you?" Which I shouldn't have asked because it set him off on a long, rambling story about some deal that had gone bad.

"So," I said, interrupting as soon as I could. "I need a bit of help and I didn't know who to call, until I remembered you are a man with all kinds of useful contacts."

"I'm like fucking Gumtree, mate. Buy and sell almost anything."

"Yeah, what I'm after is a bit of personal protection."

"Shit. You want a shooter?"

"No, no! Why do you always assume I want a gun? I just want a – I don't know – a bodyguard, I suppose. I thought you might know someone who's, like, big and scary."

"What you paying?"

"What? I don't know? What's it cost?"

"Depends on the risk, mate. Who's after you?"

"I'm not sure. Someone's paid a couple of thugs to try to scare me off a case I'm working on. I just want someone so they'll think twice about doing anything if he's hanging around."

I could almost hear him rubbing the sparse hairs on his chin. "Finder's fee?"

"Sure."

"Fifteen per cent?"

"Whatever."

"Sounds like you need Robbo."

"Robbo? That doesn't sound very scary."

"Don't judge a book, mate. Robbo's been working as a standover man for One-Hand Pete." He seemed to think that was sufficient recommendation.

"I'd need him right away. This evening at the latest."

"No worries. I'll have him wait for you at your office this arvo, yeah?"

"Yeah, all right. I might be out all day. I'll see him there at five-ish. Is that OK?"

"He'll be there."

* * * *

I met Ophelia and her bloke outside the gym and we went to a nearby café that seemed to specialise in unappetising vegan concoctions. I seemed fated to meet Ophelia McKinley when she was wearing sportswear. Today, she had on only a leotard and leggings. Or maybe she always wore stuff like that, since today's outfit must have been what she had changed into after her workout. At least the boyfriend, Fraser, was wearing boardies and a singlet, making him seem well-dressed by comparison.

As for me, I was feeling overdressed in chinos and a long-sleeved shirt. Partly it was because of what Detective Bertolissio had said about smartening myself up but mainly it was because I was trying to hide the plasters and bruises on my arms and legs. The swollen yellow lump on my left cheekbone wasn't something I could hide, although I'd seriously considered going out in a hoodie.

I grabbed an ice tea from the cold cabinet while they made elaborate orders for undrinkable smoothies and we sat together at a table with a view onto the busy street. I was glad to have somewhere to look that wasn't Ophelia's trim little body. Taking a breath and taking control, I thanked them for meeting me. I immediately had to give up my fantasy of running the interview when Ophelia demanded, "Have you caught him yet?"

I gave her a quick summary of the investigation, leaving out names, and trying to make it sound as if we'd covered lots of ground. "However," I concluded. "We haven't yet got a clear suspect so I'd like to ask you some more questions – both of you – if that's all right."

The boyfriend bridled. "Both of us? What's it got to do with me?"

Really? I thought. *Your girlfriend's father is murdered and you don't see any connection?*

"It's just some routine questions. Like, where were you on the night Everson McKinley died?"

"Me? Am I, like, a suspect now?"

"Honestly, I just want to build a clear picture of where everyone was on the night. It's just normal procedure. That way, I can eliminate everyone who needs to be eliminated."

"Well I think it's a bit bloody rich, accusing me of murder. I hardly knew the man. I met him, like, twice."

Ophelia was clearly impatient with all this. "Just answer the questions, Jacko. We don't want to be here all day."

Fraser Jackson, age 29, I reminded myself. I'd looked him up on social media. His mother had a webpage tracing the family back to the First Fleet and seemed extraordinarily proud of it considering she'd married into it. But everybody with money wanted to be a First Fleeter, as if it somehow legitimised their good fortune.

Scowling, Fraser said, "I'd have to check my calendar."

Ophelia scowled back at him. "So get your phone out."

Brows down and lips pursed, he pulled out his phone and poked at it. "I was at home."

"Do you live alone."

"I live with my parents. But I have my own flat."

"Does it have a separate entrance?"

"Of course it does."

"So, your parents can't confirm you were there?"

"They don't bloody have to. I just told you."

"Right." I glanced at Ophelia. She was frowning at him still. It made me want to press him. "What about security cameras? They'd have recorded you coming and going."

He was growing angry now. "Yeah, maybe. So what?"

"So, if I needed to confirm your alibi at some stage…"

"My fucking what?"

His growing anger was intriguing. Ophelia seemed to find it so as well. "It's just normal procedure. I'm sure the police checked Ophelia's whereabouts." I looked at her and she nodded. "Is there some reason you don't want me to check?"

He stood up and leaned over the table pointing an aggressive finger in my face. "The police is one thing, but you? You're just a fucking nobody. We don't have to sit here being insulted by a fucking dropkick like you. Offie, let's go."

Ophelia looked up at him from her chair. "It's only a few questions, Jacko."

This seemed to infuriate him even more. "Right!" he said, so loudly everybody looked at us. "If that's how you feel. Thanks for your support."

We both watched him storm out of the café. When I turned back to Ophelia, she was looking thoughtful.

"What was that about?" I asked.

"He's usually pretty laid back about things. I reckon you must have touched a nerve."

"How close are you two?"

"Sorry?"

"I mean, you're dating and all, but do you plan to live together? Get married? You know?"

"I – We haven't really talked about it. What's that got to do with anything?"

"Just curious. And what does Fraser do for a living?"

"He's – I don't know. He does some kind of trading. Arbitrage? Is that right? His father owns a brokerage and Jacko's being groomed to take over one day." She turned to look at the door her boyfriend had walked out of. "Oh, I get it. You think Jacko killed my dad so he could marry me and get his hands on my fortune. It's a bit Jane Austen isn't it?"

"I think she was against gold-digging, on the whole, and I don't recall her writing a lot of murder stories – but, yeah, basically."

She looked hard at me and I readied myself for a tirade. Instead, she said, "Even if you were right, why would he do it now? Wouldn't that be stupid? Wouldn't he have been better off tying the knot first?"

I shrugged, helplessly. "You're right, it's thin, but I've got to tell you, your dad was a pretty good bloke by all accounts. No-one I've met has even the slightest reason for killing him."

"Except me."

"Except you."

"So why don't you think I did it?"

"Well, for a start, the police no doubt did check your alibi and I'm assuming that means you weren't there that night. Of course, you could have paid someone else to do it, given them the codes to the security system, and then made sure you were seen to be somewhere else." I had a sudden flashback to last year and Detective Inspector Trevor Reid telling me I could have done the same kind of thing to murder Chelsea. *So having an alibi is a reason to be a suspect, now, is it?* I remembered saying.

"Then there's your height," I said.

She saw it immediately. "The angle of the gun. But what if I'd stood on a box just to throw you all off the scent?"

"And then there's the way you volunteered to show us your father's study and explain why you thought he'd been murdered."

"Same thing. I could have done that just so you didn't suspect me."

I grinned. "You're quite the criminal mastermind aren't you?"

She grinned back but her face quickly fell back into its habitual seriousness. "How will you ever catch him? I mean, all the people it could have been, all the variables, never knowing who's lying and who's telling the truth?"

I was asking myself the same question. "Don't worry. Even when the clues are hard to find, you just have to keep pulling on the string long enough and, in the end it all comes unravelled." Which was complete bullshit – and what I was doing felt more like pushing on a string – but I owed it to her to sound reassuring.

* * * *

I called Ronnie and got his voicemail. It went, "You have reached the voicemail of Ronnie Walker. Please leave a message after the tone." I stared at the phone in disbelief. No swearing, no rudeness, and the whole thing delivered in Karen Chan's clear, well-modulated voice with just a hint of a Chinese accent. I had been going to tell him I'd finished early with Ophelia and ask him how he was getting on with the FABClub but I was so surprised, it went right out of my head. So I called Darren Constance and arranged to meet.

As before, he left his office and met me in a café close by. He obviously didn't want me showing up at his place of work and raising questions among his mates. He looked at my face and winced.

"Nasty," he said.

"You should see the other guy." *Blood all over his bootcaps.*

"I'm sorry to take up more of your time, Mr. Constance, but I'd like to ask a couple of follow-up questions, if I may."

"Of course."

"Tell me how your relationship with Mr. McKinley ended."

He'd been relaxed and urbane for a while there but now he stiffened and withdrew a little. "It's not something I particularly want to talk about."

"Yeah, but it's something I particularly need to understand." I tried to sound regretful but the idea of going back to Ronnie without this information probably made it come out a bit pushy.

He pursed his lips and looked at his little cup of espresso for a moment. "All right. It was when his wife died. Sonny was suddenly overcome with guilt, or something. She'd known all along and he said she understood, was glad that he was able to find some solace, even. Yet, when she finally went, he had a sudden rush of conscience. He told me he should have been there for her at the end. Fully there. He had a bit of a self-flagellatory streak. I think he wanted to punish himself for his infidelity. He wasn't just into the Pre-Raphaelites because they painted pretty pictures. He bought into all that knightly chivalry and honour guff too. He said he'd fallen short of the kind of person he wanted to be and he needed to reflect on it. He said we should take a break but, of course, the break became permanent."

"You seem kind of bitter about it."

He sat back with a snort. "Wouldn't you be? I thought I was in love. But he…" His lips tightened briefly and I wondered if he was feeling anger. Then he relaxed again. He smiled. "But that was Sonny. He was a special kind of person. You know that poem? 'I could not love you half so much loved I not honour more'? Well that was Sonny all over. Yes, I was bitter for a while – still am, if I'm honest – but I can't help admiring him all the same."

He put down his tiny cup with an air of someone about to leave. But I still had questions.

"Did his daughter know about your affair?"

"I have no idea. I met her a couple of times. She was still living at home then. But it was just her popping her head round the door to tell Sonny she was off out to a club, or whatever. They didn't seem close and she buggered off not long after his wife died."

"Are you married?"

He laughed. "God no! Unlike Sonny, I realised very young where my preferences lay." He stood up. "I have to get back."

"Can you just tell me where you were on the night Professor McKinley was killed?"

"Really?"

"It's just for completeness."

He leaned down to speak confidentially. "I was at a work's do until about eleven and then I went home – with a young man from Accounts Payable."

"And the young man's name?"

"Is none of your business. But, if I ever need to prove my whereabouts, trust me, I'm covered."

I couldn't think of anything else to ask that would keep him there, so we said our goodbyes and I sat down to finish my cappuccino.

It was still an hour till I had to meet Ronnie, so I decided to have another go at Antonia Rushton at Carnarvon Fine Art. It was a longish walk and the day was hot but I decided to stretch my legs. It was a bad choice. I arrived at the little gallery drenched with sweat and cursing myself. I hung around under a nearby shop awning for five minutes to cool down a bit before going in. It didn't help much.

The shop was empty again and I wondered if Ronnie was right to question the gallery's financial health. I found myself staring at the paintings once more, wondering how artists ever made a living and who bought that kind of stuff. As before, the emaciated form of Antonia Rushton appeared at my elbow like a wraith that haunted the place. I dragged my gaze from the bright lines and swirls on the wall to the large and sunken eyes of the proprietress.

"How can I help you today, Luke?" she asked. There was something a little creepy about the intimacy of her remembering me and calling me by name. "Perhaps you'd like that gorgeous piece for your office wall? Corporate art investors are some of our best customers. Frankly, there are no other business assets you can acquire except real estate that will actually appreciate in value over the years."

I gave her a tight smile. "Didn't I read somewhere that buying and selling art is also a great way to launder money?"

She didn't bat an eye. "Do you have overseas offices? In Russia, say? Or Japan?"

"I'm afraid I haven't quite gone global, yet."

"You should. It creates so many opportunities."

"Do you have overseas offices?"

In response, she raised her eyebrows and gave an airy flick of her fingers. "Is this a social call, Luke?"

"I spoke to Nick Kryou yesterday. He was very helpful. Thanks for putting me onto him. My colleague is talking to the other FABClub members today but I wonder if I could just ask... did the club buy any works from your gallery?"

She rolled her eyes. "I wish! It would have been such a

comfortable setup with Sonny being an investor. He could have sourced all the club's artworks here. Everybody would have benefited. But, as I said, he really had no taste for new work. He liked pieces with a patina."

"You resented that?"

"God, yes! I'd have been quids in."

"So you must have been secretly pleased when he fell out with the club."

She laughed. "I've certainly never been averse to a little Schadenfreude with my Chardonnay." She studied me carefully. "You know, you've changed, Luke. Last time you were here, I have to say, you were all bumbling and deferential. Today you're so much more assertive – forceful, even. I wonder… Does it have something to do with that ugly bruise on your face?"

"You think maybe somebody knocked some sense into me?"

She laughed again. "Would you like a coffee or something?"

I said I would, even though I didn't want one really, and she took me through a bead curtain at the back of the shop into a small office with a tiny kitchenette at one end. The coffee was filtered – which I hated – and being kept warm in a round glass jug.

"The coffee is for visitors," she explained handing me a mug and turning on a kettle. "Help yourself. Sugar's there. Milk's in the fridge. "I only drink herb teas." In a dramatic voice, she added, "My work is all the stimulation I need." She spooned some leaves from a packet into a small, mesh globe which she dangled into a cup of hot water. For some reason, I remembered the Daphne du Maurier novel, *My Cousin Rachel*. Wasn't the mysterious and beautiful Rachel suspected of murder? Was that the connection? And then I remembered Rachel's herbal teas – tisanes in fact – which gave her such mystique and gave rise to the suspicion of poisoning. If only Everson McKinley had been poisoned, the case would be solved.

"What are you smiling about?"

"Nothing really. Your camomile tea reminded me of something, that's all." We sat down. She in her office chair and me in a cane armchair with a round tapestry cushion. "I'm sure the police have asked this but can you tell me where you were on the night Professor McKinley died?"

"I like that, that you always call him 'Professor McKinley'. It's respectful. Sonny was a man who deserved respect, you know."

"I do know. I've spoken to enough people now to have a fair idea of what he was like. People admired him."

She nodded, staring into the middle distance and, in that moment, she really was beautiful, fine boned and long necked, with those huge, soulful eyes so common in the late nineteenth century masterpieces McKinley loved so much. Perhaps that was what had drawn him to her in the first place.

"I was at home with Jackson and Pollock," she said.

"Who are they?"

"My cats. Burmese."

"You live alone?"

"You're never alone with a Burmese cat, Luke. They're wonderfully affectionate."

"But no-one can confirm you were there?"

She sighed as if she were growing bored. "Am I really a suspect? Is there no-one at all more likely than me? I certainly hope so, or your investigation is in real trouble."

Too bloody true, darl! "It's just a matter of completeness. Like doing a jigsaw. You need to start with all the edge pieces or you'll never complete it."

"Why are you so interested in the FABClub? It's just a bunch of blokes having a bit of fun."

It was my turn to sigh. "I'm not that interested. You said Mr. McKinley had fallen out with them. Nick Kryou confirmed it but downplayed it. I suppose I'm just clutching at straws at this point. As I said, it's hard to find a motive when the victim is so well liked."

"Money's always a good one. He had lots. But he wasn't robbed, was he?"

"Burgled," I said, before I could stop myself. I was really making an effort these days not to correct people's English.

"What?"

"He was murdered at home. Nothing was taken from the house. He wasn't burgled. Sorry, I'm just a word nerd."

"And a grammar Nazi, I bet."

"Guilty as charged. But I'm trying to give it away. People get a bit pissed off."

My phone rang. I excused myself and took a look. It was Ronnie. I accepted the call and said, "Hang on." I said goodbye to Rushton and left. I waited until I was outside the shop before I spoke again to Ronnie. "What's up?"

"Who was that you were with?"

"Antonia Rushton, the gallery owner."

"What about the gay lover?"

"I already spoke with Mr. Constance."

"And the daughter?"

"Yeah, yeah. Look, did you just call to check up on me or was there an actual reason?"

"You need to get over here."

"Over where?"

He gave me an address in Ipswich.

"What? That's miles away. It'll take me at least an hour."

"Just fucking do it. I'll meet you at the entrance to the Brookwater Woollies and I'll explain everything then. Just get your foot down, hey? No hanging about to kiss Gallery Babe goodbye."

The line went dead. Teeth clenched in anger, I glared at the screen. Why did I put up with him? Yes, he knew the job but, jeez, maybe it just wasn't worth it. I could give up the PI business, sign on at Centrelink and just live a happy life with no Ronnie Walker in it.

By a miracle, I flagged down a cab and five minutes later, I was at the car park. Two minutes after that, I was winding my way out of the CBD and heading for the Ipswich Motorway. Traffic was heavy – getting heavier every day as Christmas approached – so it was an hour and ten before I parked in a Woolworth's car park in the leafy suburb of Brookwater. By the time I'd switched off the engine and looked around, Ronnie was opening the passenger door and climbing in.

"Come on," he said. "Get your arse in gear. It's just up the road. I'll navigate."

"What the hell is all this? Where are we going?"

"Nowhere if you don't get your bloody finger out."

Increasingly furious, I restarted the car and headed back out of the car park.

"Down that way," Ronnie said. "I'll tell you when to turn."

We drove along a quiet road, lined with large, single-storey houses. It was an up-market suburb but nothing fancy.

"Well?"

"There's been another murder."

In an instant, I forgot my irritation. He could only mean another murder connected to the death of Everson McKinley.

"Who?"

"His name's Morgan Sanford. Age sixty-nine. CEO of Sanford Cement. Wife Annabelle – deceased. Sons Scott and Mark. Scott's an IT wonk, works in Dubai. Mark's a corporate shyster in Brisbane. And guess what…"

"Sanford is a member of the FABClub."

"Bingo."

"When did he die?"

"Sometime this morning."

"What?"

"Turn here."

I took a right off the little suburban road and was suddenly winding along a country lane, climbing a forested hillside.

"Here's the best part…" I stole a quick glance at my partner. He was as cheerful as I'd seen him in months. "It was an accidental death. The old fart slipped and fell into his swimming pool."

I eased off on the accelerator. "What do you mean, 'It was an accidental death'? You told me it was murder."

"There's the gate. Go on in."

I turned into a long straight drive, through a serious-looking security gate and rolled to a halt in a broad forecourt in front of a two-storey glass-and-concrete box. There were two police patrol cars, already there, their red and blue lights flashing, along with several other saloons in dark colours.

"What's going on?" I asked, but Ronnie was already climbing out of the car. I got out too and was immediately confronted by a young uniformed officer.

"I'm sorry, sir, but I'm going to have to ask you to leave," she said.

"What's all the fuss about?" Ronnie asked, coming round the car to join us.

"I'd like both of your names, please." She pulled out her notebook and wrote them down. "And your business here?"

"We have an appointment to see Morgan Sanford," Ronnie said. I looked at him, trying to work out what kind of game he was playing. "My colleague, Dr. Kelly, is a private investigator. I am his consultant. We're here investigating the murder of Everson McKinley. Are you writing all this down?"

The young constable had, in fact, stopped writing and was staring at us. "You're PIs?" she asked, as if that couldn't possibly be right. I pulled out my licence and showed it to her. She read it very carefully. She handed it back and held her hand out to Ronnie. "And yours?"

He smiled pleasantly. "As I said, he's the PI, I'm a consultant."

She frowned at him, then raised a finger. "Just wait there. Do not move from that spot. Someone will see you in a moment."

She walked off towards the house. She met another uniformed police officer there, an older man, and spoke to him for moment. They both turned to stare at us. Then the man said something and the younger officer left him and went into the house.

"We should wander round to the back of the house," I said. "We might be able to get a look at the crime scene."

"No need," Ronnie said, grinning. "I've already seen it. It was me that discovered the body."

"Jeez, mate, what the hell have you done now?"

"Relax. I came to see Sanford. No-one answered the door, so I went looking for him. He was floating, face down in his pool. It's a really nice pool, by the way. So I took a bit of a look around."

"You did what?"

"Don't worry, all the security cameras were already disabled when I got here. There's no trace of my visit, not even footprints. Look how dry the ground is. When I'd finished, I called the cops using a land-line in the house and went to wait for you at Woollies."

I took a moment to absorb it. The fact that he'd broken several laws wasn't the big issue in my mind, it was that the cops were going to suspect him of the murder. Me too, probably.

"What the hell were you thinking, coming back here? With me! You're name is probably in Sanford's diary. If he died any time close to when you first arrived, you'll be their prime suspect. You know what they're like." My own treatment by the police after Chelsea's death still rankled and my confidence in our men in blue had taken a nasty tumble.

"Shut up now," he said, smiling sweetly.

"No, I bloody won't shut up!"

"Am I interrupting something?" It was a woman's voice. I suddenly became aware of her footsteps approaching and spun round to find a tall, broad-shouldered woman in her mid-thirties striding towards us. She had short hair and a wide, firm jaw. Detective Sergeant Bronski was hurrying along behind her, looking hot and cross.

"So," she said, stopping a couple of metres in front of me. "The famous Doctor Luke Kelly. I'm DI Marr. This is DS Bronski, who you already know. And you are?" She turned her head to take a look at Ronnie. "Oh yes, the consultant."

I held out a hand. "Pleased to meet you. It's 'whom' by the way."

She ignored me. "What are you doing at my crime scene?"

"I had an appointment to see Mr. Sanford," Ronnie said.

"Why?" I was pretty sure she'd already been told.

"We're investigating the murder of Everson McKinley," I said.

"He's the one I told you about," Bronski murmured.

Marr twitched her nose in irritation. "What connection did Sanford have with McKinley?"

I saw a tiny smirk on Ronnie's lips. Probably, he was gloating because the cops hadn't made the connection. "They were in business together."

"Doing what?"

"Buying art as an investment."

"And what makes you think that had any bearing on McKinley's death?"

"I didn't until now. Now we have two suspicious deaths of rich art-fanciers who knew each other."

The detective shook her head in some kind of reflexive rejection of the notion. "McKinley shot himself and Sanford slipped and fell. The only thing I can see that connects them is your imagination."

"In that case, would you mind if we take a look at the body?"

"Yes I'd mind! This is a police investigation, not bloody amateur hour. Bronski, make an appointment for both of these gentlemen to come in and make a statement. Then make sure they leave the scene. You!" She waved over a uniformed cop. "Go stand at the gate. I don't want any more randos wandering in here while we're working." To me, she said, "Somebody called this in from a phone in this house.

Where were you at…" She looked at Bronski and he retrieved the time of the call from his notebook. "Well?"

I looked at Ronnie, pretending to consult him. "That would be while Antonia Rushton was being interviewed, wouldn't it?"

Ronnie nodded. "Seems about right."

"That was at her gallery in Arthur Street, Brisbane," I added, for good measure.

Bronski scribbled it down.

"Lucky for you, you have an alibi we can check," Marr said. "I don't want to see either of you around here again."

"What about this?" I asked, pointing to the bruise on my face. "I got a kicking in a car park by a couple of thugs trying to warn me off McKinley's investigation. I reported it at Indroo station and made a point of asking them to let you know. How do you explain this, then?"

"I don't have to explain anything to you, Kelly. For all I know, you did that to yourself. Or maybe you pissed someone off."

While I spluttered in disbelief, Ronnie said, calmly, "Don't make this more of a stuff up than you already have, Marr. We could help you a lot on this if you brought us in."

The cop stepped up close to Ronnie. She was almost as tall as him and looked him straight in the eye. "I wasn't around when you were with Homicide, Walker, but I've heard the stories. From what I hear, you burned out and went troppo, put yourself and everyone around you in danger, pissed off every mate who might have helped you, and got yourself thrown out because you were no good to anyone. That stunt you and your toy-boy pulled last year with the bikie gang nearly got you both killed. You put a lot of good cops in harm's way pulling your arses out of the fire. Some say you were a good cop, way back when, but now you're just a washed up old has-been with delusions of relevance. You should go put your feet up. Enjoy your retirement, old fella. Take a cruise or something. Just don't waste my time, hey? All this hanging around cops at work, pretending you're still part of it all, is just sad."

She turned and left, leaving a smirking Bronski to see us off the premises.

Chapter Eight

We drove in silence back to the Woolworth's car park. I kept looking at Ronnie, waiting for the explosion I was sure was coming, but he just stared out the window. When we arrived, he directed me to where his car was parked and got out.

"Follow me," he said. "I need a fucking drink."

I followed his old Volvo across Ipswich to a hotel. It was late, but they were still doing lunches.

"A bit up-market for you isn't it?" I asked, taking in the leather seats and polished wood. Ronnie scowled and made a bee-line for the bar. I went and ordered a couple of meals. The place seemed to specialise in fancy seafood but I ignored the prawn and calamari concoctions and got us a couple of plates of fish and chips. Ronnie was sitting in a booth, staring into a glass of rum when I found him. I put down the number-on-a-stick I'd been given and sat opposite Ronnie. He didn't look up. He'd bought me a schooner of something dark and cold and I took a sip as I studied him.

I was dying to know what he'd seen when he found Sanford's body but first I had to deal with whatever was upsetting him so much.

"Is it the operation?" I asked. "Are you in pain?" He

looked up briefly with a look of disbelief. "All right, not pain then. Well, it can't be what Marr said about you being washed up. You're making the cops look like a flock of galahs. Yet again. And her in particular."

He picked up his glass and swirled the amber liquid. I saw his nostrils twitch, as if he'd caught the scent of it.

"Marr's a fucking idiot," I said, growing heated. "I told you what Bertolissio said, Marr's too ambitious to do her job right. She just wants to close cases. She doesn't want puzzles. She doesn't want long investigations that might go nowhere. She just wants notches on her belt. To her, Sanford isn't a new data point in a big, complicated puzzle, he's just an unwanted complication she wants to go away. And if she can get forensics to say he might have tripped and fallen, even if she can just get them to say there isn't enough evidence to pursue a suspicious death investigation, she'll consider that a win. Even if a murderer goes free."

He put down his glass and looked at me. "I don't give a toss what Marr said. Not really. But she was right about one thing."

"What? What was she right about? Because I didn't hear one single sentence that wasn't just her trying to make us disappear so she could finish tying a nice bow around Sanford's accidental death. What? What did she say?"

He looked at me while his jaw worked. Then his eyes fell. "She called me old."

"What?" I almost shouted it, I was so astonished. "Old? She called you old? For fuck's sake, mate! Of course you're fucking old. You're the oldest bloke I know. I've met mummified corpses younger than you. You're so old, I bet your first mobile phone was the size of a brick. They were still building computers out of valves and magnets when your parents made the fatal mistake of knocking their genitals together. Was there even a Sydney Opera House back then? Was there even a Sydney? Christ! It may have come as a surprise to you, to hear Marr say it, but I have to tell you, mate, those of us who have to look at that smashed crab you call a face, day in, day out, have been painfully aware of your extreme old age for a very long time. I tell you—"

Lifting a hand, he said, "You should shut the fuck up while you've still got all your limbs." Which, coming from Ronnie, would normally have had me worried, but he was grinning, so I grinned too. He leaned back in his seat and the smile faded. "It's this fucking operation. It's getting me down."

"But you're not in pain, right?"

He sighed. "Ah, it's a bit sore but I've had knife wounds and bullet wounds that were a hundred times worse. This is nothing. It's just... It's what it means, all right? It's not a wound. It's not a disease or an accident. It's just my body letting me down. You know? Failing. Wearing out. Turning to shit."

A young woman dressed in black brought our meals, along with cutlery wrapped in paper napkins. She asked if there was anything else on the order and I said no, so she took away our number-on-a-stick. Ronnie had already started eating. Apparently, there was no degree of existential angst that could keep him from his food.

"I'm sorry, mate," I said. And I really was. "You'll get past this soon enough, you'll see."

"Yeah, right," he said, through a mouthful of chips. "And you'd know that because you're all of what, thirteen-and-three-quarters?"

The effort of trying to be nice to Ronnie was, sometimes,

exhausting. "All I'm saying is, it's a setback, not the end of the world. You can still bench push three times more than me."

"Press."

"Whatever. You know what I mean."

And it was true. Ronnie had a gym set up in one of his spare bedrooms and he worked out every day – a legacy from his days in the special forces, I reckoned. I'd watched him pushing up weights in there one day and asked if I could have a go. He told me I'd only embarrass myself and he was right. I managed fifty kilos, my arms trembling dangerously. He'd just done a hundred and fifty without the slightest tremor. Even then, he'd grumbled about being able to bench press a hundred and eighty when he was young.

"Yeah, well. We'll see. Are you going to eat that?"

As usual, he'd finished his meal and was eyeing mine, which I'd hardly had time to get started on. I grabbed a forkful of fish and a couple of chips and pushed the plate over to him. He fell on it like he could still eat a horse and chase the rider. I watched the food disappearing for a while.

"So, tell me about Sanford," I said.

He paused long enough to spear the last couple of chips and said, "I called him this morning and he said come round. So I drove out there and no-one answered the door. I noticed the light on the security camera was off, so I went exploring. I found Sanford doing his pool toy impression round the back. He had a gash on the back of his head. No other signs of a struggle. I checked out the edges of the pool and the diving board. On the very end of the board there was blood with a few grey hairs in it that were probably Sanford's."

"So, that sounds like he made some kind of mistake jumping off the board into the pool, cracked his head and died from that – or drowned."

Ronnie grinned. "I'm sure that's what Marr is thinking. Anyway, I took a look in the house. The doors were open. No signs of a struggle, no signs of forced entry."

"So?" It all sounded very much like an accident so far.

"So, there was a wet beach towel in the lounge room."

"So?"

"So, the route from the pool to the front door doesn't go through the lounge room."

"So?"

"So, imagine it. Sanford is out by the pool, catching a few rays. He's probably got his towel around his waist or across his shoulders. There's a bell at the door. He gets up and goes to answer it? Why would he make a detour to the lounge room to drop his towel on the way?"

"He wouldn't."

"Right. So he answers the door still wearing the towel and lets in the visitor, takes him through to the lounge room and offers him a drink."

"Or her."

Ronnie looked dubious. "If she was built like Detective Marr, maybe, just maybe, 'cause, listen, Sanford had a real fire in his lounge room. Big showy thing, probably never used it, but it had a set of shovels and tongs and shit next to it."

"Including a poker."

"Bingo. Big bastard, too. So, Sanford turns his back and the visitor whacks him on the back of the head with it. Probably broke his skull. So, Sanford goes down and the visitor drags him outside and dumps him in the pool. To make it look like an accident, he scrapes off the blood and hair from the poker, and wipes it onto the diving board. He then goes back and cleans up."

"That's all just speculation, hey? Based on nothing more than one displaced towel."

"Not quite. I reckoned, if Sanford was murdered in the lounge room, the killer would need to have cleared up a pool of blood, right? So I looked for any sign of it. Unfortunately, the floor in that room is all tiles. But, there is a discoloured patch in the grout, right where Sanford must have fallen."

"Or where someone spilled some wine at Sanford's last party."

"Yeah, maybe, but I bet that poker is a perfect fit for the dent in Sanford's skull."

I mulled that over. "But the cops won't even look at it, will they? They'd have no reason to send their forensic unit into the lounge room. They'll look at the diving board and the area around the pool. If they're really diligent, they'll check the routes from the car park to the pool."

"They might notice the towel and work it out."

Some would, I thought. Ronnie was good but I knew of at least one detective on the force who was just as good. I didn't know about Marr but I had a horrible feeling that, even if she had noticed the odd location of the towel, she'd rather dismiss it as irrelevant than complicate her cut-and-dried case with speculative possibilities.

"It doesn't matter," Ronnie went on. "We know the truth. Sanford was murdered. And don't you think there are some strange similarities to the McKinley case? The killer was let into the house by the victim. The victim was alone at the time. The murder weapon was something the killer found at the scene. The murder itself was staged to look like something else – suicide or an accident. And the security system was turned off."

"So, you're saying it was the same killer?"

He gave me a withering look. "I reckon it must be that PhD in philosophy that makes you so sharp."

"Yeah, that and all the fine mentoring I get from you."

He grinned and I was glad to see his dark mood had evaporated.

"What's more," he said. "We know what connects the two victims."

"The FABClub."

"The very thing!"

"But how?"

He pursed his lips and nodded thoughtfully. "While I ponder that one, why don't you go and shout us a couple more drinks?"

I pointed at the glass of rum. "You haven't finished that one, yet?"

He lifted his head and stared at me with obvious amazement. "How long have you known me?"

"Too long."

"And in all that time, have you ever seen me drink a glass of rum?"

"You've often had a glass of rum. The first time I met you, you had one."

"And was I drinking it?"

"No, you were doing what you always do, swirling it around and staring into the glass." He was right. All the times I'd seen him with a glass of rum, he'd been more intent on studying it than actually drinking it. "Except once!"

"When you bought me a second glass, unasked for. There's no point having two glasses to stare into, is there? So I drank one."

I stood up, shaking my head. "You're bloody weird, you know. So what do you want?"

"A beer would be nice."

When I got back from the bar with two cold stubbies, he was staring into the rum again. Maybe it was an aid to concentration. Maybe it gave him some strange aesthetic pleasure. The man was as mad as a bag of frogs and I wasn't going to give him the satisfaction of asking.

"Well?" I asked, sliding into my seat opposite him. The dinner plates were still on the table, cold and greasy. I pushed them down to the end, out of the way.

"You didn't ask me how it went with Nick Kryou," he said.

"Yeah, right. How did that go?" In all the excitement over the new murder, I'd completely forgotten that was on Ronnie's agenda for the morning. Now that the FABClub was suddenly front and centre in the investigation, Kryou was a key suspect. Or, at least, another future victim.

"How do you think? He just told me the same as he told you. Plus, he gave his wife as an alibi for the night of the murder. You really need to cover off basic shit like that when you talk to people, hey?"

"Yeah, I know. I was having a bad day, OK?" He nodded and seemed to understand. "And how did he seem to you?"

"When I lived in Sydney, they'd have called him a wannabe Eastie. You know, someone who aspires to live in the Eastern suburbs with the nobs. He's all front. My guess is he's made his money but he's still having to work hard to convince the skips he belongs among them."

"Skips?"

"It what the Greek immigrants used to call white Australians. Didn't they teach you anything at that university of yours?"

"I must have missed the lecture on racial slurs. When did

you live in Sydney?"

He sucked on his beer and ignored my question. "I met two more of the FABClub members: Jotham Wendell and Martin Hittman." He grinned, waiting for me to make the obvious joke.

"Jotham's an unusual name," I said.

"Biblical," said Ronnie. "I asked. He's from a very short line of Pentecostal nutjobs. Wanted to know if I'd let Jesus into my heart. Nasty piece of work. To him, Everson McKinley was basically a hippie with as much common sense as a babe in arms. I asked him if they'd fallen out over the club and he laughed. It seems he'd objected from the start in having some commie teacher in the group and he wouldn't waste his breath arguing with a fool like that. He has an alibi for McKinley's murder. He was at a charity auction – apparently they're great places to meet people and get business done."

"So, he couldn't have done it?"

"Oh, he could have done it, all right. He'd blow his own mother's head off if he thought he could make a quid. But he probably didn't. Pity, 'cause I can't think of anyone on this case I'd rather put away."

"What's he do for a living?"

"Not a lot, as far as I can tell. His business card says his company is a business re-engineering consultancy."

"And that means what?"

"Buggered if I know. Corporate raiders most likely. Asset strippers. He seems like the type who'd get job satisfaction out of 'restructuring' thousands out of work and onto the dole."

He scowled at his stubbie as if it had offended him.

"The other one's a fisho."

"Hittman's a fishmonger?" That was not what I was expecting.

"Yeah, runs a fleet of trawlers, owns a bunch of cold stores, a trucking company, even a chain of retail stores. Likes to think he's still just a simple fisherman at heart. Truth is, he's a fat cat business type. His granddad started off with a single fishing boat but daddy inherited a fleet and young Martin turned that into the fresh fish empire he runs today. The secret is 'vertical integration', or so he tells me. Anyway, he's right up himself and loves bragging about his little tax avoidance schemes. You should see his office. It's full of antique furniture. Apparently, you can buy really good stuff, stick it in your office buildings for three years while you write down its value to zero, then ship it all out to one of the five mansions you own. You learn a lot doing this job."

"Sounds like you really warmed to him."

He snarled at the world in general. "I fucking hate rich cunts. Why do they all have to be such dicks?"

"In future, we'll only take on poor clients."

His snarl focused down on me. "Anyway, Hittman wasn't in the country at the time of the murder. He was in Port Moresby negotiating the purchase of a fish-finger factory. What did you get from the daughter and her bloke?"

I gave him a two minute summary of my conversation with Ophelia and Fraser Jackson. "There was something iffy about Jackson's alibi. He got all defensive. Even Ophelia noticed it. We should probably follow that up."

Ronnie sat in silence, mulling it over. The girl in black arrived and took our empty plates away.

"The thing about having two murders," Ronnie said, out of the blue, "is that it lets you triangulate."

"Triangulate? As in finding the location of a radio broadcast?"

"What?" He looked at me as if he'd just remembered I was there.

"You know. You take a bearing on the signal from two different locations then, by simple trigonometry, you can work out exactly where it came from."

"What the fuck are you talking about?"

"Triangulation."

He looked at me as if I'd gone mad. "Well don't. Just 'cause someone says a word, doesn't mean you have to start blathering about it."

I clenched my jaw and tried not to argue. "So, you think it helps, then, having two murders?"

"It tells us a lot. First, that this whole thing is something to do with the FABClub."

"Unless Fraser Jackson killed McKinley and the Sanford murder has nothing to do with it."

He pointedly ignored me. "Second, the murderer is almost certainly a bloke."

"How come?"

"Because they were both so violent and brutal, because the first one needed someone quite tall to shoot McKinley at that particular angle, and because the second one required quite a bit of strength to drag Sanford out from his lounge room to the pool." He looked at me, waiting for me to disagree, but I didn't. He knew a lot more about brutal murders and what it took to commit them than I did, so I let him have the point.

"Third, we're looking at a serial killer, one who's cold and calculating and level-headed enough to improvise and then clean up after themselves."

"Now you're just being sexist."

He shrugged. "Maybe. You want to put a pineapple on it?"

"A pineapple?"

"Fifty bucks."

"Why is fifty bucks a pineapple? Oh, right. It's yellow."

"Wow, you should be a detective with a mind as sharp as that. So, have we got a bet?"

"Sure. Why not? I would just love to see your face if it turns out to be a chick."

He grinned. "Fat chance."

He was probably right. There were only two women connected to the case – Ophelia McKinley and Antonia Rushton – neither looked like good prospects. Actually, there were three. I'd forgotten about the beautiful Mel Bertolissio. She was tall and she might be young and fit enough to drag a body around. But my imagination recoiled at the idea of her shooting McKinley in the face with a shotgun. Besides, she had no motive at all.

"Right-o," Ronnie said, pushing away his empty beer bottle. "There's two more members of the FABClub I haven't spoken to yet. Neither of them lives around here. One's in Sydney and the other's in Canberra. So that's video calls. Then I'm going to call everyone I spoke to today – lucky me! – and ask them what they know about Sanford's death. You can do the same with Offie and her fella, your paramour at the gallery, and the dickhead at the uni. We need to know what they know about Sanford and…" He paused for emphasis. "We need to find out if there was any other connection between McKinley and Sanford outside the FABClub."

He stood up. I thought I saw him wince as he did so. "I'll see you back at the office later and we can catch up."

"What about making a statement to the police?"

"Tomorrow. I want to talk to everybody again before DI Marr gets off her arse and starts doing her job properly. Catch ya later."

And with that, he was gone. I went to the bar and got another coldie to keep me company while I made my phone calls.

* * * *

I got back to the office as most people were leaving the place. I parked and looked around carefully before I got out of the car and hurried into the lift. So far so good.

I walked quickly along the corridor to my office, unlocked the door and slipped inside, locking it behind me. Not a single thug had jumped out and whacked me with a pickaxe handle. Not one lurking bruiser had stepped out of a doorway and stuck a knife in me. Life was good. Relaxing, I crossed the open space at the front, where a receptionist might have sat, if we'd had one, and made for my desk.

"Ahem."

I won't say I screamed like a little girl, threw my hands over my head and dropped to the ground in some kind of total wuss fear response bordering on mindless panic, but that's only because it is hideously embarrassing to recall. I squinted up through my enclosing limbs to see a gigantic black fella staring down at me.

"Er…" he said.

I waited, heart pounding but he made no move to crush me like a bug – which he could easily have done.

"I didn't mean to startle you," the giant said.

As the fight-or-flight hormones slowly ebbed away, my brain began working again.

"Robbo?" I asked.

"Yeah, mate. Dicko said—"

"Right. Yes. Of course. Robbo. I thought…" I stood up and found Robbo still towered over me. "Wow, you're big. I mean… Look, I'm sorry about that. My nerves are a bit all over the place. Dicko told you why I wanted you, yeah?"

"Yeah, nah. He just said to go here and you'd have a job for me. Good money, he said."

"Did he. Well, yeah, we'll work something out, hey? Do you want a coffee or something." I went over to the espresso machine. "How long have you been sitting there? How did you even get in?"

Robbo didn't follow me, just stood like an ancient gum – except he was wearing a loose black Tee, black shorts and scuffed trainers. He wasn't all that ancient, either. He looked maybe twenty-five or so. Bright black eyes peered out of a face so folded and wrinkled, it wouldn't have looked out of place on a bloodhound.

"I went to Centre Management and they let me sit there till they closed. Then one of the girls let me in here to wait."

I checked the time. It was after six. "They shouldn't have done that. These are supposed to be secure offices. What if you'd been one of the people who want to hurt me?" He shrugged. "Yeah, right, not your problem. The thing is, there's a couple of blokes who are trying to scare me off an investigation. They got me in the car park last night and gave me a bit of a kicking. Just as a warning, right? Only I haven't stopped and I expect they'll be coming back. So I thought, if you're willing, you could, you know, hang out with me, go where I go, and be a sort of deterrent. I must say, you look the part."

"Sure," he said. I waited for questions but there weren't any.

"How much do you charge?"

He named an outrageous sum. I had been beginning to think he seemed a bit stupid but clearly he wasn't. I started to haggle but he shook his head, scowling, saying, "Nah. What I said." So I agreed and he went back to the reception area and sat down again. He pulled out his phone and began poking at it.

"So, how do we do this?" I asked.

He looked at me as if considering his strategy. "I go where you go. Anyone comes near you you don't like, I get rid of them."

"Right. Good. Simple."

I took my coffee and went to sit at my desk, glancing up at Robbo from time to time as I wrote up the day's notes. He didn't move, just stared into his phone and gave it the occasional prod or flick.

I was about to suggest getting some carry out food in when Ronnie turned up. He walked straight past Robbo with barely a glance and joined me at my desk. Robbo stood up and padded along behind him.

"So, who's your new friend?" Ronnie asked.

I gave him a grin. "That's Robbo. Robbo, meet Ronnie."

"Is he okay?" Robbo asked.

"Yeah, Ronnie's like my partner. You should look after him when he's with me, too."

"Right-o." The big man ambled back to his chair and sat down again.

Ronnie glanced over his shoulder at Robbo. To me, he said, "I understand why you'd do it. You're scared about the guys who gave you a walloping. You feel you need some protection. I'm getting old and feeble—"

"No, wait a minute. I never said anything like that."

He waved away my objection. "It's OK. You think I'm past it. That's fair enough."

"That's not it at all."

"The thing is, the big fella over there can't protect you. He's totally useless."

I saw Robbo look up at that. I leaned into Ronnie and lowered my voice. "Are you kidding? Look at him. He works as an enforcer for some underworld type called Peg-Leg Pete, or something."

Ronnie nodded. "Maybe but if I wanted to, I could lay him out in ten seconds flat."

"Mate, I know you're tough. I've seen you in action. And you've been special forces and a cop and all that but look at him. He's twice your size and he's built like a brick dunny."

Ronnie gave a wistful smile. "Size isn't everything – as I'm sure many ladies have had to reassure you over the years. The guy's big all right, but he's slow and out of condition."

"Hey!" Robbo said, his creased face puckering into a scowl.

Ronnie turned to face him. "No offence, mate, but you're a show pony. I'm sure you're pretty good at scaring some old shopkeeper into making his loan repayments but I wouldn't back you in a fight with anyone who knows what they're doing."

"What the fuck do you know?"

Ronnie stood up and so did Robbo. I hurried out of my seat to get between them. "Now wait a minute, you two. What the hell is going on here?"

"Tell you what, Luke," Ronnie said. He sounded relaxed and amiable, perfectly confident. "Let's put Robbo here to the test. Think of it as an interview for the job. Robbo, you stand between me and Luke. My challenge is to go through you and touch Luke on the chest – imagine I'm carrying a knife. If I can't do it in thirty seconds, you've got the job. If I can… well, you know where the door is."

Robbo looked at me, his dark eyes full of anxiety. "I don't want to hurt no-one," he said. "But the old fella's pissing me off."

"This is nuts," I told Ronnie. "You just had an operation. You're not in any state to go around fighting people."

Ronnie's eyes twinkled. He was enjoying himself. "Come on, Robbo. What are you scared of."

With a grunt, Robbo moved to stand between me and Ronnie.

"Don't hold back now, big fella. There'll be no hard feelings. I'm a paid assassin and I'm going to murder your boss. You just do whatever it takes to stop me. All right?"

I suppose I could have stopped it if I'd really tried but I have to confess I was kind of mesmerised by the whole proceeding. Ronnie walked towards Robbo looking alert and dangerous. Robbo stepped forward to close the gap, his massive fists balled. I saw Robbo's right hand streak upwards towards Ronnie's jaw and, in that instant, Ronnie was all action. He batted Robbo's incoming fist away as if it were an annoying fly, his other hand shot out, fist clenched and hit Robbo in the solar plexus. But Ronnie was still walking forward. His right leg crossed behind Robbo's and his right hand was suddenly gripping Robbo's throat and pushing. Everything was smooth and fluid. The big man went down like a felled tree and Ronnie stepped past him to tap me on the chest, grinning broadly.

"Fuck!" I said, as the shock of the sudden violence hit me.

I gaped, open-mouthed at Ronnie. He went to stand by the fallen bodyguard.

"You all right?" he asked.

Robbo made no attempt to get up. "When I get my breath back, maybe."

Ronnie held out a hand and helped the giant to his feet. Robbo looked shaken and was still having trouble breathing. To me, he said, "I'll be off, then."

"Wait a minute." I ran to the desk and got out the petty cash box. I took six hundred dollars from it and ran back to put it in Robbo's hand. "That's for, you know, wasting your afternoon. And give a hundred of it to Dicko, hey?"

He looked at me in silence and nodded. Then he gave Ronnie a long, lingering appraisal, before turning away and leaving.

I could feel Ronnie staring at me. "All right," I said. "I underestimated you. I should have had more faith." I went back to my desk, put the petty cash box away and picked up my tepid coffee. "How the hell do you make that shit look so effortless?"

He went back to his seat and joined me. "It's nothing," he said, airily. "All you have to do is practice every day of your life for about fifty years."

I sat down heavily, feeling like the fight – if you could even call it that – had tired me far more than it had Ronnie.

"So," he said. "Can we stop fucking about and get on with catching our murderer?"

Chapter Nine

"So, no-one you spoke to had ever heard of Morgan Sanford and you didn't get any more useful information out of anybody?"

I had to admit, that was a fair summary of my afternoon's work. Fortunately for my ego, Ronnie had also drawn a blank. The two out-of-town FABClub members knew both McKinley and Sanford, of course, but both had alibis for both murders and neither could see any reason why the members of their dumb little investment club should be targeted. The three local FABClub members were all shocked to hear of Sanford's death – it hadn't made the news by the time Ronnie told them – and they all had alibis for it.

"Maybe the club cheated somebody out of something and now she's going round getting even," I suggested.

"He. It's a he. But maybe you're right. God knows I haven't got any better suggestions. What about the daughter and the shifty boyfriend?"

"As I said, Ophelia didn't know Sanford. Hadn't ever met him or heard of him. Fraser Jackson had his phone off all day and I couldn't reach him."

"What? Someone of your generation with their phone

switched off? That smells fishier than my tax-cheating fish-botherer. Give the girl a bell and ask her where the hell he's got to."

I looked at the time, about to object but Ronnie's heavy sigh changed my mind. I dialled Ophelia's number, putting the phone on speaker.

"You again," she said in greeting.

"Being a pest goes with the job, I'm afraid."

"So?"

"I've been trying to reach Fraser Jackson but his phone seems to be off. Do you have any idea how I can reach him?"

There was a long pause. "His phone's not off. It's broken. I broke it. When I threw it at him."

I waited for her to elaborate but she didn't. "You threw it at him? May I ask why?"

Again, there was a long pause. "Shit," she said. "You might as well know. That alibi he gave for the night my dad died. Sounded dodgy, didn't it? Well, I thought so. So I went round to see his parents and I demanded to see the security footage for that night. It was quite a scene, really. Anyway, they eventually let me look at it and that's how I discovered darling Fraser had been screwing a slag of our mutual acquaintance. And it wasn't just that night, I found out later. It was plenty of others. And it wasn't just one slag, either." She fell silent.

"I'm very sorry. I wish I hadn't had to ask."

"No," she said. "It's better this way. Anyway, at least Fraser has a proper alibi, now. And even if he didn't, he will definitely not be getting his grubby paws on the family jewels."

I awkwardly thanked her for letting me know and ended the call. I felt bad for Ophelia but I also felt bad that one of our only suspects – however unlikely – had been eliminated. As I sat and pondered the unhappy lot of a private investigator with no suspects, Ronnie got up and began updating the whiteboards. It was clearly just a displacement activity because, half-way through, he threw down the pen and turned to me.

"Come on, were off."

"Off where?"

"My place."

"What for?"

"Well, I'm going to meet Karen and you're coming with me because, until we've got our man—"

"Or woman."

"—you will not leave my side."

I thought about it for all of two seconds. "Right-o. I'll need to get some stuff from my unit."

"We'll see."

"Oh shit. They're not going to burn it down again, are they?"

He grinned. "We'll see."

* * * *

Ronnie made me walk from the lift to my car on my own while he hung back and watched. Nothing happened. I climbed in, my heart beating faster, and had turned on the engine and put it in drive before I even thought that someone might have connected a bomb to the ignition. I drove out to Ronnie's place with my head full of all the ways an assassin might find to murder me – a bomb in my car, poison in my food or drink, a cut brake pipe, a sniper, a stranger in a crowd with a knife or a gun or a hypodermic, a couple of thugs with

iron bars, a severed lift cable, an electric wire in the shower…
In the end, I realised I was just running through murder
scenes from films I'd watched. Teasing myself, I added boiled
alive in hot wax and chased down a ski slope by men with
machine guns.

However, I was still nervous as a kitten by the time I
pulled up down the road from my unit block. This was
Ronnie's idea. He was going to get there first and check it
out. I couldn't see his car anywhere. I waited for ages,
realising Ronnie hadn't said how long I should wait before I
should assume he was dead in a front garden somewhere. I
wanted to phone him but I daren't in case he was stalking
someone or, worse, hiding out from armed killers.

The bang on my side window almost stopped my heart.
Ronnie's grinning face was there.

"You're all right. Get in and get your shit. Don't arse
about. Do it quick. I'll see you back at my place," He pulled
back and disappeared into the night.

I drove up to my block and got out. How could Ronnie
know it was clear? Had he been inside? Had he checked both
stairways? Did he look in every one of the hundreds of
shrubs and trees around here? All the doorways and
alleyways? Behind every parked car? For a moment, I was
completely paralysed. The certainty of doom clutched at my
throat and held me like a roo in the headlights.

Was I going to die on that street, or in my apartment?
Would I see it coming? Would I just blink out of existence?
Or would there be pain and fear and despair? I struggled to
muster any kind of equanimity. The great philosophers had
disagreed utterly over the nature of death. Aristotle thought it
was something to fear, Socrates and Plato thought we should
accept it as a liberation of the soul. Good old Epicurus said

that fear of death was what diverted us from our primary goal, which was to enjoy our lives. Marcus Aurelius, my favourite Stoic, thought that death was only the loss of the moment in which we live. But, if this moment between past and future is all we have, what a terrible loss that is!

"Good God!" I said aloud, hit by exasperation with myself. "What the hell are you doing?" I looked around. I was standing in an empty street, possibly in physical danger, and, instead of getting on with what I was supposed to be doing, I was reviewing different ideas about death from different philosophers. And now I'd started talking to myself! Ronnie was right: I was a complete dickhead.

I set off at a brisk walk, entered my building, then my apartment, swept through the unit, throwing stuff in a bag, got out, got back in the car, and got going, all before the simmering anger at my stupidity had come off the boil. If I died tonight, I wanted to die doing what I could to keep on living. And that meant getting my useless arse round to Ronnie's so we could solve the case and put away the man – or woman – who'd threatened me.

Ah hell. Ronnie was right about that, too. It was probably a man.

* * * *

Karen was already there when I arrived at Ronnie's house. She was sitting demurely at the kitchen table, straight back, knees together, ankles crossed, her outfit smart and restrained, and looking as pretty as I'd ever seen her. Ronnie was opening pizza boxes.

"Meat lover's, pepperoni, or..." He opened the last lid. "Another pepperoni?"

"So, no vegetarian option." I dropped my bag by the wall and joined them at the table. "Hi Karen."

"What took you so long?" Ronnie asked.

"I was pondering the nature of death."

"Good-o. Glad you weren't wasting your time then."

I helped myself to a slice of the pepperoni and started chewing. I was famished. Ronnie, of course, had eaten most of my lunch. He'd probably eat most of the pizzas too. He was bottomless. Karen also had a slice of the pepperoni and was chipping delicately at it with a knife and fork. *It's how she keeps that amazing figure*, I thought, surprising and embarrassing myself. I pulled my gaze away from her body and looked at Ronnie. Ronnie was watching me. He winked and I looked away, irritated.

"We're expecting a call," Ronnie said, nodding towards the phone on the table. It wasn't his phone and looked like one of the cheap burners he was so fond of.

Karen pulled a bag up off the floor. From it she extracted her outsize laptop. She cleared a space for it on the table in front of her, saying, "I should get ready."

"What's going on?" I asked.

Karen looked a bit uncomfortable and focused on her machine. Ronnie said, "Remember that little problem Karen has with her Uncle Lau?"

I'd completely forgotten about it. "Er, yes, of course," I said. Even then, I struggled to remember the details. Uncle Lau wanted her back in Hong Kong to work as a hacker for his criminal enterprise, or somesuch. Were there threats or... blackmail. That was it! Her uncle was coming to Brisbane to take her home soon but Ronnie was going to get her out of it, somehow.

"We're waiting for a call from a friend of mine in Hong

Kong," Ronnie said.

"You have a friend in Hong Kong?"

"Not usually. But I've got a mate in London who has a son in Poole in Dorset, who has a colleague in Hanoi. Today, the Hanoi guy is my friend in Hong Kong."

What the...? Was this something to do with Ronnie's naval connections? He'd been a special forces guy attached to the Navy. So maybe the London friend was an old SBS colleague, now at the Admiralty, and his son in Dorset would be serving at a navy base, meaning the guy in Hanoi was, what, a serving special forces operative?

"You're not going to blow anybody up, are you?" I looked from Ronnie to Karen. She looked as horrified as I was.

"No!" she said. "No, no!" She looked at Ronnie, open-mouthed. Now that I'd planted the suspicion, it obviously didn't strike her as far-fetched.

"Oh for fuck's sake!" he said. "Give me some credit. Who do you two think I am?" To Karen, he added, "You know what the plan is." He grabbed another slice of pizza and sat back in his chair, scowling and eating.

"I'm sorry," Karen said. "Only Luke sounded so..."

"So melodramatic? So hysterical?"

"I only meant..." I began but stopped myself. *I only meant I wouldn't put anything past you,* wasn't the right thing to say, however true it might be. "You're getting one of your, er, navy friends to do something in Hong Kong, aren't you?" I couldn't say SBS because I didn't know if Karen knew about Ronnie's past and he seemed to like to keep quiet about it.

Before Ronnie could answer, the phone rang. Ronnie put it on speaker.

"Hello, Brisbane," a male voice said. He sounded like Thomas the Tank Engine. Who did that? Ringo Starr?

"Hello, Hong Kong," said Ronnie. No names, I noticed. "Nice to hear from you. Just FYI, I've got a couple of mates with me – the tech support we spoke about and my business partner. You'll forgive me if I talk with a mouth full of pizza."

"Suit yourself, mate."

"Any trouble getting in?"

"Nothing to worry about. Couple of wankers with guns and an IT type who wet himself and passed out. They're all taking a nap in the next room."

"Sounds like fun. You ready to start?"

"if you've had enough chit-chat."

Ronnie gave Karen the nod. She swallowed hard as if her throat had gone dry. "Hello."

"Hello, darling."

"Did you get all the equipment I specified?"

"I wouldn't be standing in a gangster's office in Kowloon Bay on a nice sunny Friday evening if I hadn't brought the right tools to finish the job."

"Of course, yes. Then you need to connect the phone to one of the USB sockets on the server rack."

"Done."

"Now call the number we gave you."

A short pause. "Done."

Karen bent her attention to the screen of her laptop. After a moment, she said, "It's working. Thank you." She began typing at her usual lightning speed.

."That's all we need, mate," Ronnie said. "We can do the rest from here."

"You don't want me to wait until you're finished and remove the phone?"

"No need. We want them to know they were hacked. So,

as long as you didn't leave any prints or DNA, your part is over."

The caller laughed – presumably at the idea he would be sloppy.

"Then it's goodbye from Hong Kong. Nice working with you, Brisbane."

"You too, mate. If you're ever in the neighbourhood, I've got a coldie with your name on it."

Ronnie hung up and grinned at me. "Nice to discover I've still got mates who'll do me a favour."

"So that was someone from your old regiment?"

"Nah, mate. That was more a sort of civil servant. Not everyone I worked with stayed in the Navy. Some went into... other Departments."

My mouth fell open. Had he just enlisted an MI6 spy to help Karen solver her family problem?

He stood up and grabbed the two boxes of pizza. "Come on. We'll sit outside while Karen downloads every dirty secret her uncle ever had. You all right doing that on your own, darl?" Karen waved a hand distractedly. Ronnie grinned. "Just shout if you need me or Luke to help you with the hard bits." To me, he added, "Grab some beer and I'll see you outside."

I did as he asked, dropped a bottle off on the table next to Karen and settled into a sun-lounger out on the patio. Ronnie took a stubbie from me and waved a box of pizza at me in return. I declined the offer.

For a while we chatted about the case but it dwindled into longer and longer silences. I fetched another beer and we sat and stared into the night sky, each alone with his thoughts.

Out of the blue, Ronnie said, "Karen's not the one."

"What?"

"I know you need to get laid but mooning over young

Karen is a waste of time, mate."

"What?" My shock was slowly being replaced by indignation. "I do not need to get— No, I won't even dignify that with a response. And, as for Karen... You haven't got a clue what your talking about."

"Right-o," he said and fell silent again.

I watched him sucking on his beer and my temper rose. "I don't see what business it is of yours but what if I did fancy Karen? That would be none of your business. It would be between me and her. OK?"

"And her fiancée."

"What?"

"He'd probably have a few things to say about it."

"Her what?"

"Amazing. I bet you've never had a single conversation with her about her private life. Am I right? Of course I am. I've never known a bloke so completely self-obsessed and oblivious to everyone around him. Why you think your vocation is to be a private investigator, I'll never know. Monk? Yes. Lighthouse keeper? No worries. But PI?" He rolled his eyes. "Maybe your brain is still developing. You know, like a teenager. They say that's why they're all such total arseholes. Or maybe it's more a case of arrested development."

"She's engaged?" To my surprise, I found myself feeling disappointed. I realised I really did have it at the back of my mind that I could maybe ask her out one day.

"What do philosophers call that thing where they're the only real person in the universe and everyone else is just some kind of illusion?"

"Solipsism," I said, my mind still on Karen and her engagement. Obviously, if I fancied her, it must be in some very vague, impersonal kind of way, nothing to do with who she really was. Was I really so shallow? Did I really know what it meant to be someone's friend? To be in love with them? Was this how I'd been with Chelsea, emotionally distant, relating only to an abstraction, an idea of her? Not even a true idea but a fantasy concocted on superficial knowledge and meagre understanding?

I felt sick. The pizza I'd eaten sat like a ball of gristly sausage and congealed cheese in my stomach. I sat up, worried I might start retching. Ronnie sat up too.

"Jeez, mate, I didn't know you liked her that much. You look like you're going to lose your lunch. If you want to puke, don't do it out here, or you're cleaning it up."

"I'm all right," I said, the urge to throw up slowly passing.

Ronnie seemed strangely abashed. "I wouldn't have teased you like that if I'd known how you felt, mate."

I shook my head. "Nothing to do with Karen. It's just..." How did I explain the growing awareness of my own inadequacy as a human being that had begun when Chelsea died? How did I tell a man like Ronnie that every time I found some new evidence of what a useless partner I'd been, it felt like a nail being hammered into my heart? How did I ever get across to anyone the hopelessness of knowing that everything I learned about myself was too late, that any improvement I might make made no difference at all because she was gone.

Ronnie was perched on the edge of his sun-lounger, watching me. Karen appeared at the patio doors and I looked away.

"I should go home now," she said. "I've downloaded everything but there is so much of it. I need to sit somewhere quiet and go through it all. Also some of it's encrypted and

I've got a faster machine at home that will work better." She paused. "Is everything OK?"

"Luke's feeling a bit crook," Ronnie said. "Here, I'll give you a ride home."

"No, no!" she said. "You're not well, either. I'll get a cab. You sit down."

There was a long silence and I imagined Ronnie and Karen exchanging gestures and pulling meaningful faces. Eventually, Karen said, "The Uber is on its way. Two minutes. I'll go wait outside."

Ronnie went with her to the door and they were gone at least five minutes. By the time he came back, carrying two more stubbies, I was feeling thoroughly wretched.

I took a beer from him. It was cold and wet in my hand. I rolled the bottle across my brow.

"You want to talk about it?" he asked.

Not with you, I thought, like a reflex. But, if not Ronnie, then who? Since Chelsea died, I'd drifted away from all our mutual friends, realising they'd been Chelsea's friends really. I hadn't kept in touch with any of my uni friends, either, except on various social media. And, I suddenly saw, I hadn't made a single new friend since that day. Except Ronnie. God help me.

"I'm good," I said, trying a smile. "It's – it's probably the anniversary coming up. You know."

He nodded but he didn't look convinced. Maybe if Ronnie hadn't had his operation, I wouldn't be in such a mess. Trying to run a murder investigation all on my own had really shown me just how useless I was. Ronnie was right again. I should have chosen some other career. Something I actually knew how to do. But that narrowed my options down to a list of zero. And how could I not know Karen was engaged? I'd thought we were friends. I'd thought we'd grown close.

But I was wrong.

"How's your recovery coming along?" I asked, so I wouldn't have to keep thinking about my failures.

"Fine," he said.

"What was it you had done?"

"A hernia repair."

"Right." I nodded. "What exactly is a hernia?" I could have just googled it, I suppose, but I wanted to keep the conversation going.

"It's where the muscles of your abdominal wall come apart and your guts fall through the gap."

"Fuck, that sounds disgusting." The words, "poor bastard" and "Ronnie", had never gone together in my mind until that moment. "So, what do they do? Push everything back inside and stitch you up?"

"In my case, they put a bit of plastic mesh across the inside of my abdominal muscles and stapled it in place."

"Shit, that sounds precarious. Like you could fall apart again at any minute. Have you got hideous scars?"

"Yes, but not from the op. That was all done with keyhole surgery. Hardly left a mark."

"Even so, you should take, like, a fortnight off. Let everything heal properly." I remembered him throwing Robbo to the ground and winced – not that it seemed to cost him any effort at all.

"Do you really want that?" he asked. There was such a heavy weight of meaning in his question that I immediately knew he understood all my agonies of self-doubt. It was humiliating but I shook my head. I wouldn't stand a chance of solving the case on my own.

"It's up to you," I said, hating myself for my weakness.

He went to bed not long after. I stayed up for a while longer, staring at the stars and wondering if Ronnie would willingly give up hunting down our killer, even if it wrecked his health. The man was obsessive and driven. He was a powerhouse, an irresistible force, or, at least, he always had been. Now, tragically, he seemed to be feeling the limits of his strength, menaced by his encroaching mortality.

When I'd packed my bag to come over, I'd picked up a few books, meaning to give them to Ronnie as a present. They were all by Stoic writers – Heraclitus, Marcus Aurelius and Seneca. I thought there might be strength and comfort to be found in them for him. But I knew now I wouldn't give them to him. It would be presumptuous and he wouldn't read them anyway. Ronnie would come to terms with old age and death in his own way. He'd butt heads with decay and decline until they or he gave way. He'd go down fighting, spitting in Death's eye. Marcus Aurelius would not approve but, then again, I don't suppose Ronnie would give a fuck.

It would be much better if I hung on to those books. The Stoics had much more to say to me than to Ronnie. And I had far greater need of them.

Chapter Ten

"What are you doing?" I asked in alarm as Ronnie tore down the pictures and erased all the lines on our whiteboards.

We'd come into the office early ("Might as well get some use out of that money-pit of yours," Ronnie had explained.) and I'd gone straight over to fire up the coffee machine. When I re-joined my companion, he was busy destroying our work.

"This is all bollocks," he said. "We need to start again."

I sat down with my coffee, feeling his words as an indictment of my management of the case.

"There now," he said, stepping back to study the empty boards. "Let's see." He brandished a marker pen. "OK." He wrote "FABClub" at the centre of one board. Around it, he wrote the names of the seven members. He also added a question mark nearby and wrote "Lawyers" under it.

"Right. That's everyone who knew all the FABClub members – the people in the club and their lawyers. There may be others – like you and me and the cops – but I bet there aren't many."

"Secretaries and filing clerks will have seen the contract," I said. "They'd have access to the names, too."

He looked unhappy. "You're right. Seven members, seven lawyers, at least one secretary for each of them. That's nearly thirty people – excluding us and the cops."

He took a sip of his coffee and went back to scribbling. He added in the various people we'd spoken to. Everyone, including Ophelia McKinley, Antonia Rushton, Fraser Jackson and Scott Armitage, he moved off to the far reaches of the second board. In a distant corner, he put the heading "Also" and parked the housekeeper's and the gardener's names there. He wrote all the names from memory. Eventually, he drew a ring around the FABClub and turned to me.

"Those are our victims," he said. "We just need to know who's trying to kill them and why."

While I was impressed by his newfound energy, I wasn't entirely sold.

"We don't really know that," I said. "Sanford's murder might have been unrelated. You said yourself, there's always a motive to kill rich people. It might not even have been a murder. That's just your supposition, so far."

"Yeah, nah. I don't believe in coincidences – especially in murder cases. Those two blokes were murdered and it's got something to do with the club."

"Why?"

"Because there's no other connection between them."

"That we know about."

He pursed his lips and stared at me. I thought he was going to launch into some kind of harangue but he didn't. Instead, saying, "We need to know more about this club. We need to know what it has done that would make someone want to start killing its members."

I gave up arguing. The man was a human steamroller.

Besides, when push came to shove, I actually trusted his instincts a lot more than I trusted my doubts.

"Maybe it's one of the members killing the others," I said. "Maybe they did something to one of them and he's out for revenge."

He didn't seem to like it much but he wrote it on the board anyway. "The upside of that would be we only have five suspects," he said.

"Who could the club have wronged so badly they want to kill them?" I asked. "Someone they bought something from who felt cheated? Someone they didn't buy something from who felt slighted? Someone who wanted to join but was blackballed?"

He wrote them all down but obviously didn't like any of them.

"Did the club do anything else apart from buying art?" Ronnie asked.

"Not as far as I know."

"And there's no way anybody gets rich – richer – by killing everybody?"

"Well, yes, but only up to a maximum of three hundred K." I told him what Nick Kryou had said about it being the value of his new car. "It's not a big incentive for murder for these guys."

"If they were all dead, someone must inherit it."

"Potentially, I suppose, along with everything else that person might inherit. Some of these guys are running businesses worth hundreds of millions. The FABClub's assets would be in the noise in an estate that big."

He put down the marker and sat down. He sipped his coffee and grimaced, probably because it was cold by then.

"Nuke it," I suggested.

He nodded absently. "We're missing something. Or somebody."

I checked the time. "We told the cops we'd go in and make our statements at ten."

"Bloody cops," he grumbled, his mind clearly still on the problem.

"What are we going to do about that?" I asked.

"About what?"

"Our statement. We lied to DI Marr yesterday."

"No we didn't. We just left it a bit ambiguous about where I was and when."

"We let her think you were with me when I interviewed Antonia."

He grimaced. Apparently, even he didn't like having to lie to the police. "If it comes up…" he fixed me with a stern eye. "*If* it comes up, tell them I was outside in the car. Tell them I'm allergic to fine art bullshit. They'll believe that."

"We should talk to Marr about the case," I said. "She needs to know what we know."

"What, so she can make cracks about how fucking old I am and tell us to keep our noses out?"

"Yes," I said. "That's why."

He scowled. "You can talk to her if you like. For all the good it'll do."

* * * *

Brisbane Central Police Station was starting to feel familiar to me. I announced myself at the desk and went to sit with Ronnie. There was the usual collection of unhappy-looking people sharing the room with us. I don't suppose Ronnie and I seemed particularly happy for that matter, or even the cops on reception. We sat in silence. There was a woman of about fifty in a pink track suit with two very young boys who, between them, were making so much noise that talking was just about impossible anyway.

Finally, a young woman came out and called my name. We both stood up and went to join her.

"Which one is Mister Kelly?" she asked.

"I am. And it's Doctor Kelly." I decided on the spot it was now my policy when dealing with the cops.

She blinked, apparently not quite sure what to do with the information. "Would you follow me, please?" We all set off and she stopped. To Ronnie, she said, "If you'd care to wait in the reception area, it won't take a moment."

Ronnie scowled at her. "How do you know I'm not his brief?"

She made a visible effort not to run her eyes up and down his typically scruffy outfit. "So, are you his lawyer?"

"I'm his bodyguard."

We were beginning to attract the attention of one of the cops at the desk.

"I'll be as quick as I can," I told Ronnie and we went inside.

She led me to one of the meeting rooms I was also becoming familiar with and I took a seat.

"Someone will be with you in a minute," she said.

"Will that be DI Marr?"

She looked confused again. "I don't think the Detective Inspector is in today."

"I called less than an hour ago and I specifically asked to speak to DI Marr. I have important information about a case she's working on. They told me that would be no problem."

"Sorry. It is the weekend."

"The w—?" I took a breath. "So what about Bronski? Is he in?"

"DS Bronski?"

"Yes. How many Bronskis have you got?"

"If you'll just wait, someone will be along soon."

She beat a retreat and left me to fume. Eventually a woman in uniform appeared. She was a cheerful type with short, curly hair and a nice smile. She started explaining the process of me giving a statement but I stopped her after a couple of sentences.

"Are you on Marr's team?" I asked.

"No, I just—"

"Then get me someone who is. A detective. As senior as you can find."

She gave me an appraising look. I could almost see the categories rolling past behind her eyes and finally coming to a stop at "Troublemaker".

"Is there a problem, sir?"

"Yes, there is, and I think it's organisational and systemic. At the moment, it is manifested in the person of DI Marr and exemplified by the way she is conducting this investigation."

The cop seemed to increase her stolidity and decrease her cheerfulness, swapping one personality for another before my very eyes. "If you'd like to make a complaint, sir, the officer at the front desk can supply you with the appropriate form. But right now shall we just take your statement?" I didn't reply. Arguing was clearly useless. Marr wasn't even in the building. The cop seemed to sense that she had won. "Right-o, if you would, just tell me in your own words what happened yesterday lunchtime at the home of Mr. Morgan Sanford."

So I told her, as briefly and with as little information as I could, and left.

For some reason, it took them another half hour to call Ronnie. He was in and out in ten minutes and we went into town for a coffee.

"Still want to bring Marr up to speed on our investigation?" he asked, grinning. I shook my head. "It's nothing personal, you know. The cops just hate helpful busybodies and that goes treble for PIs. Just let them bumble along in their own merry way. We'll have our man in irons before they even admit they have a serial killer."

"A serial killer?"

"If he's going after all the FABClub members, that's what he is."

"But how could he imagine he'd get away with it? There's only five of them left. Pretty soon, it'll become obvious to everyone what's going on if they keep having accidents and killing themselves."

"Maybe. Maybe not. The cops didn't see the first two as murders. As far as I can tell, they didn't see the connection between the victims, either. Hell, two of the club members are in a different State. It's not like they all wear FABClub T-shirts, who's going to notice that seven accidental deaths or suicides all belonged to the same, insignificant little investment club? It's only our investigation that's connecting these victims at the moment. It's only us who thinks they even are victims."

"Do you reckon that's what pissed the killer off so much he sent his goons round to scare us off?"

"Yeah, reckon. It must really give him the shits that we know what he's up to." He laughed.

"But it didn't stop him, did it?"

"What do you mean?"

"Well, he warned me off, we kept on investigating, but he still went ahead and killed Sanford. Whatever he's doing this for, the risk of us finding him isn't enough to scare him off."

Ronnie's eyes lit up. "He's on the clock. He can't stop. He has to take the risk because there's a deadline. Something's going to happen and he needs this lot dead before it does."

It was another of Ronnie's wild surmises but I felt my heart beat a little faster. If it was true, it not only gave us another avenue of investigation – and we had precious few at the moment – but it meant the stakes were suddenly very much higher. We might be racing against time to stop this man before he murdered five more people.

"McKinley and Sanford died barely three weeks apart," I said. "At that rate, the other five club members would be dead within four more months."

Ronnie shook his head. "If we've really got him spooked, he'll bring his schedule forward. He needs to get this done before we find him, or before we convince the cops to take it seriously. My guess is, we've got a couple of weeks, if we're going to save anyone's life. After that, we can close the case at out leisure."

"Shit." Given our progress so far, two weeks sounded pretty optimistic.

We both sat back and thought about our new timetable for a moment. Ronnie broke the silence, asking, "So, who called you at eleven thirty last night?"

I tried not to wince visibly. I'd hoped he had been fast asleep when the call came and he wouldn't ask me about it. "It was nothing important."

His brows came down. "Mate, stop pissing about. You haven't got any friends who'd invite you to late night parties.

Your parents have given up on you as a lost cause. So who was it?"

"It's really not important." I tried to sound as nonchalant as I could. "It was Mel Bertolissio."

"For an update on the case?"

"Yeah, basically."

He stared at me hard, eyes full of suspicion until he worked it out. "She dumped us, didn't she?"

"She just felt that we'd—"

"Fucking hell."

She'd sounded drunk. In fact she'd sounded like she was at a party and was completely wasted. Even so, she'd managed to make her disappointment crystal clear and was adamant that she couldn't afford to let us just go on "dicking around and getting nowhere."

"It doesn't make any difference. I'll invoice her for the three days. It's better than nothing. We'll keep the investigation going. I don't need to make money at the PI work. You know that. Chelsea's company brings in more than I need, anyway. We'll see it through, hey? Get the bastard."

He turned his gaze to the tabletop. I could see his jaw working. "You should have told me."

"It doesn't make any difference. Honest."

"Except there's no client to bill any more."

"So? Like I said—"

"If there's no client, I'm not billing you for my time. And you should've told me. I'm not a fucking charity case. I've got my own income too."

I'd often wondered just where Ronnie's money came from. I assumed he'd have pensions from the Royal Navy and from the Queensland Police but I had no idea what they would amount to. I was perfectly happy for him to keep on billing his time to the case as long as he was working on it. It was my company. He wasn't a partner or anything.

"I didn't mean to suggest—"

"But you didn't tell me. You were going to just let me go on putting in timesheets and expenses claims like nothing had happened. I'm not your fucking Good Cause of the Week. I'm not some helpless fucking old age pensioner who needs Blue Care and Meals on Wheels."

And there it was again, Ronnie's insecurity about getting old and useless.

"Jeez, mate, that's not what I was thinking at all. I just knew you'd want us to keep going. I want us to keep going too. So I thought, 'Why complicate it? Just keep your mouth shut.' At the same time, I didn't want you giving me a lecture on how to run a business. You know how you get."

He seemed mollified and a bit sulky. "Yeah, well, someone has to remind you of the basic principles. Like: you only do work for a client if they're paying you." He grinned. "Otherwise you end up like I did, working for nothing and living on toast and beans – when I could afford it."

"I didn't mean to upset you, or to imply anything."

"I don't know what's wrong with me lately. I'm not usually so touchy."

I put on a sympathetic face. "It's probably the menopause, dear. Have you considered HRT?"

"Don't fucking push it, you mongrel."

I grinned, satisfied he was over his little wobble. "So what do we do now? If you're right about his schedule, we need to crack the whip a bit."

"Too bloody true, mate." He thought for a minute. "Let's get back to the money pit—"

"The office."

"Yeah, that. We need to hit the phones. I want to talk to the entire FABClub again – and their lawyers and their secretaries. I want to know if anyone else was ever involved with the club, in any capacity whatsoever. I want to know how the club started, who brought who into it, who joined and left, who was invited but declined. All that shit. I want to know exactly what is in their collection. I want to know where it is and who has the keys. And I want to sit down and read that contract from cover to cover. Then we're going to verify everybody's alibis – even if we have to go to Sydney and Canberra. And Port Moresby. We're going to dig into everybody's finances. Mr. Fisho likes to brag about his little tax rorts, but maybe he's just a cashed up bogan living on tick. If he is, I want to know." He stood up. "Ready to go?"

My head was reeling at the sheer volume of work ahead of us, but I got up feeling better about the case than I'd felt all week.

* * * *

The rest of the day was a whirlwind of activity. Ronnie made most of the calls while I got onto the Internet, searching for financial information, tracking down associates and checking out alibis. After I'd exhausted what I could do with stock prices and social media, I also started making calls. I had lunch delivered and we didn't stop for a second while we ate it. The office cappuccino machine got its toughest workout ever and my only break that day was to fetch sandwiches and snacks up from the shopping mall below us. By six o'clock, people had stopped answering their phones and we were both ready to call it a day. Considering it was a Saturday, we'd had a very productive day of it. Ronnie had broken out the flip chart and stand I'd bought but never used before and we'd filled page after page with notes and findings, taping them to walls and windows as we went along.

I was very pleased with our day's work but Ronnie seemed unhappy and subdued.

"Let's go home," he said, tossing a marker pen onto the table and falling back into his chair.

"What about all this?" I asked, waving an arm at the scribble-covered A1 sheets all around the room.

"It'll still be there in the morning," he said.

"I thought we'd, like, consolidate it all, or something, see what we've got."

"What we've got is fuck all." He got up, wearily, and began collecting up the empty coffee cups around him.

"But…"

"Come on, I'm sick of the sight of this place."

I got up and followed him in dumping used cups into the sink. "What's wrong? We got tons of work done."

He headed for the doorway and stopped. Turning to me, he said, "We didn't find a single credible suspect. We didn't crack a single alibi. We didn't get a single new lead. But, yes, we got tons of work done."

"Which we had to do."

He sighed. "Yeah, we did."

I trailed after him as he went down the corridor and into the lift. I'd been really pumped until then. Now I felt deflated. Maybe Ronnie was right that we hadn't moved ahead despite all the calling and checking but we'd achieved something, surely? We'd spread the net much wider and we'd ticked lots of boxes. Even I knew that detective work had to be like that, sometimes. It couldn't always be brilliant reasoning and flashes of insight. But maybe there was something I didn't know. Ronnie seemed so disappointed it really looked as though he'd expected today's work to give us some vital new clue that would blow the case right open. Maybe he was down precisely because we'd covered so much ground and it had revealed nothing useful. Maybe that was really bad sign which he had the experience to recognise and I did not.

The lift doors opened onto the underground parking space and I stepped forward. Ronnie put an arm across my chest and I caught my breath. I'd forgotten all about the beating I'd had right there, just two nights ago.

"Walk slowly to your car," he said in a quiet voice. "Don't look around 'til you get there. Then get in. Got it?" I nodded and he took his arm away.

I swallowed and set off. I could see my car, about twenty metres away. Most other people had left already so mine sat alone and I had to walk through open space, feeling exposed and vulnerable. I fought the urge to look around, even when I was sure I could hear footsteps behind me. I reached the car and turned. There were the two thugs I'd seen before. They both wore balaclavas as before. This time they both carried new-looking pickaxe handles. I had a vision of them both dropping into a hardware store on the way over to buy them.

"You must be fucking stupid," the shorter, broader one said. "Now you're going to come for a little ride."

"Who are you?" I asked, my voice betraying my fear. "Who sent you?"

"Shut the fuck up. Get walking. That way." He gestured with the pickaxe handle. I looked but didn't see the ute I was expecting. I looked back at the broad guy, the talker, and took a deep breath.

"No," I said.

His eyes narrowed and he shifted his grip on the stick. "What?"

"I said, no."

Pain exploded in my stomach as he rammed the pickaxe handle into it. I doubled over but it wasn't as bad as I'd feared. *They want to keep me on my feet so I can walk and they don't have to drag me*, I thought, straightening up. When I looked at my attackers again, through watering eyes, there seemed to be three of them.

The talker cried out in pain and dropped his stick. He fell to his knees, back arched. I blinked and saw Ronnie behind him. Incredibly, he winked at me before turning to the tall guy with the footy-player build.

"You should go," Ronnie told him.

"Fuck you," the man said and swung his stick at Ronnie.

With his usual calm and seemingly unhurried grace, Ronnie stepped close to his assailant, making the swing useless. His right arm shot up between them, the heel of his hand hitting the tall man under the chin with sickening violence, snapping the man's head back. Just as casually, Ronnie reached out with his left hand and took the pickaxe handle from him. As the big guy staggered away, dazed, Ronnie swung the stick at the talker's head. It connected with a thunk and the man toppled forward to lie face down on the concrete, not moving. Without a second's hesitation, Ronnie turned and caught up with the tall guy. Two sharp blows to the knees had him on the ground. Another to the chest had him whimpering and begging for mercy.

"Who sent you?" Ronnie asked.

The man's former belligerence had completely vanished. "I don't know. It was all done by phone. No names. Fuck sake, don't kill me. I've got a wife and bubs."

Ronnie whacked him on the arm. "They deserve better. What's your name?" He hesitated. Ronnie raised the pickaxe handle again and the man told him. "Address?" This time, he rattled it off. "And your mate?" Again, no hesitation.

"All right, Barry, you and Sleeping Beauty over there are done with us. Yeah? If I see either of you, ever again, you're dead. I know where you live. And I know you've got a wife and children. You've probably both got mothers, too. Maybe brothers and sisters."

"What the fuck?" I was pretty sure that Ronnie was bluffing but the footy player, Barry, seemed genuinely alarmed.

"You two fuckwits took the wrong contract. Why'd you take the business by phone? How'd you know he'd pay up?"

Barry struggled to move. I think he had it in mind to run for it but he'd barely started moving when he stopped and screamed in pain. "Fucking hell, man, you've broke my leg."

Ronnie tapped it with his stick and Barry cried out again. "It was an intermediary, right?"

"A what?"

"You got the business through someone you knew, yeah?"

"So?"

"So, I want his name."

"No fucking way. He'd kill me for sure."

Ronnie pulled back the stick for another swing at the broken leg. "You know, if I smash this up bad enough, You'll never walk on it again. Hell, you might even lose it. Just for one lousy name. And he'd never even know you told me." Ronnie pulled the stick back farther.

"You've got to promise," Barry pleaded.

"Last chance," Ronnie said. I looked away. I didn't want to see this.

"It's Darren McGuire!" Barry shouted.

Ronnie lowered the stick. "It better be." To me, he said, "Get in the car." I hurried to do so. I wanted to get out of there before the violence started up again. Ronnie threw the pickaxe handle down on top of Barry. "Are we ever going to see you or your mate again?"

Barry muttered something which might have been a sullen "No." Ronnie took a step towards him and he cringed and shouted, "No!"

I started up the engine and Ronnie got in the car. He didn't speak and I drove out of the car park. It wasn't easy. My whole body was trembling.

"We should call the cops. Shouldn't we? I mean, they attacked me. God knows what they had in mind." Ronnie didn't speak. "Do you suppose they'll call the cops? Or someone else, if they find them there. They're in a bad way. They probably both need a hospital." Ronnie still didn't speak. They weren't going to call the cops, I realised. And, if someone else did, there would be no charges, just bullshit stories about tripping and falling.

My mind kept drifting back to Barry, lying at Ronnie's feet. "I thought you were going to kill him," I said as we hit Coronation Drive.

He stared through the windscreen as if he was looking past the cars and buildings to a place darker and more bleak by far and said, "I don't do that any more."

Chapter Eleven

When we got to his place, he went out to his favourite spot on the patio with a bottle of beer. I put on the TV and watched the ABC news. It was all about idiotic political antics, celebrity antics, car crashes, and sports matches, none of which I found remotely interesting, but I kept watching for a long time because the flickering pictures and inane chatter drove what I'd just been through to the back of my mind.

When the doorbell rang, I seemed to wake from a trance. I found Karen standing on the doorstep, smiling.

"Hi," she said. Then she took a closer look at my face. "What's wrong? Are you OK?"

I made myself smile. "Yeah, bad day at the office. Come on in. Ronnie's out back gazing at his navel."

"I thought that was a job for philosophers."

"Don't you start. I get enough of that from the resident bogan."

Ronnie must have heard Karen arrive because he came in and greeted her with, "Ready?"

"Ready?" I asked. "Ready for what?"

Karen held up a manila envelope. "I found plenty."

"I won't be a mo," Ronnie said and disappeared upstairs.

"That from your uncle's servers?" I asked.

Karen nodded. "Lots of dirty laundry in there."

"And you're going round now to confront him. He's in the country."

"At the airport hotel. He flew in this afternoon."

"Shit." I didn't mean to say it out loud. Karen clearly took it as a bad sign.

"What's wrong. Something's wrong, isn't it? Is Ronnie all right?"

I shook my head. "Ronnie's fine – I think. Look, it's just me. I – I had a bit of a shock just now and I'm still processing it."

"You don't have to come," Ronnie said, reappearing. "Better if you don't."

"No. I want to. I'm ready when you are."

He gave me a long stare, then nodded to himself. "Right-o. You're driving."

* * * *

It took half an hour to drive out to the airport hotel from Ronnie's house, even though the traffic was light. There wasn't any obvious place to park except in the secure parking for guests, so we left the car out front and went inside. It was a big, modern, concrete slab with a couple of ten storey towers growing out of it. All around it were roads and all above it were aircraft. It was my idea of a post-apocalyptic hell but I'm not a keen traveller. Airports and air travel in general seemed more like paying for torture than for fun.

It was just after eight. We took the lift to the fifth floor in one of the towers and Karen tapped on a door. It took a long time to get a response. I could hear men's voices inside.

"You stay at the back," Ronnie told me. "If any trouble starts, run."

I felt a little miffed that he was saying this to me, not Karen, but when the door opened and a burly Chinese man filled the opening, I decided I wasn't that miffed after all. He stared at us in silence for a moment then walked back into the room We followed him in, Ronnie first, then Karen, then me.

It was a small room. A typical "standard double" type where the bed takes up most of the space. It seemed a lot smaller because it now had six people in it: an old bloke with white hair I had to assume was Uncle Lau, his two scowling heavies, and the three of us.

"Karen, you've brought friends," Uncle Lau said, pleasantly enough.

"I'm not going back with you," Karen said.

"I'm sorry about the accommodation," Uncle Lau said, ignoring her. "Can you believe you can't get a suite in this shithole? But you have a room to yourself for tonight and our flight leaves in the morning."

Ronnie spoke up. "Hey, arsehole, you're not listening."

My stomach sank. *Here we go*, I thought.

The heavy who had led us in, took a step towards Ronnie but Uncle Lau barked something in Cantonese and he retreated again.

"Your friends will have to leave if they can't behave themselves," Uncle Lau said.

"You can't make me go back," Karen said.

Uncle Lau smiled sadly. "I think you know that I can."

She tossed the manila envelope she had been holding onto the bed beside where Uncle Lau stood. He looked at it and frowned. "What is this?"

"Look at it. I have plenty more."

Ronnie moved slightly, standing between Karen and Uncle Lau. In a relaxed tone, he said, "A friend of mine broke into your offices in Kowloon last night. Perhaps you heard."

"That was you?"

"I have a lot of friends with extremely useful skills, Mr. Lau. Now, here's the deal. You leave Karen alone. You leave her family alone. You leave her friends alone. If you release any information you have about her to the police, we release what's in that envelope and a whole lot more. You will be destroyed. If you hurt Karen in any way – or anybody she loves – I will ask my friends to call on you personally."

Uncle Lau's polite manner faded away as Ronnie spoke. He was almost snarling as he snapped instructions to his two heavies. I hurried back and opened the door. I put a hand on Karen's shoulder and drew her towards me. Whatever Ronnie was going to do, he didn't have much room and I neither wanted to impede him nor get walloped by accident.

What he did was as astonishing a move as I'd ever seen him make. He casually pulled a handgun out from its hiding place and pointed it at the nearer of the two heavies. He made a show of sliding the bolt to feed a round into the chamber, taking a step back to give him a steady stance, raising the gun in a two-handed grip, and sighting along the barrel at the would-be attacker. The heavy came to a halt less than a metre from Ronnie's gun. The other one and Uncle Lau froze too.

"If I have to shoot all three of you, I will," Ronnie said. His voice was as steady as his aim. "You ought to know, I am a very, very good shot. It will be messy, trying to explain it to the police, but there's enough information in that envelope to convince a judge that I acted in self-defence against a gang of

Chinese gangsters. You'll be dead, of course – the big guy here goes down with the first shot, you go down with the second, the third… well, he might survive if he chooses to keep still – but it won't matter to you."

"The girl belongs to me," Uncle Lau said. He sounded angry still.

"No," Ronnie said. "You're forgetting about all that crap we found on your servers. You belong to Karen."

Before I could get a firm grip on her, Karen strode forward to stand beside Ronnie. She held up her phone. I couldn't see clearly but there seemed to be a big green button in the middle of her screen.

"See this?" she said, showing the screen to Lau. She sounded angry too. "All I have to do is push this button and everything I found on your server will be delivered immediately to the Australian Federal Police, the Hong Kong Police, and the PLA." She held her finger over the button. "You want me to press it?"

Uncle Lau was pop-eyed with anger but I could at last see uncertainty and fear starting to appear.

To the heavy in front of him, Ronnie said, "Back up." The man glanced at Uncle Lau and got the nod. Carefully, he stepped back as far as he could go. "Well, I'm sorry to break up the party but we have to leave now." Karen stayed where she was, finger over the button, lips pressed together. "Now, Karen."

Even from behind, I could see her reluctance as she stepped back and joined me at the door. I held it open and Ronnie retreated through it.

"I'll be waiting at the end of the corridor for the next five minutes to make sure nobody follows us out. You wouldn't be that stupid, would you, Uncle Lau?"

The old man merely glowered at us in reply.

"That's what I thought."

I let the door swing shut and we made for the lift at a trot. Ronnie did pause briefly at the end of the corridor but nobody emerged from the room. We got out of the building and into my car without any incident. But it wasn't until we were well along the freeway with no signs of pursuit that my heart stopped hammering. Ronnie was in the passenger seat and Karen was in the back. I could see her smiling in the rear-view mirror. After a while, she threw herself forward and wrapped her arms around Ronnie's neck.

"That was incredible!" she said. "Amazing. You were so brave. You saved me. And now I'm free. I am so happy I could sing."

Ronnie started to grin. "It was lucky you thought of programming that big button thing on your phone. I think that's what finally brought it home to the old mongrel."

Karen laughed happily and showed him her phone. Ronnie started laughing too.

"What?" I asked. "What's so funny?"

"The big button," Karen said, "is the remote control for my Roomba. If I push it, it starts vacuuming the floor."

Karen was happier than I'd ever seen her. She couldn't stop talking and laughing and thanking Ronnie. Ronnie was cheerful, too, happy that Karen was happy, joining in the fun. I drove in near silence, feeling like the spectre at the feast. I wasn't happy at all. Far from it. Ronnie pulling a gun on those guys had upset me greatly. It had been bad enough watching him breaking bones earlier in the evening but pulling a gun was beyond the pale. My partner was clearly unstable and dangerous. All I really wanted right then was to get as far away from him as possible and never go near him again.

What was I doing working with this maniac? What if he'd killed someone today? He could have, easily, five times over. I'd be an accessory to murder. Why would he even take a gun to a meeting like that? What kind of unstable lunatic did that kind of thing?

And he was still carrying it.

I pulled my foot off the accelerator and set the cruise control to five K under the speed limit. This was not the time to be pulled over by the cops.

I should just ditch him. He was like Lord Byron – mad, bad and dangerous to know – except without all the good bits. I could finish the case on my own. Couldn't I? I could leave tonight, say goodbye, and never set eyes on him again. He'd put those two thugs in the hospital – at least, I hoped they were in a hospital by now, so I didn't have that to worry about.

But what if whoever had sent them, sent some more? What would I do without Ronnie to look after me? It felt like I was on the horns of a dilemma for a moment then, to mix metaphors, I realised I could easily cut the Gordian knot. I'd just give up this whole PI business. I was crap at it anyway and there was just so much violence and fear involved. I wasn't the square-jawed hero type that this kind of work called for. I was just... me. I was suited to a life of thought and quiet study, not a life full of guns and danger. What the hell was I doing here, driving through the night with an armed man, on the way back from threatening and blackmailing a bunch of Chinese gangsters? Was that who I was now? If it was, I no longer recognised myself.

We took Karen back to Ronnie's place. I doubted that she would sleep but the plan was for her to stay there for the night where she'd be safe, until Uncle Lau left the country again.

"You can have the spare room," I told her as we filed in. "I'm heading off home." Ronnie looked my way with a puzzled frown. "No need for me to stay tonight. The thugs I was hiding from were last seen on a car park floor in a pool of blood." It was an exaggeration but not by much.

"Right-o, mate," Ronnie said, heading for the fridge. "I'll see you at the office tomorrow."

"What the hell, it'll be Sunday. Why don't we take the day off?" Ronnie stopped. There was a sudden stillness in the room. Somehow, he knew I was trying to distance myself. To Karen, I said, "I'll just nip upstairs and grab my toothbrush, then the room's all yours."

When I reappeared with my bag, I could hear them talking out on the patio. I popped my head out and called goodbye. Karen called back. Ronnie didn't.

Chapter Twelve

"It's a fucking tontine!"

"What?"

I moved my phone away from my ear so I could see the time. It was after three in the morning.

"Ronnie, do you know what—"

"Of course I fucking know. Listen. I've been reading that damned contract. Talk about incomprehensible legalese! But, when you get to the bottom of it, it's dead simple. It's a fucking tontine."

I felt like I knew the word but no meaning would attach to it. "What's that?"

"Oh, come on. Don't you ever watch the telly or go to the flicks?"

I staggered out of bed and opened up my laptop, typing "tontine" into Wikipedia and reading as Ronnie talked.

"Everybody knows what a tontine is. There's been a million murder mysteries based on the idea."

The Wikipedia article, about archaic life insurance schemes, wasn't looking particularly useful. "Why don't you just tell me what it means to you?"

"These idiots – the FABClub members – have set up a scheme where, as each member dies, the remaining members inherit his share of the investment."

"So?"

"So, the last man standing gets the lot! It's practically begging them to start murdering each other."

"Is it?"

"Yes! That's our motive. It's what we've been looking for all along. Come on, wake up, you dozy sod. Someone in the FABClub is killing off the other members so he can get his hands on the whole pot."

"Which is worth peanuts – at least, to these guys."

"No, it isn't. It can't be. It must be worth a fortune."

It sounded like more crazy speculation and I wanted to get back to bed. "Look, can we talk about this in the morning?"

There was a silence. His disappointment was palpable. "All right. Tomorrow. But just think about it, hey? I'll see you at the office at nine."

And, before I could object, he'd hung up.

I swore at the phone. I cursed Ronnie for a crazy old bastard with an obsessive, unstable personality. I walked about my lounge room, too agitated to sleep, or even sit down. I was supposed to be getting out of this, not being drawn in farther – especially because Ronnie had some new conspiracy theory based on old films and a dodgy grasp of legal terminology.

I made a coffee. I watched some awful sci-fi thing on Netflix. I downloaded an episode of The Simpsons in which Grandpa was involved in a supposed tontine with Mr. Burns. I re-read the contract – and, yes, it did look as if killing all the other members of the FABClub would result in the murderer getting everything they jointly owned but it was insane. How much would the art collection have to be to make it worth someone like Martin Hittman going on a killing spree?

Millions? Tens of millions? Hundreds of millions? I looked at some art auction sites to see what paintings sold for. It would have to be a da Vinci to sell for hundreds of millions but there were plenty of paintings by similarly well-known painters that sold for tens – Monet, Hockney, Bacon, those guys. The thing was, if the artists were in that league, an expert like McKinley would have spotted it instantly. Even I might notice a Degas or a Van Gough if I saw one at an auction. So how could the FABClub believe it had a collection worth three hundred thousand if there was a Renoir in amongst the dross? It beggared belief.

I got up and switched off the lights. The dawn had come and the day was already bright.

Maybe meeting Ronnie at the office was a good thing. I could explain to him that I found his behaviour erratic and dangerous and that I thought it would be better if we just called it a day and went our separate ways. I could thank him for all he'd done for me over the past year. I knew I owed him a lot. He'd helped me find Chelsea's killer and bring him to justice. More than that, he'd helped me find a purpose that felt useful and important, a way forward with my life after Chelsea.

But it would be hard. Ronnie needed this. He needed it far more than I did. Something in him had been twisted and broken by his years as a special forces operative. He'd moved to Australia and joined the police to make it right and, when that had fallen apart, he'd pushed on as a private investigator, until he'd lost his licence. I knew that working with me was his lifeline – probably the last chance he would get to exorcise the demons that plagued him. However reasonable I thought my position was, Ronnie would see it as a betrayal. He was not going to be happy.

The idea of an angry confrontation with Ronnie got me agitated again. It was about six-thirty and the morning was still fairly cool, so I got dressed and went out. I walked through the streets with no particular goal in mind but I ended up at the cemetery – perhaps because I'd walked that way so often that my feet no longer needed to be guided. Toowong Cemetery was one of the oldest in the city – a big, sprawling area, all hillsides and trees, with often picturesque graves and monuments. It was close to the botanic gardens and Mount Coot-tha, so it was nice that Chelsea was buried there. At first I'd visit to talk to Chelsea but, after a while, I came to appreciate it as a quiet oasis in the bustling city and to spend time strolling along its quiet lanes.

"Me again," I said, as I wandered up to Chelsea's grave. I didn't mind talking aloud in that place. Lots of people did it and I'd got into the habit during those first few miserable weeks after her death, when I really didn't care who saw me doing what.

Of course, there was no reply. At first, in the depths of my grief and pain, I could imagine her speaking to me, answering questions, offering advice, even making jokes. I knew it was all coming out of my own head but it was a comfort all the same. It was like having something of her still, even if all she was was a simulation of Chelsea running in my brain. These days, I didn't even have that. Try as I might, I couldn't conjure her image or her voice, not in any realistic way. Maybe I'd been a bit crazy back then. Maybe I'd been a lot crazy. I still spoke to her but she didn't answer me any more.

"Lousy night," I said. "All Ronnie's fault." I sat down on the grass at the foot of her grave. A headstone had appeared on it a few weeks after her death. Organised by her mother, Stephanie, I supposed. Stephanie and I had not spoken since a couple of days after the funeral. She certainly had not consulted me about the headstone. It was a piece of polished black granite with Chelsea's name, the dates for her twenty-five-year-long life, and the words, "Beloved daughter of Stephanie" and, below that, in quotation marks, "God called me home."

I'd flown into a rage when I first saw it. Chelsea was not in the least bit religious. She would never have said such a thing. For Stephanie to put those words into her mouth after she was dead and couldn't spit them out, was infuriating. But I calmed down again quickly enough. There was no point being angry with Stephanie, however stupid and selfish the old baggage was. She'd lost a daughter and she was doing what she had to do to get through it all, just as I was.

"I haven't told you yet, we got a case. A real one. A murder. It might even be a serial killer. Ronnie's all over it like a rash. I was too, except, now..." I was sitting about where her feet would be. Somewhere, much deeper underground than Chelsea's body, was the Legacy Way road tunnel. Whatever the symbolism of putting our dead in the Earth, it seemed to me to be totally demolished by the fact there was a four lane motorway running beneath all the bodies, thousands of people every day, cruising along down there, listening to hip-hop, arguing, talking on the phone, or whatever. They might as well have just put the road through the cemetery. But then we'd have lost all the trees, too, I suppose.

"I wish you'd met Ronnie. You'd be able to tell me how to handle him. You were always so good with people."

I fell silent. There was a butcher bird nearby practising its beautiful song at the top of its voice.

"I'm thinking of giving up the business," I said. "Not

yours, mine. Although, God knows what I'll do without it." I picked up a pebble from the ground and turned it in my fingers. In a sudden fit of anger I threw it aside. "This should have been so fucking great. I mean, I've longed for a case like this since... since... well, you know. Solving murders, catching killers, it's what it's all supposed to be about. And now that crazy old tosser has spoiled everything. He pulled a fucking gun, Chel. I can't work with a man like that. And, let's face it, I'd be as much use as a chocolate teapot without him. So that's it. It's over. I don't see any way out of it. I'm just going to have to tell him. He's going to start spewing. And I'm just going to have to hope he storms off before he kicks the shit out of me."

For a long time, I mulled it over. Then my thoughts started to drift again.

"He reckons I need to get rooted," I said. "He might be right, hey? I mean, I've always noticed women, their looks, their bodies, even when I was with you. It's just a bloke thing, right? But it was like noticing the colour of a sunset, or the shape of a tree. Yeah, there's some underlying evolutionary urge that makes them attractive, or something, but it's not like it meant anything more than, hmmm, that's nice. It wasn't something to obsess over, or to create an impulse to action. Know what I mean?

"Only, these days, it's started to get more intrusive. I'm more keen to look and, when I do, it's more distracting, it tugs at something that hasn't been tugged for a long, long time. It's affecting my concentration. But I can't imagine it. I can't imagine being close to any woman who isn't you. And that's all of them. And maybe some ancient part of my hindbrain is saying, 'Come on, man, throw me a bone. It's been nearly a year already,' and maybe my unconscious is toying with the idea, but, honestly, if I actually try to think about it, I just feel exhausted, like I want to curl up into a ball and hide until it all goes away."

I stood up again. As so often happened, telling my troubles to a patch of earth just made me feel worse. It made me feel hollow and foolish and, worst of all, it made me feel utterly and completely alone.

The sun was high now and the day was getting hot. I checked my phone. I still had plenty of time to walk over to the office and grab a coffee and a croissant along the way before Ronnie was due. "It's the small things that matter," Chelsea used to say. "Feel the sunshine, listen to the birds, taste the coffee."

* * * *

Ronnie was already there when I arrived. All the scribbled-on sheets of paper from yesterday had been pulled off the walls and windows and were now piled in a heap on the floor. The whiteboards had been scrubbed and now each contained just two words. On the left-hand board, Ronnie had written, "FABClub Members". On the right, were the words, "Darren McGuire".

I set down the paper bags of food and the cardboard cup-holder with the two coffees and went to stare at the boards. Ronnie was looking tense and excited. He descended on the bags, opened mine and found the croissant. With a moue of disdain, he grabbed the other one and started eating the meat pie.

"Breakfast of champions," he said, grinning through a mouthful. He came to stand next to me.

"Did Karen get off all right?" I asked, prevaricating.

"No idea. She was still there when I left. Sleep well?"

"Like a baby – until some dick woke me up at three in the morning."

"Bloody ripper, hey, mate." He pointed at the left-hand board. "That one's got the killer. And the other one's got the bloke who knows who he is." He took a big bite of pie and grinned. "Now we just need to put the two of them together."

I walked back to get my coffee, just to put some distance between us, really. "Ronnie," I began. I turned to face him and found him scowling back at me.

"What the fuck is going on with you?" he demanded. "Ever since we saw Uncle Lau, you've been as miserable as a bandicoot."

I took a deep breath. "I think we should give it all away. This… isn't working for me."

"What?"

"I can't do this any more."

"Do what, for fuck's sake?"

"This. The business. Working with you."

"With me? What am I supposed to have done?"

I didn't know how to say it tactfully, so I just said it. "It was the gun. That was the last straw. I can't work with someone who's so fucking mental they go around threatening to shoot people in hotel rooms."

"The gun," he said, with an ominous calmness. "That's what you think of me? You think I'm some kind of madman who would shoot three men to solve my problems?"

The way he put it reminded me of something he'd said once, something about murderers and why they did it.

"That's what you think, isn't it? We've known each other nearly a year, spent hundreds of hours together, and that's who you think I am?"

What the hell was it he'd said? *I've worked on a couple of dozen murders in my time and they all have one thing in common; for one screwed up reason or another, someone believes that they are so much more important than someone else that they can kill that other person to solve whatever problems they have.* Something like that.

"You pulled the gun," I said. "I was there."

"And you thought I would use it. Was it even loaded?"

"I – How would I know?"

"Well, you're the fucking epistemologist? Why don't you work it out? You could have known by asking me. You could have known by assuming the truth. You could have known by working it out on the basis of every bloody thing I've ever said since the day we met." His voice was getting louder, angrier. "When someone tells you that they've learned by hard and bloody experience that killing another person is the single worst crime a man can commit, when they've dedicated half their fucking miserable life to hunting down killers, lost their wife, given away everything, in the single-minded pursuit of one tiny scrap of atonement, don't you think you ought to just fucking listen, you useless, fucking pillock?"

He threw the remains of his pie at the whiteboards and stormed out, shouting, "Well fuck you!"

I stared at the empty doorway for a long while.

"Shit," I said out loud. "Shit, shit, shit."

Had his gun been loaded? I'd never thought to ask. I'd just assumed it was. Someone pulls a gun in a situation like that and everyone assumes it's loaded. Uncle Lau and his thugs certainly had. You'd have to be an idiot to believe anything else. But now Ronnie was saying it wasn't. He'd bluffed them. And, if they'd called his bluff, he'd have been left standing between Karen and two very dangerous-looking professional bodyguards. And he'd have faced them in that cramped little room knowing that he couldn't count on me for any support worth having. *If any trouble starts, run,* he'd said. That's all he could have counted on me for. He hadn't even wanted me to go with them. Karen could have run just as well on her own.

So, not a crazy bastard with a psychopathic disregard for human life, but a brave old man, doing his best to get a friend out of a tight corner by putting his own sore and probably exhausted body in harm's way. The stunt with the gun was Ronnie's only chance in that situation. What else could he have done that would have been anywhere near as effective at getting us all out of there in one piece?

Shit, shit, shit.

And I'd assumed the worst. Of course. Because he was right. I didn't know him at all, even after all we'd been through together. This whole crappy situation was my fault.

I sat down in the nearest chair and hung my head, staring at the carpet.

What was wrong with me? How could I have been so wrong about Ronnie? He'd given me enough clues. Hell, he'd practically said it as clear as day. Something had happened to him in his time serving in the UK special forces. He'd killed people. I had the impression he'd killed lots of people. He'd been trained to do it and he did it well. But it had got to him. In the end, it had changed him. I'd never asked him about it. He was wrong that I was incurious. I'd have loved to know what had happened during that time. But how can you ask a man why he stopped killing people? How do you ask him when and how his willingness to kill on command had changed into an obsessive need to hunt down the killers?

But I should have asked. I should have. Not to was just moral cowardice, a squeamish fear of an uncomfortable conversation, or of an angry rebuttal, or, perhaps worse, of getting a close and intimate look at the soul of a man who had done what he did and the torment he now lived with.

I should go after him, I thought. He'd have driven away by now, probably home, or to a pub somewhere. I needed to apologise, to explain myself, somehow, and try to get him to come back.

But I couldn't. If I was honest, I still didn't want to have that conversation. Moral cowardice doesn't go away just because you acknowledge it.

Maybe there was another way. I looked at the whiteboards. The FABClub members. And the man who knew which one of them had hired him to scare me off. I knew which one Ronnie would go after. In fact, I'd bet a million bucks that that's where Ronnie was right at that moment. It was obvious, now I thought of it. He wouldn't have gone home to sulk, not when he thought we were so close to a breakthrough. He would have been gung-ho to prise the information we needed out of Darren McGuire. To Ronnie, it wouldn't matter if I'd quit the case. What would matter would be bringing down the killer.

So, what if I let Ronnie find the killer first but I did the work that would make it stand up in court? After all, even if McGuire was talkative – even if Ronnie had to beat a name out of him – all that meant was one of the club members was in the frame. It didn't prove anything. For a real case, we needed motive, means and opportunity – and, of those, all we had was the means.

Ronnie was sure the motive had to be the value of the FABClub's assets. Which meant that, sitting in a bank somewhere, was a painting worth millions – tens of millions, most like. So, all I had to do was find myself an art expert and go take a look.

I had made the acquaintance of two art experts in the past few days. One was Antonia Rushton, the gallery owner. The other was Acting Professor Scott Armitage at QUT. Since we now believed the killer was a FABClub member and not someone specifically connected to Everson McKinley, I no longer needed to consider either of them as a suspect and could treat them as a useful resource. Of the two of them, I'd far rather spend time with Antonia Rushton. She looked a bit weird but she was pretty normal, otherwise. Scott Armitage was a cocky, sarcastic, arrogant narcissist and I didn't want to spend a second more in his company if I didn't have to. However, I had no idea what Rushton's credentials were. For all I knew, her only real skill was as a salesperson. Armitage, on the other hand was a genuine academic in a respectable art department, which, I supposed, meant he must know something about art.

Armitage it was, then.

Next, I needed a FABClub member who would give me access to the paintings. That was easier. The only one I'd met was Nick Kryou, the slimy property developer. He'd be easier to approach than either of the other two who lived locally – Martin Hittman, the tax dodging fishmonger, and Jotham Wendell, corporate raider and Christian fundamentalist.

So I gave Kryou a call.

"This is getting to be a bit of nuisance, Luke." He used a stern tone, as if to say I ought to know better than to bother the grown-ups with my silly problems.

"I know but there's something I really need your help with." I explained as quickly as I could that I'd like him to show me the club's paintings so my expert could assess their value.

"It's out of the question, mate. I just don't have the time for that kind of thing."

"I promise you it is absolutely vital to our investigation. It may also be of benefit to you. If we can establish that the collection is as valuable as we believe it is, you and the other investors may find you're sitting on a goldmine. I'll be bringing one of the best experts in the country. Who knows, you may be able to persuade him to advise your club on future purchases."

"Who's your expert?"

I hesitated but I had no doubt Armitage would be eager to be involved. "It's Professor Scott Armitage. He lectures in Fine Arts at QUT."

There was a long silence at the other end. Then he said, "I think Sonny may have mentioned him." Then he fell silent again. I was just warming up to give my sales pitch another go when Kryou said, with a heavy sigh, "Very well. We could do it this morning around eleven. But, honestly, I can't see Sonny McKinley being wrong about the valuation." He gave me an address to meet at and hung up.

I called Armitage straight away but my call went to voicemail. I gave him a quick explanation of what I needed and told him the time and place. After the call, I stared at the phone. I really needed to get him on board or I'd have to call Kryou back and reschedule. While I was staring at it, the phone rang.

"Professor Armitage," I said. "Thank you for getting back so quickly."

"Professor who?"

The voice was not Armitage's urbane drawl. It was an altogether more masculine and less educated accent.

"I – I'm sorry. I was expecting a call from someone."

193

"No worries, mate. Is that Luke Kelly, the private dick?"

"Yes. Yes it is. How can I help you?"

"Look, my name's Dan Bridgeman. You don't know me but we've got a mutual friend."

My heart thumped. Was this another threat? Did he mean Ronnie? Had something happened?

"OK," I said, cautiously.

"You're working on a case for Mel Bertolissio, right? The art prof. who got himself blown away, yeah? Are you getting anywhere with that?"

"I'm afraid I can't discuss—"

"Yeah, yeah. Thing is, I know Mel's dumped you but she's not happy about it."

What the hell was this about? "If Ms Bertolissio has any issue with how we've conducted the case—"

"Yeah, don't get your frillies in a twist, mate. I'm about to make you a happy little vegemite. I want to take over as your client."

It was such a surprise, all I could say was, "What?"

"Look, I'll whatsapp you my details and you can just carry on as before but now the invoices will come to me, not her. I was always going to be paying for it, anyway."

"But – if you don't mind me asking – why?"

"'Cause she's my bird, right. I don't like to see her unhappy. Personally, I don't give a fuck who topped the old prof but Mel does. Probably banging him at uni or something. Get her grades up, hey? Anyway, she thinks its all taking too long and it's not fair on me and all that shit. Like a few quid matters when your lady's miserable, hey? So. Are we on?"

"Er, yes. Thank you Mr…."

"Bridgeman. Call me Danno. So, how's the case going?"

"Very well, actually. We just had a big breakthrough, I think."

"Good onya. So what's going on?"

"We should really make this more formal before I go into any details." Ronnie would be proud of me. "How about I send you a contract right now? You can take a look and get back to me."

"I've seen the contract, mate. I've got it right here. Same rates? Same terms?"

"Well, yes."

"So that's no problem, then."

"Maybe I could drop by? As soon as I get that signature, I can give you a full briefing in person."

He didn't sound enthusiastic. "Yeah, no probs. I'm on the Gold Coast. Bridgeman Luxury Motors. Do you know it? Right on the main drag. Can't miss it. Whenever you like."

And, with that, he was gone. My new client, Dan Bridgeman. I thought about driving straight out there. Straight up the M1. It would only take an hour and a bit each way. But I couldn't. I had to get Scott Armitage to go with me to see the FABClub paintings. So, Bridgeman would have to wait.

I was about to call Armitage again when the phone rang in my hand. It was Armitage.

"Professor, thank you for calling back."

He laughed. "Always happy to be dragged deeper into the world of murder and intrigue. What's this you want me to do?"

I explained about the need to get a second opinion on the valuation of the FABClub's assets. "Only we have the opportunity to go there this morning and take a look. Mr. Kryou seemed very reluctant so, if we miss this chance, I'm not sure when we'll get another."

"It just so happens I've got a deskful of paperwork to get through." I started to plead my case but he cut me off quickly. "So you couldn't have picked a better time. Being Prof isn't all doe-eyed undergrads and telling people what to do, you know. Most of the time it's budget reconciliations and purchase requests. That's why I'm going to take this as a sign from God that all this crap can wait while I go off on an adventure. I'll meet you there, shall I?"

"Er, yes." I gave him the address and the time again, just to be sure, and that was that. I blinked at my phone, now silent. I'd expected him to be interested but not to drop everything with such enthusiasm. How a man of such a childish disposition was ever given a position of responsibility, I did not know but at least it had worked to my advantage. I checked the time and pulled up Google Maps.

Chapter Thirteen

The MyVault secure storage facility in Coorparoo was basically a bunch of storage sheds with a front office. I'd expected something like a bank, with the paintings in a locked box under the building, but this was just row after row of sheds with steel roller doors.

I found Nick Kryou and Scott Armitage waiting for me in the front office. We greeted one another and Kryou said he'd drive us. So we climbed into his silver Mercedes – perhaps the very one he'd said was worth as much as the collection we were about to visit – and he steered us through the maze of concrete roads between the sheds. At one point, he stopped at a high, steel-mesh fence, got out and tapped a number into a keypad beside the gate. It rolled back to let us enter and I noticed that many of the sheds were bigger than the ones we'd seen so far and some had corporate logos on them. I mentioned this to Kryou.

"Yeah, corporate storage," he said. "Martin Hittman's business rents space here and he lets us stick our paintings in a corner of one of his sheds."

"I thought it would be somewhere more secure," I said.

Kryou laughed. "Yeah, like we're going to pay bank rates to store this stuff. Do you know what that would do to our investment? Anyway, this is fine. PIN coded access, CCTV surveillance, lighting all night, eight-foot fences with razorwire, security patrols, door alarms... No-one in their right mind would try to get in here, even if there was anything valuable to steal. Most of these sheds are full of junk, anyway."

We got out at a shed with a fish in a blue circle painted on the door. Kryou went to the PIN pad and entered a number. With a certain amount of painful screeching, the door rolled up and we went in. The shed was stifling hot and full of shelving. The shelves were full of what looked like stationery supplies. In the glare from a couple of overhead fluorescent lights, Kryou went straight to the back of the shed and waited for us beside a boxy shape, swaddled in grey removalist's blankets and resting on a wooden pallet.

"Here they are," he said.

"You don't worry about controlling the temperature, or water getting in?" I asked. "Or mice?"

"Look around," Kryou said. "No damp. No mice. I agree it gets a bit hot. Here, give me a hand."

I helped him unwrap the bundle. I counted fifteen paintings in the heap. *Making each one worth about twenty thousand dollars on average*, I thought. They were all framed and were stacked in order of size, with hardboard sheets between them. It all seemed incredibly cavalier. Even if Kryou didn't think a twenty-thousand dollar painting was worth taking care of, I was horrified that anyone would think that piling them up in a shed with a blanket on them was OK. Especially since a couple of them would keep the average Australian family fed and housed for a year. I suppose I'd never really thought about what wealth meant but now I was getting a small object lesson.

None of the paintings were very large. One by one, we lifted them out and took them to the doorway where our friendly art professor could inspect them in the light. I didn't really know what we were looking at – there were abstract monstrosities, chintzy Aussie outback scenes, a portrait that seemed to have been done by a schoolkid, an Aboriginal dot painting, and on and on, each one looking less like twenty-thousand bucks than the last. I stood beside Armitage as he made a second pass through the set.

"This is the prize of the collection," he said, holding up a picture of a cat in a bed of flowers. It looked Victorian and hideously sentimental. "Minor artist but incredibly popular these days. You'd probably get a hundred K just for this one."

"Unbelievable," I said.

"Which is fortunate, because some of these are not exactly bonza. This one, for example…" He put down the shockingly expensive cat and picked up a small picture that looked like a photo-montage of sixties pop-culture icons, printed on a white canvas. "It's a pretty awful attempt at the style of Robert Rauschenberg. I wouldn't give you two cents for it but it would probably fetch a few hundred in the right auction."

"Are you finished?" Kryou asked. He sounded irritated, maybe because Armitage was bagging his investment.

"All done," said the professor, chirpily.

"Then let's put them away."

I helped him re-stack and re-wrap the pictures.

"Well?" he asked Armitage. He still sounded cross, as if the silly man had earned his permanent ire somehow.

Armitage pushed up his lower lip, squinted and wagged his head side to side. "Yeah, I reckon. Three hundred's about right, give or take. Bit under, maybe."

Kryou pursed his lips and narrowed his eyes, clearly quite angry. He turned to me and snapped, "Happy?"

I wasn't. I'd wanted Armitage to say something quite different. "Yes, of course. Thank you. You've both been incredibly helpful."

Kryou drove us back to our cars in grumpy silence. He pulled up in the car park by the front office and I thanked them both again. As I got out, he said, "I think you've wasted enough of my time on this, don't you? Sonny McKinley was a nice bloke and, if he was murdered, I'd like to see someone go to jail for it. But your investigation is using up a lot of my time and making no apparent progress. I don't know what today was supposed to achieve but it looked to me like a fishing expedition and a desperate one at that. So, unless you have a real breakthrough and you're actually closing in on your killer, I don't want to see you or your partner again. Am I being clear?"

In a weak voice, I assured him he was. He spoke to Armitage, who was still in the car.

"Professor, I'd like five minutes of your time, if that's OK."

He turned back to stare at me until I got the message and buggered off. I left them talking. At least the FABClub might get a new art expert out of this and Armitage might get some consultancy work.

* * * *

I drove back up Vulture Street into West End and found the least trendy restaurant I could to have lunch in. The food was good but my appetite was not. After a few minutes, I pushed my plate away and sipped slowly at my coffee. I was so tired after last night I was beginning to feel woozy. My thoughts kept circling round and round the morning's awful discovery but would not stand still and face it.

Three hundred's about right, give or take. A bit under, maybe.

I pulled out my phone and stared at it. I should call Ronnie and tell him. He was off on a wild goose chase. He was wasting his time. I got up his number but I couldn't bring myself to punch the call button. Maybe it wasn't that bad. Even though his theory about the so-called tontine was shot to pieces, somebody had definitely tried to frighten me off and Ronnie was almost certainly out there right now trying to hunt them down. Even if his pursuit of the shady Darren McGuire didn't lead to a FABClub member, it would lead to someone, and that someone would be a prime suspect in two murders.

I put my phone down. I even pushed it away a little. I took another sip of coffee and jumped when the phone rang.

It was Detective Bertolissio.

"How are you doing, Luke?"

"Good. Yourself?"

"Yeah, not bad. I hear you have a new client for the McKinley case."

"And you called to tell me he's a dodgy character and I should be careful?"

"Something like that."

"Thank you."

"No worries. I also had a visit from DI Marr. She seems to think you and Ronnie are interfering with a police investigation."

"Really? I thought she'd decided it was best not to investigate anything. All murders are suicides or accidents.

Isn't that the Marr philosophy?"

I heard a sigh from the other end of the line. "Do you know there are fewer than a hundred deaths by homicide in the whole of Queensland each year? That's about the same rate as the number of deaths by suicide. For any suspicious death the police are called to investigate, we could toss a coin about the cause and be right half the time."

"Or you could be DI Marr and get it wrong all the time."

"Apparently, she's changed her mind. Have you seen the breaking news?"

"I haven't had time today."

"It seems someone tipped off the media this morning about Mr Sanford's death being suspicious. There were lots of details, including several places the police should have looked for clues but failed to."

I winced. I could see how Marr would feel about that.

"She wouldn't even talk to us about Sanford," I said. "She deliberately ignored us when we said we had evidence."

"So you called the press."

"No! I mean, I didn't."

"So it was Ronnie. The Chief Inspector has re-opened the case. The Chief Constable is ropeable, as you can imagine. There's a forensic team over at Sanford's place right now. Marr would like you and Ronnie spit-roasted with a little barbecue sauce. You should probably expect a visit."

I fumed in silence for several seconds. "Did he tell them about the connection to McKinley's death?"

"What connection?"

I almost blurted out the story of the FABClub and the agreement they'd signed. But hadn't I just proven that was a red herring? "Oh, you know, two prominent Brisbane identities murdered in the space of a few weeks."

"Yes? And?" She waited for me to give her more.

"Seems like a coincidence."

"Okay." She knew I was holding back, but I didn't want to add to my troubles – and my embarrassment – by feeding her yesterday's failed leads.

"When Marr starts asking you questions," she said, "just tell her everything, hey?"

"Yes, of course. And thank you."

"For what?"

"The warning."

"Warnings. Plural."

"Right. Yes."

After we hung up, I went back to sipping my coffee and trying not to think too much, but a growing knot of anxiety in my stomach kept bringing me back to face just how stuffed my life was. The past few days had been an emotional rollercoaster. Everything had conspired to bring it all to a head. A murder investigation just dropping into my lap, Ronnie going into hospital exactly when I needed him, the case being a complete bastard with no clues, no motives and every suspect having an alibi, me stumbling my way through interviews like some kid playing at being a detective, my new best friend, DI Marr, being such a complete dick, someone taking out a contract on me, Ronnie torturing people – again – and then that stunt with the gun at the hotel...

I felt ashamed of myself all over again for thinking Ronnie was an out-of-control maniac. Of course, he was pretty wild and unpredictable, but I shouldn't have assumed he was being as crazy as I thought. I should have known him better. I should have listened when he tried to tell me about his dark and tormented soul instead of just lifting my skirts over my head and burying my face. What kind of friend does that?

What kind of person? He was right to despise me. He was right to walk out.

And now, just as I'd resolved to make it up to Ronnie by helping him solve the case, just when I'd taken some real initiative and done some real investigation work, I'd actually proven his big breakthrough was a load of rubbish.

I had to tell him but my phone seemed to repel my fingers when I tried to reach for it.

So I was back where the day had started, only for different reasons. I had no partner, not because he was a dangerous madman but because he was rightly and properly pissed off at me. And that meant I had no business because, as I'd proven so often since this case began, I was useless without Ronnie.

I didn't need to tell him that. It was one of the last things I'd said to him.

My phone rang again. For a pathetic moment, I had the hope that it might be Ronnie calling to tell me what he'd found. It was from "Unknown Number". I picked up.

"Mr. Kelly," a woman's voice said. I knew the voice.

"It's Doctor Kelly."

"Of course. I don't know why I can't keep that in mind. I wonder if you'd mind coming into the station for a chat."

"So now you want to talk. I'm actually very busy. Can we do it on the phone?"

"No, *Doctor* Kelly, we can't. I'll expect you here at two o'clock. Don't make me have to come and fetch you."

I wanted to stand on my rights but suddenly thought, *What the hell?* It would actually be a good thing to see DI Marr, tell her everything I knew and then walk away from the whole business.

"All right, then. Two o'clock. I assume you'll reserve me a visitor's car parking space."

"Yeah, right," she said and hung up.

"I'll take that as a no, then," I told the dead line.

Now, I had to call Ronnie. Marr would be after him too and he might not have had Bertolissio's warning. I tapped the buttons and got through to his voicemail. It was back to the usual, irritating recording. Obviously Karen's attempt to clean it up had not met with his approval. "If you're selling anything," Ronnie's voice said, "fuck off. Otherwise, if you really think I'll be interested, leave a message. Don't expect an answer." This time, it made me smile, thinking of DI Marr listening to it.

"Ronnie, it's Luke. Marr just called. She's spewing big-time over that leak to the media. I'm going in for an interview at two." I hesitated. "I had an independent evaluation of the FABClub paintings done this morning. They're worth exactly what Kryou said. I just thought you should know."

* * * *

And there I was, back at the good old Central Police Station, waiting to be grilled by an angry DI whom my partner had humiliated and who was now no doubt looking for someone's bones to crack between her teeth. At about one-fifty, I got a call from Terry Marchant, Ronnie's lawyer friend.

"Have you gone in yet?" he asked, cutting through the pleasantries.

"No, the appointment's at two but, if she's true to form, I expect to be kept waiting."

"Good. Don't. Someone will be with you in ten. If they call you, tell them you're waiting for your lawyer to arrive. Her name is Valentina Perofsky. I'd come myself only I'm in the middle of a kid's birthday party. Val will look after you though, don't worry."

"Is this Ronnie's idea?"

"Yes, he called me just now. He said – how did he put it? – you were about to be swallowed by a five metre croc. Colourful chap. Anyway, can't talk. Just do what Val says and you'll be fine."

He hung up without even asking whether I wanted representation. It made me nervous – like everyone knew I was in deep shit except me.

Bugger. So much for the cathartic unburdening I'd imagined.

It was about five minutes later that a short, round woman in her thirties came bustling into the reception area. She had a heavy briefcase in one hand, a bundle of papers in the other and a phone clamped to her ear with one shoulder.

"Yeah," she said into the phone, scanning the room. I gave her a wave. "Yeah," she said again. "Yeah. Too bloody true. Look, gotta go. Yeah, yeah, you too mate." She dropped her bundle on the nearest seat and pulled the phone from her ear. I got up to join her.

"G'day, you must be Luke Kelly," she said, holding out a hand. "I'm Val. Terry called, hey?"

"Er, yes." I felt like I was being drawn into a whirlwind. Even when she wasn't doing anything in particular, the woman seemed like a firework about to go off.

"Great, So fill me in."

We sat as far from everyone else as was possible and I told her all about the Everson McKinley case, our suspicions about the FABClub and the death of Morgan Sanford.

"And what's this new evidence an anonymous tipster has given to the police?" she asked.

"I honestly don't know. That was nothing to do with me."

"So, let me get this straight." She fixed me with a shrewd stare. "You have no evidence that McKinley was murdered and the police think it was suicide. You have no evidence that Sanford was murdered and the police think it was an accidental death. But both men belonged to this FABClub thing and you think that means it must be murder?"

"No! I mean, there are other reasons." I went through all the odd circumstances surrounding McKinley's death.

"OK. And Sanford?"

She had me there. I didn't want to tell her anything about Ronnie studying the crime scene before calling the cops. "Well... Obviously somebody thinks it was murder. The anonymous caller with the new evidence."

"Yes, but, why are you so sure?"

I fell back on what I'd said to Bertolissio. "It's too much of a coincidence."

The lawyer nodded, clearly choosing not to say how big an idiot, or how big a liar she thought I was. "And why does DI Marr want to see you?"

"I have no idea." Which was the truth.

She nodded to herself and was instantly out of interrogation mode and into advice mode. "When we get in there, just give brief, honest answers. Don't embellish and don't say anything you're uncomfortable with. Marr can't force you to and, if she tries, I'll stop her." I nodded. "Right-o." She dug around in her briefcase. "I'm just going to get on with some work while we wait."

I sat back and left her to it. It was almost three by the time we were called and escorted to one of the interview rooms. We waited there in silence until well after three. Marr and Bronski came into the room, scowling and businesslike, with not a word of apology and only perfunctory introductions.

"Before we start," Val said. "I would like it on the record that, after insisting he rush in to see you at very short notice, you kept my client waiting for more than an hour."

"We'll try to do better next time," Marr said with a fake smile. "OK, Luke, tell me what you know about Morgan Sanford's death."

"I don't know anything about it. I turned up at his house for an interview and you told me he was dead."

"You didn't go into his house?"

"No."

"You didn't go to his pool?"

"No."

"You didn't examine the body?"

"Christ, no."

"We had a call to Crimestoppers this morning from a call box in the Valley. What do you know about that?"

"Nothing."

"The call contained details only the killer would know."

"So you think it's a murder now?"

"We're reviewing the case. How did you know Morgan Sanford?"

"I didn't. His name came up in connection with the Everson McKinley murder. Ronnie Walker and I are investigating that case. We'd gone to meet Sanford for the first time to ask him some questions about McKinley."

"And where were you in the hour before you turned up at Sanford's house?"

"It's in my statement. You know, the one you insisted I come in and make and then couldn't be arsed to even send a detective to, despite me saying I had information about the killing."

Val put a hand on my arm. I took the hint and shut up.

The fact is I was very tired and growing a bit tetchy.

"You just told me you didn't know anything about Sanford's death."

So I had. "And I don't, but I know he was in a business arrangement with McKinley and, at the time of my statement, I believed they were both murdered because of that connection."

Marr exchanged glances with Bronski but, whatever she was looking for there, she didn't find.

"What business arrangement?" she asked.

"They were both members of an investment group that bought paintings. McKinley was the art expert and the others were just investors. They called it the Fine Art Buyer's Club."

"So why do you think someone was killing club members?"

"I don't. Not any more. The club has a weird contract, a bit like a tontine—"

"A what?" They were the first words Bronski had spoken.

"Google it," I said. "It looked like there might have been a motive for the members to kill each other if the investment was large enough. But it isn't. I had that verified independently this morning."

Bronski shook his head and muttered, "Jesus."

"So that's all you had to connect McKinley and Sanford?" Marr asked.

"Yes."

Bronski kept shaking his head. Marr stood up. "Thank you for your time, Mr. Kelly. We'll be in touch. Someone will be along to show you out."

Bronski got up too and they both left.

"It's Doctor Kelly," I called to their disappearing backs. I'm pretty sure I heard Bronski chuckle.

Val and I sat in silence until we were escorted off the premises. Outside, she stared at me with a puzzled expression for a moment before she asked, "What the hell was that all about?"

"Honestly, I'm not sure. I was expecting a savaging, not an almost-polite interview."

"Well, if you ask me, they've changed their minds and they're treating Sanford's death as a murder." I nodded. "And you and Mr. Walker seem to be on their list of suspects."

"That's ridiculous."

"Well, I hope you both have very solid alibis, because DI Marr is going to try to break them. I also hope Mr. Walker was not caught on CCTV making a call from a certain public telephone this morning – unless he has a good explanation for why he knew things about a crime that even the police did not."

My stomach seemed to have started tunnelling its way out through my lower intestine. With a dry mouth, I said, "I'm sure everything will be fine." I was fairly sure Ronnie was too good to have been caught on camera making anonymous calls to the cops. I was more worried about our story about where he was while he was stickybeaking around in Sanford's house. How many speed cameras had he driven past on his way there? What cameras at the mall in Ipswich might have caught him? How many witnesses might have seen him there? How many saw me going to the gallery to interview Antonia Rushton? Was my car photographed with no-one in the passenger seat?

"You look a bit worried, if you don't mind me saying."

"Yeah, nah. She'll be right. I must have a face the cops don't like. This isn't the first time they've tried to pin a murder on me."

She scrutinised me for a long while. "Don't talk to them again without me or Terry present," she said. "If they pull you in, just politely refuse to make any comment. Tell them you're waiting for your lawyer. OK?"

"Yeah, I remember the routine."

"Good. I've got to go." As she bustled away, she fumbled the phone back to her ear.

Chapter Fourteen

I made my way back to the car park in a daze. It was a small victory, I supposed, getting the police to take Sanford's murder seriously. Maybe they'd find the link to McKinley. If it existed. If only it hadn't taken Ronnie putting so much on the line to open their eyes.

Then it hit me, like a slap on the face, why he'd taken such a risk. It was all my fault. I'd told him I was shutting down the business, that I couldn't work with him any more. I just assumed he'd carry on trying to solve the case without me. But he couldn't. I was the one with the PI license. He'd lost his before I even met him and he was no longer allowed to practice. Our loophole was for him to be a "consultant" to my business. But if there was no business, he had no legal basis to go around interviewing suspects and gathering evidence. He was just some old guy poking his nose into private matters.

So, faced with this new obstacle, he'd done the only really effective thing he could that might get results; he'd dragged the police kicking and screaming back into the investigation – even if that meant risking himself.

And me.

If I'd known Ronnie the way I should have known him,

I'd have seen that he would do anything, risk anything, to put the killer behind bars. If I'd had half the brains I thought I had, I would have known that calling the cops was his best and most likely move.

And now we were suspects again. And Ronnie was going to be their prime suspect, if Marr ever worked out that he wasn't with me in Arthur Street that morning. And it was all my fault.

I sat in my car in the car park, feeling too weak to put it in motion and get moving again. The dim light, the low ceilings, the crowded cars, the grey concrete, the pipes and strip lights all helped. I needed a cave. I needed a hole in the ground. But this brutal, industrial bleakness would do instead.

I must have dozed off because the ringing of my phone definitely woke me. I checked the time. Had I really slept for two hours? I was hungry, too? I had missed lunch?

"Yes?"

"I'm at the office. Where are you?"

"Ronnie?"

"Jeez, mate, are you drunk?"

I gave myself a shake. "No. No, of course not. I – I was just taking a nap. I didn't get much sleep last night."

"Yeah. Right. So, you're back on the case, right? Your message said you've been looking into the FABClub assets, hey?"

I was fully awake again. "Look, mate, Marr had me in for an interview." Of course, he knew that. He'd organised the lawyer for me. Maybe I wasn't fully awake yet.

"Yeah, me too. Looks like my call managed to get the dickheads off their arses at last. Of course, now they think we did it but you can't have everything. It's better than a slap in the belly with a wet fish, hey?"

He seemed quite cheerful for a man who might get busted for obstructing the police – at the very least.

"Look, Ronnie, I'm sorry about—"

"Forget it."

"No, I was a—"

"A fucking drongo. Yeah, I know."

"I was going to say, I was a bad friend."

"Yeah, well... Forget it, hey? We're back in business and that's all that matters. Are you coming in or what?"

"Ah, sure. I'll be there in ten."

* * * *

It was more like twenty, thanks to road work on Coro Drive but Ronnie was in a good mood and it didn't seem to bother him. He'd been updating the whiteboards, I noticed, but I didn't get much chance to look before he steered me back out the door.

"What? What's the rush? Where are we going?"

"To the pub, mate. It's beer o'clock. We'll get some nosh and I'll update you on the day's doings."

It was a hot afternoon and the day had grown humid and close, with little or no breeze. I was still slightly disoriented about what day it was and what time of day thanks to my disrupted sleep. We went to the Royal Exchange Hotel – Ronnie's choice – ordered food and drinks and made our way out to the large beer garden.

"To being back in business," I said, raising my glass. Ronnie grinned and took a swig. "I understand why you called the cops this morning." I began but Ronnie jumped in and stopped me.

"Don't you want to know what I found out?" he asked.

I bit down my disappointment. He clearly was not going to let me talk about the blue we'd had, or its fallout. "From Darren McGuire?"

"Didn't take me long to find him. He's something of a celebrity in the Brisbane underworld, it seems. The bloke runs a kind of Uber for thugs. People call him and he sends them heavies. Turns out he has tons of standover men on his books just waiting for the call. I bet your mate Robbo's got a listing. He gets the requirement from clients, who are referred to him for a fee by a network of crooks, then he pairs them up with the thugs they need. He handles the payment, takes his cut and then settles with the thugs. It's a helluva business model. All done on Whatsapp."

"You spoke to him?"

"Mate, I spent the best part of two hours listening to him bragging about how well he's doing. I believe him too – one of those blokes who likes to wear his profits in heavy gold jewellery."

"So? Who was it that hired him?"

"Not hired. He just does the brokerage. The thugs are like self-employed. He just takes a commission for introducing them."

"So, who did he broker our thugs for?"

"No idea."

"What? You just said you spent two hours with him."

"He was a great bloke. Funny. Interesting. Full of stories. I really liked him."

"You—" Words failed me. "So that's why you didn't break his legs and make him talk?"

"Yeah. That and the four ex-military minders he keeps with him at all times. I tried offering him some of your money but he said his reputation was all he had to trade on and, if that was tarnished because he'd given up a client, he'd be out of business. I could see his point."

"So our two big leads both went nowhere, then? We're back to square one?"

He made a grimace. "Yeah, not really. It might be a good idea if you moved back to my place for a while."

My heart began to race. "What? What have you done?"

"Nothing. It was just, when we were chatting about his reputation, he did mention that he didn't like being made to look like a dick — you know, because he'd sent a couple of boofheads to knock you off. So he's going to set his client up with a real professional — at his own expense — to get the job done properly."

What? A professional? Like a professional assassin? Oh my fucking god! Can this thing get any worse?"

He held up his hands. "She'll be right, mate. Just stick close to me and let me do all the worrying."

"Close to you? How do I stick close to you if DI Marr turns up and arrests you?" I looked around the beer garden, at the people sitting there, at the man in the hoodie sitting on his own, at the buildings that overlooked us. "And how does sticking close to you save me from a sniper? Or a car bomb?"

"Mate, what else do you suggest?"

"Well… We could drop the case for a start, let McGuire know his intimidation tactics worked and we're no longer after his client. That should satisfy his professional pride, shouldn't it?" Ronnie's face hardened and I felt a pang of shame. "All right, all right. But this shit suddenly got real. I mean, we're still nowhere on this case. How do we dig up new leads with me looking over my shoulder all the time?"

Ronnie looked at me for a long time. So long I began to squirm. All right I was a physical coward. We weren't all special forces geriatric ninjas like Ronnie. Some of us were just ordinary people and the idea of being stalked by an assassin quite reasonably scared the shit out of us.

"Let me tell you," he said, his scrutiny complete, "how I've been keeping myself busy since my chat with McGuire. First, I went to see a friend of mine who deals in useful oddments the department stores don't usually carry. I bought two bullet-proof vests. I'm wearing mine, the other is in this carrier bag." I'd noticed the bag, of course, but hadn't thought to ask what was in it. I reached for it. "Don't be a dick," he said, pulling it away. "You can put it on in the dunny in a minute. Secondly, I checked out the office and the car park before you arrived. Thirdly, I have been keeping up a constant surveillance since we left. We weren't followed here. Fourthly, we're sitting with a wall behind us and I've got good line of sight to the entrances. Finally, no-one in the pub looks suspicious."

I leaned forwards and whispered, "What about the bloke in the hoodie?"

"Do me a favour. He'd be like number ten on my threat list. The barmaid is more likely than him. Trust me, we're safe for now."

"Shit. I don't need this. Not again. Why is it every time we investigate a case, people start trying to kill me?"

"You've just got that kind of face."

"I mean it. I used to think I lived in a civilised country, a nice place, with the rule of law and all that kind of crap."

"You do. Mostly. They build sewers underground so that people like you don't have to smell them all the time. But they're still there. The scumbags in this city like to stay out of sight, too, hidden away in dark places, otherwise all the ordinary types would hold their noses and insist somebody do something about the stench."

I reached for my beer and felt a slight tremble in my fingers. "Cute, but definitely not accurate. It might be true for the bikie gangs and your entrepreneurial friend, McGuire, but the guy we're looking for is probably living in a multi-million-dollar mansion and making speeches at the Rotary Club about his charity work. Besides, there are plenty of scumbags quite openly using laws they helped create to avoid paying taxes, to drive decent people bankrupt with defamation cases, to pollute the planet, to clear-fell forests for mines, or to build luxury hotels for their rich mates. All that shit."

Ronnie sighed. "You're such a fucking hippie." He took a swig of his beer. "That's why I like murder. There's no moral ambiguity. Taking a life is wrong. If you do it, you deserve punishment. Not like those crappy Centrelink cases we've been doing all year where you're always asking yourself if it's the perpetrator or the client who's the worst crook."

"It's usually the client," I said, feeling miserable. Chelsea always used to tell me how awful and corrupt our nice, safe society really was. I used to agree in a vague, not-really-my-problem, kind of way. But a year of wallowing in crime had really opened my eyes to what she'd meant. I still clung to the idea that civilised society needed laws but it was becoming dismally obvious that a lot of those laws were about protecting the property and wealth of those who had it and making sure those who didn't, never got the chance to get their hands on any. Maybe Ronnie was right that murder was the only unambiguously wicked crime.

"So what now?"

Ronnie sat back in his chair, let his head fall back and blew out a long breath. He stayed that way for a long time. I thought he wasn't going to say anything, I thought maybe he, too, was flat out of ideas, but he sat up quickly and leaned forward. "You know what? That valuation you had done was bullshit."

"What?"

"Think about it. The only thing that makes any sense of this is if the FABClub assets are worth a fortune."

"If the Sanford murder and the McKinley murder are related."

"Of course they're related! It's bloody obvious. How could they not be?"

It didn't seem quite so obvious to me but I wasn't going to argue. "Even if they are, we've got two valuations now that say the same thing. I know we live in a post-truth society and expertise is just a matter of opinion, and all that dingo excrement, but what makes you so much better at evaluating an art collection you've never seen than two different top experts who've actually studied it?"

"Common sense. Who is this second expert, anyway, someone your mate Dicko recommended?"

"Professor Scott Armitage, Acting head of the Department of Fine Arts at Queensland University of Technology."

"What? That wanker couldn't find his arse with both hands. What'd you ask him for?"

"Because he's probably the leading expert in the State and because I know him. The alternative was Antonia Rushton. Look, going on like a spoilt brat, trying to discredit my expert by just calling him names, is all very Trumpian but it's not exactly mature, is it? Like it or not, Armitage knows what he's talking about — at least when it comes to art."

Ronnie scowled at me, lips pursed. Slowly, he relented. "So what did he say, exactly?"

"He said three hundred thousand, give or take. He showed me some individual paintings and put a value on them. The best of the lot, he said, was a Viccy piece of schmaltz featuring a cat in a flower bed. That was worth a hundred K. The worst was some piece of rubbish that looked like an illustration torn out of a magazine article about the sixties – wouldn't give you tuppence for it, he said, or something like that."

Ronnie settled into a brooding sulk. After a few minutes watching him, I got bored.

"Shall we go?" I asked.

Maintaining his silence, he nodded and got up.

* * * *

I went back to my unit to pick up some clothes and a toothbrush. Ronnie came in with me and made a point of entering the apartment first, checking each room, and closing the blinds before he'd let me in. I put on my bullet-proof vest under my shirt while I was there. It was light and thin and not very noticeable. I wondered if something so insubstantial could stop a pea-shooter, let alone a bullet. When we went back out to the cars, Ronnie took a device from his plastic bag and unfolded it. It was a mirror on the end of a long telescopic tube. I thought it was a selfie-stick at first and couldn't understand why he was running it under the edge of my car. When I realised he was looking for bombs, not taking snaps, my stomach did a small flip.

At Ronnie's house, instead of the usual beers on the patio, we stayed inside with all the curtains drawn. Ronnie was still brooding and quiet and the atmosphere of waiting for something terrible to happen made me restless and edgy.

"Tell me about your wife," I said, out of nowhere. It amazed me when I first heard that Ronnie had once been married and, while I could quite see why she'd leave him, I had never understood how he had managed to woo and win a mate.

He slowly came out of his reverie. "It's all right," he said in a kindly voice. "You don't need to do that just because of what I said this morning."

"Do what?"

"Pretend you're interested."

"Yeah, mate, I've always been interested. Honest. I just always thought you didn't like talking about private things."

"Projection."

"What?"

"It's where you project your own thoughts and feelings onto other people. You're the one who doesn't like talking about himself. You've got a real problem with it."

"No I haven't. I just… I mean, there isn't much opportunity."

"Because you haven't got any friends?"

"I – Things have been different since Chelsea died. I kind of drifted away from my old crowd."

"Nah, mate. You haven't got any friends because you avoid people. You're not really interested in what they think and do. You don't keep up friendships because it's too much like hard work, hey? Too much effort and too little reward."

"That's just not – I was close to Chelsea. Very close."

"Were you? Were you really?"

Red hot anger burst inside me like a grenade. "Fuck you! What the fuck do you know?" I was on my feet, shouting. "You poisonous old bastard. This is what I get for trying to be nice? For showing an interest? Yeah, well, here's another pop-psychology term for you to chew on. Deflection. That's where someone asks you a question you don't want to answer and you deflect it with a load of bullshit."

I stormed out of the room and up the stairs. As before, I was staying in Ronnie's guest room. It made me angry all over again to think Ronnie felt the need for a guest room. Like he was showing off about how many friends he had and how they were always coming over to stay. I sat on the edge of the bed and fumed, then got up and walked back and forth around the bed, then sat down again and fumed.

The worst thing about it was that stupid little voice at the back of my head saying Ronnie was probably right. Not just about my lack of friends, my lack of interest, my dislike of intimacy, but about my relationship with Chelsea. It had been love. It had been everything the movies said it should be. And she'd loved me too. I knew that. But, since her death, I'd come to see how emotionally inept I'd been with her. In fact, I'd come to see myself as having been more of a pet than a real partner, a big, devoted, slobbering dog, someone she could lavish her love and caring on, asking only that my eyes were round and full of adoration when she petted me and that my tail wagged when she called my name.

Tears were rolling down my cheeks and I brushed them away angrily.

Damn you, Ronnie! How did you do it? How did you push the knife in exactly where it would hurt most?

It was what made him a great detective, I supposed, and what made me a crap one.

Slowly, my anguish subsided and all I felt was guilt and shame. Again. Ronnie was right about the projection and, even if I was right about his deflection, it was wrong of me to lash out at him just because I felt so bad about how I'd treated Chelsea. No, not just that, I told myself, determined to be honest. It was also because I felt so bad about myself, so afraid that I was incapable of loving a woman the way Chelsea had deserved to be loved. And that I was incapable of being a true friend to anyone at all.

It was a dark, moonless night. I remembered the mortal danger I was in and realised I hadn't drawn the curtains. Someone could be out there – in one of the houses opposite, maybe – watching me through the telescopic sights of a high-powered rifle. I jumped up and put the house's outer wall between me and the imagined shooter. What was the house made of? It was brick, wasn't it? Surely that would be safe? But Aussie houses were typically just a single skin of brick outside a wooden frame and a plasterboard inner wall. Chelsea used to complain about Aussie building standards. Her complaint was about a lack of insulation and wasted energy, but maybe one brick wasn't enough to stop a bullet from some kinds of rifle. I didn't really know much about all that kind of thing and maybe I should learn. Maybe, in this line of business, my life might depend on it one day. And what if the sniper had infra-red sights? What if he could see my heat signature right now through this barely-insulated wall? What if standing there was the absolute worst thing I could be doing?

In a rush, I grabbed the curtains and pulled them closed, rolling away from the window across the bed and standing against the far wall, waiting for the steel-jacketed slug to come bursting through the flimsy gyproc wall at supersonic speed and blast a hole in my chest.

It didn't happen. Of course it didn't happen. I was an idiot and a coward and Ronnie had every reason to hold me in complete and utter contempt.

I crawled onto the bed and lay on my back staring at the vague greyness of the ceiling.

Is it always going to be this hard? I asked Ronnie in my head.

I reckoned his answer would have been a resounding, "Yes!" and some choice words about what a whingeing little wuss I was. In fact, he'd never suggested it would be easy catching killers. The police couldn't always do it. When he'd been a cop, he couldn't always do it. It had obsessed him, ruined his marriage, dragged him down to some very dark places, and maybe that's where I was heading too. Somewhere worse, maybe, because, unlike Ronnie, I seemed to have no gift for the work, no reserves of self-confidence to sustain me, and definitely no hint of the physical courage and moral certainty that kept him going.

And how come I had never thought this through? Me, who prided himself of being such a subtle intellect? Why had I not seen that to hunt a murderer is to face one of the most terrible monsters in the whole world, a creature that will take human lives to achieve its ends, that will take your life, too, if you begin to pose a threat? Ronnie may have been right to say that murder is the worst of crimes and it can never be left unpunished, but he neglected to mention that to hunt a murderer is to go out into the jungle to fight a tiger with your bare hands.

I remembered the first time I had stayed in Ronnie's spare room. The murderer we were chasing had burned down my home and wanted me dead. I knew who he was back then. I just didn't know how to catch him. This time we had no idea who the killer was and it was a third-party arsehole who'd put out the contract on me as a marketing ploy to repair his damaged reputation.

For a moment, just thinking about the contract set my

heart racing again and filled my thoughts with panicky schemes to escape and hide.

"Fuck this!" I said aloud, sitting up on the bed. I was just torturing myself to no good end. I needed to focus on the case and forget the contract. As terrifying as it was that a professional killer was out there plotting my death, it was a distraction. The only thing that would make anything better would be to find McKinley's murderer. That was who had tried to get rid of me in the first place and, if he was put behind bars, maybe McGuire would reconsider the need to placate him.

I went down to the kitchen and took a coldie from the fridge. Ronnie had gone to bed – or, at least, to his room. I didn't turn on the lights. There was enough street light outside to give the kitchen a dull orange tinge. Besides, there were enough LCDs and LEDs on kitchen appliances to light up the room. I sat with the beer at the kitchen table. Perhaps I could drink enough to fall asleep. Perhaps I shouldn't think that way.

I tried to go back over the case in my mind, all the fumbled, difficult interviews with McKinley's family, associates and staff. It all seemed like a complete waste now. It felt like the real investigation only began after Ronnie found Stanford's body. In fact, the first time I actually felt like we were moving into gear was when Ronnie cleared the whiteboards and wrote the two names; "FABClub" and "Darren McGuire". But now I'd proven the FABClub was a dead end and Darren McGuire had become my personal nemesis.

And yet…

Ronnie's reasoning had been impeccable. If you accepted that Sanford's death was not a coincidence – and how could it be? – two members of the FABClub had been murdered. The only thing that connected them was the FABClub itself. And the club had a dumb contract that practically begged the members to start killing one another – but only if the club's assets were worth a very large fortune.

Which they weren't.

I went over my visit to the storage facility with Kryou and Armitage. The mere fact that the paintings were in a heap under a blanket in a storage unit testified to the fact that the club members themselves believed their collection to be of very little value. Armitage's second valuation just verified it.

And yet...

Like it or not, Armitage knows what he's talking about. That's what I'd told Ronnie, right here, less than an hour ago. And it was true. He did. He was an absolutely gold-plated, hundred per cent, dyed-in-the-wool, art expert. Ronnie could argue with that till he was blue in the face. It was a fact. It could not be denied.

And yet...

The FABClub collection had to be incredibly valuable or none of this made any sense at all. So, if Armitage really did know what he was talking about...

Shit!

I jumped to my feet, sending my chair skidding. I ran up the stairs, taking them three at a time, stumbling in the darkness. Ronnie's bedroom door was shut and I reached for the handle, stopping myself just in time. The last time I'd thrown open Ronnie's bedroom door in the night, he'd pulled a gun on me and, I was still convinced, had almost blown a hole in me. This time, I froze, slowly withdrew my outstretched hand and took a breath.

"Ronnie? Mate? It's me. I need to tell you something. Can

I come in?"

There was silence from the other side of the door. Surely he couldn't be asleep? It was barely past nine and Ronnie was not one for taking early nights. So what was he doing? Did he suppose I wasn't alone? Was that it? Did he think some thug had a gun to my head and was using me to get him off his guard?

"I'm alone, Ronnie. It's OK. I'm going to open the door now. Do not shoot me, hey? Just… relax." Heart pounding, I reached out again and took the handle, turning it slowly until I felt the latch open. "OK, I'm opening the door now and coming in. Don't get nervous. It's only me."

Slowly, slowly, I pushed the door open, cringing at the thought of that bloody big gun of his pointed at my chest. The room was dark, but lighter than the hallway, with pale street-light coming in through the window. I kept pushing the door farther as I prayed Ronnie's nerve would hold and he wouldn't blow me away. When the door bumped against the wall I almost fell to the ground in a ball but somehow managed not to make any sudden moves.

"There," I said, my voice shaky. "All alone, see?" I couldn't make out whether he was in the bed or not but it looked empty. What was he playing at? Was he hiding somewhere, watching me from a dark corner? Or maybe he couldn't see me properly. Maybe he still thought there could be someone with me. It was too much to bear. I couldn't just stand there waiting to be shot by a paranoid nutjob.

"Ronnie, I'm turning on the light. All right? Just so you can see that I'm alone." I groped the wall for the light switch and found it. "Ready? I'm turning it on now."

I flicked the switch and, for a moment, was blinded by the light. I squinted into the room but could see nobody. The bed was still made and was empty. I stepped forward and looked behind the door. Nobody. What the hell?

"Ronnie?"

Had I been talking to myself all this time? Feeling like a complete idiot, I reached for the light switch again. There was a sound, a high-pitched "thwip!" and I felt a sting on my ear. Like any other Aussie would, I assumed some vicious little flying creature had stung me. But there were other sounds; a loud thump on the wall and the gentle tinkle of falling glass.

Like the inexperienced drongo I was, I stared at the little hole in the wall, then turned and stared at the somewhat larger hole in the window.

Shit!

I fell to the ground even as the thump and tinkle of another bullet flying past my head confirmed that I was being shot at. Before the intention had even formed in my mind, I was crawling out of the lighted bedroom into the darkness of the hallway. I was on my belly at the top of the stairs before I dared look back to see if I was safe. I couldn't see the window. So that meant the shooter couldn't see me. As obvious as that line of reasoning was, I double-checked it before I dared get off the floor and scurry down the stairs.

Ronnie's bedroom was at the front of the house. Which meant the shooter was at the front too. I tried to slow my breathing and settle the hammering in my chest. Was the shooter in the gardens of the houses across the road? Would he just run around the house now to get another shot at me?

Angles, I told myself. *Work out the angles.* The hole that had appeared in the wall was about my head height but so was the hole in the window. Which meant? What the hell did that mean? Why couldn't I work it out? Why was my brain being so sluggish and slow?

Shock. Calm down.

The bullet was travelling parallel to the ground. The shooter was high up, on a roof, inside one of the houses opposite, in a tree maybe... To come and get me, they'd have to get down to the ground first. That gave me a few seconds, maybe more, to get out of there. Out the back. Hide. I'd already wasted so much time standing there like a dummy. I was still standing there!

For god's sake!

I ran to the back door, screaming with frustration when I found it was locked. Then again, when I realised it was also bolted. After what seemed like a superhuman struggle against my own clumsiness, I tore open the door and raced through. I tripped on a wire between the doorposts, flying across the pavers in the patio as cans and bottles smashed to the ground behind me. In my panic, I assumed I'd been shot. Properly this time. It took me several seconds, sprawled on the ground, waiting for the pain to hit, before I realised I'd fallen foul of some kind of booby trap. Ronnie had set booby traps at the doors so no-one could sneak in on us.

"You might have told me!" I cried between clenched teeth.

I got to my feet, unsteady on trembling legs. How long had I been lying there? Plenty of time for the shooter to get down from his perch and come looking for me – and, of course, the racket I'd made would have told him exactly where I was. I listened for the sound of running feet. And, as I did, a wave of utter despair washed over me. The patio lights had come on. When I nose-dived out the back door, the motion sensors had triggered the lights. I was a sitting duck. I might as well have gone out into the street, painted a target on my forehead and sat down in the road under a lamppost. Someone as dumb as me deserved to die. It was just the application of natural selection. Simple Darwinism. One way or another, nature would ensure that my genes would not be passed on to blight the lives of any future generations.

But I still couldn't hear footsteps. What did that mean? Was the shooter some kind of commando, like Ronnie, moving through the night like a cat? Or had I just gotten lucky and something had delayed him? Either way, sitting in a lighted garden was the absolute last thing I should be doing. I should be moving, running, however hopeless it seemed, however useless I felt.

I whirled to face the end of the garden, about thirty metres away. There was a hedge, probably a fence behind it. Then I'd be out of sight in a neighbour's garden. Maybe they'd see me, come out shouting, call the police... If I could get past that hedge, I might be safe.

I ran.

I fell. My legs were like rubber and every slight bump and dip in the lawn felt like mounds and potholes. I scrabbled back into motion, sprinting towards the hedge, realising only at the last minute that it was a dense and tangled thicket of bougainvillea. Thorns tore at my hands and face as I plunged into the bushes. Thorns snagged my clothes and scored my flesh as I fought to pull back. Horrified, I staggered back from the impenetrable mass of tough, vicious tendrils. I searched for a gap but there was none. The bougainvillea blocked the full width of the garden and extended up the sides almost to the house. I had to go back. I couldn't get out this way.

Cursing Ronnie for being such a smart-arse – while a part of me admired his clever little security trick – I raced back up the garden to the house. There was a plain wooden trellis at the side of the patio and I intended to climb it and get into the neighbour's garden. But then I heard the sound I'd been dreading, running footsteps, coming round the side of the house. I wasn't going to make it. I'd be caught out in the open with an armed assassin free to take his shot.

My mind exploded into incoherence. Something wild and feral took control of me. Instead of running away or hiding – both of which would have been useless – I charged towards the approaching footsteps. I ran fast and my hands reached out ahead of me, ready to grasp the killer's throat. I saw him as he rounded the house, and I leapt at him.

I realised that it was actually Ronnie in the microsecond before he sidestepped me and, with a quite gentle push, sent me sprawling into the flower bed to fetch up hard against a low wall.

"What the fuck are you doing?" he yelled.

My sanity snapped back into place the moment I hit the ground. "Ronnie! Christ, mate, I thought you were the shooter." I was winded and my heart was making my whole body shake with every beat.

"The shooter?" He moved closer to take a better look at me, frowning at what he saw. "You mean the bloke in the house opposite that I just disabled? That shooter?"

He wasn't making any sense. "What?" I asked. I tried to grope my way back to a more solid reality. "There were shots. Two shots. Through your bedroom window. One of them hit my ear!"

He kept staring at me. "So, you went into my bedroom – you can explain why later – and turned on the light. I saw that because I was out in the road, waiting for the hit man to make his move. There were two shots from a suppressed rifle at an upper window in the Pham house. Nice people the Phams. I hope this doesn't make them decide to move to a less dangerous suburb. I went there and waited for the shooter to come down – which he did, in quite a rush. Then I disabled him, secured him, called the cops and came back to find you… doing what exactly?"

I struggled to my feet then sat down on the wall. "I thought the shooter might come over here to finish the job."

He looked puzzled. "So you decided to beat yourself up, cut yourself and tear your clothes in some kind of fight club frenzy?"

I began to explain but I suddenly saw how ludicrous it must all look to Ronnie. I burst out laughing. It was all completely ridiculous. While Ronnie was methodically dealing with the problem, I'd been running around like a frightened rabbit, literally getting nowhere. "That fucking bougainvillea!" I gasped, laughing so much I could hardly breathe.

Ronnie watched me in silence with a small smirk on his lips until I had calmed down. I felt sick and I was trembling all over.

"Come on," he said. "You can have a shower and change your clothes while I make you a cup of tea and some supper. The cops will be here any minute now and they're going to want to talk to both of us. It's going to be a long night."

Chapter Fifteen

And it was.

Ronnie's advice going in was, "Don't try to be a clever bugger. Just tell them everything." I thought he meant about the investigation and what we'd found but the cops weren't interested in all that. They just wanted to know about the shooting. When I began to elaborate on the reasons why we were being shot at, I was told to, "Stick to the facts," even though, to me, it seemed completely relevant.

I was grilled for a good two hours at the local cop shop and signed a statement to the effect that I had been at home, two shots had been fired through Ronnie's bedroom window. I'd tried to escape but met up with Ronnie before I left the premises, and was informed by him that the shooter had been captured and the police were on their way. I then waited for the cops to arrive. Written down like that, as a single paragraph on a police form, it seemed like a lot of fuss about nothing. The fact that I had nearly died, the complex web of actions and motivations that had led up to it, the two previous murders that had put us in such jeopardy, didn't warrant a mention, it seemed. The detective on duty – Detective Sergeant White – seemed happy to have his companion take a few notes but didn't appear to want to get involved in the McKinley or the Sanford cases. "DI Marr can get into all that," he told me. "She'll probably want to follow up on this." It was obvious that his greatest wish was to drop the whole thing on her desk as soon as he walked out of the interview room and never look at it again.

"How are the Phams," I asked when he said I could go.

"The whats?"

"The family from the house the shooter used."

He shrugged. "Went to hospital for a check-up," he said. "Someone else will be taking their statements in the morning."

Ronnie was still being interviewed when I got out to the waiting room. It was about one o'clock and it felt very much like the middle of the night. There was no-one else there. I tried to make myself as comfortable as I could in a plastic chair under the cold fluorescent light and waited for Ronnie to appear. When he did, we got a lift back to his house in a police car. By then it was 2 a.m. and I was woozy with sleep. Even so, we sat for a while in Ronnie's lounge room and had a beer while we talked about what had happened. The cops had cordoned off his bedroom as a crime scene.

"You should have told me you were out patrolling – or whatever you were doing. I had no idea where you'd gone."

"Yeah, I'd have said, only I didn't think you were talking to me after you flounced off. I didn't know you were going to be prowling round the house, looking for me."

"I wasn't pr—" I clamped down on my protest. "Why do you always do that?"

"Do what?"

"Put everything in such a provocative way. Do you just like everyone to be cross with you all the time?"

He grinned. "Hey, don't forget I was the one who saved

you from beating yourself to death in the garden tonight."

I couldn't help laughing, even though I was irritated too. "I'm off to bed," I said. Then I remembered the crime scene. "Do you want me to take the couch?"

He shook his head and said I should take the bed. I needed it more.

I thanked him and stood up to go but he said, "So what were you doing in my bedroom?"

I sat back down. "I worked something out. Something important."

"About the case?"

"Yes. Professor Scott Armitage really knows what he's talking about."

"Yeah, look, if you're trying to convince me the FABClub stash is worth bugger all, I'm just not buying it. It's got to be worth a motza."

"No, you're not listening. Armitage really knows what he's talking about."

"So how could he get it so—?" He stopped as realisation dawned. "Fuck me! The bastard was lying."

I smiled and sat back. "Give the man a coconut."

Ronnie's eyes glazed over as his mind raced through all the ramifications. "Do you think he's the killer?"

"I don't know. He would certainly be someone McKinley would let into his home late at night. He would also likely have been there before so he'd know about the gun in McKinley's office and might even know something about the building security system – enough to force McKinley at gunpoint to give him the access code so he could turn it off and wipe the recordings after the murder."

"So…" Ronnie was excited now. "Someone in the FABClub asked Armitage for a second valuation – maybe after McKinley walked out on them."

"I bet whoever it was even asked McKinley to recommend another expert."

"Reckon. But Armitage spotted something. One of those paintings is worth millions. He tells the club member and, between them, they hatch a plot to keep it for themselves."

"Tens of millions. It would have to be, to make it worthwhile."

"Tens of millions?" Ronnie looked sceptical. "You've seen them. Did any of them look like they were in that class?"

I shrugged. "The whole lot's not worth a brass razoo if you ask me but what do I know?"

Ronnie fell silent again. After a while, he said, "So there's two of them."

"Maybe."

"No. Definitely. There's no way Armitage could profit from this otherwise."

"He could wait until the club sells the pictures."

"Yeah, he could but didn't Kryou say the plan was to hold them for at least ten years? It would be worth waiting for but, when the time comes, they'll probably sell them at auction and that means having other experts take a look. He couldn't risk that. No way. He needs a club member to fix it."

"Like Kryou?"

"Yeah, maybe. But it could be any of them. Did Kryou seem particularly anxious about taking you to see the paintings?"

"No. Not really. He seemed more grumpy than anything, like I was wasting his precious time. He didn't seem very happy with Armitage, either, probably because he was showing off his knowledge and acting the prat instead of getting on with things."

I yawned. It had been a long and stressful day after a short and interrupted night. My vision was getting jumpy and my muscles were going slack. If I didn't get to bed soon, I'd just fall off the chair and sleep on the floor. "Ronnie, mate..." I said.

"Yeah, yeah. Go to bed. Nothing we can do now. But tomorrow... Tomorrow we've got a very busy day." He grinned at me, looking fiendishly happy.

* * * *

I woke to the sound of pop music coming from somewhere. I was on top of the bed and fully clothed. For a moment I was completely confused as to why I wasn't at home in my own bed – until it all came back to me.

According to my phone, it was well after 10 a.m..

I changed my T-shirt and rubbed some cold water on my face, trying to avoid looking at my raddled features in the mirror. I seemed to have aged ten years since I last looked. I opened the bedroom door and the music volume went up several notches. It was coming from Ronnie's bedroom, although why he was listening to Rhianna, I couldn't have guessed. I headed down the stairs. I needed coffee, then maybe I could solve this new mystery.

I found Ronnie sitting in the kitchen, eating his way through a pile of scrambled eggs, bacon and toast. It smelled wonderful. When had I last eaten?

"Plenty in the fridge," he told me around a mouth stuffed to capacity. "Help yourself."

I did. "When did you have the time to go shopping for all this stuff?" I asked, grabbing egg boxes and packets of bacon.

"Maggie brought some things round this morning. Bloody

rippa, hey? Said she knows what I'm like when I'm on a case. God bless that woman."

"And the racket from upstairs?" I glared at the kettle. Why, if we could put a man on the Moon, could we not find a way of boiling water that didn't take forever?

"That's Doug. Odd job guy. Putting in a new window and filling the holes in the wall. Good rates, if you ever need someone. Mate, while you've been hibernating, all kinds of activities have been going on. For a start the police forensic team came, measured up my bedroom, dug out the slugs and gave it the all clear."

I felt my heart flutter at the mere mention of the shooting. My hand went up to my ear. There was a small scab. Ronnie must have noticed my involuntary movement.

"Don't worry, mate. Chicks dig scars."

"Not the kind of chicks I want to meet."

"Suit yourself."

I focused on beating and frying for a while and finally brought my assembled brekky to the table. Ronnie had finished by then and was looking at me over the top of his coffee mug. It was annoying that he was so disgustingly perky.

"The cops called." he said. "DI Marr will be with us soon."

"Great. What about the lawyer? Shouldn't we get him to sit in?"

"We'll see how it goes. We can always tell her to get stuffed if she starts getting stroppy."

I nodded and concentrated on eating.

"I've been thinking," Ronnie said. I resisted making a comment. "Today I need to see to Darren McGuire. Then we need to work out which of the FABClub members has teamed up with Professor Armitage."

"How?"

"We need to get at their finances. The one and only reason they'd start on a killing spree is if they need the money in a tearing rush. Think about it. Two people dead inside a month. Why not kill one a year? They've got the time before the paintings are sold and it would be way less suspicious. It's because the need the money soon. That's why they have to risk it. So we're looking for one of them who needs money in, say, the next few months."

"OK."

"Then we need to check alibis. The thing is, if there are two of them, they might be sharing out the dirty work. So the fact that they have an alibi for one killing but not the other wouldn't rule them out the way it would if there was just one killer. Do you see?" I nodded. "What we really need, is for the next murder to happen."

I pushed away my plate. "That's a morally questionable position."

He grinned at me. "Yet it's going to happen soon, unless we stop them."

"What about the cops? Should we tell Marr all this when she comes round?"

"Sure. It won't make a scrap of difference though. She's only just coming round to the idea that Sanford was murdered. And only then because I rubbed her nose in the evidence. By the time she accepts that it was connected to McKinley and the connection is the FABClub, they could all be dead. But tell her if you like. See where it gets you."

I began to protest that even Marr would have to take us seriously after last night but Ronnie held up a hand to stop me. "I need to sort McGuire out first, before Marr turns up."

He laid one of his burner phones on the table and began typing. I went to stand behind him so I could see. He was composing a text message.

"The first two boys you sent ended up in hospital," it said. "The next guy is also in hospital, waiting to be transferred to a police lock-up. I think they both learned their lesson. But it's you I really need to explain things to." I frowned down at it. It was kind of menacing and cryptic but I couldn't see how a professional criminal like McGuire would find it at all intimidating. But Ronnie was still busy, appending pictures to the message. The first was of a smart, suburban house. The next was the same house with a car in front and a woman ushering two schoolkids in uniform into the back. Then came a close-up shot of the woman. And then one each of the two kids. Then one of a school building. Finally, Ronnie added more text. "Your reputation is being trashed. It's costing you money. But things can get so much worse if you don't stop." He hit send.

"Fuck. Did you just threaten his wife and kids?"

He blinked at me in mock innocence. "What? Is that a morally questionable position, too?"

"But you wouldn't actually… Would you?"

He got up and gathered the dishes. "Your faith in me is touching. As ever. Thing is, McGuire knows me even less than you do. What's more, he's an evil scumbag who wouldn't hesitate to do something like that himself. And we all judge others by our own standards, don't we? I think he's going to believe me."

"And the pictures? Where did you get them?"

"I did a bit of research, found out where he lives, then went out this morning and took a few snaps. The kids were a bonus."

"But won't it just, you know, get him mad?"

Ronnie grinned at me. "Let's see. Give him a few minutes to make a couple of panicked phone calls and I'm sure he'll let us know." The doorbell rang. "That'll be Marr. Take her into the lounge room while I stack the dishwasher, hey?"

I looked at him in exasperation. How could he be so calm after what he'd just done? He ignored me and got on with his clearing up. A heavy hand rapped at the door and I stalked off to open it.

DI Marr and the ever-present Bronski didn't look very happy. With the bare minimum of politeness, they let themselves be led into the lounge room and declined offers of coffee and biscuits.

"Is Mr. Walker joining us?" Marr asked.

"Right here, Detective Inspector," Ronnie said, coming in and sitting down.

Marr looked from one to the other of us as if the family pet had just dropped us on the carpet.

"Maybe we could start by you telling me exactly what happened here last night?" she said.

I opened my mouth to speak but Ronnie beat me to it. "It's all in the statements we made last night. I assume you've read them."

Marr didn't rise to the bait. "And why is it that you think Mr. McGuire put out a hit on you?"

Ronnie was about to answer but his phone beeped. He pulled it out of his pocket to read a message. Marr went wide-eyed and stone faced. So I jumped in to answer her question.

"McGuire is a middleman who hires thugs for clients who want to frighten or hurt people. He took a job to scare us off the McKinley investigation but that didn't get him very far. So he sent his guys to take us out. But that ended up even worse for him. So he took it on himself to have us killed to protect his reputation. It was his bloke who shot at me last night."

Ronnie held his phone in front of my face so I could read it. It was the reply from McGuire. It said, "No need to get all crazy. It was just business. All done now. No hard feelings."

"Fuck," I said, amazed that it had worked.

"Would you two rather talk to me at the station?" Marr demanded angrily.

"Sorry, officer," Ronnie said, putting his phone away. "It won't happen again."

She looked at Ronnie as if she'd have liked to bite him, then she turned back to me. "So, you're accusing Darren McGuire of hiring the man we now have in custody. On what evidence?"

Ronnie jumped in. "He told me he was going to do it."

"Witnesses?"

"Sure but none who'd testify against him."

"Then it's your word against his."

Ronnie's phone rang. He fished it out and switched it off. Marr scowled. Doug, the odd-job man, popped his head in the doorway and said, "All done, mate." Marr turned her scowl on Doug. "Look, you've got company. I'll stick the invoice in the email, hey?"

"Yeah, no worries, mate. Thanks for coming round."

Ronnie turned back to Marr, just as the doorbell rang. "I'm sorry, Detective Inspector. I'll just see who that is. Luke can answer your questions. Won't be a mo."

"This is a case of attempted murder, Mr. Walker."

But Ronnie was already half-way to the door. "Won't be a mo."

"It's all to do with the McKinley case," I said, trying to

draw her attention away from Ronnie's back. "McGuire's standover tactics started as soon as we started asking questions about McKinley. You need to get McGuire in and find out who paid him to set his heavies onto us."

"There is no McKinley case," she said, jaw set. "McKinley shot himself."

"Then why did someone hire McGuire to shut us up?"

"How do you know someone hired McGuire?"

"We had it from one of the goons he sent to kill us."

"Name?"

I had a flash memory of the man lying on the floor of the car park, with Ronnie poking his broken leg with a pickaxe handle. "I don't know his name," I said. That was not something the police needed to know about.

"Pity. So you were accosted by some men in the car park of your office..." She had obviously read the statement I'd made to Sergeant Pearce at the time. "...and one of the men said that McGuire sent them?"

"Yeah, not that first time. They came again. That's when we got McGuire's name."

"But you didn't report the second attack."

"It hardly seemed worth it given that you didn't do anything when I reported the first one."

Marr nodded, lips pursed. "And then you went to visit Mr. McGuire and that's when he confessed and said he'd send another hitman to kill you?"

"Yeah, not quite. Only Ronnie went to see him."

"So you can't corroborate Mr. Walker's story?"

"I have no reason to doubt it – especially since someone shot at me about twelve hours later. What's his name, by the way? They bloke who tried to kill me."

"I'm afraid we can't discuss details of the case."

"It was Sam Weller," Ronnie said, coming back and re-seating himself. "His drivers licence was in his pocket. That was the press at the door, by the way. The street is full of them. They'd love to talk to you, Detective Inspector."

She looked furious but kept her voice calm. "What did you tell them?"

"Nothing! Well... I might have mentioned your name."

Marr's phone rang. She glanced at it and switched it off.

"Are we done here?" Ronnie asked. "I don't know about you but I've got a very busy day planned."

"Mr. Walker, whatever happened here last night, I intend to get to the bottom of it. Your neighbours are in hospital being treated for shock and minor injuries. There is another man in the hospital with a broken rib and a dislocated shoulder."

"The Phams are fine," Ronnie said. "The bloke was knocked about a bit, that's all. I found them tied up in the utility room and set them free before I called the cops. As for the arsehole with the gun, he's lucky I didn't take his fucking head off."

"So you admit to assaulting him?"

"Of course. In self defence and to protect the Phams and Luke, here. Of course, it's just my word against his. How will you ever get to the truth?"

To me, Marr said, "You were alone in the house?"

"As it happens, I was." Pointedly, I said, "I didn't know where Ronnie was."

"And what were you doing in Mr. Walker's bedroom?"

"That's what I wanted to know," Ronnie said.

"I was looking for Ronnie."

"And you," she said, turning to Ronnie, "were outside, 'patrolling the street' you said in your statement. Do you often spend your evenings prowling round the neighbourhood?"

Ronnie smiled. "Only when I've just received a credible death threat."

"And do you get those often?"

"It happens more than you might think."

"Yes, I can imagine. And you saw the shots?"

"And heard them. The rifle was suppressed but this is a very quiet neighbourhood."

"And you ran to the Phams' house to challenge the shooter?"

"Yep. I met the fucker legging it down the stairs."

Marr looked at Ronnie suspiciously. "Mr. Weller is a strong, fit man in his late twenties and he was allegedly armed with a loaded firearm. Are you telling me you just ran in there and disabled him? I have to say, you don't look like a man in his prime."

"It must be the training I received as a police officer. I always knew it would come in handy one day."

"I've looked at your record, Walker. You were not a good detective, were you?"

"Nah, mate. I was a great detective. It just turned out I was a very bad employee. You, on the other hand, are probably an excellent employee."

I saw Marr's nostrils flare but she still didn't lose it. She stood up. "Thank you both. That's all for now. We'll be in touch. We've got your prints and DNA haven't we?" The cops had taken them last night – although mine were already on record from a year ago. "Good." In a final aside to Ronnie, she said, "I should caution you about talking to the press. Carelessly mentioning details of the case could possibly prejudice any potential conviction."

Ronnie opened the door for her and Bronski and a sudden swell of shouting rose from outside as the reporters saw them emerge. Ronnie shut out the racket with a sigh.

"Right-o," he said. "That's all the bullshit over for the day. Let's get down to some real work."

Chapter Sixteen

"No." I said it as firmly as I could but Ronnie still had the expression of a man trying to persuade a reluctant toddler to put his pants on.

"Give me an alternative," he said, reasonably.

"No. It's just wrong. You just saved her from Uncle Lau and a life of crime and now you want to get her involved in our own shady dealings."

"Just tell me what else we can do?"

Knowing I shouldn't, I said, "We could take all our ideas to the cops. They don't know half of what we do. We'll give them what we know and get them to look into Armitage's bank accounts."

"Take it to the cops? That's your plan? Were you not there when DI Marr came visiting this morning? That woman would break her neck bending over backwards not to help us. She wouldn't spit in your mouth if your teeth were on fire."

"Bertolissio, then. She'd help."

"Like hell, she would. She's not that stupid. How would she justify looking into Armitage's finances? What would she tell her boss? You remember her boss, don't you? Big guy? Looks like the Marlboro Man? Wanted to put you away for killing Chelsea?"

I remembered Detective Inspector Reid all right. "It doesn't matter. It's still wrong."

"She owes us a favour."

"No she doesn't! She saved our lives, remember? As far as I'm concerned we owe her and we always will."

"Yeah, well, maybe, but she'd like to help. You'll see. If we ask her, she'll jump at the chance."

"It's immoral."

"Why does everything have to be about morality with you? You're obsessed."

"She works for me. Well, I mean, I own the company she works for."

"So what? As far as I can see, that gives her even more of a reason to help you out."

We were sitting in Ronnie's car outside the office in West End where Karen Chan worked. Ronnie had driven there without telling me why but, as soon as I'd heard his plan, I put my foot down.

"That's just so… deontological," I said.

"Da fuck?"

"Your whole morality seems to be based on duty and obligation. Well there are other ways to build an ethical system."

Ronnie was growing as exasperated as I was. "I don't want to build a fucking ethical system. I just want Karen to hack a bloke's laptop."

"We'd be putting her in danger. Again. It's not right."

"Yeah? And if she doesn't do it, a couple of murderers go free. Is that right? And you know they're going to kill again – four more times. Is that right? What was that shit about a tram and the baby on the tracks you told me once?"

"It's called the trolley problem," I said, weakly. He was right, this was a perfect example of it. Turn the wheel one way and Karen might go to prison. Turn it the other way and four people might die. On the face of it, it was a no-brainer. Except I liked Karen a lot more than I liked a handful of rich old buggers I'd never met. And, on a purely utilitarian calculation, I'd weigh her security against their lives any day.

"It's not that simple," I said, feeling dismal that all my studies had left me incapable of arguing for what should be an easy ethical decision.

There was a rap at the window and I jumped. Karen was outside, smiling in at us. We got out and joined her on the pavement.

"Hi," she said, managing to make the one syllable sound like a little tune. "I saw you from the window."

"We were just coming to see you," Ronnie said. "We've got a little job for you."

I jumped in smartly. "No we haven't."

"Ignore him, he's an idiot," Ronnie said. "We need you to hack someone's laptop."

"No, we don't. I've already explained to Ronnie why that would be a really bad idea."

"And I explained to Luke that it is our only way forward."

"We'll find another way."

"No we won't."

"Yes, we will."

Karen's head was turning back and forth as she followed our exchange. "All right," she said. "I'll do it."

We stopped glaring at one another and looked at Karen. She gave me a sweet smile and said, "If Ronnie thinks it is the only option, I think he is probably right. No offence, Luke, but he is older and wiser in these matters. In which case, it must be done. I know you want to protect me. You are always very careful not to make me feel obliged to you and I am very grateful but I want to help you if I can."

"You know how dangerous these things are, Karen," I said. "You've only just got your permanent residency and you want to get citizenship. If you're caught doing something like this, it would make that impossible. They'd send you back to Hong Kong."

She nodded. "I know. But maybe it is worth the risk to put a murderer behind bars – and to help my friends."

"That's my girl!" Ronnie said. "Now, what we need is—"

"And," I said, loudly. "There is also the danger that the killers – we've met several lately – could turn on you if they found out you were helping us."

Her expression became sober. It made her look even younger and more vulnerable. She put a hand on my arm. A butterfly could hardly have touched me more lightly. "I understand the dangers, Luke, but I want to help, honestly."

"Great," said Ronnie. "Shall we begin?"

* * * *

Karen went back inside and picked up her laptop. She also let Kazima, the CEO, know that she was off on yet another secret assignment for me. I'd met Kazima at least once a month over the past year at our regular status updates. As the majority shareholder in Chelsea's old company, I tried to take an interest in how it was getting along and Kazima, stepping into the role of CEO after Chelsea's death, had been keen to keep me involved. It was probably at the second or third of these meetings that she had said we needed to formalise Karen's relationship with me and my then-brand-new private investigation company. As usual with Kazima, she already had a solution worked out when she raised the problem. Karen was to continue with the employment contract she had but her terms would be varied so that servicing my company and running little side projects for it would become part of her job, on the condition that Kazima had a veto if she needed Karen, or thought I was abusing the arrangement. I asked her why she'd agree to something that clearly disadvantaged her operations.

"All kinds of reasons," she said. I pressed her and she eventually told me. "I want to help you. For Chelsea. I think she would want me to do that. Also…" She winked. "I don't want you poaching the best sysadmin I've ever seen."

So there was no problem about Karen coming with us.

"Where do you want to set up?" I asked. In the past, she'd done her hacking work from my lounge room or even sitting by the pool in a hotel.

"I either need his laptop, or I need to be somewhere near him while he's using it."

I tried to remember how Armitage worked. I'd been in his office. Did he have a laptop on his desk or did he use a university desktop machine? When he left the building, did he carry his laptop with him or leave it behind? Did he have one machine at home for personal use, and another at the office for university business? When we went out to the storage place, did he have a laptop bag over his shoulder?

"I'm pretty sure he has one laptop that he carries around with him," I said. "I'm sure he'd miss it if we borrowed it."

"OK," said Karen. "If I can get into the university network, I should be able to connect to his machine and poke around inside it."

"Right-o," said Ronnie and pulled out onto the road, heading for the city centre and the QUT campus.

"What do you need?" she asked.

Ronnie answered. "Bank statements. Credit cards. Any and all of his accounts. If he's received any payments, apart from his salary, we need to know who from."

"OK," she said again, as if we were asking for nothing difficult or illegal.

"And emails, texts, Facebook friends, all that. We're trying to find a connection between Armitage and one of the FABClub members."

"OK."

I gave her a worried look. "You're sure you're all right with this? In the past, you've always been sort of reticent, to say the least."

"It's time I stopped thinking so much about myself," she said. "You and Ronnie are doing a good thing. Something the police can't do. You're helping people."

"We're getting paid for it, too, don't forget," Ronnie said, grinning. "Don't go thinking we're heroes."

She grinned back at him. "Me too, thanks to Luke and Kazima. And it's a lot more interesting than installing server upgrades."

We drove on in silence. Whatever Karen's motives for helping, I couldn't shift a feeling of unease. Either she was helping us out of a misguided sense of obligation, or she really was starting to enjoy it and we'd corrupted her – something even her wicked Uncle Lau had failed to achieve.

"We need to get inside so I can plug into the network," she said, as we prowled through the campus streets looking for somewhere to leave the car. We found a spot that wasn't too far way from the Creative Industries Precinct – the very name sent Ronnie into a grumbling tirade against "pretentious dickheads" – and made our way inside.

A quick recce confirmed that Scott Armitage was in his office and had his laptop open on his desk. We had failed to find any public access points to the network and Karen was just explaining to me why she'd prefer not to use the wifi access when Ronnie said, "This way." He was standing in the open doorway of some random office along the corridor. "Careless of them to leave their door unlocked," he said.

I seriously doubted that the door had been unlocked but we hurried inside and shut ourselves in. The door had a reinforced glass window set into it and I kept watch through it on the corridor outside while Karen set up on the desk and Ronnie peered over her shoulder. I wasn't sure what I'd do if the rightful occupant came back while we were all in there but ignoring the danger was just not possible. After a while, I realised that standing outside would be a better tactic. At least then I could intercept anyone who approached. So I went out into the corridor again and tried to lounge around inconspicuously.

I'm a student, waiting to talk to my tutor, I told myself, getting into character. I should have a bag, or some books, papers in my hand, at least. I found a notice board farther along the corridor and ripped off adverts for protests and exhibitions and guest talks, until I had a sheaf of paper to go with my cover story. The corridor was very quiet. Not one of the offices seemed to be occupied. Bored, I started reading the notices I'd grabbed. Some of the events looked really interesting and I felt a pang of nostalgia for my old university days. *I should make an effort to go to things like this,* I told myself, although I knew I probably wouldn't. Lunchtime recitals by the Music Department, plays in outdoor spaces, lectures by visiting academics, writers and artists, were all things of the past. Somehow there wasn't room for such things in my new life.

"Hello." I looked up to see a woman standing just two paces away, smiling at me. "You found it, then?"

"What?" Did I know this woman? She was about my age, attractive in a sharp-featured, intelligent way. I struggled for a name but nothing came.

"You don't remember me, do you?"

"I – I..."

She looked at the sheaf of coloured paper in my hands.

"Not a map this time but you still look lost. What are you trying to find now?"

At the top of the sheaf was a page advertising a collection of Japanese ceramics. "I..." My mind was flailing helplessly for some reason why I might be standing there with an entire noticeboard's worth of posters when I suddenly placed her.

"You're the kind stranger!" I exclaimed. "I mean, the person who helped me the other day when I was lost. But... but that was at UQ, not here. Why are you here?" I hadn't meant to sound so challenging. I was just speaking my thoughts instead of behaving like a normal person.

She seemed to find it amusing. "It's my hobby. I wander around university campuses helping lost souls find their way."

I discretely moved the posters behind my back. "On behalf of lost souls everywhere, I thank you."

She acknowledged my thanks with a minimal curtsey. "So, are you studying here?" she asked. "Oh no, you said you studied at UQ. So maybe you're working here?" She frowned. "No, that's not right either. There is no arts course at UQ, so why would you be working in an arts department at QUT? You are a man of mystery."

I needed to get her off the subject. I said, "I think I've worked you out, though." She smiled, clearly enjoying this new game. "You are actually a secret agent in the employ of the State Education Department. Your mission is to seek out disoriented and confused people who are obviously under the mind control of foreign powers. I suppose you want to know the name of the evil saboteur who is directing my every action."

She smiled and glanced past me along the corridor. "What I'd really like to know is why you are trying to hide a bunch of posters you have clearly taken down from that noticeboard over there."

"What? These?" I held up the posters. She cocked her head slightly and looked puzzled but still amused as I blustered. "I was just... I was only..."

A door opened nearby and I nearly jumped up the wall. Ronnie and Karen came out. They both stopped and stared at me and the strange woman. Then Ronnie stepped forward and caught my arm. "Come on, we've got to get going. No time for chatting."

As relieved as I was, even as he dragged me off towards the exit, I craned around to get a last look at the woman. She was watching my exit with an expression of pure amazement.

* * * *

"Bloody hell, mate," Ronnie complained as we drove away. "I know I said you should get laid but I didn't mean you should start chatting up every woman you meet." Karen's eyes widened and her pupils swivelled towards me.

"I wasn't cha— I was just— She found me there. What was I supposed to do?"

Ronnie grinned. "At least tell me you got her number."

"That's not what was going on."

But it was, sort of. There was a definite hint of flirting in the air. And she was a very attractive woman – and funny – and bright... And I hadn't got her number. Or even her name. We would never meet again. The sadness I felt was well out of proportion to the significance of the encounter, yet there it was.

"Anyway," I said, doing what Ronnie might call "deflecting". "What did you get from Armitage's machine?"

"Everything," said Karen. "He has no security. His passwords are all the same. Nothing has two-factor authentication." She held up a thumb drive. "I have all his bank accounts, credit cards, phone accounts, emails, social media accounts, browsing history, location history, everything. He does use an encrypted messaging system but he'd left himself logged into it, so I could just download all the messages in clear."

"So, if our boy is conspiring with one of the FABClub members, we've got him."

"We should go to the office and take a look at it all," I said.

"Well duh," Ronnie said and I realised we were already on Coronation Drive heading for Toowong.

When we arrived, Karen went straight to work, printing out reams of Scott Armitage's personal information. Ronnie had asked for the last three months – which was lucky because the printer quickly ran out of toner and I wasn't sure our last new cartridge would have been enough for any more. We soon settled into a routine of poring through the life of Scott Armitage, grabbing extra sheets from the constantly-rattling printer as we each ran out. I got the bank statements, including the credit cards. Karen got the itemised phone bills and Ronnie took the emails and other text messages. I made a list of phone numbers for each of the FABClub members and Karen wrote a program that, line by line, checked Armitage's phone calls against each of them. She was finished well before Ronnie and I were. And, before heading back to her actual job, delivered the disappointing news that Armitage had never spoken to anyone from the FABClub – at least not on the phones we knew about.

Ronnie and I pressed on in silence for the next two hours.

"This bloke's a complete fucking jerk," Ronnie announced at last, throwing a handful of emails on the table. "I've never heard anyone more up themselves. Talk about figjam. Have you found anything yet?"

I sat back and pressed my fingers into my eyes. "Nothing worth knowing. You know, he's got a separate credit card account that he uses to pay for his porn site subscriptions? How devious is that?"

"No big cash deposits around the time of McKinley's murder?"

"Nothing at all. And I've been through everything. I was going though it all again but I think this is a waste of time. If he's in league with the killer, he's been very careful not to leave any electronic traces. If he's using a pre-paid phone to talk to his partner, I can't even find the day he bought it. Plenty of candidate purchases, but nothing definitive. He probably got it from a newsagent or something and buys charge cards from the supermarket. Is there nothing in his email at all?"

"Nah. But I tell you, if I was on the receiving end of some of these snarky little messages, I'd have gone round and made him eat his keyboard. I don't know how people put up with him."

"Shall we call it a day?"

He stared at the piles of paper, lips pursed in frustration for a long time.

"It must be him," he said at last. "I don't care if we can't find anything. Nothing else makes sense.

I pulled out my phone. It had rung twice while we were working but I hadn't answered. I checked my messages. The first call was from my mum, asking what we were doing for my dad's birthday – which I had completely forgotten about. The second call was from Dan Bridgeman, our new client.

"Luke," it said. "It's Danno. Listen, mate, I've been expecting an update. You're still on the case, hey? Why don't you come by? We should meet. This arvo would be good."

I checked the time.

"Fancy a drive out to the Gold Coast?" I asked Ronnie. "Our new client wants to see us."

"Tough choice," he said. "Waste our time here, or waste it there. Are you driving?"

"Yeah, sure."

"Is he going to feed us?"

"I don't suppose so."

"Then we're eating on the way. It's the middle of the afternoon and I haven't had my lunch yet."

I stood up. I was hungry too. "We can grab a pie on the way out."

"And a roast beef sandwich with gravy."

"Whatever."

* * * *

It took about two hours to get from the office to Bridgeman Luxury Motors. It was a broad, low, glass-fronted building in a sea of beamers and mercs parked in the lot outside. Inside were more beamers and mercs and a couple of Porches. Pride of place seemed to go to a gleaming pink Cadillac that dwarfed all the other cars. There was Christmas bunting everywhere, along with "Summer Sale" stickers. Out near the road was a gigantic half-inflated balloon person that kept flopping and falling then jerking upright. The impression was not one of quiet luxury but of frenetic, gaudy bad taste. It might have looked out of place elsewhere but on the Gold Coast, it seemed, nothing was too tacky.

A salesman zeroed in on us like a guided missile and exploded into his spiel. Ronnie looked at him with distaste and walked away.

"Father and son, is it?" the salesman asked.

"What? No! Christ no! We're here to see Mr. Bridgeman. I'm Luke Kelly."

The man's smile stayed rigidly in place but the interest in his eyes vanished. "I'll get someone to help you." He turned to a distant corner of the showroom and waved. A young woman appeared from out of the shadows and minced towards us in an overly-tight pencil skirt and high heels. "Jilly will take care of you," he said and walked briskly away.

Jilly was the kind of buxom teen who might well be working a second job as a hot schoolgirl porn model. She smiled expectantly at me and I repeated what we were here for. "Follow me," she said and minced away. Ronnie, who had appeared at my elbow as soon as the salesman left, nudged me and winked, nodding towards the girl's ample buttocks. I mouthed "Fuck off," at him but he kept up the pantomime until we reached Bridgeman's office.

"Two gentlemen to see you, Danno," she said. Bridgeman came around his desk to greet us and Jilly minced away. Both Bridgeman and Ronnie stared after the girl. I made a point of not doing so.

"I'm Luke Kelly," I said, holding out my hand. Bridgeman turned to me with a smile and took it. "And this is my associate, Ronnie Walker."

"You're the ex-cop, right?" he said, shaking Ronnie's hand.

Ronnie looked him in the eye and said, "Yeah, that's right."

Bridgeman was about forty, very slightly taller than Ronnie, with very short fair hair and blue eyes. He was good looking, in a mean, street-fighter kind of way. There was something hard, even cruel about him that his big, wolfish smile seemed to emphasise rather than soften. I thought about the beautiful, elegant Mel Bertolissio and felt anxious for her being this man's girlfriend.

He showed us to seats – deep, leather-upholstered chairs around a marble coffee table – and sat back, relaxed and in control, the king of his domain.

"So, tell me what I'm getting for all this money you charge."

I glanced at Ronnie, but he clearly thought this was my show. So I launched into a summary of the case. As I spoke, Jilly minced back in with a tray of coffee, placed it on the table between us and minced out again. From the moment she appeared to the moment she was gone, Ronnie and Bridgeman stared at her. I kept my mind on the report and my eyes off the girl and managed to get through it to the end.

As we helped ourselves to coffee and Tim Tams, Bridgeman said, "So you've got fuck all, really."

"I wouldn't say that," I said, feeling defensive. "We've interviewed lots of potential suspect, eliminated a great many—"

Ronnie held up a hand to stop me. "We're progressing with our enquiries," he said.

Like a snake, Bridgeman slowly swung his gaze over to Ronnie. "And are you ever going to catch anybody?"

Ronnie's lips curled into a small grin. "Sure. One day. Do you care?"

Bridgeman grinned back and shook his head. "Couldn't give a flying fuck who done it. But I do care about how much it's going to cost me."

Ronnie cast his eyes about the office, somehow he managed to convey the idea that Bridgeman had plenty of money. "I thought this was a present for your girlfriend."

"Mate, if your pitch is that you're in the same market as handbags and jewellery, you probably need to check your marketing strategy."

"Ronnie's point is," I said, cutting in. "A murder investigation is unpredictable and complicated. As such, it's impossible for us to say quite how long it might take."

Bridgeman was unimpressed. "So you'd like a blank cheque, is that what you're saying?"

"We have a suspect," I said, hoping to sound as if we were close to completion.

"Really? Because the names you've mentioned so far – the ones I recognise – have all been serious businessmen. You think the likes of Nick Kryou and Martin Hittman are serial killers?"

"You know Nick Kryou?" Ronnie asked, suddenly fully engaged.

Bridgeman appeared to notice the change in tone and

considered Ronnie in silence for a moment. "Sure," she said. "He's part of the Parkland Cove development consortium. Building a load of shit houses for yuppies out at Miami. Is he your suspect?"

"No," said Ronnie. "Should he be?"

"How would I know? Met him a couple of times. Seems okay."

"Is there any reason he might need money in a hurry?"

"What kind of money are we talking about? You know what those big developments are like. It's a high stakes game. The other names in the consortium are much bigger players than Kryou – you know, national and international brands. I figured Nick had someone big behind him."

"Big step up for him, then," Ronnie said.

"Sure, puts him in a different league."

Ronnie nodded and sat back to ponder in silence. Bridgeman continued to study him.

"So, what else can we tell you, Mr. Bridgeman?" I said, hoping we could wrap it up. But Ronnie was nowhere near finished.

"What about Hittman?" he asked. "What can you tell us about him?"

After that, he went through all the FABClub members, one by one, living and dead, and pumped Bridgeman for every scrap of gossip he could get. Our client knew something about three of them – Kryou, Hittman and Wendell – but not the two out-of-towners, nor McKinley and Sanford. Ronnie wound up with Scott Armitage but Bridgeman had never heard of him.

"Thanks, Danno," Ronnie said, standing. "That was really helpful."

Bridgeman stood, too. "Yeah? So one of those blokes is

the killer?"

"Could be. You know not to mention any of this to anyone else, hey?"

"Sure. So which one is it?"

I stood up. "It's too soon to say with certainty and, without certainty, we'd be leaving ourselves open to defamation charges."

"Right," said Bridgeman, clearly unconvinced.

"If you talk about what we just said..." Ronnie didn't seem sure that Bridgeman had really taken his point. "...you might tip off the killer that we're onto him. Other people might die as a result. You might even put yourself in danger. There have already been two attempts on Luke's life in the past few days. You understand, don't you?"

Bridgeman looked at me as if he really couldn't understand why anyone would want to kill me but he said, "Yeah, yeah. Heavy shit. I get it."

* * * *

We left soon after. It was early evening and the rush hour traffic was already dying down. The ocean was not far from us as we walked to the car and I was almost sure I could hear it over the sounds of the traffic.

"Do you have to do that?" Ronnie asked as we got in.

"Do what?"

"Give people your business card."

I knew exactly where this was going. "It's a perfectly good name."

"You saw his face, yeah? It's embarrassing."

"Look, maybe you're right. I'll think about it."

"Hoo-bloody-ray! It's only taken a year to get you to see

what everybody else sees in an instant."

I sulked in silence for a moment. "Do you want to get some chips and sit on the beach?"

"Reckon. There's a place down that way." He pointed South along the coast.

"How do you know? Never mind. Just navigate."

Ronnie's recommendation turned out to be pretty good although more of a bustling night-spot than the traditional daggy fish and chip joint I'd imagined. We took our food and bottled drinks down onto Broadbeach and stared at the ocean for a moment before trudging through the sand to sit down to enjoy our picnic. The sun was setting rapidly and the waves flashed gold. There was a grumble of noise from the streets behind us and a periodic roar from the ocean ahead as waves broke on the beach. Joggers passed up and down the strand between us and the water. Couples sauntered along barefoot and close. About half a kilometre to the North, there seemed to be a party going on. The fish was hot and scalded my fingers.

"It's fucking Kryou," Ronnie said into the gathering gloom.

"You can't be sure."

"You reckon?"

"And now you want Karen to hack his data. What makes you think he'd be any less careful than Armitage?"

"We don't need that," he said. "Maybe not, anyway. We just need to know what kind of pressure the... What was it?"

"The Parkland Grove development?"

"Yeah, that. I'll bet you the investors are expecting him to come up with a few million in the next few months and our man hasn't got it."

"We could dig around, I suppose."

"Yeah," he said, staring at the ocean as if it were his personal nemesis. He didn't seem to want to talk any more so I attended to my meal in silence.

"Ready?" I asked after he'd finished his food as well as everything I'd left.

"It's funny that the sea smells the same wherever you go," he said. "The land doesn't."

For Ronnie, this was deep scientific insight. "Dimethyl sulphide," I said, wanting to encourage this new mood of enquiry.

"What?"

"That's what gives the sea its smell. It's released by sea life."

"Jesus fucking Christ on a stick," he growled and got to his feet. "Let's go before you start telling me about the life-cycle of bloody seaweed."

"I was just—"

"Being a smart-arse? Yeah, I know."

Chapter Seventeen

I woke up convinced that Chelsea was asleep in the bed beside me. It was a feeling I hadn't had for weeks but which had been horribly common in the months after she'd died. I got up quickly, showered, made a coffee and thawed a croissant. My unit had a small balcony and I sat out there with my breakfast, enjoying the morning while it was still cool enough to do so. Inside, every surface was strewn with paper from the research I'd done into Nick Kryou, his company and all the property developments he'd been involved with during the past two years. I knew Ronnie would have spent the evening – probably all night, knowing him – doing the same kind of research. But all he'd said on parting last night had been, "See you tomorrow."

One thing that had surprised me about being a private investigator was how useless the Internet was as a research tool. Yes, it was way better than having to go to libraries, visit government departments and trawl through newspaper archives. But it was nothing at all like you see in the movies, where the investigator, with a few quick searches, has a complete dossier on his suspect, their schedule for the week and architect's drawings of their secret lair. Trying to find out anything from public websites about the finances of companies, individuals, and especially of projects, was like an Easter egg hunt where everyone you asked was part of the conspiracy to keep the information hidden.

I had found one or two useful things, though, through a painful process of putting together scraps of information and constructing timelines from obfuscated statements and announcements. I'd get into it with Ronnie when I got to the office. But, first, I was going to savour an excellent croissant, with real butter and fine, English marmalade, and a perfect cappuccino that smelled like nectar must have smelled to the gods of ancient Greece.

Ronnie could wait. Murder could wait. This blissful moment could not.

Even though we only have three days?

Damn it, brain, won't you ever shut up?

Despite Dan Bridgeman's increasing interest in what we were doing for him, his parting shot after our visit had been, "You've got three days to wrap this up. After that, Mel's just going to have to make do with new shoes or a pony, like other girls."

It doesn't matter, I told myself, trying to recapture the mood. *We were going to keep on investigating after Mel dropped out and we'll keep on investigating after Bridgeman drops out. We won't be pressured by arbitrary deadlines. Neither Ronnie nor I are in it for the money.* Yet I drank down my coffee even though it was still hotter than I liked it, and I ate my croissant just a little faster than I might have.

Ronnie's car was parked in one of our spaces at the office. I felt the bonnet. It was cold. So, I wasn't too surprised to see him at the whiteboards. And I wasn't surprised that everything that was once on them had changed again. One of the boards had a line down the middle, with Armitage at one side and Kryou at the other. The other board had two timelines that stretched over a period of weeks, annotated in detail with the movements of both Armitage and Kryou. Heavy vertical bars marked the deaths of McKinley and Sanford.

Ronnie and I grunted greetings at one another. I went to look at the board with our two suspects on it. There seemed to be potted biographies under each name – Ronnie had obviously been researching them – but there was nothing much about Kryou's finances or his business activities.

"OK, do you want to hear what I found?" I asked, going to the cappuccino machine.

"Let me guess, you've been digging into the money side. I didn't bother because I knew you'd be into that."

"I reckon I got something.' He came and joined me, leaning on the counter while I worked. "First the Parkland Grove development. It was years getting approvals and doing feasibility studies and the like. Lots of local opposition but certain councillors were all for it. It's pretty big – shopping mall, a leisure complex, loads of new units, including a massive high-rise that will make the Q1 building look like a younger sibling, all at a price tag of over six billion dollars."

Ronnie whistled to show how impressed he was. "How does a little runt like Kryou get his snout into a trough like that?"

"'Specialist services' according to what I've read. It's all shrouded in obfuscation but, reading between the lines, Kryou helped with certain introductions, brought certain influential people to the party, and so on."

"You mean the corrupt little shit organised the bribes that got the local council and the state government on board."

"That's what it looks like. In return, they gave him a slice of the pie. But here's the rub. The funding for the various phases of the project falls due at particular milestones. They haven't needed masses of money yet because nothing's been built but that all changes with Phase Three, which starts in April. Then the consortium members need to cough up some very big money. I don't know but I'm guessing that Kryou has to put in a big chunk of cash, too, so he can keep his feet under the table."

"How big?"

"I just don't know. It would depend on what kind of deal he's done with the consortium. I wouldn't even know how to find that out."

"We hack him, or we break into his offices."

"Yeah, right, but, before you go all special forces on this one, there's more. I think I know where Kryou was planning to get the money. About two months ago, he was expecting a huge payout from one of his other projects – a hotel in Cairns. But it didn't happen. That freak, out-of-season cyclone – what was it? Albert? Andy? You know the one – it took out the hotel and half the infrastructure it relied on. And... there was a problem with the insurance. Like, he wasn't covered – at least, according to the local press."

"Fuck."

"Fuck, indeed. I can't be certain, but I think Nick Kryou is about twenty million dollars short of where he needs to be right now."

"Maybe more. Whatever he sunk into that hotel would have been borrowed from the banks. He's going to need to start paying that back – or at least find a nice big source of security. It explains why he can't just borrow the money he needs."

"So he definitely can't default on his Parkland Grove

commitments because that would be how he keeps the banks happy and manages to stay solvent. Unless he can get his hands on tens of millions of dollars in the next couple of months, Nick Kryou is going down the gurgler, big time."

I'd been laying out the documents I'd based my conclusions on and Ronnie had been leafing through them as we spoke. He raised a couple of sheets to me. "This is good work, Luke."

"It's mostly supposition and wishful thinking, actually. Not a scrap of what we have is what the courts would call evidence."

He just grinned and took the coffee I handed him. "There's an old Scottish saying: 'Many a mickle maks a muckle.'"

I blinked. "And that means?"

"It means, it all adds up. You're right, we haven't got a solid piece of evidence anywhere but what we have got is a plausible, coherent story that explains everything we know." He went and sat down. "Got any bikkies?" I found a half-empty packet in a cupboard and went to join him.

"And this is it," he said, chomping down on a Monte Carlo. He pulled a face and examined it. "Stale," he said, pushed the rest into his mouth and reached for another. "Right-o. A couple of years ago, Kryou and a bunch of other businessmen got together to have some fun speculating in the fine art market. They found a tame art professor to help them out and formed a little club. It went well for a while until the art professor got a bit up himself and they fell out. The enthusiasm waned and they lost interest in buying art but their little stash sat in a storage unit waiting for their investment to mature.

"Then one of them falls on hard times. In fact, he's in a

real bind. A freak cyclone has trashed his cash-flow and his path to a bright and mega-wealthy future is suddenly blocked. He starts looking around, desperate to raise a shitload of cash in a very short time. We can only suppose that one of the things he looks at in his desperation is the FABClub's pile of disappointingly-worthless daubings. He's probably thinking that if there's a hidden gem in there after all, he might be miraculously saved. He can't call McKinley. The man's a goody-two-shoes and anyway, if there was something there, McKinley has already failed to spot it. So he goes to number two on the list of Queensland's art specialists, just like you did, our boy Armitage. And in him, he finds a fellow sociopath with no moral compass and an unhealthy respect for filthy lucre.

"Probably, Kryou was thinking that, even if Armitage found nothing, they might be able to pull off some kind of scam, but Armitage does find something. He finds a painting worth at least, what, thirty million? Something like that. And then a new plan hatches.

"They can't just announce to the club that they've struck gold. Have you got any more of these?" He waved the empty biscuit bag at me. I shook my head. "Yeah, 'cause there's seven of them in the club and that's only four million and change each. Kryou needs twenty. He can't just nick the picture and sell it at an auction because a painting worth at much would attract international attention. It would be all over the news and one of the club members – McKinley in particular – might recognise it. If he sold it on the black market to some crook collector, he might only get a fraction of what it was worth.

"Then Kryou has a brainwave."

"Why Kryou? Why not Armitage?"

"Because only Kryou knows the terms of the tontine."

"It's not really a…"

Ronnie held up a finger to silence me. "So he makes a deal with Armitage. There are six murders to be done and the prize is thirty million bucks. So, Armitage does one or two and Kryou does the rest, meaning Kryou keeps the bulk of the proceeds."

"I know which painting it is," I said as the realisation hit me.

"Tell me in a minute. Obviously McKinley has to go first. He's the only one who might accidentally discover the true value of the painting. Equally obviously, Armitage has to do McKinley. Their plan is that every death will look like an accident or suicide and Armitage can see how it might be staged using the old shotgun that McKinley keeps on display in his office.

"Holy crap!" He sat bolt upright, spilling his coffee. "No-one's thought to check the cartridges."

"What? No. Surely the cops would have…" But would they? If McKinley had killed himself, he must have kept the gun loaded or have had a couple of shells in the case with it. But if McKinley was murdered, the killer would have had to bring cartridges, either because the gun was not loaded, or in case there was no ammo about.

I darted over to my desk where the piles of printout from yesterday were sitting. Somewhere in his credit card purchases there might be a record of him buying a box of shotgun cartridges.

"It won't be there," Ronnie said. "He's careful, right. There's no way he'd make a mistake like that."

But I scanned the printouts all the same. If I could just find it, we'd have our first piece of real evidence. I studied every line of every purchase before the day of the shooting. Then I studied them all over again. I looked up at Ronnie and he could see from my face that I'd found nothing.

"Told you. Anyway, once McKinley was dead and the police had decided it was suicide, it's Kryou's turn. The murder had gone off perfectly. There's one small fly in the ointment and that's us."

"Two small flies."

"So Kryou makes a call. He's probably used McGuire's services before, putting pressure on reluctant tenants, or whatever. So scaring us off doesn't seem like too big a deal. Then he gets on with whacking Sanford on the head and throwing him in the pool. And the cops are buying that one too. The plan is still going great except…"

"There's still those two flies in the ointment."

"It's starting to get messy for the killers now. We won't shut up and we won't die. The cops have re-opened the Sanford case and then that idiot McGuire puts you and me on the front page with a second botched assassination."

"What? We're on the front page? I didn't see anything?"

"It's in the Courier Mail. I suppose you only read The Guardian."

"Well… Yes. Have you got a copy?"

"In the car. Don't worry, the photographer got your good side."

"Wow! This could be good for business, hey?"

"Right, because people like hiring PIs who get shot at."

"No, no, because no publicity is bad publicity, yeah?"

He shook his head in dismay. "Come on. Let's go somewhere where I can get a snack."

I stood up to go and froze. "Shit! A snack! God, I nearly missed it." I dived back into the pile of credit card records and after an agonising age of searching, found it again. I held it up to show Ronnie.

"On the Saturday before McKinley's death, Scott Armitage bought a coffee and a pie at a servo in Aratula."

Ronnie looked confused. "And…?"

"Aratula. It's a small town on the New England Highway. It's a hundred, maybe a hundred and fifty kilometres south of where he lives. What was Armitage doing out there? What possible reason could he have for a long drive into rural Australia just then?"

"I don't know. A family outing?"

"What do you find out in the country that you don't find here in the city?"

"Jeez, I don't know, mate. Cows? What's your point?"

"I think he was on an outing to find a shop that sold shotgun ammo."

Ronnie considered it. "You can buy ammo in Brissy. Why go all that way?"

"What? Why would anyone sell ammo in a major city?"

"I don't know, 'cause nut jobs like to go out and shoot things at the weekend?"

"Huh." It was a surprise but, on the other hand, "because nut jobs" explained most of what was weird about modern life. "Anyway, Armitage is a sly bastard. His first instinct is to hide his activity and cover his tracks. Anything here in the city would seem to risky. There'd be CCTV. Someone might recognise him. I don't know. It just feels like something he'd have done."

Ronnie looked unconvinced. "OK, so he's out prowling the countryside looking for ammo – which we know he must have bought with cash because the purchase isn't in the records we have. Why did he pay for his snack at Aratula with a credit card?"

"He slipped up. He's only human. He made a mistake. Probably did it without thinking. Who uses cash these days?"

"I do."

"Right! Old people and crims."

Ronnie scowled. "All right, maybe you're onto something. So what? How many gun shops are down that road? How many hardware shops? Produce shops? It could be a lot. And it was a couple of months ago. Do you think anyone would remember Armitage after all that time?"

"Jeez, mate, I don't know. I just had the idea."

"Well—"

We both stopped and turned at the sound of the office door being pushed open. Detective Sergeant Bronski and two uniformed cops came striding in.

"Ronald Walker," Bronski said, in a no-nonsense voice. "I'd like you to accompany me to the station to answer questions about your involvement in the death of Morgan Sanford."

Ronnie sighed and rolled his eyes. "OK," he said and got to his feet. "No probs." To me he said, "Call Terry and tell him I'm with the Keystone Cops. Meanwhile, you should pursue that new lead, OK?"

"Yeah, no worries," I said. I spoke to his back as he was already being led out of the office.

For a while, I sat there blinking at the empty doorway. Then I pulled out my phone and found the lawyer's number. *I need this on speed dial*, I thought.

* * * *

The New England Highway, despite proclaiming itself "The

National Highway" on billboards along the way, was mostly a two lane country road with passing places here and there. It was a bumpy road, with a noisy surface, and, for kilometres at a stretch, a quilt of patches and repairs. By the time I reached Aratula, I was already sick of it. I found the service station Armitage had used on the opposite side of the road – meaning, I reckoned, he'd gone there on the way back from wherever he'd been. I pulled in and went to the shop and restaurant area. I bought a coffee and a pie and flashed my photo of Armitage at the teenage girl behind the counter. Her eyes lit up when I told her I was a PI on a case and she took it out to the back and showed it around. However, nobody remembered him, which I took to be a dismal omen.

My plan was to stop at each town on the highway that had a population at least the size of its post-code. Since Queensland post-codes are four digits and start with a '4', Aratula itself didn't qualify – by about an order of magnitude. I called Ronnie from the car park and got his answering service. I left a message asking him to call me to let me know how it had gone with the cops.

When I left, heading roughly South, the road rose into the Great Dividing Range and for a while I drove through beautiful hills and dense forest, with tantalising glimpses of magnificent views that I daren't stare at because the road became increasingly winding and difficult. Eventually I got stuck behind a group of big trucks grinding their way slowly up and then down the steep slopes. It gave me more time to enjoy the scenery but my pleasure was paid for in frustration. At the other side of the hills, the road levelled out again and the speed picked up but it was still a long, tedious drive through endless monoculture farmland before I reached Warwick. This was a town big enough to have several shops that sold shotgun ammo and I wasted a good hour going round them all with absolutely nothing to show for it. The risk of missing some little shop selling hardware or animal feed that might also sell ammo kept me poring over Google far longer than I should have.

Beyond Warwick, the drive was more interesting but the road was in worse condition. I was getting tired and it was well past lunchtime. The sheer lack of any towns on the highway big enough to be worth investigating was a surprise to me – although I suppose it shouldn't have been. Sixty kilometres ahead of me was the country town of Stanthorpe and, another sixty beyond that was Tenterfied. By then I'd have driven about three hundred kilometres and crossed the state border into New South Wales. I decided that, if I didn't find anything in Tenterfield, I'd give up.

Signs of habitation and roadside retail outlets heralded the approach to Stanthorpe. My first order of business was to find a place to have a feed. The speed limit dropped and the road became dual carriageway. The turning into the town was on my left but, just as I got there, I noticed a place on my right that looked so much like the storage facility I'd visited with Kryou that I did a double-take. Rows of storage units behind a high wire-link fence. I was so taken with the finding that I almost missed my turning. I pulled off the road as soon as I could and began searching on my phone. It was, indeed, a storage facility – managed by an estate agent in the town. I don't know why it was so interesting to me at the time, it felt like some kind of synchronicity, I suppose. I was so taken with it, I almost went to the agent to see if Armitage had a unit there. But common sense prevailed. There was absolutely no reason why he should or why I'd find anything interesting there if he had. Even so, I made a note of the address, the agent's address, and the enquiries phone number.

Lunch was an excellent pizza in a very Italian little restaurant. There were even people – half-a-dozen tiny, dark-skinned old ladies – sitting at another table speaking Italian as they ate cake. I asked the waitress where I could buy ammo in the town and she looked at me as if I had just confessed my plan to conduct a mass murder at the local school. So I explained what it was all about and she gave up waitressing on the spot and sat down with me at the table to hear more. I showed her Armitage's photo on the off-chance he had been in there but she didn't recognise him. In the end, she was asking me far more questions than I was asking her and it was quite a struggle to get away. She even suggested we get together for a drink later. It didn't occur to me that she might be coming on to me until I was in the car, driving away.

See? I told Ronnie in my head. *I'm not obsessed with sex. It was the last thing on my mind.* However, after that, I couldn't stop kicking myself for being such an idiot because she really had been very cute.

The first place I tried was a hardware store, just up the road. There was a gun shop nearby and I planned to walk over there next. It was a small place, with curious items for sale – sacks of animal food, chainsaws, piping and pumps, wheelbarrows, agricultural chemicals, ride-on mowers – things I might never buy in my whole life but which were obviously central to the lives of many locals. And there, in a locked cabinet beside the counter, was a display of ammunition. I wished I had Ronnie with me because, judging by the huge variety in types and sizes, ammunition was clearly a more complicated matter than I had previously suspected.

"Yeah, mate," said a man at my elbow. He wore the shop's logo on his shirt and he had the dusty appearance of someone who man-handled sacks of alpaca food for a living.

"G'day," I said. I don't know why. It wasn't something I'd normally say. I'd just caught the mood of the place, I suppose. The shop guy didn't bat an eyelid and I hurried on. "I'm looking for a bloke who might have been in here to buy ammo a few weeks ago."

"You a cop?"

"No, I'm a private investigator." I reached for my card but thought better of it. "Systematic Doubt" raised enough eyebrows in the city. Out here in the country, it would be an embarrassment. Maybe that's how Ronnie felt about it all the time. "I'm from Brisbane," I said, as if it explained something. I pulled out Armitage's picture and showed it to him. "This is the bloke. Do you, or maybe one of the others here, remember seeing him? His name is Armitage and he'd have bought shotgun cartridges for a – a shotgun."

He studied the picture for a very long time. Then he said, "I'll go ask Steve." He took the picture and disappeared through a side door. I waited, browsing a shelf of pet care products until another man appeared from the side door holding Armitage's picture and a hard-cover notebook.

"How are ya? How ya doin'?" he asked.

"I'm good. Are you Steve?"

"Steve? Nah, mate."

"OK. Have you seen that bloke?"

"Yeah, reckon. Came in a few weeks ago." My heart thumped. "I remember him 'cause he was asking about shotgun ammo but I reckon he didn't know one end of a gun from the other. Which is odd, like, 'cause you can't buy ammo without a firearms licence. So you'd think he'd know what gauge his own gun was."

"Did you check his licence?"

"Dead right! Looked like a townie. No offence. Reckoned he was up to something."

"And?" *Please tell me you wrote down his name,* I pleaded in my head.

He looked at me steadily. "And you're a private investigator."

I didn't get his point for a moment. "Right! Yes!" I pulled out my licence and handed it to him. *Another townie, probably up to something.* "As you can see," I added, to speed up his long study of my credentials. "I'm licensed to conduct investigations within the State of Queensland."

He nodded and handed the license back. "I've never met a private investigator. I always thought they were, like, just on the telly."

"Nope. It's a real thing." He seemed about to start asking me about my work so I cut him off with, "Am I right in thinking you made a record of Mr. Armitage's purchase?" I pointed at the notebook.

He grinned and tapped his nose. "Copied his details from the firearms license he showed me."

"Can I take a look?"

"His name wasn't Armitage," he said. "I knew there was something shifty about that bloke. What's he done?"

Not Armitage? Damn! If he had used a fake license… a false name… I reached for the book. "May I look?"

He looked disappointed that I wasn't going to share more, but he opened the book anyway and turned back a handful of pages. He showed me the entry. In a round, legible hand, he had written. "1 case 12 gage ammo. Sold to…"

My heard leapt again and I broke into a smile. "Can I get a photocopy of this?"

He thought about it and said, "Yeah, reckon."

"And he told you his name was Nicholas Kryou?"

"Showed me his driving licence."

"Did he now?" I could have hugged the man.

Maybe he thought I would because he hurried off to the little office behind the counter, saying, "I'll get you that copy."

* * * *

On the road from Stanthorpe back to the highway, I called Ronnie. He picked up.

"Are you OK?" I asked.

"Yeah, no worries."

"I thought they might arrest you."

"Nah, even Marr isn't that daft. She's got nothing and she knows it. She was just fishing."

"Well, I've got something. Something fantastic."

I told him what I'd found in Stanthorpe. He made appropriately appreciative noises.

"So, we've got evidence of collusion between Kryou and Armitage to illegally procure ammunition to be used in the commission of a crime," I said, liking the way it sounded.

"You got the make and manufacturer of the shells did you? Batch number? That kind of thing?"

"What? Er…"

"The exact time and date of the sale?"

"I got the date…"

"Was there any in-store CCTV footage from that day?"

I swung the car around in a U-turn. "I've just done a U-ie and I'll be back there in five minutes."

I called him again after I'd gone back to the shop and gathered every last detail I could.

"OK. Got it all. They only keep their CCTV recordings for a month so we're out of luck there. However, I got the name and address of the bloke who served Armitage and he says he'd be happy to tell the cops the man in the picture was the man who presented himself as Nick Kryou."

"That'll have to do."

"People here are incredibly friendly, you know. I can't believe how much trouble they all went to. I think I'm going to retire here."

"Yeah? They probably wouldn't have been so helpful if they'd known that was going to happen."

"Funny. But this is good, right? This is real, solid evidence, hey?"

"Yeah, don't go wetting your panties just yet. It's good but it will only be what we need if forensics can match the shot in McKinley's body and wall to the particular cartridges Armitage bought. I reckon a flash lawyer could do a lot with any scrap of doubt about that."

"So we take this to the cops?"

I could feel his reluctance. "Reckon. Can't see what else to do with it. At the very least, it should get the McKinley case re-opened."

He was nowhere near as excited about all this as I'd hoped. A heavy weight of disappointment settled on me. "OK, I'll see you when I get back, hey? Should be two or three hours."

"Right-o. Come round to my place and I'll give you a feed. Maggie brought me a lasagne that would feed a regiment. Good grub, though."

I hung up just as I arrived at the highway. The storage place was exactly opposite me, row upon row of blue metal sheds with cream doors, standing behind a high fence topped with barbed wire. On impulse, I crossed the road and drove around to the side where the entrance gate was. I got out and looked around. There was no front office or double rings of fencing as with the place in Brisbane. This was a much more humble affair, with a simple padlock and, from what I could see, a single security camera watching the gate. Even though we were just a few kilometres from the town centre, the area surrounding the facility was all country lanes and farmland.

What the hell are you doing here? I asked myself. It was like some kind of obsessive behaviour. Just because I'd checked out one storage place, didn't mean I had to check them all. Angry with myself, I got back in the car and drove back to the highway and then home without stopping.

Chapter Eighteen

Chelsea wasn't there when I woke up the next day. Last night, home late from Ronnie's and exhausted, I'd dreaded going to sleep because I might feel her ghostly presence once again in the bed when I woke. Yet, for all the pain these strange echoes of her caused, I was sad when it didn't happen. It was awful to know that, one day, I'd stop feeling her next to me in bed, I'd never hear her voice again when I spoke to her at the cemetery, and she'd be gone. Completely gone. And I'd have lost her for good.

I took my breakfast out onto the balcony as I had done the day before but I couldn't recapture the blissful mood of yesterday. My croissant was just bread, my coffee was just a drink, and I finished both as quickly as I could and drove in to the office.

"Are you still good with the plan?" Ronnie asked as I made my way to the cappuccino machine. This time there was no new material on the whiteboards. All that was new was the packet of evidence I'd gathered in Stanthorpe, sitting on my desk.

We'd talked about Ronnie's plan until far too late in the night. It wasn't much of a plan, as far as I was concerned. He was going to confront Armitage, tell him everything we knew, show him the documentary proof we had, and persuade him to come with us to the cops. The idea was that Armitage would make a deal to save himself by turning on Kryou. It all seemed to hinge on Ronnie's assessment of Armitage's character.

"He's a narcissist," Ronnie had argued. "All he thinks about is how wonderful he is. Once we put it to him that he doesn't deserve to be locked up for this, that Kryou is the real villain, he'll find himself in total agreement. After all, he's the good guy, here – in his own mind, anyway."

"Do public prosecutors here do that kind of deal? Could he really bargain his way out of jail?"

"Not a cat in Hell's chance! But he doesn't know that. Everyone's idea of how the justice system works is based on what they see on American TV shows. Shit, people even dial 911 when they should be dialling triple zero! I used to get people asking me what 'precinct' I worked at, and telling me to back off because they knew their 'Miranda rights'. One guy wanted to talk to the 'District Attorney' before he'd tell me anything."

It still seemed like a massive risk to me. If we told Armitage what we knew, what would there be to stop him saying, "Thank you very much," and catching the first flight to a non-extradition country? But we'd had this discussion round and round, so I told Ronnie I was still OK with the plan.

"When do you want to go?" I asked.

"Oh, no rush," he said, smiling a fake smile. "I thought we'd sit around here for half an hour watching you drink that coffee before we did anything useful."

I gritted my teeth, switched off the machine, picked up the packet of evidence and we left.

As we neared the car park for the Creative Industries department at UQ, a cop car passed us, going the other way. Behind it was a big, blue Range Rover with DI Marr at the wheel and Bronski beside her. She didn't notice us, even when I almost ran up the kerb.

"What the hell are they doing here?" Ronnie growled.

"Armitage wasn't with them," I said. I'd made a point of looking in both cars as they passed. "They haven't arrested him."

I parked and started to get out. Ronnie put a hand on my arm.

"Just a sec. Let's think about this." I settled back in my seat. "Armitage is part of the McKinley investigation, not Sanford. Marr's position – as of my interview yesterday – was that the two are unconnected and that McKinley is still a suicide. So why is she here, talking to Armitage?"

I started speaking but he carried on. "The only thing that connects Armitage to Sanford is the FABClub – through McKinley. So, what changed, since yesterday, to make DI Marr take that connection seriously?"

Again I opened my mouth but again he pressed on. "It was you."

"What?"

"It was your visit to Stanthorpe. Somehow, going there and asking questions triggered this. Do you think you were followed?"

"Followed? No. I mean... I didn't take any particular precautions. Why should I? But... No, I'd have noticed, surely." I remembered that, during our pursuit of Chelsea's murderer, Ronnie had followed me around Brisbane for half a day without me suspecting a thing. "Why would they do that?"

"Maybe they didn't. You need to call your contact at the ammo shop right now and find out what happened. If someone went in there after you asking questions, we need to know who it was."

"What, now?"

"Yes, now. Or have you got something else planned?"

I pulled out my phone and delved into my notes, extracting the phone number of the bloke in the hardware store. I made the call through the car so Ronnie could hear it. A woman in the office picked up and it was about five minutes, that felt like thirty, before they found the man I'd spoken with.

"How are you doing?" he asked.

"I'm good. Look, did someone else come into your shop yesterday asking about Armitage?"

"Nah, mate. Just the cops."

"The cops? What did they want?"

"Well, I called them."

"Why? Why would you do that?"

"Well, we all got to talking about what you said and Mike – he's the manager – he said we had a duty to report this Armitage fella to the cops because, you know, he committed a fraud. I said we should call you and ask whether we should but you didn't leave us a number." I remembered reaching for my card and thinking better of it. *Jesus Christ! That bloody stupid name!*

"I'm in the book," I said, plaintively.

"Not in the Granite Belt Informer," he said, winning the point. No, I was not in their local phone book. This was all my fault.

"So you called the cops?"

"Yes, we did. Next thing we knew there was a lady

287

Detective Inspector from Brisbane chewing Mike's ear off for interfering with a police investigation. She said we never should have talked to you at all."

"Yeah, well, that's all bullshit. She's just worried that her arse is going to need covering because she's made a complete cock-up of this investigation. Look, I'm sorry you had to deal with her. I should have left you a number. Did she say anything else? About Armitage, I mean."

"Nah, mate, just that she'd be dealing with this now and I shouldn't talk to you again."

"Right. Well, thanks."

"No worries, mate."

After the call ended, Ronnie said, "You didn't leave your number?"

"I was going to but…"

He shook his head, sadly. "So now DI Marr knows that Armitage bought some shotgun ammo, using Nick Kryou's firearms licence and ID. I think we can safely assume she can connect the dots to McKinley's so-called suicide and the FABClub. She's probably running through every conversation she ever had with us, she's re-read all our statements, and she's rushing the new information through forensics to see if the cartridges Armitage bought are a match to the ones that killed McKinley. She's having a road to Damascus moment and not liking it one bit, I reckon. Right now, she's kicking herself for not having listened to what we said but, real soon, she's going to start deciding we deliberately misled her and hid evidence from her."

"What?"

"Come on. You know none of this is going to be her fault."

He was right, of course. Marr needed a scapegoat or two

and we were the perfect choice.

"But," he said. "As usual, she's screwed this up. She could have been the one that turned Armitage and got him to finger Kryou but she still doesn't know the half of it."

"Like what?"

"Like stuff we've deduced that she'll take forever to catch up with. Like that Armitage killed McKinley and Kryou killed Sanford. I'll bet you she's gone blundering in there to tell Armitage that she's onto him but the fact that she hasn't arrested him means he and Kryou are still free to use that to their advantage."

"But what can they do? Even Marr will work it all out in time. She's got the link between Armitage and Kryou now, the link between both of them and McKinley, as well as the link between both of them and the weapon in the McKinley murder."

"Well, what would you do if you were the killer? Bear in mind that you're sitting on a very portable asset worth tens of millions of dollars?"

"You think they're going to run for it?"

"They're both smart guys. I'm sure they've got a contingency plan."

"Shit! We need to get up there to Armitage right now. Maybe we can still persuade him to dob in Kryou."

Ronnie pointed out the window. "We might just be a bit late."

A man had emerged from the Creative Industries building and was hurrying across the street to the car park. Ronnie slid down low in his seat and so did I. It was Armitage. He had a bag stuffed to overflowing with stuff, as if he'd thrown together everything from his office he couldn't bear to leave behind. He looked around anxiously and dashed to his car, throwing the bag in the boot. He reversed out of his parking space so fast that the car rocked on its suspension. Then he sat there for a few seconds – probably to get over the scare he'd just given himself – before he drove off at a more moderate speed.

I started the car, meaning to go after him.

"No need to follow him," Ronnie said.

"What? Why?"

"We know where he's going, don't we?"

Home to get his passport and pack a bag? But then where? The airport? It took me a second but I got there. "The storage place at Coorparoo. He needs the painting."

"Off we go, then."

* * * *

We took about fifteen minutes to get from the Gardens Point campus to the MyVault secure storage facility in Coorparoo. If Armitage had, indeed, gone home first to pack, we'd easily have time to get in there and stake out the storage unit with the fish logo on it. However, getting in there would be an issue.

I pulled up in front of the office and we went in to talk to the bloke on duty. He didn't seem too impressed with my PI credentials.

"Mate, you'd be surprised how often I get PIs in here – and cops and journos. They all want to take a look at someone's private stuff. But, you know what? I never let them. Not without a warrant. You got a warrant?"

Ronnie pulled out his wallet and began casually counting the notes inside.

"Don't even think about it," the man said. "Even if you

had a million dollars in there, there are so many security cameras watching us right now, I wouldn't show the slightest interest."

"Perhaps you'd be more interested if we went to my car?" Ronnie said. "We're having engine trouble. Maybe we could look under the bonnet together?"

"Look," I said, scowling at Ronnie. "We're all here to stop crimes being committed, not to join the criminal fraternity. Is that the only way in or out of this storage place?" I pointed to the gate that Ronnie and I had just driven through.

"Yeah," the bloke said. "It's part of the secure design of the facility. Single point of access and egress."

But I was no longer listening to him. A silver Mercedes had just pulled out of one of the inner gates and was moving slowly towards the exit.

"Fuck!" I said and Ronnie looked too.

"Is that Nick Kryou's car?" he asked me.

"Yeah," the bloke behind the counter answered. "He came in a few minutes ago to pick something up."

I ran for the door but Ronnie didn't. "Did he say where he was going?"

"Taking a holiday? Taking a break? Something like that."

"Come on," I said, holding the door open. "We need to get after him."

"Anything else?" Ronnie asked. "Any suggestion he was going overseas? That kind of thing?"

The security guy scrunched up his face in concentration. "Nah. He asked where the servos were around here. Said he had a long drive ahead of him and he needed to fill up."

"Can we go now?"

Ronnie thanked the bloke and sauntered after me.

I ran ahead to get the car started, calling out the window,

"What the hell are you doing? Come on."

"Calm down," Ronnie said, climbing into the passenger seat. "We can't follow him."

"Why not?"

"Because he'll be looking out for a tail and he'll spot us. We'd need a whole bunch of cars to pull it off."

"But you followed me once. You're good at it. You've been trained."

"Yes, I have. And that's why I'm telling you, if your mark is watching for a tail, one car isn't enough." I began objecting that we'd definitely lose him forever if we didn't do something right now but he cut me off. "Listen, the chances are good he's not leaving the country – not right away, anyway. He's got something else planned. Something where the cops won't stop him at the airport with a stolen painting in his possession. We just need to work it out."

I was hyped up on adrenaline, ready for a chase, so I made an effort to calm myself down and focus on the problem. Where would Kryou go to lie low for a while? How long would he need to be away? How would he get himself and the picture out of the country? At the very least he'd need to arrange for it to be safely packed and ready to travel. That would be true whatever he did, whether he posted it, or took it with him on a plane, or a boat, or whatever. He was going to need hours at the minimum, maybe days to arrange something. And that would need a hotel, or a friend's house. Or...

"Kryou has a firearms license. He already owns a shotgun."

Ronnie gave me a look half curiosity and half irritation.

"It's quite hard to get a licence," I explained. "The bloke at the shop was explaining the conditions and the length of time it took. But Kryou's already got one." Ronnie was flicking through screens on his phone. "But the easiest way to get a shotgun license…"

"Would be if he had a rural property."

"Bingo! And we know where that is."

"We do? Of course we do!"

He pulled the envelope of evidence against Armitage from the glove box and pulled out the photocopies of the firearms licence. The image showed a small plastic card, quite similar to a Queensland driver's licence, with Kryou's photo on it and the class of gun he was allowed to own. Attached to that sheet was another, with the image of the back of the card. Like a driver's license, this one had the licensee's address on the back.

He went back to his phone. "Do you know a place called Amiens?"

"What, like the World War One battle in France?"

"Nah, mate, in Oz. It looks like it's down south near that place you went to look for ammo shops."

"What, near Stanthorpe? That's where Kryou's property is? Bloody hell. That's why he sent Armitage down there to buy shells. 'Cause he knew the place. And his license wouldn't look out of place. Damn! And you know what else there is down there?"

Ronnie was studying a map on his phone. "An airport for a start. What else?"

"A storage place just like the one we're sitting in – only smaller."

Ronnie put his phone down. "So, Kryou has a hideout, out in the sticks but close to an airport and a storage facility. If the cops don't know where he is – and I'm betting there's no record of this place at his office or his home – he could probably sit it out there until he's made a deal to sell the painting, then hire a plane to take him anywhere he likes to offload it and collect his money. After that he'd just slip out of the country."

"And Armitage?"

"Probably meeting him at the hideout. He'd want to be with him to collect his cut of the sale. Also, Kryou might need him to make the right contacts."

I picked up my own phone and began typing a search. "It's a Rauschenberg."

"What is?"

"The painting. I told you I knew which one it was. Armitage made a big show of telling me how worthless it was. It made Kryou really mad at the time but I thought he was just grumpy about other stuff. Then I realised it was because Armitage was having a bit of fun at my expense."

"So what's a… what?"

I pulled up an image and showed it to him. It was a print, very much like the one I'd seen in the FABClub collection. "A Rauschenberg. This one sold at auction a couple of years ago for twenty-eight million dollars."

"US or Aussie?"

"Aussie. But this one might well fetch more. Let's call it a round thirty million."

"And Kryou needs twenty. That is, he needed twenty. All that has gone by the board now the cops are onto him. Even if they can't pin Sanford's murder on him, or get him for conspiracy to murder McKinley, there's no way he can go on knocking off FABClub members now. No-one would believe accidental deaths or suicides after this."

"Which means he can't get the painting by inheriting it and he can't save his investment in Parkland Grove. I guess he must really hate us."

"Oh yeah. It might have been just business last time he tried to knock you off but I reckon it'd be very, very personal if he tries again."

It was not a pleasant thought but not as scary as it probably should have been. Maybe I was getting used to working with sociopaths. "So... Our work here is done."

"Pardon?"

"I mean, we just tell the cops where Kryou and Armitage are, they swoop in, and Bob's your uncle."

"No way!"

"Yes, way! What do you think we can possibly do now? They're holed up in a remote shack in Woop-Woop and we know Kryou has at least one shotgun. I know you have insane visions of us creeping through the night with infra-red goggles and... and rappelling ropes, to make some kind of dramatic citizen's arrest, but that's just the incipient senility talking. The reality is, you're a pensioner who's into dog shows and I'm a philosopher with a weird phobia about getting my head blown off. Let me explain this as clearly as I can; we need to go to the cops because anything else is stupid."

Ronnie's face set into a scowl and my heart sank. "Picture this," he said. "DI Marr gets a visit from her two favourite private dicks. They tell her all about respectable Brisbane business identity, Nick Kryou who, desperate for a steaming heap of money, and with the help of a foppish art teacher, has set about murdering other business folk to get his hands on a very valuable painting. 'How do you know the painting's valuable?' the incisive Detective Inspector asks. 'Oh it must be,' we say, 'or the rest of it wouldn't make any sense.' 'And where's your proof of its value?' asks the Detective. 'Oh, we have no proof,' we say. 'We just feel it in our bones.' 'Good enough for me,' says Marr and sends us on our way. Now, normally, DI Marr would just go back to knitting socks, or whatever she does all day, but because we've raised some pretty substantial suspicions about Armitage, she sets her knitting aside and phones the Stanthorpe police. She asks them to take a look at an address in Amiens to see if there's a couple of shifty-looking blokes hiding under the bed there. They report that there was no-one home. Meanwhile, our two murderers, thanking DI Marr in their hearts for the handy tip-off, disappear into the night, never to be seen again."

"All right," I snapped, irritated that it was a disturbingly plausible scenario. "So what are we going to do?"

He grinned at me. "Well, first, we find a pub and get some lunch." It was still early but I let it pass. "Then we fill up your tank and drive down to Stanthorpe for a little vacation."

I closed my eyes and took a long breath.

"Luke, mate, I don't know exactly what we're going to do. Not yet. But I know what we're not going to do. We are not going to let two cold-blooded killers go free. Not while there's a chance in hell we can stop them."

Chapter Nineteen

The drive to Stanthorpe was long and tedious, the quick hop over the hills of the Scenic Rim being the one break in a seemingly endless series of flat roads and farmland.

"Chelsea always said farms were deserts," I said, breaking yet another long spell of silence. "All of this was beautiful forest, teeming with life, not so long ago. Then the farmers clear-felled everything and left this desert in its place – nothing, as far as the eye can see except grass and food crops, all poisoned regularly so nothing can live there."

"Yeah, those bastards. How dare they feed everybody?"

"I'm just saying, it gives you a different perspective on farming and country living."

"I can feel my mind expanding with every word you speak."

"You're a miserable old bastard. Why can't you just have a normal conversation like anybody else? Why do you have to be so confrontational?"

"Why do you have to start every deep and meaningful conversation with, 'Chelsea always used to say...'? Don't you have any original thoughts?"

That shut me up. I liked to think of myself as a thinker. I was a doctor of philosophy for heaven's sake! But Chelsea was the one who thought more about real life – social issues, politics, human relationships, where our food comes from, what our lifestyle does to the planet, how we take so much for granted. She made me realise that I had spent my life studying abstractions, many of which didn't really connect all that well with real life as we live it. And, since she died, I had thought more and more about the things she'd said, things that had been striking enough at the time but which I had failed to give the consideration I now saw they deserved.

"To be honest," I said. "I don't think I do. I mean, leaving aside the issue of whether any of us ever has a truly original thought. I think I've spent a lot of my life skating on the surface of things."

Ronnie was quiet for a long time. Then he said, "Do you want some music?"

It was a deliberate provocation. Ronnie and I could never agree on what kind of music to play and he always preferred silence to anything I liked.

"What the hell is wrong with you?" I demanded, growing angry. "I was conceding your point. You can't even win an argument now without being obnoxious?"

His jaw set and he breathed out through his nose. "Here's the thing. I agree. Life is shit. But so what? Nobody cares except a few bleeding heart liberals who get all choked up about koalas going extinct. If anyone cared, they'd do something about it. They'd stop eating meat, they'd vote Green, they'd ban live exports. But they don't. They like meat. They like exports. They hate self-righteous pricks who don't want them to exploit their own country and live high on the hog for as long as they can. So the system that generates massive food waste and grows more crops for animal fodder than for human consumption goes on. It goes on and prospers with the blessing of the whole damned country.

"So what good does it do for you to sit there maundering on about monoculture deserts and lamenting the poor, dead sugar gliders? Absolutely no good at all. You're not doing anything to change things. You're not coming up with ideas. You're not even raising anybody's awareness. So what are you doing? You're indulging yourself. You're making yourself feel more virtuous. You're pretending you're on the side of the Angels but you're doing nothing except pissing me off.

"So why don't you save all that self-serving bullshit for your blog, or your memoirs, or your social justice warrior Facebook groups, and just focus on things that you are willing and able to actually do something about? Like catching killers. You want my views on agriculture in Australia? I don't give a fuck. Nobody gives a fuck. Nothing I say or do or think or weep over is going to make a scrap of difference. So I'm not going to waste my time on it. You want to put an end to the system that leads to all that waste and destruction? Change human nature. If you can't do that, just shut the fuck up and let me think about the things that actually matter."

I drove in stunned silence. Ronnie's outburst had shocked me in all kinds of ways. For a start, I'd never have guessed he knew anything about any of all that. For another, his critique of my impotent middle-class angst about the environment was disturbingly near the knuckle. Chelsea had actually done things. She had stopped eating meat. She did vote Green. Me? Well I just didn't have the strength of will to put my money where my mouth was and keep it there consistently. On top of that, Ronnie's obvious belief that there was nothing to do about any of the ills that plagued the world because it was basically "human nature" to crap in your own nest, was depressingly difficult to argue against. What was even worse, his view made it a kind of pragmatic, psychological problem, not a philosophical one at all. And there were other ramifications. Was I wrong to be concerned? Had Chelsea been wrong? Was I wrong to think I was thinking more deeply about real life now than I used to? Maybe I was just skating off into new and equally shallow waters, not plumbing the depths at all.

"All right, I'll shut up," I said, gloomily.

"Good 'cause I don't want to have to start slapping you around. We're coming up to Warwick. That's just about sixty K from this Amiens place. I reckon we'll find a place to stay here. Stanthorpe's too small. They might spot us."

"Fine."

"Oh for God's sake, don't sulk. Look, you've been doing great on this case. You've done some good work. We're only here, now, because of you. So don't spoil it all by being a prat. This is the end game, mate. Just stay focused and we'll put both those ratbags behind bars. All right?" Before I could answer, he started giving me directions to a motel – a smart little place close to the town centre. We took two rooms. Ronnie and I didn't even have the debate about it any more. After a year of working together, he just accepted that I would not budge on having my own room and that was that.

Lying on my bed, staring endlessly at yet another strange ceiling as the daylight faded away, I asked myself for the ten thousandth time if it was all worth it. Of course, the answer would be yes – as it had been ten thousand times in a row – but the past few days had been pretty intense and I was emotionally wrung out. It wasn't the two attempts on my life, the beating, the disruption and dislocation. It wasn't even the constant sparring with Ronnie, the frustrations of being harassed by the cops, the never-ending anxiety, or the frequent social awkwardness of having to question people who resented being suspected of crimes. Of course, it was all that, too, but the worst thing was the endless insecurity, the knowledge that I wasn't actually very good at this and yet people's lives literally depended on me getting it right. Lately – maybe ever since Chelsea had died – I felt like I was doing Life wrong, that I sucked at being an adult and the other adults could all see it. It wasn't just my job – although my choice of career alone would probably keep a therapist busy for years – it was everything about me. And Ronnie, God help me, Ronnie had become my closest friend, my teacher and my guide. And we didn't even like each other. We were just, sort of, co-dependent. I fed his need for redemption for a life I daren't even ask too much about, and he fed my need to be something more than the hollow creature I'd found wandering in the ruins of my life with Chelsea.

And there it was. The knock at the door. Ronnie wanting to go to a pub to eat and drink and plan our next move. For a moment, I stubbornly resisted it. I fought the impulse to be drawn back into the fray, to re-engage with that dour and dangerous man but, at the second knock, I got up and answered the call.

* * * *

"Nice place," I said, looking around at the pub. "Sort of old fashioned. The kind of thing you don't see in Brissy any more." I hadn't noticed the name as we entered but I doubted I'd ever be back.

"Yeah," Ronnie said, pushing away his plate. I pushed

mine – still half-untouched – towards him without waiting for him to ask. "It's no wonder you're so fucking scrawny," he said, by way of thank you.

"So, what do we do now?" I asked. Although we knew where Armitage and Kryou were staying, we couldn't just barge in on them and make an arrest. They weren't actually wanted for anything. And, although we knew they were probably planning to flee the country, sell a stolen painting worth millions and avoid justice for two murders, there was nothing we could do about it.

I had to wait for Ronnie to stop stuffing his face before he replied. "We break into their shed at that storage place we passed on the way in."

"What?" As usual, he'd managed to surprise me. "Why? And how do we even know they've got one and, if they do, which one it is?"

"They've got one, all right. I called the estate agent that manages the place."

"What, and they just told you?"

"Not quite. I pretended to be Kryou. I said I needed to rent a second unit but I wanted it as close to my first one as possible. By the time we'd finished discussing what they had available and where, the nice lady on the phone had said the number of the one I wanted to find at least a dozen times. I didn't even have to pretend I'd forgotten the number. Piece of cake."

"Wow, if the private investigation business gets boring, you could make a mint running phishing operations for hacker collectives."

He ignored me. "We'll go when it's good and dark – about nine o'clock?"

"You know it will never be really dark there? It's right next to the highway and that junction is all lit up at night."

"That's why we'll be going in from the back." I tried to remember what was around the storage facility fence. Nothing much, as far as I recalled. If there was a farmhouse at the back, it was far enough away that no-one would see us.

"How do we cut through the fence?"

"With bolt cutters."

"Which we haven't got."

"Actually… While you were watching the porn channel and pleasuring yourself, I took a drive out from the motel and found the local Bunnings. I bought a few things we might need. They're in the back of the car. The receipt's in the bag for my expenses claim."

I blinked at him, not knowing where to start. The fact that he'd borrowed my car? The fact that I hadn't noticed? Or his tendency to buy stuff on expenses without agreeing it first? "I wasn't watching porn," was what came out of my mouth. "I was reflecting on my life."

He grinned at me and winked. "Is that what you kids are calling it now? Anyway, we're all good to go."

I took a deep breath, trying to re-focus. "OK. Do you want to tell me why we're breaking into Kryou's storage unit?"

"To steal his painting." He held up a hand to stop me spluttering all over him. "Think about it. There's still a small chance the cops will find his property at Amiens. If they do, there's a small chance they'll go there with a warrant. If they did that, they might just find his precious painting. And, don't forget, he's on the run now and that painting is all that stands between him and penury. If he gets busted and does time, it's his insurance for his old age. I can't see Kryou being happy about a future where he's living on a state pension, can you?

So, he'll hide it, somewhere where the cops won't think to look, and where he can keep it hidden for many, many years if he has to."

"So the painting's sitting in a storage unit in Stanthorpe. And we're going to steal it. Because…?"

"Because then Kryou and Armitage can't leave." He gave a little shrug. "And maybe I can think of some way to use it as bait in a trap."

It was actually quite clever but I could see a small flaw in the plan. "You realise, of course, that breaking into that storage place is illegal? And, if we get caught, we could be the ones doing time?"

"Who dares, wins, baby."

It wasn't even his motto. He'd been in the SBS, not the SAS. The SBS motto was something about "guile and strength." When I thought about it, though, both seemed to fit his personal philosophy remarkably well.

"All right, so we're doing a bit of burglary tonight." I knew I might as well concede because Ronnie would just go and do it on his own if I didn't help him. "Did you case the joint while I was allegedly pleasuring myself?" I knew he hadn't. We were sixty kilometres from the storage place and he hadn't had time.

"I did, as a matter of fact. Just a satellite surveillance, of course, and a few photos taken on a drive-by, but it will have to do." Right. He'd looked at Google. "But you've seen it with your own eyes. So you can fill in the gaps in my intel."

We both got out our phones and studied maps and images of the storage facility for the next half hour. Ronnie knew exactly where Kryou's storage shed was and we eventually settled on the best spot to park, where to cut the fence, and how to get into the shed. Ronnie always carried a set of lockpicks but he'd bought a cordless drill, just in case. The rest would be a matter of grabbing the painting and legging it.

We took a stroll up and down the main streets of the town. It was a lovely, warm summer evening. Every shop window was full of Christmas decorations, even though the big event was still about four weeks away. I wondered, idly, about getting a tree for the office. I felt a frisson of anxiety about not having even thought about what to get my parents for Christmas. It was followed by a vague resentment that something as dumb as Christmas might distract me from the important work I was doing. It was a weird feeling, like Christmas was for other people, ordinary people, people who didn't get shot at, who didn't have to break into places in the dark, who weren't hiding out in a strange town, hunting a pair of dangerous killers. I don't think I'd ever felt it before – that sense of being an outsider, like I was walking around that nice little country town wearing my own face as a disguise so the people there wouldn't see the unnatural creature I'd become. I wondered if Ronnie always felt like that. I was about to say something when he nudged my arm.

"Perfect!" He stopped outside a two-screen cinema. "Some stupid sci-fi crap. Just the thing to kill a couple of hours."

"You don't like sci-fi?" The film was another Marvel blockbuster. I'd seen every one as it came out when I was a teenager but I hadn't bothered in a long time.

"What, gorgeous hotties, running around in Lycra bodystockings? What's not to like?"

"Are you serious?" The thought of a sitting through endless jittery fast cuts, fight-scenes and blaring music didn't seem all that perfect to me. I was wound up enough already.

"It'll take your mind off things. Come on."

So we went in, bought popcorn for Ronnie, and spent the next two hours being bombarded by sound and flashing light in what felt more like the brainwashing scene from *A Clockwork Orange*, than something you might do for fun.

However, it did actually take my mind off things.

Chapter Twenty

Like any good battle plan – or bad one, for that matter – ours did not survive beyond the first encounter with the storage facility.

It took the best part of an hour to drive down the almost-deserted highway to Stanthorpe again. Ronnie saw the sign for the storage place and said, "Head's up." It was the first word either of us had spoken in half an hour. I turned off the highway and onto the little road that ran around two sides of the outer fence. At Ronnie's insistence, I cut the headlights and we relied on the spillover light from the highway junction to guide us. The facility was basically a square. I drove slowly along the edge facing the road, heading south, then turned left and drove east past the entrance. Ronnie had his face pressed up against the window on his side, staring intently as we crawled passed row after row of corrugated steel sheds. Everything was neat and clean and utterly deserted. The fence was about two metres of chain link with another metre of barbed wire strung across the top. Getting in would be no real problem as long as we weren't observed.

Reaching the end of the fence, I planned to turn left again and head north across a field. This was the back of the facility, farthest from the road, and our best bet for sneaking inside.

I had barely begun the turn when I slammed on the brakes, the ABS rattling as we skidded over the sandy soil. A hundred metres across the field, almost exactly at the spot we were heading for, was a silver Mercedes.

"Shit," said Ronnie, possibly because I'd surprised him with my abrupt stop.

"It's Kryou's car," I said, needlessly. "Now what do we do?"

"Turn off the engine. There's only one reason he'd be here right now and that's to grab the painting."

It didn't make sense. "He could do that in the morning." Ronnie got out of the car, closing the door quietly after him. I got out too. "He doesn't have to steal it."

"And yet, here he is."

In the dark, at that distance, I couldn't make out much detail around Kryou's car. We crossed the field and crouched down among some shrubs growing in a pile of boulders. Ronnie pulled out a small pair of binoculars and peered along the fence at Kryou's car.

"He's cut through the fence."

"Oh good," I said. Based on my limited past experience, I hadn't been looking forward to wielding the heavy, cumbersome bolt cutters. "But why is he here? What's he doing?"

Ronnie ignored my questions. "Come on," he said, and began making his way towards the Merc, bent low and sticking close to the scrubby bushes along the fence line.

"Quite right," I said, to myself. "The only way we'll find out is by sneaking up on the crazy murderer with the shotgun and asking him."

"Shut the fuck up," Ronnie hissed over his shoulder.

"This is a bad idea," I grumbled but Ronnie kept going.

We reached Kryou's car and used it as cover as we peered through the fence. The inside of the facility was brightly lit by small lamps mounted on the walls of the storage sheds, so it was quite easy to see what was going on.

"Kryou's storage unit is down that row, near the far end," Ronnie said, pointing. "Let's go."

He started to rise but I grabbed his shirt from behind and pulled him down.

"What the hell are you doing?" I demanded. He said something similar at the same time.

"What are you going to do if you find him?" I asked. "The idea was to keep him from running off, not to confront him. You can't arrest him. You can't just knock him about. What's the plan here?"

"I want to know what he's up to. This doesn't make sense. We've misread it somehow. I'm not going to risk losing him."

"And what if he sees you?"

"Then... we'll just have to improvise."

We glared at one another for several seconds.

"What do you want to do?" he asked. "Go away? Call the cops?"

"I don't know. But letting him see us is stupid."

"He's not going to see us. I'm just going to take a look. Are you coming, or what?"

Obviously, I couldn't stop him. "All right. Just a look."

He was off on the instant, creeping round the car, across the grass, through the hole in the fence and over the concrete road of the storage place to flatten himself against the end wall of a run of storage units. I could hardly keep up with him as I stumbled over the grass and fumbled my way through the fence. It snagged my T-shirt and rattled loudly as I pulled myself free. Ronnie glared back at me.

"Wait here. It's best if I go on alone," he whispered.

"It was an accident."

"Just wait here."

He moved to the corner of the building, then poked his head out and back, so fast I couldn't believe he'd had the chance to see anything. However, it seemed to satisfy him because he immediately set off running across the concrete to the end of the next row of storage units. That was the one in which Kryou's shed was. Angry that Ronnie had dismissed me as useless, I also ran across and joined him. I almost tripped over my own feet when I noticed the body lying on the ground between the rows of sheds.

I grabbed Ronnie's arm. "Did you – Did you see what I just saw?"

He looked at me as if he was wondering quite where to thump me. "Security guard," he said.

Of course, now he'd said it, I realised the man had been wearing a blue uniform.

"Shouldn't we...?" *Help him*, I was about to say, but that wasn't possible. If Kryou was around and armed, we couldn't do a thing for the guard without putting ourselves in danger.

"Why don't you go back to the car and call the cops?" he said. "Get an ambulance." His voice was steady but his anger was there in every syllable. At first I assumed it was anger aimed at me but then I realised it was directed at Kryou. And then I realised why.

"The guard is dead, isn't he?"

"Another murder." Another reason to take Kryou and Armitage down, his tone said.

"But why? What's so important that they have to come

here tonight and break into their own storage unit?"

"That's what I'm going to find out. Now you go and make that call."

"No way!"

"What?"

"I know you. You're going in there to stop him. You've got a murder right here to get him on. You can even legally make a citizen's arrest. Well I won't let you. I mean, not alone. I'm going too."

The glared at me but the corner of his mouth turned up. "You know you're a complete fuckwit?" he asked. "But you're not a coward. Not when it comes down to it."

"Oh yes I am. If you weren't such a crazy old bastard, hell bent on getting us both killed, I'd be at home right now having a cup of Milo and watching Netflix."

He grinned. "Come on, then."

He did his head-bobbing-around-the-corner thing again and then crept out into the road between the storage sheds. I gave him a couple of seconds and followed. It was easy to see which one was Kryou's. They all had up-and-over doors and there was only one door that was up a little and protruding slightly. There was a light on inside and, despite the well-lit exterior, a bright patch spread across the concrete. It was half-a-dozen sheds down from us, which felt far too close. The concrete road was clear but there was a light dusting of sand which made every footfall crunch. It must have been a tiny sound but to me it felt like we were walking over bags of crisps.

All too soon, Ronnie reached the shed door. He got down on his knees, put his head near the ground and took a look inside. He stood up quickly and fell back against the wall, staring up at the sky. I daren't speak to ask him what he'd seen. He took maybe three deep breaths through his nose then stood in front of the door and, game as Ned Kelly, threw it up and open. He stepped straight inside. I hurried to get in there after him.

And then I wished I hadn't.

I don't know what I was expecting to see. I suppose I hadn't given it any thought. The two conspirators, packaging up their painting for travel, perhaps? Working at a table with bubble-wrap and duct tape. Probably the last thing I expected was to find Nick Kryou on his knees, hacking the body of Scott Armitage into pieces with a machete.

Kryou had on an apron and yellow rubber gloves. The apron had the words, "Everything Tastes Better With Bacon" just visible through the blood. The body of Scott Armitage was naked, with an arm and half of each leg stacked beside it. It was on its back on a large polythene sheet. Blood was smeared everywhere, even on Kryou's face. He was staring up at Ronnie, open mouthed and wide eyed. But that's all I saw before I turned aside and threw up.

"Caught in the act, hey?" Kryou said and giggled.

It was so incongruous and creepy, I turned back to look at him. He was climbing to his feet, the long knife still in his hand. Apart from the body on the floor, a large suitcase and a couple of packing crates nearby, the shed was empty. There was an odd smell, a little like uncooked meat. I began retching again when I realised it was Armitage's blood.

"He must have really pissed you off," Ronnie said.

Kryou looked down at the body. Ronnie shifted his weight forward.

"He insisted on coming with me," Kryou explained. "But my plan doesn't have room for leeches and parasites."

Ronnie slid a foot forward, apparently just making himself

comfortable, but I could see what he was doing and, surely, Kryou would notice too. I looked at the long knife in the man's hand. Blood was still dripping from it.

"So, you told him you had to come here tonight because...?"

"That's right. I had to do it tonight." He seemed distracted but excited too. "My trip's all planned. I have to leave tonight. And I don't have room for him." He smiled. It was an incongruously sad smile. "Except as luggage."

"I think you've totally lost it, mate."

"It's possible." Kryou seemed confused, as if he was finding it hard to focus on the here and now, despite his peril. "It was all so simple. I had every step planned, with contingencies and emergency plans. I don't think the cops would ever have worked it out, even with the whole club dead except me. Hittman was going to be a traffic accident. Wendell was going to be stung by an irukandji jellyfish." He laughed. "It was quite brilliant. All spread out over a few months and three different states. But... I don't know. Somehow, it all ended up here." He waved a hand at the dismembered corpse on the floor.

"It wasn't all that brilliant. We were onto you as soon as Sanford died. Even McKinley wasn't a convincing suicide."

The smile faded from Kryou's face and a snarl replaced it. His grip on the machete tightened. I supposed he was remembering the part we'd played in bring him to this point. I realised Ronnie had moved imperceptibly closer. Did he think he could tackle an armed man? I didn't know. But he probably did. I'd seen him lay out a bigger, younger man who attacked him with a knife.

"And now you're going to jail," Ronnie said. "It probably doesn't seem such a great idea now, does it?" He was goading

Kryou. He wanted him to attack.

"You don't know what was at stake," Kryou said. "It was worth any gamble."

"You're joking. For a better car and a bigger house?" The sneer in Ronnie's voice sounded completely genuine. "You're an idiot." He took a step forward, offering himself to Kryou's attack. "Or was it all about acceptance? About being one of the fat cats? The one per cent? Being allowed to join the right clubs and know the right people? 'Cause that's just pathetic."

Anger flashed in Kryou's eyes, but he still didn't bite.

"Why here?" I asked, deciding I should join in, perhaps help Ronnie by providing some kind of distraction. I walked away from Ronnie, keeping my distance from Kryou, so that he couldn't watch both of us at the same time. "I mean, you could have butchered the poor, stupid bastard at your Amiens property. Why bring him here to do it?"

Kryou gave a wan smile. "My sister's staying there. What a time for the silly cow to take a holiday!" He looked at me from under lowered brows, as if he'd just remembered something that really annoyed him. "You should be dead." He looked like he'd be happy to fix that problem himself.

"Your man McGuire wasn't up to the job. Another brilliant plan that went sideways, hey?"

"You cocky little shit! You think you know everything 'cause you've dug up a few names and crap like that." He held up his machete and pointed it at Ronnie. "And you just stop right where you are." Ronnie held up his hands and pulled a "Who, me?" face. Kryou took a couple of quick steps back and moved behind the packing crates. It would make any attack by Ronnie a lot more difficult. Maybe it even gave Kryou the advantage.

"So what happens next?" Ronnie asked. "If we stand here

long enough, someone will find that dead security guard out there and call the cops. Besides, you've got to meet someone tonight, haven't you? You knew it was all over when Armitage told you the cops had been to see him. You probably thought there was still some chance of getting clear of the mess you were in. You even thought you just might keep the cops guessing. But when Armitage insisted on going with you, you knew it was all over. You couldn't take him and you couldn't shake him loose. So you had to kill him. And that was it. You'd never be able to make that look like an accident. The best you could do was to make sure no-one ever found the body. But then there was the security guard. Bit of bad luck, that. After that, it didn't matter how many you killed or where you left them, did it?"

Kryou frowned and glanced down at Armitage's dismembered body. "That's a really good point. I don't know why I'm chopping this disgusting bastard up at all now you mention it."

"You probably went a bit nuts," Ronnie suggested, helpfully.

A bit? I thought. Kryou had found himself in a deep hole and had stupidly chosen to keep on digging. Now he was looking up at the sides falling in on him but digging had become his only option.

Kryou looked at Ronnie long and hard. "How much?"

It took me by surprise but Ronnie knew exactly what he meant. "You're completely screwed, mate. Bodies everywhere. All you've got left in the world is that painting and that's nowhere near enough to buy your way out of this."

"Perhaps you don't realise how much it's worth."

"Thirty million, give or take," I said. "Less than half that on the black market."

His lips went thin and taught over clenched teeth. He pointed the machete at me. "One more word and you will be the next to die."

And that's when Ronnie made his move. He pushed himself forward with a grunt and, before Kryou could react, he had grabbed the hand holding the machete and wrenched it up and over. As Ronnie slammed into the packing cases, the machete flew free and Kryou fell back and out of sight behind the boxes.

Ronnie fought for his balance then ran round to finish Kryou. But he stopped dead as he rounded the boxes. He stared open mouthed for a second at whatever he saw back there.

There was a massive explosion. It was stunning. It overwhelmed my senses. The shed rattled and rang with the force of it, as if it had been hit everywhere at once with sledgehammers. I saw Ronnie fly backwards like someone had pulled him on a rope. My hands went up by reflex to cover my head. I saw Ronnie land on his back. He landed hard, like a dumped sack. There was a blackened hole in the front of his shirt, smoke curling up from it, red blood beginning to ooze through the blackness.

My heart was hammering so much it shook my body. I saw Kryou climb to his feet behind the crates, clinging to them to help himself up. He looked as shocked and dazed as I was. In his hand was a double-barrelled shotgun. It must have been behind the crates all along. I looked again at Ronnie. He hadn't moved.

Shit!

But Kryou was moving. He was lifting the gun, bringing its long barrel up and around to point at me. Without thinking, I began to run. I was only a couple of paces inside the shed. It would only take me two, maybe three seconds to get out. But I didn't have three seconds, or even two. I had one at the most. I'd taken one step already. My time was up.

I dropped and rolled just as the shed shook to another blast from the shotgun and an answering clang as the shot crashed into the door of the shed opposite. I was sprawled across the concrete, just outside the shed. I scrambled to turn and saw Kryou pulling two more cartridges out of his pocket. My ears were ringing and everything was eerily quiet. He looked up from reloading the shotgun and our eyes met briefly. I got all the way up and ran.

Chapter Twenty-One

I ran like a man being chased by a homicidal maniac with a double-barrelled shotgun. I was almost to the end of the row of sheds, before I realised I'd gone the wrong way. I looked back and saw Kryou emerge from the shed. He saw me too and fired. Even outside, even with my ears still ringing, the noise was tremendous. I grabbed the door-frame of the last shed and swung myself around the corner. I cried out in pain as the skin of my palm tore.

I took a moment I couldn't spare to orient myself and threw my body into a sprint for the back fence. That's where the hole was. That's how I'd get to my car. That was my only hope. Or could I climb the fence anyway? I could jump up it, scrabble to the to and throw myself over. The barbed wire would cut me but that seemed like a very minor inconvenience. But how long would it take? How long until Kryou appeared and found me hanging on the fence, a sitting duck? I saw the back fence, saw Kryou's car. But where was Kryou? If he was behind me, I might make it but, if he had gone round the other way, he'd cut me off.

I skidded to a halt on the sandy concrete. I had to know before I dare run out there and expose myself. I'd be able to hear his footsteps, surely? My own had been so loud. I tried to listen but my heart was thumping and my breath was rasping. Worse, my ears were still ringing. A horrible panic gripped me. I had to move. I was standing out in the open and he'd be there any moment. I ran for the hole in the fence. I crossed the concrete, stumbled as I hit the uneven grass. I was still fifty metres from the hole.

"Kelly!"

It was a scream of manic fury. I turned towards the sound and fell even as I saw Kryou fire. Vicious stabs of pain jabbed at my arm and thigh. I hit the ground hard and it knocked the wind out of me. The shot had gone over me, I reckoned. I'd just caught the edge of it. I raised my head, cautiously, to peer at Kryou. He was peering right back at me. But he was in the bright light of the storage units and I was in the dim outer reaches. He wasn't sure if I was dead and he couldn't see me very clearly. I kept still. He broke his shotgun, pulled out the spent cartridges and reached into his pocket for fresh ones but he didn't find any. In disgust, he threw the gun aside. He began walking towards his car, then stopped. He slapped his forehead in a pantomime of having forgotten something, and set off back into the rows of storage sheds. I could hear him talking to himself, calling himself an idiot, cursing me and Ronnie.

The painting, I told myself. *He's going back for the painting.* Which would mean he'd be coming back again in a minute or so. I could run for the car now. I'd make it, probably. But what if he came back with the machete, or more ammo for the shotgun? What if he saw me get into my car? He could easily catch my sedate four-wheel drive in his sleek Mercedes. Would he try to run me off the road? Would he kill us both in a suicidal crash? I wouldn't put anything past him in the state he was in.

But, if he got into his car first, I could follow him, find out where he was going and try to stop him. The bastard had killed Ronnie. I felt the first flicker of anger as I acknowledged to myself what I'd seen. He'd killed Ronnie. Murdered him. The anger grew. He wasn't going to get away with it. I would stop him. I'd track him down, thwart him, get him, make him pay.

So I lay in the grass, blood oozing from my wounds and hoped that playing dead would be the best tactic. If it wasn't, if he came for me with the machete, I would tear his heart out with my bare hands.

I saw him emerge from around the edge of the sheds. He was carrying the painting under one arm. He didn't have the machete. He glanced my way but that was enough to convince him I was dead or near enough not to be a nuisance. He went straight to his car and got in. The lights came on. The reversing lights flickered as he found drive and he pulled away. I jumped up and limped at a crouch along the fence until I reached the hole. The pain in my leg and arm was bad but tolerable. In a way, I welcomed it. It sharpened my focus, amplified my anger. Kryou's car swung around the corner as I passed through the fence. I straightened up and ran. I ran to where my car was parked at the corner of the fence. There I could see the brightly-lit highway. After a few seconds, a silver Merc appeared, heading north towards Warwick.

I sprinted to the driver's door and got in. I gunned the engine and wrenched the stubborn machine into a tight U-turn, shooting off after him, wheels skidding. As soon as I was underway, I told the phone to call triple-zero.

"I want the cops. And an ambulance." I said cutting across the opening spiel. I gave them the address of the storage place. "There are three people dead there. Or two. Probably three." I wasn't sure about the security guard. "One was shot. The other two, I don't know. The killer is Nicholas Kryou. He's in a silver Mercedes heading north on the New England Highway. I'm in pursuit now."

The operator asked for my name. "I'm Luke Kelly. I'm a private investigator." I turned onto the highway. It curved away but it was empty and I could see Kryou's tail lights a long way ahead. I slammed the accelerator to the floor. "Look, you should call Detective Inspector Marr in Brisbane. She's going to want to know about this. It's her case although she'd done fuck all about it." I pulled myself up. I mustn't let my anger distract me. "I've got to go."

The operator started asking me to return to the crime scene and wait for the cops but I hung up. Kryou's lights had flared. He was braking. I took my foot off the pedal. He'd barely got started but he was already turning right off the highway. What was there? Where was he going? I stabbed at the map display, trying to get some kind of heads up. But before I'd made the stupid thing give me a map, I saw a road sign for the airport and I knew.

I braked hard. I was amazed to find I was doing a hundred and fifty. Slowing enough for the exit was touch and go. I took the turn with my ABS hammering and the car rocking on its suspension. Forcing myself to calm down, I turned off my headlights and tried to let Kryou gain a bit more distance. Away from the main road, I was immediately on little country roads, winding between open paddocks and sprawling country businesses. Driving without lights was dangerous but I didn't want to let Kryou know he was being followed. For a while I was travelling parallel to the highway, close enough to see the flashing lights of a police patrol car racing north. I reckoned that was the one they'd told to go after Kryou. Which meant I was on my own.

The only good thing about airports, even little country aerodromes, is that they are always well signposted. Even in the dark on those crappy roads, I managed to find my way there. From time to time I'd glimpse Kryou's lights in the distance. He was several minutes ahead of me by the time I found myself among the terminal buildings – such as they were.

I suppose I'd imagined a place that had people, cars, activity, even at night. What I found was a silent, dark place that seemed completely abandoned. I stopped the car and got out to get my bearings. There was a tiny, cream-coloured hut that served as the terminal. There didn't seem to be any other infrastructure except a couple of big sheds that must have been hangars; no refuelling facilities, no emergency services, and not a plane in sight. If it hadn't been for a bright half moon, the whole area would have been a giant black void. Even in the moonlight, I struggled to get the layout. The aerodrome looked like one massive field with a handful of unlit buildings. My hearing was coming back but I heard no sound anywhere, except a light wind, some distant cattle and a few frogs. If Kryou was here, his car engine was off and I couldn't hear him speaking to anyone.

The need to do something became a physical sensation, a maddening tension in my muscles, a crawling itch on my skin. I got back in the car, turned on the engine and then the lights. I crawled forward then swept out a complete circle, headlights on full beam. And there they were, not fifty metres away, Kryou's car and a small, twin-engined plane. There were two men taking bags from Kryou's boot and pushing them into a hatch on the side of the plane. They stopped dead as my beam caught them and so did I.

The tableau lasted a couple of seconds before Kryou began gesticulating and shouting. The other man ran towards the cockpit while Kryou threw open one of the rear doors of his Merc and pulled out the painting that had cost so many lives.

"It's not even a good painting!" I shouted, driving towards them. "It's rubbish!"

By the time I screeched to a halt, banging into Kryou's rear bumper, he was jamming the painting into the aircraft's hatch. I jumped out, yelling, "Oh no you don't you murdering bastard!" but my words were lost as the plane's engine roared into life.

Kryou slammed the hatch shut and turned to face me. We were just a few metres apart. He shouted something I couldn't hear but I didn't need to. I could see from his body language that he was challenging me to try to stop him. With barely a thought for the obvious craziness of taking on a deranged murderer with my bare hands, I charged at him, screaming in rage. This was the man I'd just seen shoot Ronnie. I was going to tear him apart.

Kryou was not a big man. A couple of inches shorter than me, maybe. He wouldn't have lasted ten seconds in a fight with Ronnie. He was an office worker, not a street fighter. But, on reflection, he probably went to the gym a couple of times a week and was ten or fifteen kilos heavier than me. Whereas most people would have described him as a fit and active forty-something, those same people would probably have described me as a scrawny academic type. So when I ran straight into one of Kryou's fists and found myself dazed and lying on the ground, I shouldn't have been all that surprised. Kryou, his face set in a mask of hatred, grabbed me by the collar, lifted my upper body to a more convenient height and thumped my face several more times. When he'd had enough of that, he dropped me, stood up and kicked me in the stomach and ribs for a while. He might have done more but the other man, obviously the pilot, came around the tail of the plane and shouted something that might have been "What the fuck?" Kryou shouted back, "Shut up and get back in the plane." The pilot hesitated and then did as he was told. Kryou, without another word, went off to join him in the cockpit.

I groaned and rolled over, trying to get up. Everything hurt. Some things hurt so much I cried out as I struggled to my feet. The plane's engine bellowed into the night. Warm, stinking fumes blew back at me. The plane was moving, rolling slowly forward. The tail knocked against my head, quite gently, but enough that I fell down again. I screamed in frustration as I watched the little aircraft trundle away from me.

It's on a taxiway, I thought, *heading for the runway. It won't go fast until it gets there. But when it does...*A little plane like that would need no time at all to get up to speed and take off. I had to catch it quickly, while it was still possible. For a wild moment, I thought about running after it, jumping on, pulling the door open and dragging Kryou out. But, even driven by rage and still dizzy from my pummelling, I could see how completely insane that was. No, I needed the car. I needed to catch up and block the runway.

I got up again and ran for the car. I ran into it and had to hang on to stop myself falling down. I was probably more dizzy than I knew. I shook myself and got behind the wheel. The engine screamed into life as I floored it but I had to waste precious seconds manoeuvring past Kryou's Merc before I could give chase. My door slammed shut as I took off after the plane, surprising me that I hadn't thought to close it. It didn't matter. All that mattered was stopping that plane.

Ahead of me, I could see it turning onto the runway and my stomach sank. Its engines belched smoke as they revved up to accelerate. I swerved off the bitumen onto the grass, cutting the corner to try to reach the runway ahead of the plane. It was probably a bad idea. The ground was rough and my car bounced and swerved almost out of control as I pushed it hard to gain speed.

I hit the runway just behind the tailplane but lost ground as I took the turn and the car's rear end swung out and threatened a full spin. Yet I kept control somehow and surged after the plane. I was catching up fast. I passed the tail again and moved out to pass the wing. I was going to make it. We were going at almost a hundred kph and I had plenty of speed yet. I felt exultant, wildly triumphant.

"I've got you now, you bastard!" I screamed as I moved alongside the wing.

Then, to my horror, I saw the wheel below the wing lift off the ground.

I shouted, "No!" and swung the wheel. I don't know what possessed me. In that moment, the only thought in my head was to stop Kryou getting away. The car veered into the aircraft. I ducked as the fuselage filled the windscreen. I barely felt the impact as I hit it.

And then the world was a whirling, dizzying confusion of screeching, thundering sound and fleeting, impossible sights. At times, I was weightless. At others I was slamming into the side of the car, or the roof. I saw the entire tail section of the plane twirling away across the runway. I saw my hands floating in the air in front of me. I saw a propeller, churning up the ground as it ran away across the grass. And tiny pieces of glass, like a crystal rainstorm, hung in front of my eyes, then darted away, sideways.

Chapter Twenty-Two

I woke up in a hospital bed, three days later.

My mother was there, reading a book. She was in a mustard-yellow armchair that looked uncomfortable. She sat awkwardly and looked tired.

When I woke again, Mum was gone and Kazima Abbas was in the mustard-yellow armchair. She saw my eyes open and hurried to my bedside.

"Hi," she said. It was amazing how much a single word could communicate – concern, affection, a query about my welfare, and a greeting. I wasn't quite sure what Kazima was doing there. She was the CEO of Chelsea's company, not really a friend. At least, I hadn't thought so.

I tried to answer her but nothing came out. She reached over and picked up a beaker of water with a straw. She put the straw in my mouth. It seemed overly familiar but I forgave her when I felt the cool liquid in my parched mouth.

"What?" I said.

"You're in hospital," she said. "In Brisbane." I tried to look around but my head was restrained. "Don't try to move. You've got a neck brace and your arm's in a cast and your foot's in a cast and I don't know what else. You nearly killed yourself."

I remembered the runway, the plane lifting off the bitumen, me turning the wheel.

"I rolled the car, didn't I?" It was quite hard to speak. My head felt fuzzy and my tongue wasn't quite under my control.

"Big time! It's a write-off. You smashed up an aeroplane, too."

So I did. Christ alive, what was I thinking? "Kryou and the pilot?"

"Don't worry. They're both alive and the police have them."

I felt a rush of relief. I hadn't killed anybody.

"When...?"

"When can you leave?" I tried to nod, but couldn't. "In a few days, they said. It seems the multiple air bags and all the other safety features in your car were worth every penny. You broke a couple of things, you got a bad concussion and you wrenched your neck rather badly, but it could have been very, very much worse. You were so lucky." She reached out and squeezed my hand.

"Thank you," I said, a little embarrassed. "For being here."

She smiled. "Karen and I have been taking turns – a couple of days on, a couple of days off. Your mum and dad were here too for the first couple of days but when it was certain you were going to make a full recovery, we persuaded them to let us young 'uns carry the burden. Nice people. Karen'll be so mad it wasn't her turn when you woke up. Ronnie... couldn't be here, of course."

I closed my eyes and saw him lying on his back, his chest smashed. I felt a tear run down my face.

"You rest now," Kazima said. She sounded anxious. "I'll tell the nurse you're awake. Then I'll go and phone your mum and dad. And Karen. Wow, there are all kinds of people who want to know you're all right." She squeezed my hand again and left. I wanted her to tell me who all these people were who were so concerned. Apart from the people she'd mentioned, I couldn't think of anybody. And then I remembered the cops. DI Marr would definitely want to know. DS Bertolissio might be interested.

* * * *

My mum and dad were there within the hour and camped out at my bedside for the final three days of my stay in hospital. By the time I was discharged, their duet on the theme of "How could you do something so stupid?" had grown just a little repetitive. I politely declined their offer to let me stay with them until I had my casts removed. They left me on the sofa in my unit with a fridge full of ready meals, my crutch, my phone and the TV remote within reach, and cushions piled all around me.

The cops had come to see me in hospital, to ask me questions and take a statement. Then DI Marr came, Bronski in tow, as usual. She'd been almost penitent, thanking me awkwardly for my "help" in catching Kryou, and assuring me that no-one was going to prosecute me for attempted murder, or wilful damage of an aircraft – a possibility I hadn't even considered until she said it. Apparently, I could also have been done for leaving the scene of a crime when I left the storage place and several other misdemeanours, too, but the public prosecutor didn't think it was in the public interest to pursue such things.

"We don't approve of vigilantes, Mr. Kelly," she said, gruffly, as if the effort of being nice to me needed some kind of counterweight.

"Doctor. And I'm not a vigilante. I'm a licenced PI."

"Yeah, well… All said and done, I reckon you did us all a favour taking that nutter down. And it took guts."

It was grudging but it was strangely uplifting to a man who'd been sinking ever deeper into the doldrums. "Taking that nutter down" had come at an appalling cost and it was hard now to see how it could possibly have been worth it.

I sat on the sofa and dozed while the TV ran through cop shows and medical dramas. A buzz from the door snapped me out of it. I fought with my crutch and dragged my aching body to the entry buzzer at the door.

"Luke?"

"Yes?"

"It's Alexandra Bertolissio."

"Oh, right. Come on up."

By the time I'd limped back to the sofa and struggled to fall into it without killing myself, she was inside and closing the door. She came over to me and her quick eyes took in the neck brace and the casts.

"Ah," she said. "Too soon?"

"No, no." I waved her to a chair. "If you'd like a coffee or something, just help yourself. I don't think I'm quite up to working the machine yet without falling over."

She shook her head but stood up again and headed for the kitchenette. "Let me get you one – if I can work out how to use this starship navigation console over here."

I talked her through the workings of the cappuccino machine and she brought back two coffees and freshly defrosted croissants from the freezer. I thanked her profusely.

"Is there much pain?" she asked.

"They've got me on something strong enough to keep it

tolerable. Some sort of synthetic opioid. I'll probably need a month in rehab afterwards but, right now I'm popping pills like a teenager at a party."

She smiled, weakly. "You were lucky. It's incredible that you hit that plane and all three of you survived."

Sheepishly, I said, "I wasn't really thinking straight. From the minute I saw…" *Ronnie's body*, I was going to say but I couldn't get the words out. "…what I saw in that shed, I was sort of on autopilot. All I could think of was stopping Kryou."

"Well, you certainly did that. Mel thinks you're wonderful. Not quite as wonderful as she thinks she is herself though. You should hear her crowing about how she just *knew* McKinley had been murdered. Her boyfriend is getting a lot of credit too, 'for never giving up on her.'" She pulled a sour face.

To change the subject, I asked, "What's with the pile of papers?" I'd been dying to know since she arrived with a thick wad of newspapers under one arm.

"I thought you might like to see what the press has been saying about you over the past few days. I salvaged this lot from the week's recycling." She started opening and folding newspapers so that I could see the relevant articles without needing to struggle with them. "You should start with this."

It was a copy of the *Courier Mail.* On the front page was a photo of a wrecked light aircraft with my car, hideously battered, standing on its roof nearby. The headline was, "Tontine Killer Meets His Match". Underneath, in bold, "Genius detective stops serial killer in spectacular airport showdown." There were a couple of paragraphs along these lines.

"Genius?" I said, looking up.

"It's the philosophy degree. It got the press very excited." She handed me a copy of *The Guardian* from the same day. Under a photograph of Kryou, bloodied but still on his feet, being led away by cops, was a considerably more restrained piece about the crash and the bodies found at the storage facility. Most of the quotes in both articles came from DI Marr, who described my pursuit of Kryou as "reckless" and "dangerous."

The papers from the next couple of days also had articles about Kryou although no longer on the front page. The painting had survived the crash, it seemed, and was found lying in the grass the next morning. Ronnie and I were "local heroes". The Mayor of Stanthorpe wanted us to get medals. Detective Chief Inspector Adams wanted tighter controls on the licensing of private investigators.

"Wow," I said. "I'm famous."

The last paper Bertolissio handed me was that morning's Guardian. It had a small piece deep inside commenting that I'd be out of hospital soon and that Ronnie was doing well after a second round of surgery.

I read the paragraph three times. I looked up at Bertolissio.

"What the hell?"

"What?"

"Ronnie. It says he's in the Princess Alexander Hospital."

"Yes?"

"But he's dead. I saw him die. He was shot, point blank, with a shotgun, right here." I tapped my chest. Bertolissio seemed confused. I noticed her glance at the bandage on my head. "I'm not crazy. I saw it."

"Luke, Ronnie's OK. He survived. They took him by helicopter to Brisbane. He's at the PA now. Good God! Did nobody think to tell you?"

I grabbed my crutch and began struggling to get up. Bertolissio was at my side in an instant, helping.

"I've got to get over there. I've got to see him."

She tried to help me hobble to the door. "I'll take you there right now. The car's just outside."

"Oh, God! I thought he was dead. I saw it. I saw him die. He was on the ground, on his back. There was a hole—"

I couldn't speak. I couldn't breathe. A wave of dizziness passed through me. I leaned against the door. Bertolissio held me so I wouldn't fall.

"He's alive? He's really alive?"

She smiled up at me. "Yes, he is. I'm so sorry no-one told you."

"I – I didn't even ask. I was so sure."

Ronnie was alive! It felt like a miracle. It felt… wonderful. Tears sprang from my eyes. I wasn't even embarrassed. Bertolissio was OK. She'd understand.

"I thought he'd died without even knowing I'd stopped Kryou," I said, realising as the words came out, how important that had been to me. "He'd have hated that. I'd have hated that."

"Come on," she said, still smiling. "Let's go see him. I'll drop you there and get back to work."

* * * *

Ronnie was in a public ward. Two nurses and a doctor were standing around his bed when I arrived. They were all laughing. The doctor was a middle-aged woman with a handsome, well-tanned face. As I limped over to the bed, she turned to me and said, "So, it's the genius detective at last."

Everyone laughed. I didn't quite know what to say or do. I just wanted to talk to Ronnie.

"I was just discharged," I told him. "I didn't even know you were alive."

"He nearly wasn't," the doctor said. "I thought I'd never stop pulling shotgun pellets and lumps of Kevlar out of him. What a mess!"

"Kevlar?" Ronnie had worn his bullet-proof vest? How had I not noticed?

"But the real Christmas miracle," the doctor went on, "was my brilliant reconstruction of his ribcage. We printed off a whole sternum and joined up twenty-two different pieces of bone. It was like building one of those plastic models of the Opera House. Even so, if he hadn't been so fit and healthy…" She shook her head in wonder. "This man's blood is definitely worth bottling. In fact, I think I'll grab a couple of litres before I let him go home."

Astonished as I was, I just wished she'd shut up and go away. I looked again at Ronnie and realised he was covered in plaster and that some kind of elaborate framework of metal pins and wires surrounded his chest.

"Will he be all right?"

"All right? Why the man's practically a cyborg!" Ronnie grinned at me. "Ah well, must press on. Can't stand here admiring my handiwork all day."

She strode off, nurses hurrying in her wake, and I watched until she left the ward.

"I think she fancies me," Ronnie said, with a wink. Given that his eyes were about the only part of his upper body still free to move, I couldn't help laughing.

I carefully arranged a chair by the bed so I'd be able to see Ronnie without either of us turning our heads, and lowered myself into it. "I was hoping I wasn't going to have to see your ugly mug again," I lied, grinning.

"Yeah. What do I have to do to get away from you? A shotgun to the chest didn't work. Maybe I'll try explosives next time."

I nodded, sympathetically. "Well, I tried ramming an aeroplane at a hundred kilometres an hour and that didn't work, either."

"Somebody up there wants us to go on tormenting each other."

"Looks like it. Meanwhile, you're lying around here flirting with the doctors and taking it easy while I carry our heavy caseload all on my own." In fact, to my knowledge, there wasn't a single thing in the in-tray except the monthly bills.

"It's hard work but someone's got to do it. So, when does that lot come off?"

"About six weeks, they said. Yours?"

"About the same, maybe longer. It would heal faster if I could stop breathing."

"Hey, don't let me stop you."

"All right, that's enough chit-chat. Tell me what happened."

It was my turn to grin. "Haven't you seen the papers? The Genius Detective cracked the case and single-handedly brought down the Tontine Killer."

Ronnie grinned back. "He's confessed to everything, you know. Not that the cops needed a confession. He was still wearing the apron with Armitage's blood all over it when they arrested him. You're welcome, by the way."

"For what?"

"I don't actually remember doing it, but it seems that when the medics arrived, I came round briefly and sent the cops out to the airport."

"How did you know we'd gone to the airport?"

"It was obvious. Anyway, the cops got there just in time to see you total a twin-engine Cessna."

"Thanks. Turns out they've decided not to prosecute."

"Yeah but someone's bound to sue you. Just wait and see. I used to get sued twice a year, back in the day. Of course, I had the QPS to pay the settlements. Hey, do you reckon that's why they gave me the elbow?"

"Wow, this is really cheering me up." I made a mental note to call my insurance company about what my ludicrously expensive professional indemnity and public liability insurances actually covered.

"So tell me the story. Last I remember, I was bravely tackling a machete-wielding madman. What happened next?"

And, in an instant, I was back in that shed with smoke rising from a hole in Ronnie's chest and Kryou swinging his gun round to shoot me. All the lightness of our banter disappeared.

"I thought you were dead," I said. "I thought he'd killed you."

"But you got away." Ronnie's voice was incredibly gentle. Kind, even. "You got out of that shed and saved yourself – and me   somehow." My eyes refocused on the hospital. Ronnie in the bed, his blue-grey eyes fixed on mine. "Go on," he said. "How did you do it?"

"I only got as far as the door before he fired again," I said. And then the story began to flow.

I managed to get it all out before a nurse came to shoo me away.

"Where's the cute one?" Ronnie complained as she started fussing around him. "I think I'm ready for my bed bath."

The nurse rolled her eyes at me. "There's always one on every ward." She glared at Ronnie. "They think they're funny."

"He probably pulled legs off spiders as a boy," I told her. To him, I said, "Just leave the staff alone. No-one thinks you're funny. And the cute one thinks you're a gross old pervert – as any normal person would."

He grinned back at me. "Feels good, doesn't it?"

"What? Teasing people?"

"No, dickhead, getting your man."

I looked down at our bandaged bodies. "And this is all worth it?"

"Fuck yes! I'd do it all again. And so would you."

* * * *

I rested up for a few days, receiving my parents, Kazima and Karen like a pampered billionaire greeting flunkies. They brought delicacies, they pandered to my whims and they ran around the unit making food and tidying the place. Mum even brought a tiny Christmas tree and did my laundry. It was agreed that I would spend Christmas Day with them. I began to feel like the proverbial bird in a gilded cage.

So, I picked up my laptop and called a taxi. They sent a special mini-van with invalid access and, even though I could have managed without it, it made the trip so much more comfortable. I took it to the office, hobbling through the door for the first time in well over a week. It was depressingly messy, with paper piled and strewn on every surface and unwashed coffee cups everywhere, including a couple still half full on which brightly-coloured mould was floating. Even my cappuccino machine was unusable until I'd given it a thorough cleaning.

So I set to and, even one handed with a crutch, it didn't take all that long before I'd got the place looking normal again and the smell of mould was replaced by the smell of disinfectant.

I treated myself to a cappuccino, watching people moving around in the street outside as I drank it. Then I opened my laptop and, again with one hand, began writing up the final notes on the case. That took a lot longer but it was strangely satisfying to close it all off like that. The last act of administration I did was to write a brief summary for our client, Daniel Bridgeman, and to create an invoice to go with it. I opened up the office email app and sent off both report and invoice.

"The end," I said and sat back.

It was only then that I realised there were scores of emails in the inbox. Our normal daily count of work emails was some small fraction of one. So to find dozens after only a week-and-a-bit away was puzzling. Had we got onto a spam list? I began reading through the subject lines; "Can you help me?", "My father has gone missing", "Someone is stealing my garden ornaments", "My wife is cheating on me", "I think I'm being followed", were just the first few. They went on like this for page after page.

"Oh my god!" I said aloud. I pushed away from the desk, still staring at the screen. This was business. These were all potential clients. I'd been in the papers and now everyone wanted me to take their cases. It was shocking. Overwhelming. I felt my heart begin to flutter. I wasn't ready. I was still getting better. This was too much.

A woman's voice from across the room interrupted my

rising panic.

"Hello? Is this the Genius Detective agency?"

"We're clo—" I began and stopped dead. "Hang on. You're the woman from the university. Both universities." She smiled and walked in.

"'The woman from the university.' So that's how you have me pegged. Well, I suppose it could be worse. At least it's not 'That bloody awful woman,' or 'That crazy woman who's been stalking me.'"

I struggled to my feet. "I... er... what?"

She laughed. "Don't look so alarmed. I'm not really a crazy woman. It's just... Look, we met a couple of times and it was like a weird kind of accident. But I thought we got on pretty well. Didn't you?" I opened my mouth but nothing came out, so she went on. "And then I saw you in the paper and thought, 'Crikey! I know this bloke!' It was like fate or something. So I thought I'd come and say hello. That's all right, isn't it? Only, I didn't really expect you to look like an extra from a Mummy movie. So I'm thinking my timing kinda sucks. Look..." She delved in her handbag and pulled out a business card. "Maybe we should, I don't know, start over from the very beginning, or something. This is me." She handed me the card. It said, "Megan Thomas, Principal Consultant, HotMM."

She saw my puzzled expression, no doubt, and said, "It's an acronym for 'Heart of the Matter Media'. I do press releases for the unis and other labs around Brisbane. That kind of thing."

"Hot MM sounds like a radio station," I said.

"Yeah, I get that a lot."

"One that only plays the top two thousand songs."

"Bit geeky, that one. I've only heard it M times."

Laughing, I grabbed one of my own business cards from my desk. I handed it over. "And that's me."

"Systematic Doubt? What, as in Descartes?"

"Yes! At last, someone who understands."

"Oh, I'm definitely a Descartes buff. I even know the three-word quote."

"*Cogito ergo sum*," we said, together.

"In fact, I was thinking of doing a book of three-word quotes from the world's great philosophers. Like Nietzsche: 'God is dead.' Socrates: 'I know nothing.'"

I joined in. "Plato: 'I knew Socrates'"

"Bertrand Russell: 'Ban the bomb.'"

We both laughed and it trailed off into a self-conscious silence.

"I'm changing the company name," I said. "Nobody likes it."

"The Luke Kelly Agency? Your name is your brand, right?"

"I was thinking The Featherfoot Agency."

"Wow, even more obscure. Nice."

We laughed again.

"I should go," she said. "You look like you might fall over at any moment."

I looked down at my casts. "This is temporary. I'll be a new man after Christmas. Well, in the new year, anyway."

"That's a shame, I was just starting to like the old man."

"So I should call you, right? In January sometime."

"We can get a coffee or something."

"This may be the painkillers talking but I think we're past the getting a coffee stage. In fact, this is like our third date already. I'll call you and we'll have dinner." I had no idea why I was being so bold. It just seemed easy.

She gave me a lovely smile. "It's a date," she said. "Merry Christmas."

She stepped forward and kissed me on the cheek – in a small gap of skin between the plaster on my broken nose repair and the bandage around my half-shaven head. It reminded me what a hideous sight I must be. But it also thrilled me beyond all reason.

After she'd gone, I sat down again and stared at the empty doorway. For a long time I was in a "What the hell just happened?" kind of daze. Then I was just happy and excited. Then the guilt began to creep in. January would be the anniversary of Chelsea's death. Was that really the best time to be starting up a new relationship?

I needed to talk to someone. If Ronnie hadn't been encased in medical technology, I might even have called him because, for the life of me, I couldn't think of anyone else. Besides, as my dear old friend Jean-Paul Sartre well knew, when you have a difficult decision, the best person to ask is the one who will give you the advice that conforms to your secret desire. And, for sure, Ronnie would be all, "Yeah, mate, go for it!"

The only other person who might understand was Chelsea. I wanted to walk down to the cemetery and have a chat but I ached in every joint and fibre. Even the idea of taking a cab was daunting – at least until I could take some more painkillers. So I got out my phone, got up a map of the area and oriented myself as near as possible to Chelsea's grave.

"I hope you don't mind," I said. I was alone. I could talk out loud. "I feel like I've been shot, pummelled and finished off in a tumble dryer." As usual these days, Chelsea – or the simulation of her that ran in my mind – wasn't very talkative, but I was pretty sure she'd let me off for not dragging myself over to the graveyard.

"So, what did you think of Megan? She's not at all like you. I mean, she's pretty and clever and all that but she's not... you. In fact, she's more like me, I reckon. A total geek. Only funny and together. Well, you saw her. You know what I mean."

The silence was profound. Perhaps my chats with Chelsea were finally coming to an end. A great sadness filled me. And fear. If I couldn't talk to Chelsea, it would be like losing her all over again. And I'd be on my own. Truly and totally. Forever.

"I want to go out with her," I said, hearing the defiance in my own voice. "I like her. I think that maybe we could be good together. She seems to see it too. It's a miracle. Impossible. But, when we were talking just now, making stupid philosophy jokes and laughing, I was happy. It was the first time since you died." I felt my throat close and tears well up in my eyes. "It's been a really long time. But I think, maybe, if I don't screw things up, there's a chance this could be really good. I mean, I've missed you. I've missed being happy. But you're not there any more, not even in my head."

The tears broke loose and ran into the nose plaster. "I'm sorry, Chelsea. I didn't love you very well, just... lots. And now I'm moving on and you're still dead and I'll never be able to make any of it right."

For a while I just sat there and breathed. I listened for any word, felt for any hint of a response, but it was like a phone when the signal's gone. Not even a dial tone. Not even static. Just blank emptiness. "Goodbye," I said into the silence.

Thank You

Thank you for reading *Bright City Lost Souls,* the second of my Luke Kelly crime novels. I really hope you enjoyed it as much as I enjoyed writing it. If so, I'd be grateful if you'd leave a review on one of the book retail sites, your blog, or pasted to a wall on the nearest underpass. There will be more books about Luke's adventures. To stay informed of when new books of mine are about to appear, please visit my website and sign up for my newsletter.

About the Author

I am a writer living in Queensland, Australia. A former research scientist, IT consultant and award-winning software designer, I now live and write – mostly science fiction and crime – in a quiet corner of the Australian bush with my wife, Christine, and a Tonkinese cat called Minsky.

Other Books By Graham Storrs

Crime Stories

Sisters: The Complete Short Story Collection

The Luke Kelly Crime Series:

Bright City Deep Shadows
Bright City Lost Souls
Bright City Dark Love
Bright City Old Wounds

Science Fiction

Cargo Cult
Heaven is a Place on Earth
Mindrider
Time and Tyde

The Timesplash Series:

Timesplash
True Path
Foresight

Novels in the Placid Point Universe

The Rik Sylver Trilogy:

The Credulity Nexus
The Sentience Machine
The Dissonance Factor

The Canta Libre Trilogy:

Emissaries
Supplicants
Warriors

The Deep Fracture Trilogy:

Loner's Deep
Omega Point
Nadezhda

Contact the Author

I am always happy to hear from readers, so don't be shy. And if you enjoyed this book, don't forget to post your review.

Follow me on Twitter: @graywave

or on Facebook:
facebook.com/GrahamStorrsAuthor

For an up-to-date list and full details of all my novels and short stories, visit cantalibre.com